Sandstorm

BY JAMES ROLLINS

Sandstorm

ᚷᚻᚾᛁᚼᚷᚷᚷ᛫ᚲᛒ

James Rollins

HARPER LUXE

An Imprint of HarperCollinsPublishers

SANDSTORM. Copyright © 2004 by Jim Czajkowski. All rights reserved. Printed in the United States of America. No part of this book may be used or reproduced in any manner whatsoever without written permission except in the case of brief quotations embodied in critical articles and reviews. For information address HarperCollins Publishers, 10 East 53rd Street, New York, NY 10022.

HarperCollins books may be purchased for educational, business, or sales promotional use. For information please write: Special Markets Department, HarperCollins Publishers, 10 East 53rd Street, New York, NY 10022.

FIRST HARPERLUXE EDITION

HarperLuxe™ is a trademark of HarperCollins Publishers

ISBN: 978-0-06-206652-7

11 12 13 14 ID/OPM 10 9 8 7 6 5 4 3 2 1

To Katherine, Adrienne, and RJ,
the next generation

Acknowledgments

I impose on too many people. First, Carolyn McCray must be acknowledged and worshiped for her ceaseless friendship and guidance from the first word to the last . . . and beyond. And Steve Prey for his arduous and detailed help with schematics, logistics, artwork, and sound input of a critical nature. And his wife, Judy Prey, for putting up with Steve and me and the many last-minute, desperate requests I've made on her time. The same above-and-beyond efforts were faced, accepted, and exceeded by Penny Hill (with the help of Bernie and Kurt, of course). For help with details in the novel, I must thank Jason R. Mancini, senior researcher for the Mashantucket Pequot Museum. And for help with languages, Diane Daigle and David Evans. Additionally, the book would not be what it is without my chief advisers, who rake me over the coals on a regular basis, in no particular order: Chris Crowe, Michael Gallowglas, Lee Garrett, David Murray, Dennis Grayson, Dave Meek, Royale Adams, Jane O'Riva, Kathy Duarte, Steve Cooper, Susan Tunis, and Caroline Williams. For the map used here, I must acknowledge its source: *The CIA World Factbook 2000*. Finally, the four people who continue to remain my most loyal supporters: my editor, Lyssa Keusch; my agents, Russ Galen and Danny Baror; and my publicist, Jim Davis. And as always, I must stress any and all errors of fact or detail fall squarely on my own shoulders.

DOSSIER MAP FILE

DEPT OF DEFENSE CODE:
ALPHA42—PCR

SIGMA FORCE

ARABIAN PENINSULA

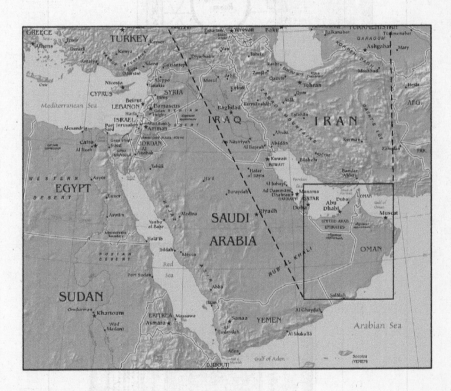

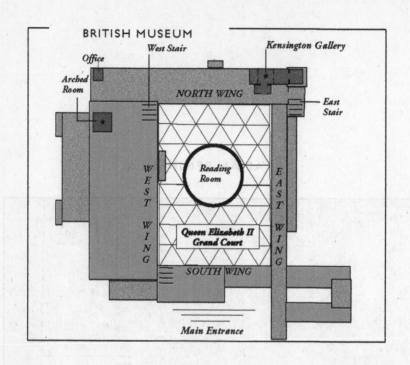

BRITISH MUSEUM

Office

Arched
Room

West Stair

Kensington Gallery

NORTH WING

East
Stair

W
E
S
T

W
I
N
G

Reading
Room

E
A
S
T

W
I
N
G

Queen Elizabeth II
Grand Court

SOUTH WING

Main Entrance

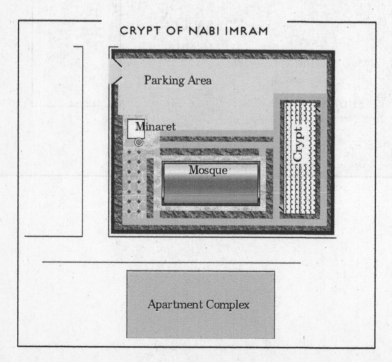

CRYPT OF NABI IMRAM

Parking Area

Minaret

Mosque

Crypt

Apartment Complex

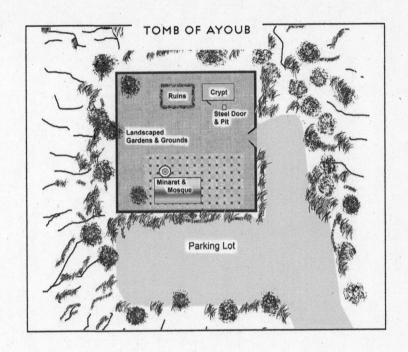

TOMB OF AYOUB

Ruins

Crypt

Steel Door
& Pit

Landscaped
Gardens & Grounds

Minaret &
Mosque

Parking Lot

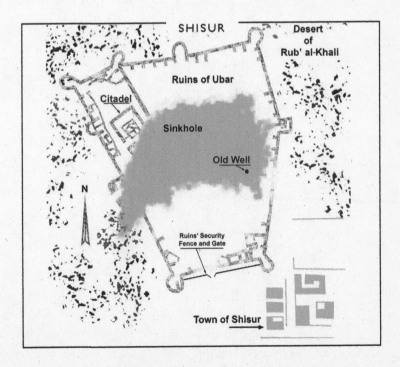

SHISUR

Desert
of
Rub' al-Khali

Ruins of Ubar

Citadel

Sinkhole

Old Well

N

Ruins' Security
Fence and Gate

Town of Shisur

PART ONE

Thunderstorm

ᚷᛁᛟᚾ�(ᛉᚷ∘(ᛒ

1

Fire and Rain

ᛟᛉᛝᛊᛁᚻᛉᚻᛁᛉᚺᛉᛉ

November 14, 01:33 A.M.
The British Museum
London, England

Harry Masterson would be dead in thirteen minutes.

If he had known this, he would've smoked his last cigarette down to the filter. Instead he stamped out the fag after only three drags and waved the cloud from around his face. If he was caught smoking outside the guards' break room, he would be shit-canned by that bastard Fleming, head of museum security. Harry was already on probation for coming in two hours late for his shift last week.

Harry swore under his breath and pocketed the stubbed cigarette. He'd finish it at his next break . . . that is, if they got a break this night.

Thunder echoed through the masonry walls. The winter storm had struck just after midnight, opening with a riotous volley of hail, followed by a deluge that threatened to wash London into the Thames. Lightning danced across the skies in forked displays from one horizon to another. According to the weatherman on the Beeb, it was one of the fiercest electrical storms in over a decade. Half the city had been blacked out, overwhelmed by a spectacular lightning barrage.

And as fortune would have it for Harry, it was *his* half of the city that went dark, including the British Museum on Great Russell Street. Though they had backup generators, the entire security team had been summoned for additional protection of the museum's property. They would be arriving in the next half hour. But Harry, assigned to the night shift, was already on duty when the regular lights went out. And though the video surveillance cameras were still operational on the emergency grid, he and the shift were ordered by Fleming to proceed with an immediate security sweep of the museum's two and a half miles of halls.

That meant splitting up.

Harry picked up his electric torch and aimed it down the hall. He hated doing rounds at night, when the museum was lost in gloom. The only illumination came from the streetlamps outside the windows. But now, with the blackout, even those lamps had been extinguished. The museum had darkened to macabre shadows broken by pools of crimson from the low-voltage security lamps.

Harry had needed a few hits of nicotine to steel his nerve, but he could put off his duty no longer. Being the low man on the night shift's pecking order, he had been assigned to run the halls of the north wing, the farthest point from their underground security nest. But that didn't mean he couldn't take a shortcut. Turning his back on the long hall ahead, he crossed to the door leading into the Queen Elizabeth II Great Court.

This central two-acre court was surrounded by the four wings of the British Museum. At its heart rose the great copper-domed Round Reading Room, one of the world's finest libraries. Overhead, the entire two-acre courtyard had been enclosed by a gigantic Foster and Partners–designed geodesic roof, creating Europe's largest covered square.

Using his passkey, Harry ducked into the cavernous space. Like the museum proper, the court was lost to darkness. Rain pattered against the glass roof far over-head. Still, Harry's footsteps echoed across the open space. Another lance of lightning shattered across the sky. The roof, divided into a thousand triangular panes, lit up for a blinding moment. Then darkness drowned back over the museum, drumming down with the rain.

Thunder followed, felt deep in the chest. The roof rattled, too. Harry ducked a bit, fearing the entire structure would come crashing down.

With his electric torch pointed forward, he crossed the court, heading for the north wing. He rounded past the central Reading Room. Lightning flashed again, brightening the place for a handful of heartbeats. Giant statues, lost to the darkness, appeared as if from nowhere. *The Lion of Cnidos* reared beside the massive head of an Easter Island statue. Then darkness swallowed the guardians away as the lightning died out.

Harry felt a chill and pebbling of gooseflesh.

His pace hurried. He swore under his breath with each step, "Bleeding buggered pieces of crap . . ." His litany helped calm him.

He reached the doors to the north wing and ducked inside, greeted by the familiar mix of mustiness and ammonia. He was grateful to have solid walls around him again. He played his torch down the long hall. Nothing seemed amiss, but he was required to check each of the wing's galleries. He did a fast calculation. If he hurried, he could complete his circuit with enough time for another fast smoke. With the promise of a nicotine fix luring him, he set off down the hall, the beam of his torch preceding him.

The north wing had become host to the museum's anniversary showcase, an ethnographical collection portraying a complete picture of human achievement down the ages, spanning all cultures. Like the Egyptian gallery with its mummies and sarcophagi. He continued hurriedly, ticking off the various cultural galleries: Celtic, Byzantine, Russian, Chinese. Each suite of rooms was locked down by a security gate. With the loss of power, the gates had dropped automatically.

At last, the hall's end came into sight.

Most of the galleries' collections were only temporarily housed here, transferred from the Museum of Mankind for the anniversary celebration. But the end gallery had always been here, for as far back as Harry could recall. It housed the museum's Arabian display, a priceless collection of antiquity from across the Arabian Peninsula. The gallery had been commissioned and paid for by one family, a family grown rich by its oil ventures in that region. The donations to keep such a gallery in permanent residence at the British Museum was said to top five million pounds per annum.

One had to respect that sort of dedication.

Or not.

With a snort at such a foolish waste of good money, Harry splayed his torch's spot across the engraved brass plate above the doorway: THE KENSINGTON GALLERY. Also known as "The Bitch's Attic."

While Harry had never encountered Lady Kensington, from the talk among the employees, it was clear that any slight to her gallery—dust on a cabinet, a display card with a smudge on it, a piece of antiquity not properly positioned—was met with the severest reprimand. The gallery was her personal pet project, and none withstood her wrath. Jobs were lost in her wake, claiming even a former director.

It was this concern that kept Harry a few moments longer at his post outside the gallery's security gate. He swept his torch around the entrance room with more than casual thoroughness. Yet again, all was in order.

As he turned away, withdrawing his torch, movement drew his eye.

He froze, torch pointing at the floor.

Deep within the Kensington Gallery, in one of the farther rooms, a bluish glow wandered slowly, shifting shadows with its passage.

Another torch . . . someone was in the gallery . . .

Harry felt his heart pounding in his throat. A break-in. He fell against the neighboring wall. His fingers scrambled for his radio. Through the walls, thunder reverberated, sonorous and deep.

He thumbed his radio. "I have a possible intruder here in the north wing. Please advise."

He waited for his shift leader to respond. Gene Johnson might be a wanker, but he was also a former RAF officer. He knew his shit.

The man's voice answered his call, but dropouts ate most of his words, interference from the electrical storm. " . . . *possible . . . are you sure? . . . hold until . . . are the gates secure?*"

Harry stared back at the lowered security gates. Of course he should have checked to see if they had been breeched. Each gallery had only one entrance into the hall. The only other way into the sealed rooms was through one of the high windows, but they were wired against breakage or intrusion. And though the storm had knocked out main power, the backup generators kept the security grid online. No alarms had been raised at central command.

Harry imagined Johnson was already switching cameras, running through this wing, bearing down on the Kensington Gallery. He risked a glance into the five-room suite. The glow persisted deep in the gallery. Its passage seemed aimless, casual, not the determined sweep of a thief. He did a quick check on the security gate. Its electronic lock glowed green. It had not been breached.

He stared back at the glow. Maybe it was just the passing of some car's headlights through the gallery's windows.

Johnson's voice over his radio, cutting in and out, startled him. *"Not picking up anything on the vid . . . Camera five is out. Stay put . . . others on the way."* Any remaining words disappeared into the ether, fritzed by the electrical storm.

Harry stood by the gate. Other guards were coming as backup. What if it wasn't an intruder? What if it was just the sweep of headlights? He was already on thin ice with Fleming. All he needed was to be made a fool of.

He took a chance and raised his torch. "You there!" he yelled. He thought to sound commanding, but it came out more of a shrill whine.

Still, there was no change in the wandering pattern of the light. It seemed to be heading even deeper into the gallery—not in panicked retreat, just a meandering slow pace. No thief could have that much ice in his veins.

Harry crossed to the gate's electronic lock and used his passkey to open it. The magnetic seals released. He pulled the gate high enough to crawl under and entered the first room. Straightening, he lifted his torch again. He refused to be embarrassed by his momentary panic.

He should've investigated further before raising the alarm.

But the damage was done. The best he could do was save a bit of face by clearing up the mystery himself.

He called out again, just in case. "Security! Don't move!"

His shout had no effect. The glow continued its steady but meandering pace into the gallery.

He glanced back out the gate to the hall. The others would be here in under a minute. "Bugger it," he mumbled under his breath. He hurried into the gallery, pursuing the light, determined to root out its cause before the others arrived.

With hardly a glance, he passed treasures of timeless significance and priceless value: glass cabinets displaying clay tablets from Assyrian king Ashurbanipal; hulking statues of sandstone dating back to pre–Persian times; swords and weapons from every age; Phoenician ivories depicting ancient kings and queens; even a first printing of *The Arabian Nights*, under its original title, *The Oriental Moralist*.

Harry swept forward through the rooms, slipping from one dynasty to another—from the times of the Crusades to the birth of Christ, from the glories of Alexander the Great to the ages of King Solomon and Queen Sheba.

At last, he reached the farthest room, one of the largest. It contained objects more of interest to a naturalist, all from the region: rare stones and jewels, fossilized remains, Neolithic tools.

The source of the glow became clear. Near the center of the domed chamber, a half-meter globe of blue light floated lazily across the room. It shimmered, and its surface seemed to run with a flame of prismatic blue oil.

As Harry watched, the globe sailed through a glass cabinet as if it were made of air. He stood stunned. A sulfurous smell reached his nostrils, issuing forth from the ball of cerulean light.

The globe rolled over one of the crimson-glowing security lamps, shorting it out with a sizzling *pop*. The noise startled Harry back a step. The same fate must have been dealt to camera five in the room behind him. He glanced to the camera in this room. A red light glowed above it. Still working.

As if noting his attention, Johnson came back on his radio. For some reason, there was no static. *"Harry, maybe you'd better get out of there!"*

He remained transfixed, half out of fear, half out of wonder. Besides, the phenomenon was floating *away* from him, toward the darkened corner of the room.

The globe's glow illuminated a lump of metal within a glass cube. It was a chunk of red iron as large as a calf, a *kneeling* calf. The display card described it as a camel. Such a resemblance was dodgy at best, but Harry understood the supposed depiction. The item had been discovered in the desert.

The glow hovered over the iron camel.

Harry backed a cautious step and raised his radio. "Christ!"

The shimmering ball of light fell through the glass and landed upon the camel. Its glow winked out as quickly as a snuffed candle.

The sudden darkness blinded Harry for a breath. He lifted his torch. The iron camel still rested within its glass cube, undisturbed. "It's gone . . ."

"Are you safe?"

"Yeah. What the hell was that?"

Johnson answered, awe in his voice, *"A sodding lightning ball, I think! I heard stories from mates aboard warplanes as they flew through thunderclaps. Storm must have spit it out. But bloody hell if that wasn't brilliant!"*

It's not *brilliant* anymore, Harry thought with a sigh, and shook his head. Whatever the hell it was, it at least saved him from an embarrassing ribbing from his fellow guards.

He lowered his torch. But as the light fell away, the iron camel continued to glow in the darkness. A deep ruddy color.

"What the hell now?" Harry mumbled, and grabbed his radio. A severe static shock bit his fingers. Swearing, he shook it off. He raised his radio. "Something's odd. I don't think—"

The glow in the iron flared brighter. Harry fell back. The iron flowed across the camel's surface, melting as if exposed to a wash of acid rain. He was not the only one to note the change.

The radio barked in his hand: *"Harry, get out of there!"*

He didn't argue. He swung around but was too late.

The glass enclosure exploded outward. Stabbing spears pierced his left side. A jagged shard sliced clear through his cheek. But he barely felt the cuts as a wave of blast-furnace heat struck him, searing, burning away all the oxygen.

A scream lay upon his lips, never to be aired.

The next explosion ripped Harry from his feet and threw his body clear across the gallery. But only flaming bones hit the security gate, melting themselves into the steel grating.

01:53 A.M.

Safia al-Maaz awoke in a dead panic. Sirens rang from all directions. Flashes of red emergency lights strobed the bedroom walls. Terror gripped her in a vise. She could not breathe; cold sweat pebbled her brow, squeezed from her tightening skin. Clawed fingers clutched the bedsheets to her throat. Unable to blink, she was trapped for a moment between the past and the present.

Sirens blaring, blasts echoing in the distance . . . and closer still, screams of the wounded, the dying, her own voice adding to the chorus of pain and shock . . .

Bullhorns boomed from the streets below her flat. "Clear out for the engines! Everyone pull back!"

English . . . not Arabic, not Hebrew . . .

A low rumble rolled past her apartment building and off into the distance.

The voices of the emergency crews drew her back to her bed, back to the present. She was in London, not Tel Aviv. A long strangled breath escaped her. Tears rose to her eyes. She wiped them with shaky fingers.

Panic attack.

She sat wrapped in her comforter for several more breaths. She still felt like crying. It was always this way, she told herself, but the words didn't help. She gathered the woolen comforter around her shoulders, eyes closed, heart hammering in her ears. She practiced the breathing and calming exercises taught to her by her therapist. Inhale for two counts, out for four. She let the tension flow away with each breath. Her cold skin slowly warmed.

Something heavy landed on her bed. A small sound accompanied it. Like a squeaky hinge.

She reached out a hand, met by a purring welcome. "Come here, Billie," she whispered to the overweight black Persian.

Billie leaned into her palm and rubbed the underside of his chin across Safia's fingers, then simply collapsed across her thighs as if the invisible strings supporting the cat had been sliced. The sirens must have disturbed him from his usual nighttime haunting of her flat.

The low purr continued on Safia's lap, a contented sound.

This, more than her breathing exercises, relaxed the taut muscles of her shoulders. Only then did she notice the wary hunch in her back, as if fearing a blow that never came. She forced her posture straight, stretching her neck.

The sirens and commotion continued half a block from her building. She needed to stand, find out what was happening. Anything simply to be moving. Panic had transmuted into nervous energy.

She shifted her legs, careful to slide Billie onto the comforter. The purring halted for a moment, then resumed when it was clear he was not being evicted. Billie had been born in the streets of London, alley feral, a wild fluff of matted fur and spit. Safia had found the kitten sprawled and bloodied on the flat's stoop with a broken leg, covered in oil, hit by a car. Despite her help, he had bitten her in the fleshy meat of her thumb. Friends had told her to take the kitten to the animal shelter, but Safia knew such a place was no better than an orphanage. So instead, she had scooped him up in a pillow linen and transported him to the local veterinary clinic.

It would have been easy to step over him that evening, but she had once been as abandoned and alone as the kitten. Someone had taken her in at the time, too. And like Billie, she had been domesticated—but neither ended up completely tamed, preferring the wild places and rooting through lost corners of the world.

But all that had ended with one explosion on a bright spring day.

All my fault . . . Crying and screams again filled her head, merging with the sirens of the moment.

Breathing too hard, Safia reached to the bedside lamp, a small Tiffany replica depicting stained-glass dragonflies. She flicked the lamp's switch a few more times, but the lamp remained dark. Electricity was out. The storm must have knocked down a power line.

Maybe that was all the commotion.

Let it be something that simple.

She swung out of bed, barefoot, but in a warm flannel nightshirt that reached her knees. She crossed to the window and twisted the blinds to peer through to the street below. Her flat was on the fourth floor.

Below, the usually quiet and dignified street of iron lamps and wide sidewalks had become a surreal battlefield. Fire engines and police cars jammed the avenue. Smoke billowed despite the rain, but at least the fierce storm had faded to the usual London weep. With the streetlamps darkened, the only illumination came from the flashers atop the emergency vehicles. Yet, down the block, a deeper crimson glow flickered through the smoke and dark.

Fire.

Safia's heart thudded harder, her breath choked—not from old terrors, but from newborn fears for the present. The museum! She yanked the blinds' cords, ripping them up, and fumbled with the lock to the window. She pushed the sash open and bent out into the rain. She barely noted the icy drops.

The British Museum was only a short walk from her flat. She gaped at the sight. The northeast corner of the museum had crumbled to a fiery ruin. Flames flickered from shattered upper windows while smoke belched out in thick gouts. Men, cowled in rebreathing masks, dragged hoses. Jets of water sailed high. Ladders rose into the air from the back of engines.

Still, worst of all, a gaping hole smoked on the second floor of the northeast corner. Rubble and blackened blocks of cement lay strewn out into the street. She must not have heard the explosion or just attributed it to the storm's thunder. But this was no lightning strike.

More likely a bomb blast . . . a terrorist attack. *Not again* . . .

She felt her knees grow weak. The north wing . . . her wing. She knew the smoking hole led into the gallery at the end. All her work, a lifetime of research, the collection, a thousand antiquities from her homeland. It was too much to fathom. Disbelief made the sight even more unreal, a bad dream from which she would awake at any moment.

She fell back into the security and sanity of her room. She turned her back on the shouts and flashing lights. In the darkness, stained-glass dragonflies bloomed to life. She stared, unable to comprehend the sight for a moment, then it dawned. The power was back on.

At that moment, the phone on her nightstand rang, startling her.

Billie raised his head from the comforter, ears pricked at the jangling.

Safia hurried to the phone and picked up the receiver. "Hello?"

The voice was stern, professional. "Dr. al-Maaz?"

"Y-yes?"

"This is Captain Hogan. There's been an accident at the museum."

"Accident?" Whatever had happened was more than just an *accident*.

"Yes, the museum's director has requested I call you into the briefing. Can you join us in the next hour?"

"Yes, Captain. I'll be there immediately."

"Fine. Your name will be left at the security blockade." The phone clicked as the captain hung up.

Safia stared around her bedroom. Billie thumped his tail in clear feline irritation at the night's constant interruptions. "I won't be gone long," she mumbled, unsure if she spoke the truth.

Sirens continued to wail outside her window.

The panic that had woken her refused to fade away completely. Her worldview, the security of her position in the staid halls of a museum, had been shaken. Four years ago, she had fled a world where women strapped pipe bombs to their chests. She had fled to the safety and orderliness of academic life, abandoning fieldwork for paperwork, dropping picks and shovels for computers and spreadsheets. She had dug herself a little niche in the museum, one where she felt safe. She had made a home here.

But still disaster had found her.

Her hands trembled. She had to grip one in the other to fight another attack. She fancied nothing more than to crawl back into bed and pull the comforter over her head.

Billie stared at her, eyes reflecting the lamplight.

"I'll be fine. Everything's okay," Safia said quietly, more to herself than to the cat.

Neither was convinced.

02:13 A.M. GMT (09:13 P.M. EST)
Fort Meade, Maryland

Thomas Hardey hated to be disturbed while he worked on the *New York Times* crossword puzzle. It was his Sunday-night ritual, which also included a neat snifter of forty-year-old Scotch and a fine cigar. A fire crackled in the fireplace.

He leaned back in his leather wingback chair and stared at the half-filled puzzle, punching the nub on his Montblanc ballpoint pen.

He crinkled a brow at 19 down, a five-letter word. "Nineteen. The sum of all men."

As he pondered the answer, the phone rang on his desk. He sighed and pushed his reading glasses from the tip of his nose up to the line of his receding hairline. It was probably just one of his daughter's friends calling to discuss how her weekend date had fared.

As he leaned over, he saw the fifth line was blinking, his personal line. Only three people had that number: the president, the chairman of the Joint Chiefs, and his second-in-command at the National Security Agency.

He placed the folded newspaper on his lap and tapped the line's red button. With that single touch, a shifting algorithmic code would scramble any communication.

He lifted the receiver. "Hardey here."

"Director."

He sat straighter, wary. He did not recognize the other's voice. And he knew the voices of the three people who had his private number as well as he knew his own family's. "Who is this?"

"Tony Rector. I'm sorry for disturbing you at this late hour."

Thomas shuffled his mental Rolodex. Vice Admiral Anthony Rector. He connected the name to five letters:

DARPA. *The Defense Advanced Research Projects Agency.* The department oversaw the research-and-development arm of the Department of Defense. They had a motto: *Be there first.* When it came to technological advances, the United States could not come in second place.

Ever.

A tingling sense of dread grew. "How may I help you, Admiral?"

"There's been an explosion at the British Museum in London." He went on to explain the situation in great detail. Thomas checked his watch. Less than thirty minutes had passed since the blast. He was impressed by the ability of Rector's organization to gather so much intelligence in such a short time.

Once the admiral finished, Thomas asked the most obvious question. "And DARPA's interest in this blast?"

Rector answered him.

Thomas felt the room go ten degrees cooler. "Are you sure?"

"I already have a team in place to pursue that very question. But I'm going to need the cooperation of British MI5 . . . or better yet . . ."

The alternative hung in the air, unspoken even over a scrambled line.

Thomas now understood the clandestine call. MI5 was Britain's equivalent of his own organization. Rector wanted him to throw up a smoke screen so a DARPA team could whisk in and out before anyone else suspected the discovery. And that included the British intelligence agency.

"I understand," Thomas finally answered. *Be there first.* He prayed they could live up to this mission. "Do you have a team ready?"

"They'll be ready by morning."

From the lack of further elaboration, Thomas knew who would be handling this. He drew a Greek symbol on the margin of his newspaper.

$$\Sigma$$

"I'll clear the way for them," he said into the phone.

"Very good." The line went dead.

Thomas settled the phone to the cradle, already planning what must be done. He would have to work quickly. He stared down at the unfinished crossword puzzle: *19 down.*

A five-letter word for *the sum of all men.*

How appropriate.

He picked up a pen and filled in the answer in block letters.

SIGMA.

02:22 A.M. GMT
London, England

Safia stood before the barricade, a yellow-and-black A-frame. She kept her arms folded, anxious, cold. Smoke filled the air. What had happened? Behind the barricade, a policeman held her wallet in his hand and compared her photo to the woman who stood before him.

She knew he was having a hard time matching the two. In hand, her museum identification card portrayed a studious thirty-year-old woman of coffee-and-cream complexion, ebony hair tied back in an efficient braid, green eyes hidden behind black reading glasses. In contrast, before the young guard stood a soaking, bedraggled woman, hair loosely plastered in long swaths to her face. Her eyes felt lost and confused, focused beyond the barriers, beyond the frenzy of emergency personnel and equipment.

News crews dotted the landscape, haloed by the spots from their cameras. A few television trucks stood parked half up on the sidewalks. She also spotted two British military vehicles among the emergency crews, along with personnel bearing rifles.

The possibility of a terrorist attack could not be dismissed. She had heard such rumblings among the crowd and from a reporter she had to sidestep to reach the barricade. And not a few cast suspicious glances in her direction, the lone Arab on the street. She'd had firsthand experience with terrorism, but not in the manner these folks suspected. And maybe she was even misinterpreting the reactions around her. A form of paranoia, what was termed hyperanxiety, was a common sequela to a panic attack.

Safia continued through the crowd, breathing deeply, focusing on her purpose here. She regretted forgetting her umbrella. She had left her flat immediately after getting the call, delaying only long enough to pull on a pair of khaki slacks and a white floral blouse. She had donned a knee-length Burberry coat, but in her hurry, the matching umbrella had been left in its stand by the door. Only when she reached the first floor of her building and rushed into the rain did she realize her mistake. Anxiety kept her from climbing back up to the fourth floor to retrieve it.

She had to know what had happened at the museum. She'd spent the past decade building the collection, and the past four years running her research projects out of the museum. How much had been ruined? What could be salvaged?

Outside, the rain kicked up again to a steady downpour, but at least the night skies were less angry. By the time she reached the makeshift security checkpoint that cordoned off access, she had been soaked to the bone.

She shivered as the guard satisfied himself with her identification.

"You're clear to proceed. Inspector Samuelson is awaiting you."

Another policeman escorted her to the southern entrance of the museum. She stared up at its pillared facade. It had the solidness of a bank vault, a permanence that could not be doubted.

Until this night . . .

She was ushered through the entrance and down a series of stairs. They passed through doors marked MUSEUM STAFF ONLY. She knew where she was being taken. To the subterranean security suite.

An armed guard stood watch at the door. He nodded at their approach, clearly expecting them. He pulled the door open.

Her escort passed her on to a new fellow: a black man dressed in civilian clothes, an undistinguished blue suit. He stood a few inches taller than Safia, hair gone completely gray. His face looked like well-worn leather. She noticed a gray shadow of stubble across his cheeks, unshaven, called from his bed most likely.

He held out a hard hand. "Inspector Geoffrey Samuelson," he said as firmly as his handshake. "Thank
you for coming so quickly."

She nodded, too nervous to speak.

"If you'll follow me, Dr. al-Maaz, we need your
assistance in investigating the cause of the explosion."

"Me?" she managed to force out. She passed a break
room, crowded with security staff. It appeared the
entire staff, all shifts, had been summoned. She recognized several of the men and women, but they stared at
her now as if she were a stranger. The murmur of their
chatter fell silent as she passed. They must have known
she had been called in, but they didn't seem to know
the reason any more than she did. Still, suspicion was
plain behind the silence.

She held her back straighter, irritation sparking
through her anxiety. These were her coworkers, colleagues. Then again, they were all too aware of her past.

Her shoulders slumped as the inspector led her
down the hall to the farthest room. She knew it housed
the "nest," as it was nicknamed by the staff, an oval-
shaped room whose walls were completely covered
with video-surveillance monitors. Inside, she found
the room almost deserted.

She spotted the head of security, Ryan Fleming,
a short but stout man of middle years. He was easily

distinguished by his entirely hairless pate and beaked nose, earning him the nickname the "Bald Eagle." He stood beside a lanky man wearing a crisp military uniform, including a sidearm. The pair leaned over the shoulders of a technician who was seated at a bank of monitors. The group glanced over to her as she entered.

"Dr. Safia al-Maaz, curator of the Kensington Gallery," Fleming said as introduction. Straightening, he waved her over.

Fleming had been on staff since before Safia had assumed her position. A guard at the time, he had worked his way through the ranks to become chief of security. Four years ago, he had foiled the theft of a pre-Islamic sculpture from her gallery. It was this diligence that had won him his current position. The Kensingtons knew how to reward those who had done right by them. Ever since then, he had been particularly protective of Safia and her gallery.

She joined the group by the video bank, followed by Inspector Samuelson. Fleming touched her shoulder, his eyes wounded. "I'm so sorry. Your gallery, your work . . ."

"How much was lost?"

Fleming looked sick. He simply pointed to one of the monitors. She leaned toward it. It was a live feed. In black and white, she saw a view down the main hall of the north wing. Smoke roiled. Men, masked in protective suits, worked throughout the wing. A collection of them gathered before the security gate that led into the Kensington Gallery. They appeared to be staring up at a figure tied to the grating, a gaunt, skeletal shape, like some emaciated scarecrow.

Fleming shook his head. "The coroner will be allowed in shortly to identify the remains, but we're sure it's Harry Masterson, one of my men."

The frame of bones continued to smoke. That had once been a man? Safia felt the world tilt under her, and she fell back a step. Fleming steadied her. A conflagration of a magnitude powerful enough to burn the flesh off the bone was beyond her comprehension.

"I don't understand," she mumbled. "What happened here?"

The man in military blue answered, "That's what we're hoping you can shed some light on." He turned to the video technician. "Rewind back to zero one hundred."

The technician nodded.

The military man turned to Safia as his order was carried out. His face was hard, unwelcoming. "I'm Commander Randolph, representative of the Ministry of Defence's antiterrorist division."

"Antiterrorist?" Safia stared around at the others. "This was a bombing?"

"That's yet to be determined, ma'am," the commander said.

The technician stirred. "All ready, sir."

Randolph waved her to the monitor. "We'd like you to watch this, but what you're about to see is classified. Do you understand?"

She didn't, but she nodded anyway.

"Play it," Randolph commanded.

On the screen, a camera showed the rear room of the Kensington Gallery. All was in order, though the space was dark, lit only by security lights.

"This was taken just after one o'clock," the commander narrated.

Safia watched a new light float in from a neighboring room. At first, it appeared as if someone had entered, bearing aloft a lantern. But it soon became clear that the source of light moved on its own. "What is that?" she asked.

The technician answered, "We've studied the tape with various filters. It appears to be a phenomenon called ball lightning. A free-floating globule of plasma jettisoned from the storm. This is the first time in history one of the bloody buggers has been caught on film."

Safia had heard of such lightning displays. Balls of charged air, luminescent, that traveled horizontally over the ground. They appeared on open plains, inside houses, aboard airplanes, even within submarines. But such phenomena rarely caused any harm. She glanced back to the live-feed monitor with its smoking charnel house. Surely this wasn't the cause of the blast.

As she pondered this, a new figure appeared on the monitor, a guard.

"Harry Masterson," Fleming said.

Safia took a deep breath. If Fleming was right, this was the same man whose bones smoked on the other monitor. She wanted to close her eyes, but couldn't.

The guard followed the glow of the lightning ball. He seemed as mystified as those in the room with her. He raised his radio to his lips, reporting in, but there was no audio with the footage.

Then the ball lightning settled atop one of the display pedestals, one holding up an iron figure. It fell across it and winked out. Safia winced, but nothing happened.

The guard continued to talk into his radio . . . then something seemed to alarm the man. He turned just as the display cabinet shattered outward. A moment later, a second explosion appeared as a flash of white, then the screen went black.

"Hold that and rewind four seconds back," Commander Randolph ordered.

The footage froze and reversed, frames clicking back. The room reappeared out of the flash, then the cabinet re-formed around the iron figure.

"Freeze there."

The image stopped, shuddering slightly on the monitor. The iron artifact could be seen clearly within its glass display. In fact, *too* clearly. It appeared to shine with a light of its own.

"What the hell is that?" the commander asked.

Safia stared at the ancient artifact. She now understood why she had been called into this briefing. No one here understood what had happened either. None of it made any sense.

"Is that a sculpture?" the commander asked. "How long has it been there?"

Safia could read his mind, the barely hidden accusation. Had someone slipped a bomb into the museum disguised as a sculpture? And if this were true, who would be the one most likely to cooperate with such a ruse? Who but somebody on the inside? Somebody tied to an explosion in the past.

She shook her head at the questions and the accusations. "It . . . it's not a sculpture."

"Then what is it?"

"The iron figure is a fragment of *meteorite* . . . discovered in the Omani Desert near the end of the nineteenth century."

Safia knew that the artifact's history dated much further back. For centuries, Arabian myths spoke of a lost city whose entrance was guarded by an iron camel. The wealth of this lost city was supposedly beyond comprehension. Such were its riches that scores of black pearls were said to be scattered near its entrance like so much trash. Then, in the nineteenth century, a bedouin tracker led a British explorer to the place, but he found no lost city. What he discovered was merely a chunk of meteorite half buried in the sand that looked roughly like a kneeling camel. Even the black pearls were found to be just bits of blasted glass, formed by the heated impact of the meteorite into the sands.

"This camel-shaped meteorite," Safia continued, "has been a part of the British Museum's collection since its founding . . . though it had been relegated to the storage lockers until I found it in the catalog and added it to the collection."

Inpector Samuelson broke the silence. "When did this transfer happen?"

"Two years ago."

"So it's been there quite some time," the inspector said pointedly, glancing toward the commander as if this satisfied some earlier quarrel.

"A meteorite?" the commander mumbled with a shake of his head, clearly disappointed that his conspiracy theory had not panned out. "That makes no sense."

A commotion drew everyone's attention to the door. Safia saw the director of the museum, Edgar Tyson, force his way into the security room. The usually dapper man wore a wrinkled suit that matched his worried expression. He tugged at his small white goatee. Only now did Safia wonder at his conspicuous absence. The museum was the man's life and livelihood.

But the reason for his notable absence soon made itself clear. In fact it followed at his heels. The woman swept into the room, her presence almost preceding her form, like a surge before a storm. Tall, a full hand span over six feet, she wore a full-length tartan overcoat, dripping water, yet her sandy-blond hair, cut to the shoulders, was dry and coiffed to gentle curls that seemed to shift with their own breezes. Apparently she had not forgotten her umbrella.

Commander Randolph straightened, stepping forward, his voice suddenly respectful. "Lady Kensington."

Ignoring him, the woman continued her search of the room, her eyes settling on Safia. A flash of relief. "Saffie . . . thank God!" She hurried forward and hugged her tightly, mumbling breathlessly in her ear,

"When I heard . . . you work late so many nights. And I couldn't reach you on the phone . . ."

Safia hugged her back, feeling the tremble in the other's shoulders. They had known each other since they were children, been closer than sisters. "I'm all right, Kara," she mumbled into her shoulder.

She was surprised by the depth of genuine fear in the otherwise strong woman. She had not felt such affection from her in a long time, not since they were young, not since the death of Kara's father.

Kara trembled. "I don't know what I would've done if I'd lost you." Her arms tightened around Safia, both comfort and need.

Tears rose in Safia's eyes. She remembered another hug, similar words. *I won't lose you.*

At the age of four, Safia's mother had died in a bus accident. With her father already gone, Safia was placed in an orphanage, a horrible place for a child of mixed blood. A year later, the Kensington estate took Safia on as a playmate for Kara, put up in her own room. She barely remembered that day. A tall man had come and collected her.

It had been Reginald Kensington, Kara's father.

Because of their closeness in age and a shared wild nature, Kara and Safia had become fast friends . . . . sharing secrets at night, playing games among the date and palm trees, sneaking out to the cinema, whispering of their dreams under bedcovers. It had been a wonderful time, an endless sweet summer.

Then, at the age of ten, devastating news: Lord Kensington announced Kara would be traveling to England to study abroad for two years. Distraught, Safia had not even excused herself from the table. She had run to her room, panicked and heartbroken that she'd be returned to the orphanage, a toy put back in a box. But Kara had found her. *I won't lose you,* she had promised amid tears and embraces. *I'll make Papa let you come with me.*

And Kara had kept her word.

Safia went to England with Kara for those two years. They studied together, as sisters, as best friends. When they returned to Oman, they were inseparable. They finished their schooling in Muscat together. All seemed wonderful until the day Kara returned from a birthday hunting trip, sunburned and raving.

Her father had not returned with her.

Killed in a sinkhole was the official story, but Reginald Kensington's body had never been found.

Since that day, Kara had never been the same. She still kept Safia close to her, but it was more from a desire for the familiar than from true friendship. Kara became engrossed in finishing her own education, in taking over the mantle of her father's enterprises and ventures. At nineteen, she graduated from Oxford.

The young woman proved a financial savant, trebling her father's net worth while still at the university. Kensington Wells, Incorporated, continued to grow, branching into new fields: computer technology platforms, desalination patents, television broadcasting. Still, Kara never neglected the fountainhead of all her family's wealth: *oil*. In just the last year, Kensington surpassed the Halliburton Corporation for the most profitable oil contracts.

And like Kensington's oil ventures, Safia was not left behind. Kara continued to pay for her education, including six years at Oxford, where Safia earned her doctorate in archaeology. Upon graduation, she remained under the employ of Kensington Wells, Inc. Eventually she came to oversee Kara's pet project here at the museum, a collection of antiquity from the Arabian Peninsula, a collection first started by Reginald Kensington. And like his former corporation, this project also prospered under Kara's mantle, growing into the single largest collection in the entire world. Two months ago, the ruling family in Saudi Arabia had attempted to buy the collection, to return it to Arabian soil, a deal rumored to be worth in the hundreds of millions.

Kara had declined. The collection meant more to her than money. It was a memorial to her father. Though his body had never been found, here was his tomb, this lone wing in the British Museum, surrounded by all the wealth and history of Arabia.

Safia stared past her friend's shoulder to the live-feed monitor, to the smoky ruin of her hard work. She could only imagine what the loss would mean to Kara. It would be like someone desecrating her father's grave.

"Kara," Safia began, attempting to soften the blow that would come, to hear it from someone who shared her passion. "The gallery . . . it's gone."

"I know. Edgar already told me." Kara's voice lost its hesitancy. She pulled out of the embrace, as if suddenly feeling foolish. She stared around at the others gathered here. The familiar tone of command entered her demeanor. "What happened? Who did this?"

To lose the collection so soon after rejecting the Saudis' offer had clearly piqued Kara's suspicion, too.

Without hesitation, the tape was once again played for Lady Kensington. Safia remembered the earlier admonishment about the secrecy of what the footage revealed. No such warning was given to Kara. Wealth had its privileges.

Safia ignored the replay on the monitor. Instead she studied Kara, fearing how this might devastate her.

From the corner of her eye, she caught the final flash of the explosion, and then the monitor went black. All during the viewing, Kara's expression remained unchanged, a marble relief of concentration, Athena in deep thought.

But at the end, Kara's eyes slowly closed. Not with shock and horror—Safia knew Kara's moods only too well—but with profound relief. Her friend's lips moved in a breathless whisper, a single word, caught only by her own ears.

"Finally . . ."

2

Foxhunt

◊∘५Y▥५X

Patience was the key to any successful hunt.

Painter Crowe stood upon his native lands, the land his father's tribe named Mashantucket, the "much wooded land." But where Painter waited, there were no trees, no birdsong, no whisper of wind across the cheek. Here it was the chime of slot machines, the chink of coins, the reek of tobacco smoke, and the continual recycling of lifeless air.

Foxwoods Resort and Casino was the largest gambling complex in the entire world, surpassing anything found in Las Vegas or even Monte Carlo. Located outside of the unassuming hamlet of Ledyard,

Connecticut, the towering complex rose dramatically from the dense woods of the Mashantucket reservation. In addition to the gambling facility with its six thousand slot machines and hundreds of gaming tables, the resort was home to three world-class hotels. The entire facility was owned by the Pequot tribe, the "Fox People," who had hunted these same lands for the past ten thousand years.

But at the moment, it was not a deer or a fox being hunted.

Painter's quarry was a Chinese computer scientist, Xin Zhang.

Zhang, better known by his alias, *Kaos*, was a hacker and code breaker of prodigious talent, one of China's finest. After reading his dossier, Painter had learned respect for the slim man in the Ralph Lauren suit. During the past three years, he had orchestrated a successful wave of computer espionage upon U.S. soil. His latest acquisition: plasma weapons technology out of Los Alamos.

Painter's target finally shoved up from the pai gow table.

"Would you like to color out, Dr. Zhang?" the pit boss asked, standing over the table like a captain at the prow of his boat. At seven in the morning, there was only the lone player . . . and his bodyguards.

The isolation required Painter to spy upon his quarry from a safe distance. Suspicions could not be aroused. Especially not so late in the game.

Zhang shifted the pile of black chips toward the dealer, a woman with bored eyes. As the dealer stacked the winnings, Painter studied his target.

Zhang proved the stereotype of the Chinese as *inscrutable*. He had a poker face that gave no obvious *tell*, no idiosyncratic tic that denoted a good or a bad hand. He simply played his game.

Like he did now.

None would guess from the man's appearance that he was a master criminal, wanted in fifteen countries. He dressed like a typical Western businessman: a sharply tailored suit in an understated pinstripe, a silk tie, a platinum Rolex. Still, there remained a certain austere aesthetic quality to him. His black hair was shaved around the ears and back, leaving only a crisp crown of hair on top of his head, not unlike a monk. He wore a pinched set of eyeglasses, circular lenses, faintly tinted blue, a studious countenance.

At last the dealer waved her hands over the stack of chips, showing her empty fingers and palms to the security cameras hidden in the black mirrored domes in the ceiling.

"Fifty thousand dollars even," she finished.

The pit boss nodded. The dealer counted out the amount in thousand-dollar chips. "More good luck, sir," the boss acknowledged.

Without even a nod, Zhang departed with his two bodyguards. He had been gambling all night. Dawn already glimmered. The CyberCrime forum would resume in another three hours. The conference covered the latest trends in identity theft, infrastructure protection, and myriad other security topics.

In two hours, a breakfast symposium put on by Hewlett Packard would commence. Zhang would make the transfer during that meeting. His American contact was still unknown. It was one of the main objectives of the ops here. Besides securing the weapons data, they sought to flush out Zhang's stateside contact, someone tied to a shady network that traded in military secrets and technologies.

It was a mission that must not fail.

Painter followed the group. His superiors at DARPA had personally tapped him for this mission, in part for his expertise in microsurveillance and computer engineering, but more importantly, for his ability to blend in at Foxwoods.

Though only half-blooded, Painter had inherited enough of his father's features to pass as a Pequot Indian. It did take a few trips to a tanning salon to enrich his complexion and brown contact lenses to hide his mother's blue eyes. But afterward, with his shoulder-length hair the color of a raven's wing, presently tied back in a tail, he did look like his father. To finish his disguise, he wore a casino suit with the symbol of the Pequot tribe embroidered on the pocket, a tree atop a knoll framed against a clear sky. Who looked beyond a suit anyway?

From his position, Painter remained wary as he followed Zhang. His eyes never focused directly upon the group. He watched peripherally and used natural cover to the best advantage. He stalked his quarry through the neon woodlands of blinking machines and wide glades of green felt tables. He maintained his distance and varied his pace and direction.

His earpiece buzzed with Mandarin. Zhang's voice. Picked up by the microtransceiver. Zhang was heading back to his suite.

Painter touched his throat microphone and subvocalized into the radio. "Sanchez, how are you picking up on the feed?"

"Loud and clear, Commander."

His co-agent on this mission, Cassandra Sanchez, was holed up in the suite across the hall from Zhang's, manning the surveillance array.

"How is the subdermal holding?" he asked her.

"He'd better access his computer soon. The bug is running low on juice."

Painter frowned. The "bug" had been planted yesterday on Zhang during a massage. Sanchez's Latino features were dark enough to pass for Indian. She had implanted the subdermal transceiver during a deeptissue massage last night, the prick of penetration unfelt as she dug her thumbs in deep. She covered the tiny puncture wound with an anesthetic smear of surgical bond. By the time the massage was over, it had sealed and dried. The digital microtransceiver had a life span of only twelve hours.

"How much time left?"

"Best estimate . . . eighteen minutes."

"Damn."

Painter focused his full attention back on his quarry's conversation.

The man kept his voice low, meant for his bodyguards only. Painter, fluent in Mandarin, listened. He hoped Zhang would give some indication when he would retrieve the plasma weapons file. He was disappointed.

"Have the girl ready after I've showered," Zhang said.

Painter tightened a fist. The "girl" was thirteen, an indentured slave from North Korea. *His daughter,* he had explained to those who even thought to ask. If this had been true, *incest* could be added to the long list of charges to which Zhang was guilty.

Following them, Painter skirted around a change booth and set off down a long bank of machines, paralleling his quarry. A jackpot rang out from a dollar slot machine. The winner, a middle-aged man in a jogging suit, smiled and looked around for someone to share his good fortune. There was only Painter.

"I won!" he cried jubilantly, eyes red-rimmed from playing all night.

Painter nodded. "More good luck, sir," he answered, repeating the pit boss's earlier words, and strode past the man. There were no real winners here—except the casino. The slot machines alone netted eight hundred million dollars last year. It seemed the Pequot tribe had come a long way from its 1980s sand-and-gravel business.

Unfortunately, Painter's father had missed out on the boom, abandoning the reservation in the early eighties to pursue his fortune in New York City. It was there he met Painter's mother, a fiery Italian woman who would eventually stab her husband to death after seven years of marriage and the birth of their son. With his mother on death row, Painter had grown up in a series of foster homes, where he quickly learned it was best to keep silent, to be unseen.

It had been his first training in stealth . . . but not his last.

Zhang's group entered the Grand Pequot Tower's elevator lobby, showing their suite key to the security guard.

Painter crossed past the opening. He had a Glock 9mm in a holster at the base of his back, covered by his casino jacket. He had to resist pulling it out and shooting Zhang in the back of the head, execution style.

But that would not achieve their objective: to recover the schematics and research for the orbital plasma cannon. Zhang had managed to steal the data from a secure federal server, leaving a *worm* behind. The next morning, a Los Alamos technician by the name of Harry Klein accessed the file, inadvertently releasing the data worm that proceeded to eat all references of the weapon while defecating a false trail that implicated Klein. That bit of computerized sleight of hand cost investigators two weeks as they pursued the false trail.

It had taken a dozen DARPA agents to filter through the worm shit and discover the true identity of the thief: Xin Zhang, a spy positioned as a technologist with Changnet, a telecom upstart out of Shanghai. According to the CIA's intelligence, the stolen data was on the suitcase computer in Zhang's suite. The hard drive had been trip-wired with an elaborate encryption defense. A single mistake in attempting to access the computer would wipe out everything.

That could not be risked. Nothing had survived the worm at Los Alamos. Estimates were that the loss would set the program back by a full ten months. But the worst consequence was that the stolen research would advance China's program by a full five years. The files contained some phenomenal breakthroughs and cutting-edge innovations. It was up to DARPA to stop it. Their objective was to gain Zhang's password and retrieve the computer.

Time was running out.

Painter watched from the reflection in a *Wheel-of-Fortune* slot machine as Zhang and his bodyguards stepped into an express elevator that led to the private suites that topped the tower.

Touching his throat mike, Painter whispered, "They're heading up."

"Got it. Ready when you are, Commander."

As the doors squeezed closed, Painter rushed over to a neighboring elevator. It had been crisscrossed with bright yellow tape, lettered in black: OUT OF ORDER. Painter ripped through it while punching the button. As the doors parted, he ducked through. He touched his throat mike. "All clear! Go!"

Sanchez answered, *"Brace yourself."*

As the elevator doors shushed closed, he leaned against the mahogany paneling, legs wide.

The car shot upward, driving him toward the floor. His muscles tensed. He watched the glowing numbers climb upward, ever faster. Sanchez had rewired this car for maximum acceleration. She had also slowed Zhang's elevator by 24 percent, not enough to be noticed.

As Painter's car reached the thirty-second floor, it decelerated with a shudder. He was lifted off his feet, hung in the air for a long breath, then fell back to the floor. He ducked through the doors as they opened, careful not to disturb the taped entry. He checked the neighboring elevator. Zhang's car was three floors away and climbing.

He needed to hurry.

Painter raced down the hall of suites. He found Zhang's room number. "How are we positioned?" he whispered.

"The girl is handcuffed to the bed. Two guards are playing cards in the main room."

"Roger that." Sanchez had placed pencil cameras in the room's heating vents. Painter crossed the hall and keyed his way into the opposite suite.

Cassandra Sanchez sat nestled among her electronic surveillance equipment and monitors like a spider in a web. She was dressed in black, from boots to blouse. Even her leather shoulder holster and belt matched her outfit, carrying her .45 Sig automatic. She had customized the pistol with a Hogue rubberized grip and mounted the thumb catch for her magazine release on the right side to accommodate her left hand. She was a deadly-accurate marksman, trained like Painter in Special Forces before being recruited into Sigma.

Her eyes greeted him with the sparkle of the endgame.

His own breath quickened at the sight of her. Her breasts pushed against the thin material of her silk blouse, snugged tight by the shoulder holster. He had to force his eyes up to maintain proper contact. They had been partners for the past five years and only recently had his feelings for her deepened. Business lunches turned into drinks after work, and finally long dinners. But still, certain lines had yet to be crossed, a distance tentatively maintained.

She seemed to sense his thoughts and glanced away, never pressing. "About time the bastard got up here," she said, turning her attention back to her monitors. "He'd better burn those files in the next quarter hour or— *Shit!*"

"What?" Painter stepped to her side.

She pointed to one of the monitors. It showed a three-dimensional cross section of the upper levels of the Grand Pequot Tower. A small red X glowed within the structure. "He's heading back down!"

The X marked the tracer built into the microtransceiver. It was dropping through the levels of the tower.

Painter clenched a fist. "Something's spooked him. Has there been any communication with his room since he entered the elevator?"

"Not a whistle."

"The computer is still there?"

She pointed to another monitor, a black-and-white image of Zhang's suite. The suitcase computer still rested on the coffee table. If not for the encryption, it would've been so easy to break in and abscond with the computer. But they needed Zhang's codes. The planted bug would record every keystroke he made, capturing the code. Once that was obtained, they could lock down Zhang and his men.

"I've got to get back down there," Painter said. The tracking device was built on such a small scale that it had a range of only two hundred yards. Someone had to be close at all times. "We can't lose him."

"If he's wise to us—"

"I know." He headed for the door. Zhang would have to be eliminated. They'd lose the files, but at least the weapons data wouldn't make it back to China. That

had always been their fallback plan. They had safeguards built upon safeguards. There was even a small
EM grenade affixed inside one of the suite's ventilation grates. At a moment's notice, they could activate it,
triggering an electromagnetic pulse that would activate
the computer's self-defenses to wipe the data. China
must never gain the research.

Painter rushed down the hall and crossed back to
the taped-off elevator. He ducked inside. He spoke into
his radio's throat mike. "Can you get me down there
ahead of him?"

"Better grab your balls," she answered.

Before he could take her advice, the elevator dropped
from under him. He was weightless for a long stretch,
stomach riding up into his throat. The elevator plummeted in a free fall. Painter fought down a surge of
panic, along with a rise of bile. Then the car's floor
came crashing up. There was no way to hold himself
upright. He fell to his knees. Then the slowing eased
and the elevator came to a gliding stop.

The doors whisked open.

Painter stumbled to his feet. Thirty floors in less
than five seconds. That had to be a record. He pushed
through the doorway and out into the elevator lobby.
He glanced to the numbers above the express elevator
Zhang had taken.

He was only a floor away.

Painter took a few steps back, near enough to cover the door, but not close enough to arouse suspicion, posing again as casino security.

The doors opened on the main floor.

Painter spied indirectly, using the reflection of the polished brass elevator doors across from the express. *Oh, no . . .* He swung around and crossed in front of the elevator. No one was in the cage.

Had Zhang gotten off on another floor? He stepped into the vacant elevator. Impossible. This was the express. There were no stops between here and the floor of suites above. Unless he had pulled the emergency stop, then forced the doors open to make his escape.

Then Painter spotted it. Taped to the back wall. A glinting bit of plastic and metal. The microtransceiver. The bug.

Painter felt his heart pound against his rib cage as he stepped into the elevator. His vision tunneled on the bit of electronics taped to the wall. He ripped it free, examining it closely. Zhang had lured him away.

Oh, God . . .

He touched his throat mike. "Sanchez!"

His heart continued its heavy thudding. There was no answer.

He swung around and punched the elevator button, marked simply SUITES. The doors closed too slowly.

Painter paced the tiny compartment, a caged lion. He tried his radio again. Still no response.

"Goddamnit . . ." The express began its climb. Painter pounded a fist against the wall. Mahogany paneling cracked under his knuckles. "Move, you fucker!"

But he knew he was already too late.

02:38 P.M. GMT
London, England

Standing out in the hall, steps from the Kensington Gallery, Safia could not breathe. Her difficulty was not from the stench of wood smoke, burned insulation, or the residual scorch of electrical fires. It was the wait. All morning long, she had watched investigators and inspectors from every British bureau traipse in and out. She had been barred.

Official personnel only.

Civilians were not allowed to cross the streamers of yellow tape, the cordons of barricades, the wary eyes of military guards.

Half a day later, she was finally being allowed inside, to see firsthand the destruction. In this final moment, her chest felt as if it were clamped in a giant stone fist. Her heart was a panicked pigeon, beating at her rib cage.

What would she find? What was salvageable?

She felt stricken to the core, devastated, as ruined as the gallery.

The work here was more than just her *academic* life. After Tel Aviv, she had rebuilt her *heart* here. And though she had left Arabia, she had not abandoned it. She was still her mother's daughter. So she had rebuilt Arabia in London, an Arabia before terrorists, a tangible account of her land's history, its wonder, its ancient times and mysteries. Surrounded by these antiquities, walking the galleries, she heard the crunch of sand underfoot, felt the warmth of the sun on her face, and tasted the sweetness of dates freshly picked. It was home, a safe place.

But it was more than all that. Her grief went deeper.

At her core, she had built this home, not just for herself, but also for the mother she barely remembered. At times, when working late at night, Safia caught the faintest wisp of jasmine in the air, a memory from childhood, of her mother. Though they couldn't share their life, they could share this place, this bit of home.

Now it was all gone.

"They're letting us in."

Safia stirred. She glanced to Ryan Fleming. The head of security had kept vigil with her, though it looked like he'd had little sleep.

"I'll stick with you," he said.

She forced air into her lungs and nodded. It was the best she could manage as thanks for his kindness and company. She followed the other museum staff forward. They had all agreed to help with the cataloging and documenting of the gallery's contents. It would take weeks.

Safia marched forward, both drawn to and fearful of what she would find. She rounded past the last barricade. The security gates had been removed by the coroner's office. She was thankful of that. She had no desire to see the remains of Harry Masterson.

She stepped to the entrance and stared inside.

Despite the preparation in her head and the brief glimpse from the video cameras, she was not ready for what she found.

The bright gallery was now a blackened cavern system, five chambers of charred stone.

Breath caught in her chest. Gasps arose behind her.

The firestorm had laid waste to everything. The wallboard had been incinerated down to the base blocks. Nothing remained standing except for a single Babylonian vase in the center of the gallery. It stood waist-high, and while scorched, it had remained upright. Safia had read reports of tornadoes doing the same, cutting a swath of total devastation while leaving a bicycle resting on its kickstand, untouched in the middle of it all.

It made no sense. None of it did.

The place still reeked of smoke and several inches of sooty water covered the floor, left over from the deluge of the fire hoses.

"You'll need rubbers," Fleming said, placing a hand on her arm, guiding her over to a line of boots. She pulled into a set numbly. "And a hard hat."

"Where do we even begin?" someone muttered.

Properly outfitted now, Safia stepped into the gallery, moving as if in a dream, mechanical, eyes un-blinking. She crossed through the rooms. When she reached the far gallery, something crunched under her boot heel. She bent down, fished through the water, and retrieved a stone from the floor. A few lines of cuneiform etched its surface. It was a piece of an Assyrian tablet, dating back to ancient Mesopotamia. She straightened and stared across the ruin of the Kensington Gallery.

Only now did she note the other people. Strangers in her home.

Folks labored in pockets, talking in hushed tones, as if in a graveyard. Building inspectors examined the infrastructure while fire investigators took readings with handheld devices. A pack of municipal engineers argued in a corner about budgets and bids, and a few policemen stood guard by the collapsed section of the exterior wall. Workmen were already constructing a crude plank blockade to cover the opening.

Through the gap, she spotted gawkers across the street, held back by cordons. They were surprisingly persistent considering that the morning drizzle had turned into sleet by the afternoon. Flashes of camera bulbs flickered in the gloom. Tourists.

A surge of anger flamed through her numbness. She wanted to throw the lot of them out of here. This was her wing, her home. Her anger helped focus her, bring her back to the situation at hand. She had a duty, an obligation.

Safia returned her attention to the other scholars and students from the museum. They had begun to sift through the debris. It was heartening to see their usual petty professional jealousies set aside for now.

Safia crossed back toward the entrance, ready to organize those who had volunteered. But as she reached the first gallery, a large group appeared at the entrance. At the forefront strode Kara, dressed in work clothes, a red hard hat emblazoned with the insignia for Kensington Wells. She led a team of some twenty men and women into the gallery. They were identically outfitted, wearing the same red hard hats.

Safia stepped in front of her. "Kara?" She had not seen the woman all day. She had vanished with the head of the museum, supposedly to help coordinate the various investigative teams of the fire and police. It seemed a few billion in sterling garnered some authority.

Kara waved the men and women into the gallery. "Get to work!" She turned to Safia. "I've hired my own forensic team."

Safia stared after the group as they tromped like a small army into the rooms. Instead of weapons, they carried all manner of scientific tools. "What's going on? Why are you doing this?"

"To find out what happened." Kara watched her team set to work. Her eyes had a feverish shine, a fiery determination.

Safia had not seen such a look on her face in a long time. Something had sparked an intensity in Kara that had been missing for years. Only one thing could bring about such fervor.

Her father.

Safia remembered the look in Kara's eyes as she had surveyed the videotape of the explosion. The strange relief. Her one spoken word. *Finally* . . .

Kara stepped out into the gallery. Already her team had commenced digging samples from various surfaces: plastics, glass, wood, stone. Kara crossed to a pair of men carrying metal detectors, sweeping them along the floor. One pulled a bit of a melted bronze from some debris. He set it aside.

"I want every fragment of that meteorite found," Kara ordered.

The men nodded, continuing the search.

Safia joined Kara. "What are you *really* seeking here?"

Kara turned to her, eyes ablaze with determination. "Answers."

Safia read the hope behind the set in her friend's lips. "About your father?"

"About his death."

4:20 P.M.

Kara sat in the hall on a folding chair. The work continued in the galleries. Fans whirred and rattled. The mumble and chatter of workers in the wing barely reached her. She had come out to smoke a cigarette. She had long given up the habit, but she needed something to do with her hands. Her fingers trembled.

Did she have the strength for this? The strength to hope.

Safia appeared at the entryway, spotted her, and stepped in her direction.

Kara waved her off, pointed to the cigarette. "I just need a moment."

Safia paused, staring at her, then nodded and headed back into the gallery.

Kara took another drag, filling her chest with cool smoke, but it did little to settle her. She was too unbalanced, the adrenaline of the night wearing thin. She stared at the plaque beside the gallery. It bore a bronze likeness of her father, the founder of the gallery.

Kara sighed out a stream of smoke, blurring the sight. *Papa* . . .

Somewhere out in the gallery, something fell with a loud bang, sounding like a gunshot, a reminder of a past, of a hunt across the sands.

Kara drifted into the past.

It had been her sixteenth birthday.

The hunt had been her father's gift.

The Arabian oryx fled up the slope of the dune. The antelope's white coat stood out starkly against the red sands. The only two blemishes to its snowy hide were a black swatch on the tip of its tail and a matching mask around its eyes and nose. A wet crimson trail dripped down its wounded haunch.

As it fought to escape the hunters, the oryx's hooves drove deep into the loose sand. Blood flowed more thickly as it kicked toward the ridgeline. A pair of tapered horns sliced through the still air as the muscles of its neck wrenched with each painful yard gained.

A quarter mile back, Kara heard its echoing cry over the growl of her sand cycle, a four-wheel all-terrain vehicle with thick knobby tires. In frustration, she gripped the handles of her bike as it flew over the summit of a monstrous dune. For a breathless moment, she lifted out of her seat, airborne, as the cycle bucked over the ridge.

The angry set to her lips remained hidden behind a sand scarf, a match to her khaki safari suit. Her blond hair, braided to the middle of her back, flagged behind her like a wild mare's tail.

Her father kept pace on another cycle, rifle carried across his back. He had his own scarf dropped around his neck. His skin was tanned the color of saddle leather, his hair gone a sandy gray. He caught her glance.

"We're close!" he yelled above the whining growl of their engines. He gunned his engine and sped down the windward side of the dune.

Kara raced after him, bent over her cycle's handlebars, followed closely by their bedouin guide. It had been Habib who had led them to their quarry. It had also been the bedouin's skilled shot that had first wounded the oryx. Though impressed with his marksmanship, shooting the antelope on the fly, Kara had become furious upon learning the wounding had been deliberate, meant not to kill.

"To slow . . . for the girl," Habib had explained.

Kara had rankled at the cruelty . . . and the insult. She had been hunting with her father from the age of six. She was not without skill herself and preferred a clean kill. Purposely wounding the animal was needlessly savage.

She cranked the throttle, kicking up sand.

Some, especially back in England, raised their eyebrows at her upbringing, considering her a tomboy, especially with no mother. Kara knew better. Traveling half the world, she had been raised with no pretensions about the line between men and women. She knew how to defend herself, how to fight with fist or knife.

Reaching the bottom of the dune now, Kara and their guide caught up with her father as his cycle bogged down in a camel wallow, a patch of loose sand that sucked like quicksand. They passed him in a cloud of dust.

Her father bulled the bike out of the wallow and gave chase up the next dune, a massive six-hundred-foot mountain of red sand.

Kara reached the crest first with Habib, slowing slightly until she could see what lay beyond. And it was lucky she had. The far side of the dune fell away as steeply as a cliff, ending in a wide plain of flat sand. She could have easily tumbled tail over head down the slope.

Habib waved for her to stop. She obeyed, knowing better than to proceed. She idled her bike. Stopped now, she felt the heavy heat drop like a weight on her shoulders, but she barely noticed. Her breath escaped her in a long awed sigh.

The view beyond the dune was spectacular. The sun, near to setting, tempered the flat sand to sheer glass. Heat mirages shimmered in pools, casting an illusion of vast lakes of water, a false promise in an unforgiving landscape.

Still, another sight held Kara transfixed. In the center of the plain, a lone funnel of sand spiraled up from below, vanishing into a cloud of dust far overhead.

A sand devil.

Kara had seen such sights before, including the more violent sandstorms that could whip out of nowhere and vanish just as quickly. Still, this sight somehow struck her deeply. The solitary nature of this tempest, its perfect stillness in the plain. There was something mysterious and foreign about it.

She heard Habib mumbling beside her, head bent, as if in prayer.

Her father joined them then, drawing back her attention. "There she is!" he said, panting and pointing at the base of the steep slope.

The oryx struggled across the open plain of sand, limping badly now.

Habib held up his hand, stirring out of his prayer. "No, we go no farther."

Her father frowned. "What are you talking about?"

Their guide kept his gaze ahead. His thoughts were hidden behind dark Afrika Corps goggles and a woolen Omani headcloth, called a shamag.

"We go no farther," Habib repeated thickly. "This is the land of the nisnases, the forbidden sands. We must turn back."

Her father laughed. "Nonsense, Habib."

"Papa?" Kara asked.

He shook his head and explained, "The nisnases are the bogeymen of the deep desert. Black djinns, ghosts that haunt the sands."

Kara glanced back to the unreadable features of their guide. The Empty Quarter of Arabia, the Rub'
al-Khali, was the world's largest sand mass, dwarfing even the Sahara, and the fantastic tales flowing out of the region were as many as they were outlandish. But some folk still held these stories to be true.

Including, apparently, their guide.

Her father throttled down his bike's engine. "I promised you a hunt, Kara, and I won't disappoint you. But if you want to turn back . . ."

Kara hesitated, glancing between Habib and her father, balanced between fear and determination, between mythology and reality. Here in the wilds of the deep desert, all seemed possible.

She stared at the fleeing animal, limping across the hot sands, every stride a struggle, its path etched in pain. She knew what she had to do. All this blood and agony had started for her benefit. She would end it.

She pulled up her sand scarf and gunned her engine. "There's an easier way down. Off to the left." She rode along the ridgeline, heading toward a more gentle section of the dune face.

There was no need to glance over her shoulder to feel her father's wide smile of satisfaction and pride. It shone on her as bright as the sun. Still, at the moment, it offered no real warmth.

She stared out across the plain, past the lone oryx, to the solitary spiral of sand. While such sand devils were commonplace, the sight still struck her as strange. It hadn't moved.

Reaching the gentler slope, Kara tilted her bike down toward the flat plains. It was steep. She and her cycle skated and skidded down the face, but she kept the bike stable on the loose sand. As she struck the rough plain, her wheels bit with the firmer traction, and she sped away.

She heard her father's bike at her heels. The sound reached their quarry, too. The oryx's pace increased with an agonized toss of its head.

It was less than a quarter mile off. It would not be long. On level ground, their ATVs would ride the animal down, and a quick, clean shot would end its misery, end the hunt.

"She's going for cover!" her father called to her, pointing an arm. "Making for the sandstorm!"

Her father shot past her. Kara gave chase, bent low. They pursued the wounded creature, but desperation gave it swift speed.

The oryx trotted into the storm's edge, heading toward its center.

Her father cursed thickly but continued racing ahead.

Kara followed, dragged in her father's wake.

Nearing the dust storm, they discovered a deep hollow in the sand. Both bikes braked at the lip. The dust devil rose from the hollow's center, as if it were burrowing into the desert, casting sand high into the air. The dust column had to be fifty yards across, the bowl a good quarter mile.

A smoking volcano in the sand.

Traces of blue energy laced through the devil with unnervingly silent crackles. She could smell the ozonelike odor. It was a phenomenon unique to the sandstorms of the dry desert: static electricity.

Ignoring the sight, her father pointed to the bottom of the bowl. "There she is!"

Kara looked down. Limping across the floor of the hollow, the oryx made for the thicker dust, the twisting cyclone near the center.

"Loosen your rifle!" her father called.

She remained frozen, unable to move.

The oryx reached the edge of the devil, legs shaking, knees buckling, but it fought for the denser cover of the swirling sand.

Her father swore under his breath and dove his bike down the slope.

Fearful, Kara bit her lower lip, pushed her cycle over the edge, and headed after him. As soon as she dipped down, she felt the static electricity trapped in the hollow. The hairs on her skin crackled against her clothes, adding fuel to her fear. She slowed, her rear tires sinking into the sandy slope.

Her father reached the bottom and spun the bike to a stop, almost toppling it over. But he kept his seat, twisting around with the rifle on his shoulder.

Kara heard the loud crack of his Marlin rifle. She stared toward the oryx, but it was already into the dust storm, a mere shadow now. Still, the shadow lurched, falling.

A kill shot. Her father had done it!

Kara suddenly felt a surge of foolishness. She had let her fears control her and had lost her place in the hunt. "Papa!" she called out, ready to praise him, proud of his dogged pragmatism in this hunt.

But a sudden scream strangled any further words. It came from the sand devil, issuing as if from some dark hell, a horrible cry of agony. The dark shadow of the oryx thrashed in the heart of the devil, blurred by the whirling sand. The agonized wail tore from its throat. It was being slaughtered.

Her father, still straddling the cycle, struggled to get his vehicle turned around. He stared up at her, eyes wide. "Kara! Get out of here!"

She couldn't move. What was happening?

Then the wailing cry cut off. A horrible smell followed, the stench of burning flesh and hair. It rolled up and out of the hollow, cresting over her, gagging her. She saw her father still fighting his bike, but he had wallowed his wheels. He was stuck.

His eyes found her still frozen in place. "Kara! Go!" He waved an arm for emphasis. His tanned face was deathly pale. "Honey, run!"

Then she felt it. A stirring in the sand. At first it was just a gentle tug, as if gravity had suddenly increased. Sand particles began to dance and tumble down, quickly becoming rivulets, flowing down in a curving path, heading toward the sand devil.

Her father felt it, too. He gunned his engine, wheels spinning in the sand, casting up flumes of dust. He screamed at her, "Run, goddamnit!"

This shout jolted her. Her father seldom screamed— and never in panic.

She kicked up her engine, strangling the throttle. She saw to her horror that the dusty column had grown wider, fed by the inexplicable currents in the sand. It stretched toward where her father remained bogged in the sand.

"Papa!" she cried to him in warning.

"Go, child!" He finally freed his cycle by sheer force of will. Straddling the bike, he chased the cycle around, chewing up sand.

Kara followed his example. She swung around, gunned her engine, and fled back up the slope. Beneath her bike, the sand sucked at her, as if she were in a whirlpool, being drawn backward. She fought the sands with all her skill.

Finally reaching the bowl's rim, she glanced over her shoulder. Her father was still near the bottom, his face muddy with sand and sweat, eyes squinted in concentration. Over his shoulder, the swirling sand closed in, towering, sparking with traceries of static electricity. It covered the entire floor.

Kara found herself unable to look away. At the heart of the dust devil, a darkness grew, spreading wider and growing blacker, more massive. The spats of static electricity did little to illuminate it. The scent of burned flesh still tinged the air. The prior warning of their guide filled her heart with terror.

Black ghosts . . . the nisnases.

"Papa!"

But her father was mired in the deeper, stronger currents of the whirlpool, unable to escape. The column's edge brushed over him as it grew and spread. His eyes met hers, frantic not for himself, but for her.

Go, he mouthed—then he was gone, vanished into the darkness that filled the devil.

"Papa . . . !"

A horrible scream followed.

Before she could react, the column of sand exploded outward with blinding force. She was ripped from her seat and tossed high in the air. Tumbling, she toppled end over end. Time stretched until the ground rose up and struck her. Something snapped in her arm, a flash of pain that was barely noted. She rolled across the sand, coming to a stop facedown.

She lay there for several breaths, unable to move. But fear for her father rolled her on her side. She stared back toward the smoking volcano in the sand.

The devil was gone, snuffed away. All that was left was a smudgy dustiness hanging in the air. She fought to sit up, gasping and cradling her injured arm. It made no sense. She stared in all directions.

The sands lay flat all around her, untouched by track or print. Everything was gone: no sandy hollow, no bloodied oryx, no sand-scarred cycle.

She stared out at the empty sands. "Papa . . ."

A cry from the gallery drew Kara back to the present. Her cigarette, forgotten in her fingers, had burned to the filter. She stood and stomped it out.

"Over here!" the call repeated. It was one of her technicians. "I found something!"

08:02 A.M. EST
Ledyard, Connecticut

Painter Crowe crouched low on the elevator floor as the doors rolled open on the top floor of the Grand Pequot Tower. Ready for an ambush, he had his Glock pointed forward, a round chambered, his finger resting on the trigger.

The elevator bay was empty.

He listened for a long-held breath. No voices, no footsteps. Distantly a television could be heard blaring the theme of *Good Morning America*. It wasn't a particularly good morning for him.

Easing up, he risked a glance out the door, covering with his weapon. Nothing. He kicked out of his shoes and placed one so it would hold open the door in case he needed a fast retreat. In his socks, he took three fast steps to the opposite wall and checked the immediate area.

All clear.

He cursed the lack of manpower. While he had the backing of hotel security and the local police, who were already covering all the exits, any additional federal agents had been limited out of respect for Indian sovereignty.

Besides, the mission was supposed to be a simple nab-and-collar. The worst-case scenario was that they would have to destroy the research data rather than having it fall into Chinese hands.

Now it had all gone to hell. He had been duped by his own equipment. But he had a larger fear at the moment.

Cassandra . . .

He prayed he was wrong about her, but he held out no real hope.

He slid along the wall of the elevator lobby. It opened into the middle of the hallway. Numbered suites marched off in both directions. Keeping low, he swept both right and left. Empty. No sign of Zhang or his bodyguards.

He headed down the hall.

His senses sharpened to a razor's edge. At the click of a door lock behind him, he swung around, dropped to a knee, pistol pointed. It was only one of the hotel guests. Down the far hall, an older woman appeared in a bathrobe. She picked up her complimentary copy of *USA Today* resting on the doorstep and retreated back inside, not even noticing the armed gunman down the hall.

Painter twisted back around. He hurried the dozen steps to his suite's door. He tested the handle. Locked. He reached with one hand for his key; the other held his Glock pointed at Zhang's door across the hallway. He swept his key across the electronic lock. The green light flashed.

He shoved the door open while pressed against the wall outside.

No shots. No cries.

He sprang through the door. He stopped five feet inside, legs splayed in a shooter's stance. He had a clear view into the main room and the bedroom.

Empty.

He hurried forward and checked the bedroom and bathroom. No hostiles . . . and no sign of Cassandra. He returned to the bay of electronic equipment. He checked the monitors. They still showed various shots of Zhang's suite across the hall. They had cleared out. The computer was gone. There was only one occupant still in the suite.

"God . . . no . . ."

He raced back out the door, abandoning caution. He crashed across the hall and fumbled out the security passkey that opened all the rooms in the tower. He forced his way into Zhang's suite and sprinted through the main room and into the bedroom.

She hung naked from a rope attached to a ceiling fan. Her face had purpled above the noose. Her feet, which had still been kicking on the monitor, now dangled slackly.

Holstering his gun, Painter hurdled over a chair and leaped through the air. He yanked a dagger from a wrist sheath and sliced the rope with a single swift cut. He landed heavily, tossed the knife, and caught the body as it fell.

Twisting at the hips, he brought her down upon the bed, then fell to his knees. His fingers fought the noose's knot.

"Goddamnit!"

The rope had snugged deep into her thin neck, but the noose finally let go of its victim. He pried the rope loose. His fingers gingerly checked her neck. Not broken.

Was she still alive?

As answer, a shuddering gasp rattled up her frame and out her mouth.

Painter bowed his head in relief.

Her eyes rolled open, panicked and lost. More coughs rattled through her. Arms fought an invisible enemy.

He tried to reassure her, speaking in Mandarin. "You're safe. Lie still. You're safe."

The girl looked even younger than thirteen. Her naked body was bruised in places where a child should not be bruised. Zhang had sorely used her, and afterward left her behind, dangling by a rope, meant to delay him, distract him from the pursuit.

He sat back on his heels. The girl began to sob, curling in on herself. He didn't touch her, knowing better than to try.

His LASH communicator buzzed in his ears. *"Commander Crowe."* It was the head of hotel security. *"There's a firefight at the north tower exit."*

"Zhang?" He gained his feet and rushed to the balcony window.

"Yes, sir. Report is he's using your partner as a human shield. She may have been shot. I have more men on the way."

He shoved the window open. It was safety-secured and only opened enough to shove his head through. "We need those roadblocks up."

"Hang on."

The sound of squealing tires reached him. A Lincoln Town Car careened from the valet parking lot and headed toward the tower. It was Zhang's personal car, on its way to pick him up.

Security came back on the radio. *"He's broken out of the north exit. He still has your partner."*

The Town Car reached the corner of the tower.

Painter swung back inside. "Get those damn roadblocks up!" But there wouldn't be enough time. He had put in the emergency call less than four minutes ago. Law enforcement here mostly dealt with drunken fights, DUIs, and petty thefts, not matters of national security.

He had to stop them.

Bending down, he retrieved his knife from the floor. "Stay here," he said softly in Mandarin. He rushed to the main room and used the dagger to pry off the ventilation grille. It snapped open with a pop of screws. He reached within and grabbed the black device hidden inside. The EM grenade was roughly the size and shape of a football.

Palming the device, he fled to the suite's door and out into the hall. Still without his shoes, he sprinted down the carpeted hall. He analyzed a quick schematic in his head, coordinating where the north exit was in relation to his location on this floor. He did a best-guess estimate.

Eight doors down he stopped and pulled out his security key again. He swiped it through the electronic lock and shoved the door open as soon as it flashed green. "Security!" he hollered, and raced into the room.

An older woman, the same one he had spotted earlier, sat in a chair reading *USA Today*. She tossed the paper in the air and clutched her robe to her throat. "*Was ist los?*" she asked in German.

He hurried past her to the window, reassuring her that nothing was wrong. "*Nichts, sich ungefähr zu sorgen, fraulein,*" he answered.

He slid the window open. Again it was only enough to stick his head through. He glanced down.

The Lincoln Town Car idled below. The rear door to the sedan slammed shut. Shots rang out. Slugs pelted the side of the car as its tires squealed and smoked, but the car had been bulletproofed, an American-built tank.

Painter leaned back and shoved the football-shaped device out the window. He depressed the activation button and threw the grenade straight down with all the force in his shoulder, hoping for a Hail Mary pass.

He pulled his arm back inside. The wheels of the Town Car stopped squealing as it gained traction. He sent a prayer to the spirits of his ancestors. The EM pulse range was only twenty yards. He held his breath. What was that old saying? *Close only counts in horse-shoes and hand grenades.*

As he held his breath, the muffled *whump* of the grenade finally sounded. Had he been close enough?

He leaned his head back outside.

The Town Car reached the near corner of the tower, but rather than making the turn, it swerved uncontrollably and struck a row of parked cars head-on. The front of the Lincoln climbed up the hood of a Volkswagen Passat and came to a crooked rest.

He sighed.

That was the good thing about EM pulses. They didn't discriminate about what computer systems they fried. Even those that operated a Lincoln Town Car.

Below, uniformed security personnel poured from the exit and quickly surrounded the disabled car.

"*Was ist los?*" the old German woman repeated behind him.

He turned and hurried across the room. *"Etwas Abfall gerade entleeren."* Just dumping some garbage. He crossed quickly down the hall to the elevator lobby. Retrieving his shoes from the jammed elevator door, he hit the button for the main floor.

His stunt had stopped Zhang's escape, but it had also surely wiped out the computer he carried, destroying the research data. But that was not Painter's main concern.

Cassandra.

He had to get to her.

As soon as the doors opened, he rushed across the gambling floor, where pandemonium reigned. The firefight had not gone unnoticed, though a few people still sat calmly in front of their slot machines, pushing their buttons with dogged determination.

He crossed to the north exit and had to run through a series of blockades, flashing his identification, frustrated at being held back. Finally he spotted John Fenton, head of security, and called out to him. He ushered Painter through the shattered exit. Safety glass crunched underfoot and the telltale taint of gunpowder hung in the air.

"I don't understand why the car crashed," Fenton said. "Lucky for us, though."

"Not just luck," Painter said, and explained about the EM pulse and its twenty-yard range. "A few guests are going to have a hard time starting their cars this morning. And there'll probably be a few fried televisions on the first floors."

Outside, Painter saw that the local security had things in hand. Additionally, a row of charcoal gray police cars, lights flashing, wound through the parking lot, circling down upon the site. The MP Tribal Police.

Painter searched the area. Zhang's bodyguards were down on their knees, fingers laced behind their heads. Two bodies were sprawled on the ground, security coats draped over their faces. They were both men. Painter crossed to them and peeled one suit back. Another bodyguard, half his face gone. He didn't have to check the other. He recognized Zhang's polished leather shoes.

"He shot himself," a familiar voice said from amid a group of security men and a pair of EMTs. "Rather than be captured."

Painter turned and saw Cassandra step forward. Her face was pale, her smile shy. She was only in her bra. Her left shoulder was lost in a bandage.

She nodded to a black suitcase a few feet away. Zhang's computer.

"So we lost the data," he said. "The EM pulse wiped it."

"Maybe not," she said with a grin. "The case is shielded with a copper Faraday cage. It should've been insulated from the pulse."

He sighed with relief. *So the data was safe. All was not lost . . . that is, if they could retrieve the pass code.* He stepped toward Cassandra. She grinned at him, eyes still shining. He pulled his Glock and pressed it to her forehead.

"Painter, what are you—" She stepped back.

He followed, never letting his gun drop. "What's the code?"

Fenton moved to one side. "Commander?"

"Stay out of it." He cut the security chief off and maintained his attention on Sanchez. "Four bodyguards and Zhang. Everyone is accounted for here. If Zhang was onto our surveillance, then there was a good chance he alerted his contact at the conference. They would have fled together in order to complete the exchange."

She tried to glance to the bodies, but he restrained her with his gun. "You can't think it was me?" she said, with a half laugh.

He pointed his free hand, never letting his weapon drop. "I recognize the handiwork of a forty-five, like the Sig Sauer you carry."

"Zhang took it from me. Painter, you're being paranoid. I—"

He reached to a pocket and pulled out the bug he found taped to the elevator wall. He held it toward her.

She stiffened, but refused to look at it.

"No blood, Cassandra. Not a trace. Which means you never implanted it like you were supposed to."

A hard edge sharpened her face.

"The computer code?"

She simply stared at him, coldly dispassionate now. "You know I can't."

He searched this stranger's face for the partner he knew, but she was long gone. There was no remorse, no guilt, only determination. He didn't have the time or the stomach to break her. He nodded to Fenton. "Have your men cuff her. Keep her under constant guard."

As she was being secured, she called over to him. Her words were plainly spoken. "Painter, you'd best watch your back. You have no idea what a shitload of pain you just stepped into."

He picked up the computer suitcase and walked away.

"You're swimmin' in the deep end, Painter. And there are goddamn sharks all around you, circling and circling."

He ignored her and crossed toward the north entrance. He had to admit something to himself: he simply didn't understand women.

Before he could escape back inside, a tall figure in a sheriff's hat blocked his way. It was one of the MP Tribal Police. "Commander Crowe?"

"Yes?"

"We have an urgent call dispatched through our offices holding for you."

His brow crinkled. "Who from?"

"From an Admiral Rector, sir. You can speak to him on one of our radios."

Painter frowned. Admiral Tony "The Tiger" Rector was the director of DARPA, his commander in chief. Painter had never spoken to him, only seen his name on memos and letters. Had word already reached Washington about the mess out here?

He allowed himself to be led to one of the parked gray cars, lights still flashing atop it. He accepted the radio. "Commander Crowe here. How may I help you, sir?"

"Commander, we need you back in Arlington immediately. There's a helicopter on its way to collect you."

As if on cue, the bell beat of a helicopter sounded in the distance.

Admiral Rector continued, "You'll be relieved by Commander Giles. Debrief him on the current state of your operation, then report here as soon as you land at Dulles. There'll be a car waiting for you."

"Yes, sir," he responded, but the connection was already dead.

He stepped out of the car and stared at the gray-green helicopter sailing over the surrounding wood-lands, the lands of his ancestors. A sense of misgiving rang through him, what his father called "distrust of the white eyes." Why had Admiral Rector called him so abruptly? What was the urgency? He couldn't help but hear an echo of Cassandra's words.

You're swimmin' in the deep end, Painter . . . and there are goddamn sharks all around you, circling and circling.

3

Matters of the Heart

ᛒᚻᚷᚷᛃᛣᛃᚲᛣᛁᛜᚲᛁᚷᚤᛃᛁᚤᛃᚻᚷᚲᚻᚻ

"Over here! I found something!"

Safia turned to see one of the men armed with a metal detector call to his partner. *What now?* The pair had been turning up bits of bronze statuary, iron incense burners, and copper coins. Safia splashed over to see what had been discovered. It might be significant.

Across the gallery, Kara appeared at the entrance to the wing, having heard the shout, too. She joined them.

"What have you found?" she asked with cold authority.

"I'm not sure," the man said with a nod to his detector. "But I'm getting a very strong reading."

"A piece of the meteorite?"

"Can't tell. It's under this block of stone."

Safia saw that the block had once been the torso and lower limbs of a sandstone statue, toppled onto its back. Despite the fact that the upper limbs and head had been blasted away, she recognized the figure. The life-size statue had once stood guard by a tomb in Salalah. It dated to 200 B.C. It depicted a man with an elongated object lifted to his shoulder. Some thought it looked like a rifle, but actually it was a funerary incense lamp, borne on the shoulder.

The destruction of the statue was a tragic loss. All that remained now were the torso and two broken legs. Even these were so blasted by the heat that the sandstone had melted and hardened into a crust of glass over its surface.

By now, others of Kara's red-hatted forensic team gathered around them.

The man who made the discovery pointed his metal detector at the ruined statue. "We'll have to roll the block out of the way. See what's under it."

"Do it," Kara said with a nod. "We'll need crowbars."

A pair of men slogged away toward the stash of work tools.

Safia stepped protectively forward. "Kara, wait. Don't you recognize this statue?"

"What do you mean?"

"Look closer. This is the statue your father discovered. The one found buried by that tomb in Salalah. We need to preserve what we can."

"I don't care." Kara pulled her aside by the elbow. "What's important is that there could be a clue to what happened to my father *under* there."

Safia tried to pull her aside, keeping her voice low. "Kara . . . you can't really think anything of this has to do with your father's death?"

Kara waved to the men with the crowbars. "Give me one of those."

Safia remained where she was. Her gaze swept around the other rooms of the gallery, contemplating it all in a new light. All her work, the collection, the years spent in study . . . was it more than just a memorial to Reginald Kensington for Kara? Had it also been a quest? To gather research material all in one place, to determine what actually happened to her father out in the desert so long ago.

Safia remembered the story from when they were both girls, told amid much weeping. Kara had been convinced something supernatural had killed her father. Safia knew the details.

The *nisnases* . . . the ghosts of the deep desert.

Even as girls, she and Kara had investigated these tales, learning all they could about the mythology of the *nisnases*. Legend said they were all that remained of a people that once inhabited a vast city in the desert. It went by many names: Iram, Wabar, Ubar. The City of a Thousand Pillars. Mentions of its downfall could be found in the Koran, in the tales of *The Arabian Nights*, and among the Alexander Books. Founded by the great-grandchildren of the biblical Noah, Ubar was a rich and decadent city, filled with wicked people who dabbled in dark practices. Its king defied the warnings of a prophet named Hud, and God smote the city, driving it into the sands, never to be seen again, becoming a veritable Atlantis of the deserts. Afterward, tales persisted that the city still remained under the sands, haunted by the dead, its citizens frozen into stone, its fringes plagued by evil djinns and the even nastier *nisnases*, savage creatures of magical powers.

Safia had thought Kara had set aside such myths as mere fables. Especially when investigators had attributed her father's death to the sudden opening of a sinkhole in the desert. Such death traps appeared not uncommonly in the region, swallowing lone trucks or the unwary wanderer. The bedrock below the desert was mostly limestone, a porous rock pocked by caverns worn by the receding water table. Collapses of these caverns occurred regularly, often accompanied by the exact phenomenon described by Kara: a thick, roiling column of dust above a whirlpool of swirling sand.

A few steps away, Kara grabbed one of the crowbars, meaning to add her own shoulder to the effort. It seemed she had not been convinced by those earlier geologists' explanation.

Safia should have guessed as much, especially with Kara's dogged persistence about ancient Arabia, using her billions to delve into the past, to gather artifacts from all ages, to hire the best people, including Safia.

She closed her eyes, wondering now how much of her own life had been guided by this fruitless quest. How influential had Kara been in her choice of studies? In her research projects here? She shook her head. It was too much to grasp at the moment. She would sort the matter later.

She opened her eyes and stepped toward the statue, blocking the others. "I can't let you do this."

Kara motioned her aside, her voice calm and logical. "If there's a piece of the meteorite here, salvaging it is more important than a few scratches on a broken statue."

"Important for whom?" Safia attempted to match Kara's stolid demeanor, but her question came off more as an accusation. "This statue is one of only a handful from that age in Arabia. Even broken, it's priceless."

"The meteorite—"

"—can wait," Safia said, cutting off her benefactor. "At least until the sculpture can be moved safely."

Kara fixed her with a steely gaze that broke most men. Safia withstood the challenge, having known the girl behind the woman.

Safia stepped toward her. She took the crowbar, surprised to feel the tremble in the other's fingers. "I know what you were hoping," she whispered. Both knew the history of the camel-shaped meteorite, of the British explorer who had discovered it, how it was supposed to guard the entrance to a lost city buried under the sands.

A city named Ubar.

And now it had exploded under most strange circumstances.

"There must be some connection," Kara mumbled, repeating her words from a moment ago.

Safia knew one way to dispel such a hope. "You know that Ubar has already been found." She let these words sink in.

In 1992, the legendary city had been discovered by Nicolas Clapp, an amateur archaeologist, using satellite ground-penetrating radar. Founded around 900 B.C. and located at one of the few watering holes, the ancient city had been an important trading post on the Incense

Road, linking the frankincense groves of the coastal Omani Mountains to the markets of the rich cities of the north. Over the centuries, Ubar had prospered and grown larger. Until one day, half the city collapsed into a giant sinkhole and was abandoned to the sands by the superstitious townfolk.

"It was only an ordinary trading post," she continued.

Kara shook her head, but Safia was unsure if she was negating her last statement or resigning herself to the reality. Safia remembered Kara's excitement upon hearing of Clapp's discovery. It had been heralded in newspapers around the globe: FABLED LOST ARABIAN CITY FOUND! She had rushed out herself to see the site, to help in the early excavation. But as Safia had stated, after two years of digging up potsherds and a few utensils, the site turned out to be nothing more exciting than an abandoned trading post.

No vast treasures, no thousand pillars, no black ghosts . . . all that was left were those painful memories that haunted the living.

"Lady Kensington," the man with the metal detector called out again. "Maybe Dr. al-Maaz was right about not moving this bloody thing."

Both women turned their attention back to the toppled statue. It was now flanked by both of the team members with detectors. They held their devices to either side of the blocky torso. Both metal detectors were beeping in chorus.

"I was wrong," the first man continued. "Whatever I detected is not *under* the stone."

"Then where is it?" Kara asked irritably.

The other man answered, "It's *inside* it."

A stunned moment of silence followed until Kara broke it. "Inside?"

"Yes, ma'am. I'm sorry. I should've thought to triangulate earlier. But I never thought anything could be inside the stone."

Safia stepped forward. "It's probably just some random iron deposits."

"Not from the readings we're getting here. It's a strong signal."

"We'll have to break it open," Kara said.

Safia frowned at her. *Bloody hell.* She dropped to her knees beside the sculpture, soaking her pants. "I need a flashlight."

She was handed one by another member of the team.

"What are you going to do with that?" Kara asked.

"Peek inside." Safia ran her hand over the heat-blasted surface of the statue. The sandy surface was now fused glass. She planted the flashlight facedown on the statue's bulky torso and flicked it on.

The entire glassy surface of the statue lit up. Details were murky through the dark crystalline crust. Safia didn't see anything unusual, but the glass was only two inches thick. Whatever they were looking for might be deeper in the stone.

Kara gasped behind her. She was staring over Safia's shoulder.

"What?" She began to pull away the flashlight.

"No," Kara warned. "Move it toward the center."

Safia did so, bringing the wash of light over the middle of the torso.

A shadow appeared, a lump in the center of the statue, lodged deep, at the point where glass became stone. It shone a deep crimson under the light. The shape was unmistakable—especially given its position inside the torso.

"It's a heart," Kara whispered.

Safia sat back, stunned. "A human heart."

8:05 P.M.

Hours later, Kara Kensington stood in the private lavatory outside the department of the ancient Near East.

Just one more . . .

She shook a single orange pill into her palm. *Adderall, a prescription amphetamine, twenty milligrams.*

She weighed the pill in her hand. So much kick in such a small package. But maybe not enough. She added a second tablet. After all, she'd had no sleep last night and still had much to do.

Tossing back the pills, she dry-swallowed them, then stared at her reflection in the mirror. Her skin looked flushed, her eyes a bit too wide. She ran a hand through her hair, trying to fluff some body back into it. She failed.

Bending down to the tap, she turned the cold spigot, soaked both hands, and pressed them to her cheeks. She took deep breaths. It seemed like days rather than hours since she had been woken from her bed back at her family estate in the village of Blackheath. News of the explosion had her chauffeured limo racing through the stormy streets to reach the museum.

And now what?

Throughout the long day, various forensic teams had gathered all the necessary samples from the gallery: charred wood, plastics, metals, even bone. Finally, a few slag fragments of the meteorite had been picked out of the rubble. All initial evidence suggested that an electrical discharge had ignited some volatile compo-nents deep in the chunk of meteoric iron. No one was willing to say what those components were. From here, the investigation would be carried out in labs both in England and abroad.

Kara could not hide her disappointment. Witnessing the glowing ball of lightning on the video footage had drawn her back to the day her father had vanished into the dust cloud, a spiral of sand sparking with similar crackles of bluish electricity. Then the explosion . . . another death. There had to be a connection between the past and present.

But what? Was it just another dead end, like so many times in the past?

A knock on the door drew her attention from her reflection.

"Kara, we're ready for the examination." It was Safia. In her friend's voice, she heard concern. Only Safia understood the weight around Kara's heart.

"I'll be right out."

She dropped the plastic pill vial back into her purse and snapped the satchel closed. Already the initial surge of drug-induced energy took the edge off her despair. With one last futile sweep of her hair, she crossed to the door, unlocked it, and pushed out into one of the more handsome research quarters—the famous Arched Room of the British Museum.

Built in 1839, the two-story vaulted chamber, located in the west section of the museum, was of early Victorian design: double galleries of library shelves, pierced iron walkways and stairs, arched piers leading into recessed alcoves. The very bones of the place harkened back to the times of Charles Darwin, of Stanley and Livingston, of the Royal Society of scientists, where researchers wore jackets with tails and gathered studiously among the stacks of books and ancient tablets. Never open to the public, the department of the ancient Near East now utilized the room as a student center and reserve archive.

But today, deserted of all but a select few, it served as a makeshift morgue. Kara stared across the room to the stone cadaver, headless and armless, resting atop a wheeled stretcher. It was all that was left of the ancient sculpture found in the north wing. Safia had insisted that it be rescued from the rubble and brought up here, out of harm's way.

Two halogen lamps lit the body, and an array of tools rested atop a neighboring library bench, set up like a surgeon's table with scalpels, clamps, and thumb forceps. There were also various-size hammers and brushes.

Only the surgeon was missing.

Safia snapped on a pair of latex gloves. She wore safety glasses and a tightly cinched apron. "Ready?"

Kara nodded.

"Let's crack this old man's chest," a young man called with the usual crass enthusiasm of an American.

Kara, well familiar with all who worked in her gallery, knew Clay Bishop, a grad student out of Northwestern University. He fiddled with a digital camcorder resting on a tripod, standing in as the group's videographer.

"A little respect, Mr. Bishop," Safia warned.

"Sorry," he said with a crooked grin that belied any true remorse. He was not unhandsome for a gaunt bit of Generation X. He wore jeans, a vintage concert T-shirt depicting the Clash, and Reeboks that might have once been white, but this last was only a rumor. He straightened, stretching, showing a strip of his bare belly, and ran a hand over the stubble of his red hair. The only modicum of studiousness to the grad student was the pair of thick, black-rimmed glasses, uncool enough to be fashionable nowadays. "We're all set here, Dr. al-Maaz."

"Very good." Safia stepped under the halogen lights, positioning herself beside the spread of tools.

Kara circled to view from the far side, joining the only other person observing the autopsy: Ryan Fleming, head of security. He must have arrived when she had gone to the loo. He nodded to her, but his stance stiffened at her approach, nervous at her proximity, like most of the museum staff.

He cleared his throat as Safia took measurements. "I came down here when I heard about the discovery," he mumbled to Kara.

"Why might that be?" she asked. "Is there a security concern?"

"No, it was simple curiosity." He nodded to the sculpture. "Not every day we find a statue with a heart hidden inside it."

That was indeed true, though Kara suspected it was a *different* matter of the heart that had drawn Fleming down here. His eyes spent more time examining Safia than the strange statue.

Kara allowed him his puppy-dog crush and turned her attention to the prone sculpture. Beneath the shell of blasted glass, a deeper glow of crimson took up the lamplight.

A heart, a human heart.

She leaned closer. While the heart appeared life-size and anatomically correct, it had to have been sculpted from some type of ore since the forensic team's detectors had picked up its presence. Still, Kara almost expected to see it beat if she waited long enough.

Safia leaned over the statue with a diamond-tipped tool. She carefully scored the glass, forming a perfect square around the buried heart. "I want to preserve as much as possible."

Next she placed a suction-cup device atop the glass square and gripped the handle. "I expect the interface between the glass and the sandstone beneath to be weak."

Safia grabbed a rubber mallet and tapped firmly along the inside edge of the glass square. Small cracks appeared, following the prescored lines. Each pop drew a wince from everyone. Even Kara found her fingers balling up.

Only Safia remained calm. Kara knew her friend's propensity for panic attacks during stressful situations, but whenever Safia labored in her own element, she was as hard as the diamonds on her glass cutter . . . and as sharp. She worked with a Zen-like calmness and focused concentration. But Kara also noted the glint in her friend's eyes. Excitement. It had been a long time since Kara had seen such a glimpse in Safia, a reminder of the woman she used to be.

Maybe there was hope for her yet.

"That should do it," Safia said. She returned the mallet and used a tiny brush to sweep stray chips away, keeping her work surface pristine. Once satisfied, she gripped the suction handle and applied a bit of pressure, first pushing in one direction, then the other, gently rocking the square. Finally, she simply pulled straight up, lifting the block of glass cleanly away.

Kara stepped closer, staring into the statue's opened chest. The heart was even more detailed than she had first imagined. Each chamber was distinct, including tiny surface arteries and veins. It rested perfectly in its sandstone bed, as if the sculpture had formed naturally around it, a pearl inside an oyster.

Safia carefully freed the glass from the suction device and flipped it over. There was an imprint of the heart's upper surface in the glass. She turned to the camera. "Clay, are you getting a good shot of all this?"

Crouched by his camera, he bounced up and down on his heels. "Oh, man, this is fantastic."

"I take that as a yes." Safia placed the glass on the library table.

"What about the heart?" Fleming asked.

Safia turned and peered into the open chest. She tapped the handle of a tiny brush against the heart. The ring was heard by all. "Metal for certain. Bronze, I'd guess, from the ruddy color."

"That almost sounded hollow," Clay commented, shifting the camera tripod to get a better view in the chest cavity. "Do it again."

Safia shook her head. "I'd best not. See how the sandstone lips over the heart in places. It's locked in there fairly well. I think we should leave it untouched. Other researchers should see this in situ before we disturb it."

Kara hadn't dared breathe for the past minute. Her heart hammered in her ears, and not from the amphetamines. *Had no one else noticed it?*

Before she could ask, a door slammed farther back in the Arched Room. Everyone jumped slightly. Footsteps approached. Two men.

Safia tilted the halogen light to shine down the hall. "Director Tyson."

"Edgar." Kara stepped forward. "What are you doing here?"

The head of the museum stepped aside to reveal his companion. It was the inspector from Central London homicide. "Inspector Samuelson was with me when I heard the news of your brilliant discovery. We were just finishing up, and he asked if he might see the astounding find for himself. How could I refuse, considering how much help he's been?"

"Certainly," Kara said in her best diplomatic tone, hiding a flash of irritation. "You're just in time." She waved them over to the makeshift morgue, giving up her space. Her own discovery would have to wait a little longer.

Fleming nodded his greeting to his boss. "I guess I've seen enough myself. I should go check on the night shift." He stepped away, but not before turning to Safia. "Thank you for allowing me to observe."

"Anytime," she said distantly, distracted by the exposed heart.

Kara noted how the head of security's eyes lingered on Safia, then turned away, wounded, as he left. Safia was forever blind to all but her work. She had let greater men than Fleming slip from her life.

Inspector Samuelson stepped up to fill the security chief's spot. He had his suit jacket over one arm, sleeves rolled up. "I hope I'm not intruding."

"Not at all," Safia said. "It's a fortunate discovery."

"Indeed."

The inspector leaned over the statue. Kara was certain more than plain curiosity had drawn him here. Coincidences were causes for investigation.

Edgar stood at the inspector's shoulder. "Simply brilliant, isn't it? This discovery will draw attention from all around the world."

Samuelson straightened. "Where did this statue come from?"

"It was discovered by my father," Kara said.

Samuelson glanced to her, one eyebrow cocked.

Kara noted how Edgar stepped back, eyes on his toes. It was a tender subject to broach.

Safia pushed up her safety goggles and continued the explanation, relieving Kara of the need. "Reginald Kensington had financed an archaeological team to oversee the excavation for the construction of a new mausoleum at a tomb in the town of Salalah on the Omani coast. He discovered the statue buried beside the older tomb. It was a rare discovery: to find a pre-Islamic statue, one dating to 200 B.C., in such pristine shape. But the tomb had been revered for two millennia. Thus the site was not overly trampled or desecrated. It's a true tragedy to have such a perfectly preserved artifact destroyed."

Samuelson was not stirred. "But its destruction also allowed this new discovery. There's a balance in that. The same can't be said for poor Harry Masterson."

"Of course," Safia said quickly. "I didn't mean to imply that . . . his death was not the *true* tragedy. You're most correct."

Samuelson glanced around at those gathered. His eyes lingered a bit longer on the grad student, Clay Bishop. Whatever he saw there, he found wanting. His eyes drifted back to the statue. "You mentioned a tomb, near where this statue was found."

"Yes. The tomb of Nabi Imran."

"A pharaoh or something?"

Safia smiled. "This wasn't an Egyptian tomb." Like Kara, she knew the inspector was playing dumb. "In Arabia, the most famous tombs are those that mark the graves of people from the Bible or the Koran. In this case, a figure from *both*."

"Nabi Imran? I don't recall that name from any Bible class."

"Actually he was quite significant. You have heard of the Virgin Mary?"

"Vaguely." He said this so sincerely he drew another smile from Safia.

She had been teasing out the revelation, but she finally relented. "Nabi Imran was Mary's father."

01:54 P.M. EST
Arlington, Virginia

Painter Crowe sat in the backseat of the silver Mercedes S500 sedan. It glided smoothly down Interstate 66 from Dulles International, heading east toward Washington, but they weren't going that far. The driver, a taciturn fellow built like a linebacker, signaled and took the Glebe exit in Arlington. They were almost to DARPA headquarters, less than half a mile away.

He checked his watch. Only a couple hours ago he had been in Connecticut, confronting a partner he had trusted for the past five years. His thoughts shied away from Cassandra, but still circled around the sore subject.

They had been recruited out of Special Forces at the same time: he from the Navy SEALS, she from the Army Rangers. DARPA had chosen them for a new, highly secretive team within the organization, code-named Sigma Force. Most in DARPA were unaware of its existence. Sigma's objective was search and seizure, a covert militarized team of technically trained agents who were sent into high-risk situations to obtain or protect new research and technologies. Where the Delta Force had been established as an antiterrorist squad, Sigma was started to protect and maintain the technological superiority of the United States.

No matter the cost.

And now this call back to headquarters.

It had to be a new mission. But why the urgency?

The sedan traveled down North Fairfax Drive and pulled into the parking lot. They ran a gauntlet of security measures and were soon sliding into an empty spot. Another man, barrel-chested and expressionless, stepped forward and opened the door.

"If you'll follow me, Commander Crowe."

Painter was led into the main building, escorted to the office suite of the director, and asked to wait while his attendant proceeded forward to announce his arrival. Painter stared at the closed door.

Vice Admiral Tony Rector had been the head of DARPA for as long as Painter had been in service there. Prior to that, he had been the head of the Office of Information Awareness, the intelligence-gathering wing of DARPA, critical after September 11 in monitoring data flowing across computer networks in search of terrorist plots, activities, and financial transactions. The admiral's intelligence, expertise, and evenhanded management had eventually won him the directorship of DARPA.

The door opened. His escort waved him forward, stepping aside and allowing Painter to pass. Once he was through, the door closed behind him.

The room was paneled in dark mahogany and smelled vaguely of pipe tobacco. A matching mahogany desk stood in the center. Behind it, Tony "The Tiger" Rector rose to shake his hand. He was a large man, not fat, but someone who had once been well muscled now gone a little soft as he crossed his sixtieth year. But flesh was all that was *soft* about the man. His eyes were blue diamonds, his hair slicked and silver. His grip was iron as he shook Painter's hand and nodded him to one of the two leather chairs.

"Have a seat. I've called up Dr. McKnight. He'll be joining us."

Dr. Sean McKnight was Sigma's founder and director, Painter's immediate superior, an ex–Navy SEAL who had gone on to earn a Ph.D. in both physics and information technology. If Dr. McKnight was being called in, then all the big boys were coming to play. Whatever was going down was significant.

"May I ask what this is in regard to, sir?"

The admiral settled into his own chair. "I heard about the bit of unpleasantness up in Connecticut," he said, sidestepping the question. "The boys down in the Advanced Technology Office are waiting for that spy's suitcase computer to be delivered. Hopefully, we'll be able to retrieve the plasma weapons data from it."

"I'm sorry we—I failed to obtain the password."

Admiral Rector shrugged. "At least the Chinese won't be getting their hands on it. And considering all you faced, you did a fine job up there."

Painter held back asking about his former partner. Cassandra was most likely heading to a secure site to be interrogated. From there, who knew? Guantánamo Bay, Fort Leavenworth, or some other military prison? It was no longer his concern. Still, an ache throbbed in his chest. He hoped it was only indigestion. He certainly had no reason to feel any pangs over Cassandra's fate.

"As to your question," the admiral continued, drawing him back to the moment, "something was brought to our attention by the Defense Sciences Office. There was an explosion over at the British Museum last night."

Painter nodded, having listened to the news on CNN on the way here. "Lightning strike."

"So it's been reported."

Painter heard the denial and sat straighter. Before he could inquire, the door opened. Dr. Sean McKnight strode into the room, a gale barely suppressed. His face was red, his brow damp, like he'd run all the way here.

"It's been confirmed," he said quickly to the admiral.

Admiral Rector nodded. "Take a seat, then. We don't have much time."

As his boss sat in the remaining leather chair, Painter glanced over. McKnight had worked with DARPA for twenty-two years, including a stint as the director of its Special Projects Office. One of his first "special projects" had been the formation of Sigma Force. He had envisioned a team of operatives who were both technologically savvy and militarily trained—"brains and brawn," as he liked to say—who could operate with surgical precision to secure and protect classified technologies.

Sigma Force was the result.

Painter had been one of the first recruits, handpicked by McKnight after Painter had sustained a broken leg during a mission in Iraq. While he had been recuperating, McKnight had taught him the value of honing his mind as well as his body, putting him through an academic boot camp that was tougher than his BUDS training to become a Navy SEAL. There was no person on the planet whom Painter held in higher esteem.

And now to see him so shaken . . .

McKnight sat near the edge of his seat, back straight. It looked like he had slept in the charcoal suit he wore, appearing all his fifty-five years at the moment: his eyes crinkled with worry, lips tight, sandy gray hair uncombed.

Something was clearly wrong.

Admiral Rector swiveled a plasma monitor on his desk toward Painter. "Commander Crowe, you should view this footage first."

Painter shifted closer, ready for some answers. The screen's desktop filled with a black-and-white video.

"This is the security surveillance for the British Museum."

He sat silently as the video rolled. A guard appeared on the screen, entering a museum gallery. It didn't take long. As the explosion ended the tape, whiting out the screen, Painter sat back. His two superiors studied him.

"That luminous sphere," he said slowly. "That was ball lightning, if I'm not mistaken."

"Indeed," Admiral Rector confirmed. "It was the same assessment that drew the attention of a pair of researchers with the Defense Sciences Office who were in London. Ball lightning has never been caught on film."

"Or been that destructive," Dr. McKnight added.

Painter recalled a lecture he'd heard during his Sigma Force training in electrical engineering. Ball lightning had been reported from the times of the early Greeks, seen by groups of people and reported in many places. Its rarity had kept it a mystery. Theories for its formation varied from free-floating plasma caused by the ionization of air during thunderstorms to the vaporization of silicon dioxide from the soil after lightning struck the ground.

"So what happened at the British Museum?" he asked.

"This." Admiral Rector had removed an object from a desk drawer and placed it on his blotter. It looked like a blackened piece of rock, about the size of a softball. "We had it shipped on a military jet this morning."

"What is it?"

The admiral nodded for him to pick it up. He did and found the object unusually heavy. Not rock. It felt dense enough to be lead.

"Meteoric iron," Dr. McKnight explained. "A sample from the artifact that you saw explode a moment ago."

Painter placed the chunk back on the desk. "I don't understand. Are you saying the meteor caused the explosion? Not the ball lightning."

"Yes and no," McKnight answered cryptically.

"What do you know of the Tunguska explosion in Russia?" Rector asked.

The sudden shift in subject caught Painter off guard. His brow furrowed as he dredged up old history. "Not much. Something about a meteor strike, back in 1908, somewhere up in Siberia, caused a big blast."

Rector leaned back. " 'Big' is a bit of an understatement. The explosion uprooted a forest for forty miles around, over an area about half the size of Rhode Island. The blast liberated the energy equivalent of two thousand atomic bombs. Horses were knocked over four hundred miles away. *Big* just doesn't quite cover the extent of the explosion."

"There were other effects, too," McKnight said. "A magnetic storm created a vortex for six hundred miles all around. For days afterward, the night skies were luminescent from the amount of dust, bright enough to read a newspaper by. An EM pulse wrapped itself halfway around the world."

"Christ," Painter mumbled.

"Those who witnessed the blast from hundreds of miles away reported seeing a streaking bright light in the sky, as brilliant as the sun, trailing a tail of iridescent colors."

"The meteor," Painter said.

Admiral Rector shook his head. "That was one theory. A stony asteroid or comet. But there are several problems with that theory. First, no meteor fragments have ever been found. Not even any telltale iridium dust."

"Carbonaceous meteors usually leave an iridium fingerprint," McKnight said. "But such a finding was never unearthed in Tunguska."

"And there was no crater," the admiral added.

McKnight nodded. "The force of the blast was forty megatons. Prior to that, the last meteor to even come close to such force struck Arizona some fifty thousand years ago. And it was only three megatons, a mere fraction of Tunguska, and it left a massive crater a mile wide and five hundred feet deep. So why no crater, especially when we so clearly know the epicenter of the blast due to the radial felling of the trees outward from ground zero?"

Painter had no answer to this . . . or to the more immediate question in his mind: *What did any of this have to do with the British Museum?*

McKnight continued. "Since the time of the explosion, there have also been interesting biological consequences noted in the region: an accelerated growth of certain ferns, an increase in the rate of mutations, including genetic abnormalities in the seeds and needles of pine trees and even ant populations. And humans have not escaped the effect. The local Evenk tribes in the area demonstrate abnormalities in their Rh blood factors. All clear indications of some radiological exposure, most likely gamma in origin."

Painter tried to wrap his mind around a craterless explosion, unusual atmospheric effects, and residual gamma radiation. "So what caused all this?"

Admiral Rector answered, "Something quite small. About seven pounds."

"That's impossible," he blurted.

The admiral shrugged. "If it was ordinary matter . . ."

The mystery hung in the air for a long moment.

Dr. McKnight finally spoke. "Newest research as of 1995 suggests that what struck Tunguska was indeed a meteor—but one composed of *antimatter*."

Painter's eyes widened. "Antimatter?"

He now understood why he had been called into this briefing. While most folks considered antimatter to be the realm of science fiction, it had become reality in the past decade with the production of antimatter particles in laboratories. Leading the forefront in this research was CERN Laboratories in Geneva, Switzerland. The lab had been producing antimatter for close to two decades using a subterranean Low Energy Antiproton

Ring. But to date, an entire year's production of anti-protons by CERN would produce only enough energy to flicker a lightbulb for a few moments.

Still, antimatter was intriguing. A single gram of antimatter would produce the energy equivalent of an atomic bomb. Of course, someone would first have to discover a cheap, readily available source of antimatter. And that was impossible.

Painter found his eyes on the lump of meteoric iron resting atop Admiral Rector's desk. He knew that the upper atmosphere of the Earth was under constant bombardment by antimatter particles in cosmic rays, but they were immediately annihilated when they came in contact with atmospheric matter. It had been postulated that there might be asteroids or comets in the vacuum of space composed of antimatter, left over from the Big Bang.

He began to connect some of the dots in his head. "The explosion at the British Museum . . . ?"

"We've tested some of the debris from the blasted gallery," McKnight said. "Metal and wood."

Painter remembered his boss's statement upon arriving here. *It's been confirmed.* A cold lump formed in the pit of his belly.

McKnight continued, "The blast debris bears a low-level radiation signature that matches Tunguska."

"Are you saying that the explosion at the British Museum was caused by antimatter annihilation? That *that* meteor is actually antimatter?"

Admiral Rector rolled the blasted fragment back and forth with a finger. "Of course not. This is ordinary meteoric iron. Nothing more."

"Then I don't understand."

McKnight spoke up. "The radiation signature can't be ignored. It's too exact to be random. Something happened. The only explanation is that somehow the meteor had antimatter stored within it, in some unknown stabilized form. The electrical discharge by the ball lightning destabilized it and created a cascade effect with the resulting explosion. Whatever antimatter had been present was consumed during the blast."

"Leaving only this shell behind," the admiral said, nudging the stone.

Silence settled over the room. The implications were enormous.

Admiral Rector picked up the chunk of iron. "Can you imagine the significance if we're right? A source of almost unlimited power. If there is some clue as to how this is possible—or better yet, a *sample*—it must not fall into other hands."

Painter found himself nodding. "So what is the next step?"

Admiral Rector stared hard at him. "We can't let word of this connection leak out, not even to our own allies. Too many ears are connected to too many mouths." He nodded for Dr. McKnight to continue.

His boss took a deep breath. "Commander, we want you to lead a small team over to the museum. Your cover has already been established as American scientists specializing in lightning research. You're to make contacts when and where you can. While there, your objective is simply to keep your ears to the ground and to note any new discoveries that might be made out there. We'll continue research here with all departments mobilized. If any further investigation on-site is needed in London, your team will be our go-to people."

"Yes, sir."

There was a flicker of eye contact between Admiral Rector and Dr. McKnight, an unspoken question.

Painter felt an icy finger trace his spine.

The admiral nodded again.

McKnight turned to face Painter. "There is one more factor here. We may not be the only ones working this angle."

"What do you mean?"

"If you remember, the director mentioned a pair of researchers from the Defense Sciences Office over in London."

"The ones who investigated the ball-lightning sighting."

"Correct." Again a flicker of contact between Painter's two superiors. Then his boss fixed him with a hard stare. "Four hours ago, they were found shot, execution style, in their room. The place was ransacked. Several items were stolen. The Metropolitan Police are considering it a robbery homicide."

Admiral Rector stirred behind his desk. "But I never could stomach coincidences. They give me heartburn."

McKnight nodded. "We don't know if the murders are connected to our line of investigation, but we want you and your team to proceed as if they were. Watch each other's backs and keep alert."

He nodded.

"In the meantime," the admiral said, "let's just hope they don't discover anything significant out there until you get across the Pond."

09:48 P.M. GMT
London, England

"You have to remove the heart."

Safia glanced up from her measurements with a tiny silver caliper. The Arched Room of the museum lay dark all around. There were only the three of them left: Kara, Clay, and herself. Edgar and the inspector had left twenty minutes ago. It seemed the exacting measurements and notations of minutiae had not held their interest, diminishing the momentary wonder of the statue's origin as a funerary sculpture for the tomb of the Virgin Mary's father.

Safia returned to her measurements. "I'll remove the heart eventually."

"No, *tonight*."

Safia studied her friend closer. Kara's face was limned in the halogen spots. The stark light bled all the color from her face, but Safia noted the silvery sheen to her skin, the wide cast to her pupils. She was high. Amphetamines again. Three years ago, Safia had been one of the few who had known Lady Kensington's monthlong "vacation abroad" had actually been a trip through rehab in an exclusive private clinic down in Kent. How long had she been using again? She glanced to Clay. Now was not the time to confront her.

"What's the hurry?" she asked instead.

Kara's eyes darted around the room. Her voice lowered. "Before the inspector arrived, I noted something. I'm surprised you haven't seen it yet."

"What?"

Kara leaned over and pointed to one of the exposed sections of the heart, specifically the right ventricle.

"Look at this raised line here." She traced it with the tip of the caliper.

"One of the coronary arteries or veins," Safia said, amazed at the artistry.

"Is it?" Kara pointed. "See how perfectly horizontal the top section is, then it drops down vertically at both ends at ninety degrees." She followed the vessel's course. Her fingers shook with a characteristic amphetamine tremor.

Kara continued, "Everything on this heart is so naturally rendered. Da Vinci would have a hard time being so anatomically precise." She stared over to Safia. "Nature doesn't like ninety-degree angles."

Safia leaned closer. She traced the lines with her fingers, as if she were reading Braille. Doubt slowly faded to shock. "The ends . . . they simply stop abruptly. They don't blend back down."

"It's a letter," Kara said.

"Epigraphic South Arabian," Safia agreed, naming the ancient script from the region, a script that predated Hebrew and Aramaic. "It's the letter *B*."

"And look at what we can see of the upper heart chamber."

"The right atrium," Clay said behind them.

They both glanced at him.

"I was premed before I realized the sight of blood had such a . . . well, negative effect on what I had for lunch."

Kara returned to the sculpture and pointed her caliper again. "A good portion of the upper atrium is still obscured by the sandstone encasement, but I think that's another letter hidden under there."

Safia leaned closer. She felt with her fingers. The tail end of exposed vessels ended abruptly as they did on the first one. "I'll have to work carefully."

She reached for the array of picks, chisels, and tiny hammers. With the proper tools in hand, she set about with the precision of a surgeon. Hammer and chisel to break away the larger chunks of brittle sandstone, then pick and brush to clear away. In a matter of minutes, the right atrium was cleared.

Safia stared down at the crisscrossing of what appeared to be coronary vessels. But they mapped out a perfect letter.

It was too complex for mere chance.

"What letter is that?" Clay asked.

"There's not a direct corresponding letter in English," Safia answered. "The letter is pronounced somewhat like the sound *wa* . . . so in translations it's often listed *W-A* or even *U,* as that's what it sounds like orally. Though in truth, there are no vowels in Epigraphic South Arabian script."

Kara met her eyes. "We have to remove the heart," she repeated. "If there are more letters, they'd be on the opposite side."

Safia nodded. The left side still remained locked in the stone chest. She hated to disturb the statue any further, but curiosity drove her to pick up her tools without argument. She set to work. It took her a full half hour to remove the sandstone clamped around the heart. Finally, she attached the suction clamp and gripped the handle with both hands. With a prayer to the old gods of Arabia, she pulled evenly up, using all the muscles in her shoulders.

At first, it appeared to be stuck, but it was merely heavier than she had anticipated. With a determined grimace of effort, she lifted the heart free of the chest. Bits of sandstone and loose grains showered down. At arm's length, she swung the prize around to the library table.

Kara hurried over to join them. Safia placed the heart on a square of soft leather chamois to protect it, then unfastened the suction clamp. The heart rolled slightly, once released. A small sloshing sound accompanied it.

Safia glanced at the others. Had they heard it, too?

"I told you I thought the thing was hollow," Clay whispered.

Safia reached and rocked the heart on the chamois. The center of gravity rolled with the rocking. It reminded her oddly of one of those old Magic 8 Balls. "There's some type of fluid in the center."

Clay backed up a step. "Great, it had better not be blood. I prefer my cadavers desiccated and wrapped like mummies."

"It's sealed tight," Safia assured him, examining the heart. "I can't even spot a way to open it. It's almost like the bronze heart was forged around it."

"Riddles wrapped inside riddles," Kara said, and took her turn rolling and checking the heart. "What about more lettering?"

Safia joined her. It took them half a moment to orient themselves and find the two remaining chambers. She ran her finger over the largest, the left ventricle. It was smooth and bare.

"Nothing," Kara said, surprised and baffled. "Maybe it wore away."

Safia checked more thoroughly, painting it with a bit of isopropyl alcohol to clean its surface. "I see no scoring or trace. It's too smooth."

"What about the left atrium?" Clay asked.

She nodded, turning the heart. She quickly spotted a line arcing cleanly over the face of the atrium.

"It's the letter *R*," Kara whispered, sounding slightly frightened. She collapsed down on a chair. "It can't be."

Clay frowned. "I don't understand. The letters *B, WA* or *U,* and *R*. What does it spell?"

"Those three ESA letters should be known to you, Mr. Bishop," Safia said. "Maybe not in that order." She picked up a pencil and drew them out as they should be spelled.

Clay scrunched his face. "ESA is read like Hebrew and Arabic, from right to left, opposite of English. *WABR . . . UBR*. But the vowels are excluded between consonants." The young man's eyes widened. "*U-B-A-R*. The goddamn lost city of Arabia, the Atlantis of the sands."

Kara shook her head. "First a meteorite fragment that was supposed to guard Ubar explodes . . . and now we find the name written on a bronze heart."

"If it is *bronze*," Safia said, still bent over the heart.

Kara was shaken out of her shock. "What do you mean?"

Safia lifted the heart in her hands. "When I pulled the heart out of the statue, it seemed way too heavy, especially if it's hollowed out and full of liquid. See where I cleaned the left ventricle with the alcohol? The base metal is much too red."

Kara stood, understanding dawning in her eyes. "You think it's *iron*. Like the meteorite fragment."

Safia nodded. "Possibly even the *same* meteoric iron. I'll have to test it, but either way it makes no sense. At the time of the sculpture's carving, the peoples of Arabia didn't know how to smelt and work iron of this quality, especially a masterful piece of art like this. There are so many mysteries here, I don't even know where to begin."

"If you're right," Kara said fiercely, "then that drab trading post unearthed in the desert back in 1992 is a far cry from the whole story. Something is yet undiscovered." She pointed to the artifact. "Like the true heart of Ubar."

"But what do we do now? What's the next step? We're no closer to knowing anything about Ubar."

Clay was examining the heart. "It's sort of strange that the left ventricle has no letters."

" 'Ubar' is only spelled with three letters," Safia explained.

"Then why use a four-chambered heart and spell the letters in the direction of blood flow?"

Safia swung around. "Explain yourself?"

"Blood enters the heart from the body through the vena cava into the right atrium. The letter *U*." He poked a finger at the stumped large vessel that led to the right upper chamber and continued his anatomy lesson, tracing his way. "It then passes through the atrioventricular valve to the right ventricle. The letter *B*. From there, the blood leaves for the lungs via the pulmonary artery, then returns oxygen-rich through the pulmonary vein to the left atrium. The letter *R*. Spelling out 'Ubar.' So why does it stop there?"

"Why indeed?" Safia mumbled, brow furrowed.

She pondered the mystery. The name Ubar was spelled in the path that blood traveled. It seemed to imply a direction, a flow toward something. A glimmer of an idea formed. "Where does the blood go after it leaves the heart?"

Clay pointed to a thick arched vessel at the very top. "Through the aorta to the brain and the rest of the body."

Safia rolled the heavy heart, followed the aorta to where it ended, and stared inside the stump. A plug of sandstone was jammed in there. She had not bothered to clean it out, too busy concentrating on the surface of the chambers.

"What are you thinking?" Kara asked.

"It's like the writing is pointing somewhere." She returned the heart to the table and began to clean away the sandstone from the end of the aorta. It crumbled away easily. She sat back at what she found beyond the sand.

"What is that?" Clay asked, staring over her shoulder.

"Something prized more than blood itself by the ancient peoples of Arabia." She used a pick to pry a few crystalline chunks of the dried resin onto the table. She could smell the sweet aroma given off by the crystals, preserved throughout the long centuries. It was a scent from a time before Christ.

"Frankincense," Kara said, awe in her voice. "What does it mean?"

"It's a signpost," Safia answered. "As the blood flows, so do the riches of Ubar." She turned to her friend. "The clue must point toward Ubar, to the next step on the road to its doorway."

"But where does it point?" Kara asked.

Safia shook her head. "I'm not sure, but the town of Salalah is the beginning of the famous Incense Road."

She nudged the bits of crystalline frankincense. "And the tomb of Nabi Imran lies within that city."

Kara straightened. "Then that's where we must begin the search."

"Search?"

"We must put an expedition together immediately." Kara spoke rapidly, eyes wide. But it was not the amphetamines fueling her excitement. It was hope. "In a week's time, no later. My contacts in Oman will make all the necessary arrangements. And we'll need the best people. You, of course, and whomever you see fit."

"Me?" Safia asked, her heart skipping a beat. "I . . . I'm not . . . I haven't done fieldwork in years."

"You're going," Kara said firmly. "It's time for you to quit hiding in these dusty halls. Get back out in the world."

"I can coordinate data from here. I'm not needed in the field."

Kara stared at her, looking as if she was going to relent as she had in the past. Then her voice dropped to a husky whisper. "Saff, I need you. If something's truly out there . . . an answer . . ." She shook her head, close to tears. "I need you with me. I can't do it by myself."

Safia swallowed, struggling with herself. How could she refuse her friend? She stared at the fear and hope in Kara's eyes. But in her head, old screams still echoed.

She could not silence them. Blood of children still stained her hands. "I . . . I can't . . ."

Something must have broken in her face because Kara finally shook her head. "I understand." But from her clipped tone, she didn't. No one did.

Kara continued, "But you were right about one thing. We'll need an experienced *field* archaeologist on board. And if you're not going, I know the perfect person."

Safia realized whom she meant. *Oh, no . . .*

Kara seemed to sense her distress. "You know he's had the most field experience in the region." She rummaged in her purse and pulled out her cellular phone. "If we're going to succeed, we're going to need Indiana Jones."

4
White Water

ΦΥΥΧϟΙΦħΧϟ)

"I'm not Indiana Jones!" he yelled into the satellite phone's headset to be heard over the jet boat's motor. "Name's Omaha . . . Dr. Omaha Dunn! Kara, you know that!"

An exasperated sigh answered him. *"Omaha? Indiana? What bloody difference does it make? All your American names sound the same."*

He crouched over the wheel, racing down the crooked river gorge. Cliffs flanked both sides of the muddy Yangtze as it twisted and turned through a section aptly named the Narrows. In a few years, Three Gorges Dam would flood this entire region to the tranquil depth of two hundred feet, but for now, submerged rocks and wicked rapids remained a constant danger as the fierce river choked through the squeeze.

But rocks and rapids weren't the *only* danger.

A bullet pinged off the boat's hull. A warning shot. The pursuers rapidly closed the distance in a pair of black Scimitar 170 bow riders. Damn fast boats.

"Listen, Kara, what do you want?" His jet boat hit a swell and bumped airborne for a breath. He lifted from his seat, gripping tighter on the boat's steering wheel with one hand.

A yelp of surprise sounded behind him.

Omaha yelled over a shoulder. "Hang on!"

The boat struck the water with a jolt.

A moan followed. "Now you tell me."

A glance behind confirmed that his younger brother, Danny, was all right. He was sprawled in the stern, his head buried in a supply cabinet under the rear seat. Beyond the stern, the twin black speedboats continued their pursuit.

Omaha muffled the phone's receiver with his hand. "Get the shotgun."

His brother fell out of the supply chest, dragging the weapon clear. He pushed up his glasses with the back of his wrist. "Got it!"

"And the shells?"

"Oh, yeah." Danny dove back in.

Omaha shook his head. His brother was a renowned paleontologist, having earned his Ph.D. at twenty-four, but oftentimes he put the scatter in scatterbrained. Omaha lifted the phone. "Kara, what's this all about?"

"What's going on?" she asked instead.

"Nothing, but we're sort of in the middle of something here. Why did you call?" There was a long pause. He didn't know if it was due to the time lag in the satellite communication between London and China or merely thoughtful silence on Kara's part. Either way, it gave him too much time to think. He hadn't seen Kara Kensington in four years. Not since he had broken off his engagement with Safia al-Maaz. He knew this wasn't a casual call. Kara sounded serious and clipped, flaring worry for Safia in him. He couldn't end the call until he knew she was okay.

Kara spoke. *"I'm putting together an expedition into Oman. I'd like you to lead the field team. Are you interested?"*

He almost hung up again. It was a stupid business call. "No thanks."

"This is important . . ." He heard the strain in her voice.

He groaned. "What's the time frame?"

"We gather in Muscat in one week. I can't give you the details over the phone, but it's a major discovery. It may rewrite the history of the entire Arabian Peninsula."

Before he could answer, Danny pushed up next to him. "I loaded both barrels." He held the gun out to Omaha. "But I don't know how you're going to hold them off with nothing more than salt shot."

"I'm not. You are." He pointed the phone behind him. "Aim for their hull. Just rattle 'em enough to buy me some time. I've got my hands full here."

Danny nodded, swinging around.

He pulled the phone back to his face and heard Kara in midrant. ". . . wrong? What is all this about shooting?"

"Calm down. Just chasing off some big river rats—"

The shotgun blast cut him off.

"Missed," Danny swore behind him.

Kara spoke. "What about the expedition?"

Danny cranked the next shell. "Should I shoot again?"

"Yes, goddamnit!"

"Brilliant," Kara said, misinterpreting his outburst. "We'll see you in Muscat in a week. You know the place."

"Wait! I didn't—"

But the connection was severed. He threw the phone headset down. Kara damn well knew he hadn't been agreeing to the expedition. As usual, she had taken advantage of the situation.

"I hit one of the boat's drivers in the face!" Danny yelled, his voice surprised. "It's heading for shore. But watch out! The other's flanking starboard!"

Omaha glanced to the right. The sleek black Scimitar raced up alongside them. Four men in worn gray uniforms, former soldiers, crouched low. A bullhorn lifted. Mandarin spilled out in commanding tones that basically meant "Throttle down . . . or die!" To punctuate this demand a rocket launcher appeared and was pointed at their boat.

"I don't think throwing salt at them is going to help this time," Danny said, sinking into the other seat.

With no choice, Omaha pulled back on the throttle and slowed the boat. He waved an arm in admitted defeat.

Danny opened the glove compartment. Inside was a perfectly preserved trio of fossilized tyrannosaurus eggs, worth their weight in gold. Discovered in the Gobi Desert, they had been destined for a museum in Beijing. Unfortunately, such a treasure was not without its admirers. Many collectors bought and sold such items on the black market—for princely sums.

"Hang on," Omaha whispered to his brother.

Danny closed the glove compartment. "Please don't do what I think you're going to do . . ."

"No one steals from me. I'm the only grave robber around these parts."

He flipped open the thumb switch that protected the nitrous feed to the pulse jets incorporated into the Hamilton 212 turbo impeller. He had salvaged the boat from an outfitter out of New Zealand. It had raced tourists through Black Rock River outside of Auckland.

He eyed the next twist of the crooked river.

Thirty yards. With a little luck . . .

He punched the button. Nitrous gas poured into the impeller, igniting the pulse jets. Licks of flame spat from the twin exhausts, accompanied by a throaty scream of the jets. The boat's bow shot up; the stern dug deep.

Shouts erupted from the other boat. Caught off guard, they were too slow bringing the rocket launcher to bear.

Omaha shoved the throttle wide open. The boat rocketed across the water, a torpedo of aluminum and chrome.

Danny scrambled to belt himself in his seat. "Ohmygod . . . !"

Omaha simply kept his stance in front of the wheel, knees half bent. He needed to feel the balance of the boat under him. They reached the jag in the river. He risked a glance over his shoulder.

The other boat sped toward them, struggling to keep up. But their pursuers had one distinct advantage. A flash of fire marked the launch of a rocket-propelled grenade, a black-market Chinese RPG Type 69, with a lethal radius of twenty meters. They didn't have to be close.

Omaha tore the wheel to the right, canting the boat high up on the port side. They skimmed the water, plowing around the corner.

The grenade rocketed past, just missing the stern.

Clearing the bend, Omaha straightened the boat and shot it down the center of the river. The explosion ripped into the opposite cliff face. Boulders and rocks rained down amid a cloud of smoke and dust.

He eked more speed out of the jets, barely touching the water now. The boat handled as if it were on ice.

Behind him, the other boat appeared around the smoky bend, racing after them. They were loading another grenade into the launcher.

He couldn't give them another chance to get a clear shot at him. Luckily the Narrows were in a cooperative mood. The twists and crooked bends kept them out of sight for a fair stretch, but it also forced Omaha to cut the nitrous feed and slow their own boat.

"Can we outrun them?" Danny asked.

"I don't think we have a choice."

"Why not turn over the eggs? It's not worth our lives."

Omaha shook his head at his brother's naïveté. It was hard to believe they were brothers. They were both the same six-foot-two, the same sandy-blond hair, but Danny looked as if he had been put together with wire and bone. Omaha was built broader and rougher around the edges, hardened by the world, his skin burned by suns from six out of the seven continents. And the ten years that separated younger brother from older had marked his face with lines, like the rings of a tree: sun crinkles at the corners of his eyes, deep furrows across his brow from too much frowning and not enough smiling.

His brother remained unmarked, smooth, a blank slate waiting to be written upon. He had finished his doctoral program only last year, speeding through Columbia as if it were a footrace. He suspected that a part of Danny's rush through school had been the desire to join his older brother in the wider world.

Well, this was it: long days, few showers, stinking tents, dirt and sweat in every crack. And for what? To have some thieves pilfer their find?

"If we gave them the eggs—"

"They'd kill us anyway," Omaha finished, tweaking the boat around another sharp turn in the river. "These folks don't leave trails behind them."

Danny searched behind the stern. "So we run."

"As fast as we can."

The whine of the Scimitar's motor ratcheted up as the other boat cleared the bend behind them. They were closing the distance. He needed more speed, hoping for a short stretch of open water, one long enough that he could open the nitrous wide and put some distance between them again, but not *too* long a stretch that their pursuers could take another potshot.

He wrangled the boat back and forth through a narrow switchback. Worry made him miss spotting a hidden rock. The boat jarred into it, hung up for a breath, then with a screech of aluminum dragged free again.

"That couldn't have been good," Danny commented.

No, it wasn't. His brows furrowed deeper. Through his feet, he felt a persistent tremble in the boat. Even on flat water. Something had torn.

Again the sound of the Scimitar's engine whined louder.

As Omaha rounded another bend, he caught a glimpse of their pursuers. Seventy yards behind. He faced around and heard Danny groan. The river ahead boiled and frothed with white water. This section of the river pinched between high walls. A long straight stretch of river—*too* long, *too* straight.

If there had been a place to run the boat aground and take their chances overland, he would've done it. But they had no choice. He continued down the gorge, studying the flows and alert for rocks. He mapped the plan in his head.

"Danny, you're not going to like this."

"What?"

A quarter of the way down the rapids, he spun the boat into an eddy and skipped it around in a tight circle, pointing the bow back upriver.

"What are you doing?"

"The boat's corked," he said. "There's no way we can outrun them. We're going to have to take the fight to them."

Danny nudged the shotgun. "Salt shot against a rocket launcher?"

"All it takes is the element of surprise." That and perfect timing.

Pushing the throttle forward, he edged back into the current, this time working upriver. He followed the map in his head: skirt around that drop, around that deep boil, edge clear of the rock splitting the current, take the calmer side. He aimed for a standing, refractory wave as it humped over a boulder, worn smooth by the constant churn of water.

The whine of the other boat grew as it approached.

"Here they come . . ." Danny pushed up his glasses.

Over the lip of the wave, Omaha spotted the bow end of the Scimitar clear the corner. He shifted his thumb and flipped the cover over the nitrous feed. He twisted the nozzle to full feed. It was all or nothing.

The Scimitar rounded the bend and spotted them. It must appear that they were floundering, turned ass backward by some mean boil or whirlpool.

The other boat slowed, but momentum and the current brought the Scimitar into the rapids. Their pursuers were only ten yards away now. Too close to use the grenade launcher. Shrapnel from the explosion would risk their own boat and lives.

It was a momentary standoff.

Or so it seemed.

"Grab tight!" Omaha warned as he punched the nitrous injector.

It was like someone had ignited a case of TNT under their stern. The boat bolted forward, slamming into the standing wave, striking the boulder hidden beneath. The bow climbed the flat rock, driving the stern down. The twin pulse jets shot the aluminum frame straight up. They went airborne over the wave, flying high, trailing fire.

Danny hollered—then again, so did Omaha.

Their boat sailed over the Scimitar, but it was not meant for true flight. The nitrous cut out, the flames died, and their boat came crashing down atop the fiberglass Scimitar.

The jolt knocked Omaha on his ass. Water flooded over the gunwales, swamping him. Then the boat bobbed back up. "Danny!"

"I'm fine." He was still strapped to his seat, looking dazed.

Crawling forward, Omaha searched beyond the rail.

The Scimitar lay shattered in pieces, floating in different directions. A body, facedown, bobbled among the debris. Blood trailed through the muddy waters, forming its own river. The smell of fuel fogged the air. But at least the current was dragging them safely away from the wreckage in case it exploded.

Omaha spotted two men clinging to flotsam, heading down into the raging rapids with their makeshift floaters. They seemed to have lost interest in dinosaur eggs.

Climbing back into the seat, he checked the engine. It coughed and died. No hope there. The aluminum frame was bent, the keel pocked, but at least they were seaworthy. He broke out the paddles.

Danny unbuckled and accepted one of the paddles. "What now?"

"Call for help before that other boat comes to investigate."

"Who're you going to call?"

12:05 A.M. GMT

Safia was carefully wrapping up the iron heart in acid-free specimen paper when the phone on the bench rang. It was Kara's mobile phone. She had left it behind as she retreated to the lavatory again. To freshen up, she had told Safia and Clay. But Safia knew better. More pills.

The phone continued to ring.

"You want me to get that?" Clay asked, folding up the camera tripod.

Safia sighed and picked it up. It might be important. "Hello," she said as she flipped it open.

There was a long pause.

"Hello?" she offered again. "Can I help you?"

A throat cleared, sounding far away. *"Safia?"* It was said in a soft, stunned voice. One she knew all too well.

Blood drained to her feet. "Omaha?"

"I . . . I was trying to reach Kara. I didn't realize you were there, too."

She fought her tongue free from the shock. Her words came out stiff. "Kara's . . . indisposed at the moment. If you'll hold, I'll get—"

"Wait! Safia . . ."

She froze from lowering the phone, holding it as if she had forgotten how to use it.

With the phone pulled away from her ear, Omaha's voice sounded tinny. "I . . . maybe . . ." He struggled for words, finally settling on a neutral question. "If you're over there with her, then you must know what this is all about. What sort of expedition am I being shanghaied into?"

Safia put the phone back to her ear. She could handle shoptalk. "It's a long story, but we found something here. Something extraordinary. It points to a possible new history about Ubar."

"Ubar?"

"Exactly."

There was another longish pause. "So this is about Kara's father."

"Yes. And for once, Kara may be onto something significant."

"Will you be joining the expedition?" This question was asked woodenly.

"No, I can be more help here."

"*Nonsense!*" The next words gushed out loudly. She had to hold the phone away again. "*You know more about Ubar and its history than anyone on the face of the Earth. You must come! If not for Kara, then for yourself.*"

A voice suddenly spoke at her shoulder, having eavesdropped on Omaha's tinny words. "He's right," Kara said, stepping around. "If we're going to solve this riddle and any more we come across, we need you on-site."

Safia stared between the phone and her friend, feeling trapped.

Kara reached over and took the cell. "Omaha, she's coming."

Safia opened her mouth to protest.

"This is too important," Kara said, cutting her off, speaking both to Omaha and Safia. Her eyes shone glassily with the surge of drug-induced adrenaline. "I won't accept no . . . from either of you."

"*I'm in,*" said Omaha, his words an electronic whisper. "*Matter of fact, I could use a little help getting out.*"

Kara lifted the phone, turning the conversation private. She listened for a while, then nodded as she spoke. "Are you ever *not* in trouble, Indiana? I have your GPS coordinates. A helicopter will be out to re-trieve you within the hour." She snapped the phone closed. "You're truly better off without him."

"Kara . . ."

"You're going. In a week's time. You owe me that." She stormed off.

After an awkward moment, Clay spoke up. "I wouldn't mind going."

She frowned. The grad student knew nothing about the real world. And maybe that was a good thing. She sensed she had started something that was best left for-ever buried.

5

High-Wire Act

YY7YI⊕Y)ჳΙႶℲX

November 15, 02:12 A.M. GMT
London, England

Hours after Kara had stormed off, Safia sat in her dark office. The only light came from a lime-shaded banker's lamp atop her walnut desk, illuminating a sea of paper and thumbed journals. How could Kara expect her to be ready to leave for Oman in a week's time? Especially after the explosion here. There was still so much to attend to.

She couldn't go. That was that. Kara would simply have to understand. And if she didn't, that wasn't Safia's concern. She had to do what was right for herself. She had heard that often enough from her therapist. It had taken her four years to gather some semblance of normalcy in her life, to find security in her days, to sleep without nightmares. Here was home, and she wasn't going to forsake it for a wild-goose chase into the hinterlands of Oman.

And then there was the prickly matter of Omaha Dunn . . .

Safia chewed the eraser end of her pencil. It was her only meal in the past twelve hours. She knew she should leave, nip out for a late dinner at the pub on the corner, then try to catch a few hours of sleep. Besides, Billie had been sorely neglected over the past day and would need attention and a spot of tuna to assuage his hurt feelings.

Still, Safia could not move.

She kept running over her conversation with Omaha. An old ache throbbed in the pit of her belly. If only she hadn't picked up the phone . . .

She had met Omaha ten years ago in Sojar, when she was twenty-two, fresh from Oxford, researching a dissertation on Parthian influences in southern Arabia. He had been stranded in the same seaside city, awaiting approval from the Omani government to proceed into a remote section of disputed territory.

"Do you speak English?" were his first words to Safia. She was working behind a small table on the dining terrace of a small hostelry overlooking the Arabian Sea. It was the haunt of many students doing research in the region, being cheap as chips and serving the only decent coffee around.

Irritated at the interruption, she had been curt. "As a British citizen, I should hope I speak better English than you, sir."

Glancing up, she discovered a young man, sandy blond hair, cornflower blue eyes, a dusky trace of beard, wearing scuffed khakis, a traditional Omani headcloth, and an embarrassed smile.

"Excuse me," he said. "But I noticed you had a copy of *Arabian Archaeology and Epigraphy 5*. I was wondering if I could glance at a section."

She picked up the book. "Which section?"

"'Oman and the Emirates in Ptolemy's Map.' I'm heading into the borderlands."

"Truly? I thought that region had been closed to foreigners."

Again that smile, only it had grown a mischievous edge. "So you caught me. I should've said I *hope* to be traveling to the borderlands. I'm still awaiting word from the consulate."

She had leaned back and eyed him up and down. She switched to Arabic. "What do you plan to do up there?"

He didn't miss a beat, responding in Arabic himself. "To help settle the border dispute by proving the ancient tribal routes of the local Duru tribes, confirming a historical precedent."

She continued in Arabic, checking his knowledge of the region's geography. "You'll have to be careful in Umm al-Samim."

"Yes, the quicksands," he said with a nod. "I've read about that treacherous stretch." His eyes flashed with eagerness.

Safia relented and passed him her copy of the periodical. "It's the only copy from the Institute of Arabian Studies. I'll have to ask you to read it here."

"From the IAS?" He had taken a step forward. "That's the Kensington nonprofit, isn't it?"

"Yes. Why?"

"I've been trying to reach someone in authority over there. To grease some wheels with the Omani government. But no one would return my calls or letters. That place is a tough nut to crack, like its sponsor, Lady Kara Kensington. Now there's a cold fish if there ever was one."

"Hmm," she said noncommittally.

After making their introductions, he asked if he could share her table while he read the article. She had nudged the chair in his direction.

"I heard the coffee's quite good here," he said as he sat.

"The tea's even better," she countered. "But then again, I'm British."

They had continued in silence for a long while, reading their respective journals, each occasionally eyeing the other, sipping their drinks. Finally, Safia noticed the terrace door swing open behind her guest. She waved.

He turned at the arrival of the newcomer to their table. His eyes widened.

"Dr. Dunn," Safia said, "may I introduce you to Lady Kara Kensington. You'll be happy to know she speaks English, too."

She had enjoyed watching color blush to his cheeks, caught off guard, blindsided. She suspected such didn't happen often to the young man. The three of them spent the rest of the afternoon talking, debating current events in Arabia and back home, discussing Arabian history. Kara left before the sun set, heading off to an early business dinner with the local chamber of commerce, but not before promising to help Dr. Dunn with his expedition.

"I guess I owe you at least dinner," he had stated afterward.

"And I suppose I must accept."

That night, they shared a leisurely dinner of wood-fired kingfish, accompanied with spiced *rukhal* bread.

They talked until the sun sank into the sea and the skies filled with stars.

That was their first date. Their second date wouldn't be for another six months, after Omaha was finally freed from a Yemeni prison for entering a holy Muslim site without permission. Despite the penal setback, they continued to see each other off and on, across four out of the seven continents. One Christmas Eve, back at his family's home in Lincoln, Nebraska, he had dropped to a knee by the couch and asked her to marry him. She had never been happier.

Then a month later, everything changed in one blinding flash.

She shied away from that last memory, standing up finally from her desk to clear her head. It was too stuffy in her office. She needed to walk, to keep moving. It would be good to feel the breeze on her face, even the damp chill of London's winter. She retrieved her coat and locked up her office.

Safia's office was located on the second floor. The stairs down to the first floor were at the other end of the wing, near the Kensington Gallery, which meant she would have to pass the explosion site again. Not something she wanted to do. But she had no choice.

She set off down the long dark hall, illuminated by the occasional red security lamp. Usually she enjoyed the empty museum. It was a peaceful time after the daily bustle. She would often wander the gated galleries, staring at cabinets and displays, comforted by the weight of history.

No longer. Not this night.

Circulating fans had been set up like guard towers on long poles the entire length of the north wing, whirring and rattling noisily, trying and failing to disperse the reek of charred wood and burned plastics. Space heaters dotted the floor, snaking orange cords, set up to dry out the halls and galleries after the pumps had drained the worst of the sooty water. It made the hall swelter, like the damp warmth of the tropics. The line of fans stirred the air only sluggishly.

Her heels tapped the marble floor as she passed the galleries displaying the museum's ethnographical collection: Celtic, Russian, Chinese. The damage from the explosion grew worse the nearer she approached her own gallery: smoke-stained walls, ribbons of police tape, piles of swept plaster, broken glass.

As she passed the opening to the Egyptian exhibit, she heard a muffled tinkle behind her, like breaking glass. She stopped and glanced over a shoulder. For a moment, she thought she spotted a flicker of light from the Byzantine gallery. She stared for a long breath. The opening remained dark.

She fought down a growing panic. Since the attacks had begun, she had difficulty distinguishing real danger from false. Her heart thudded in her throat, and the hairs on her arms tingled as a nearby fan rotated its pass over her, whirring asthmatically.

Just the headlamps of a passing car, she assured herself.

Swallowing her anxiety, she turned back around to discover a dark figure looming in the hall outside the Kensington Gallery.

She stumbled back.

"Safia?" The figure lifted a hand torch and flicked it on, blinding her with its brightness. "Dr. al-Maaz."

She sighed with relief and hurried forward, shielding her eyes. "Ryan . . ." It was the head of security, Ryan Fleming. "I thought you had gone home."

He smiled and flicked off the torch. "I was on my way when I was paged by Director Tyson. It seems a pair of American scientists insisted that they review the explosion site." He walked her toward the opening to the gallery.

Inside, two figures dressed in identical blue jumpsuits moved through the dark gallery. The only illumination came from a pair of lamp poles in each room that cast weak pools of light. In the dimness, the investigators' instruments glowed brightly. They appeared to be Geiger counters. In one hand, each of them held a compact base unit with a lighted computer screen. In the other, they carried meter-long black wands, attached to the base unit by a coiled cord. They slowly worked one of the gallery rooms in tandem, sweeping their instruments over singed walls and piles of debris.

"Physicists out of M.I.T.," Fleming said. "They flew in this evening and came directly here from the airport. They must have some pull. Tyson insisted I accommodate them. 'Post haste,' to quote our esteemed director. I should introduce you."

Still edgy, Safia tried to bow out. "I really must be getting home."

Fleming had already stepped into the gallery. One of the investigators, a tall man with ruddy features, noted him, then her.

He lowered his wand and strode rapidly forward. "Dr. al-Maaz, what good fortune." He held out a hand. "I had hoped to speak to you."

She accepted his hand.

"I'm Dr. Crowe," he said. "Painter Crowe."

His eyes, piercing and attentive, were the color of lapis, his hair long to the shoulder, ebony black. She noted his tanned complexion. Native American, she guessed, but the blue eyes were throwing her off. Maybe it was just the name. *Crowe.* He could easily be Spanish, too. He had a generous smile that was also reserved.

"This is my colleague Dr. Coral Novak."

The woman shook Safia's hand perfunctorily with only the tiniest nod. She seemed anxious to return to her survey.

The two scientists could not be more different. Compared to her darkly handsome companion, the woman seemed devoid of pigment, a pale shadow. Her skin glowed like freshly scrubbed snow, her lips thin, her eyes icy gray. Her naturally white-blond hair was cropped short. She stood as tall as Safia, lithe of limb, but still carried a certain sturdiness to her frame. It could be felt in her firm handshake.

"What are you searching for?" Safia asked, taking a step back.

Painter lifted his wand. "We're checking for radiation signatures."

"Radiation?" She could not hide her shock.

He laughed—not condescendingly, only warmly. "Don't worry. It's a specific signature we're looking for, something following lightning strikes."

She nodded. "I didn't mean to disturb you. It was nice meeting you both, and if there's anything I can do to facilitate your investigation, please let me know." She began to turn away.

Painter stepped after her. "Dr. al-Maaz, I had meant to hunt you down. I have a few questions that I would like to discuss with you. Maybe over lunch."

"I'm afraid I'm very busy." Those eyes caught hers. She was trapped, unable to look away. She read the disappointment in his pinched brow. "May-maybe something could be arranged. Try me in my office in the morning, Dr. Crowe."

He nodded. "Very good."

She tore her gaze away and was saved further humiliation by Ryan Fleming. "I'll escort you out," he said.

She followed him into the hall, refusing to glance back. It had been a long time since she had felt so foolish, so flustered . . . by a man. It must be an aftershock of her unexpected conversation with Omaha.

"We'll have to take the stairs. The lifts are still out."

She kept in step with Fleming.

"Odd bunch, them Americans," he continued as they descended the flights to the first floor. "Always in such a hurry. Had to come this very night. Insisted that the readings they sought would deteriorate. It had to be now."

Safia shrugged as they reached the bottom and passed the short way to the employee-side exit. "I don't think that's so much an idiosyncrasy of Americans as it is of scientists in general. We're a surly and determined lot."

He nodded with a smile. "I've noticed." He used his passkey to unlock the door to keep the alarm from sounding. He pushed the door wide with his shoulder, stepping out to hold it open for her.

His eyes were on her, oddly shy. "I was wondering, Safia. If you had the time . . . maybe . . ."

The gunshot sounded like no more than a cracking walnut. The right side of Ryan's head exploded against the door, splattering blood and brain matter. Bits of skull ricocheted off the metal door and into the hallway.

Three masked gunmen crowded through the open door before Ryan's body hit the ground. They rammed Safia into the far wall, pinning her, choking her, one hand over her mouth.

A gun appeared, pressed against the center of her forehead. "Where's the heart?"

Painter studied the red needle on his scanner. It jittered up into the scale's orange range as he passed the detection rod over a blasted display cabinet. A significant reading.

The device had been designed by the nuclear labs at White Sands. Rad-X scanners were capable of detecting low-level radiation. Their particular devices had been specially calibrated to detect the unique decay signature of antimatter annihilation. When an atom of matter and antimatter collided and obliterated, the reaction liberated pure energy. That was what their detectors had been calibrated to sniff out.

"I'm picking up a particularly strong reading over here," his partner called to him. Her voice was matter-of-fact, all business.

Painter crossed to her. Coral Novak was new to Sigma, recruited from the CIA only three years ago. Still, in the short time since her hiring, she had earned a Ph.D. in nuclear physics and was already a black belt in six disciplines of martial arts. Her IQ was off the charts, and she had almost an encyclopedic knowledge on a wide range of subjects.

He had heard of Novak, of course, even met her once at a district meeting, but they had only the short hop from Washington to London to better acquaint themselves. Not nearly enough time for two reserved people to form any relationship, beyond a stiffly professional one. He couldn't help comparing her to Cassandra, which only exacerbated his reticence. Similar traits between the women tweaked his suspicion, while discordantly, the few differences made him wonder about his new partner's competence. It made no sense. He knew this.

Only time would sort it out.

As he stepped beside her, she pointed her detection rod at the melted ruin of a bronze urn. "Commander, you'd better double-check my findings. I'm reading a signature all the way into the red range."

Painter confirmed it with his own scanner. "Definitely hot."

Coral dropped to a knee. Wearing thin lead gloves, she examined the urn, rolling it carefully. A rattle sounded inside. She glanced up at him.

He nodded for her to investigate. She reached through the mouth of the urn, searched a moment, then pulled free a thimble-size chunk of rock. She rolled it in her gloved palm. One side was blast-blackened. The other was red, metallic. Not rock . . . *iron.*

"A piece of the meteor," Coral said. She held it out for Painter to scan. The readings indicated the item was the source of the strong reading. "And look at my ancillary readings. Besides Z-bosons and gluons against the background gamma, as expected with antimatter annihilation, this sample is emitting very low levels of alpha and beta radiation."

Painter frowned. He had little background in physics.

Coral shifted the sample into a lead specimen jar. "The same radiation pattern found from decaying uranium."

"Uranium? Like used in nuclear facilities."

She nodded. "Nonpurified. Perhaps a few atoms trapped in the meteoric iron." She continued to study her readings. Her brow creased with a single line, a dramatic response in the stoic woman.

"What is it?" he asked.

She continued to fiddle with her scanner. "On the flight over here, I reviewed the results from DARPA's researchers. Something troubled me about their theories of a stabilized form of antimatter trapped in the meteor."

"You don't think such a thing is possible?" It was certainly a stretch of plausibility. Antimatter always and instantly annihilated itself when in contact with any form of matter, even oxygen in the air. How could it exist here in some natural state?

She shrugged without looking up. "Even if I accepted such a theory, the question arises of *why* the antimatter happened to ignite at this time. Why did this particular electrical storm trigger it to explode? Pure chance? Or was there something more?"

"What do you think?"

She pointed to her scanner. "Uranium decay. It's like a clock. It releases its energy in set, predictable ways, spanning millennia. Perhaps some critical threshold of radiation from the uranium caused the antimatter to begin to destabilize. It was this instability that allowed the shock of the electrical discharge to ignite it."

"Sort of like a timer on a bomb."

"A nuclear timer. One set millennia ago."

It was a disturbing thought.

Still, Coral's brow remained creased. She had another concern.

"What else?" he asked.

She sat back on her heels and faced him for the first time. "If there is some other source of this antimatter—some mother lode—it may be destabilizing, too. If we ever hope to find it, we'd best not drag our feet. The same nuclear time clock could be ticking down."

Painter stared at the lead sample jar. "And if we don't find this lode, we'll lose all chance of discovering this new source of power."

"Or worse yet." Coral glanced around the burned-out shell of the gallery. "This could occur on a much more massive scale."

Painter let this sobering thought sink into him.

In the heavy silence, a scuffle of steps echoed up from the nearby stairwell. He turned. A voice carried to them, the words muffled, but he recognized Dr. al-Maaz's voice.

A prickle of warning raced through Painter. Why was the curator returning?

Stronger words reached him, a tone of command, the speaker unknown. "Your office. Take us there."

Something was wrong. He remembered the fate of the two Defense Sciences officers, shot execution style in their hotel room. He swung to Coral. Her eyes had narrowed.

"Weapons?" he whispered.

They hadn't had time to arrange for sidearms, always a difficulty in gun-shy Britain. Coral bent and tucked up the cuff of her pant leg to reveal a sheathed knife. He hadn't known she had it. They had flown commercial to substantiate their covers. She must have stashed the weapon in her checked luggage, then donned it when she used the restroom at Heathrow.

She slid free the seven-inch-long dagger, titanium and steel, German from the look of it. She held it out to him.

"Keep it . . ." He grabbed instead a long-handled spade from a nearby pile of tools one of the salvage teams had left.

Footsteps approached the stairwell opening. He didn't know if it was merely museum security, but he wasn't taking any chances.

Painter signaled Coral his plan, then flicked off the nearby lamp pole, plunging the entrance into gloom. The pair took positions on either side of the opening to the blasted wing. Painter took the post closest to the stairwell, behind a stack of wooden pallets. He could peer between the slats yet still remain in shadow. On the opposite side of the entrance, Coral crouched behind a trio of marble plinths.

Painter kept a hand raised. *On my mark.*

From his hiding place, he kept an unblinking watch on the doorway. He didn't have long to wait. A dark figure slid quickly through and took a position flanking the stairwell opening. He was masked, an assault rifle on his shoulder.

Certainly *not* museum security.

But how many others were there?

A second figure appeared, similarly attired and armed. They searched the hall. The rattle of the fans remained the only sound. Between them, a third masked figure stepped into view. He clutched Safia al-Maaz by the elbow, a pistol shoved into her ribs.

Tears ran down Safia's pale face. She trembled with each step as she was dragged forward. She struggled to breathe, gasping, "It's . . . it's in my office safe." She pointed her free arm down the hall.

Her captor nodded for his companions to continue.

Painter slid back slowly, made eye contact with his partner, and signaled their marks. She nodded, shifting position with smooth ease.

Out in the hall, the curator's eyes searched the entrance to the Kensington Gallery. Of course, she must know the Americans were still here. Would she inadvertently do or say something to give them away?

Her feet slowed, and her voice rose sharply. "Please . . . don't shoot me!"

Her captor shoved her forward. "Then do as we say," he snarled.

She tripped and stumbled, but kept her feet. Her eyes again searched the gallery's entrance as the pair drew nearer.

Painter realized her terrified outburst had been an attempt to pass on a warning to the American scientists, to send them into hiding.

His respect for the curator grew.

The pair of masked riflemen on point glided forward, passing Painter's hiding spot. Their weapons swept over the blasted gallery. Discovering nothing, they continued down the hall.

A couple of yards behind the guards, the third man dragged Safia al-Maaz. She searched the gallery glancingly. Painter noted the flash of relief as she found the nearest rooms deserted.

As the pair passed his position, Painter signaled his partner.

Go!

Coral sprang past the cluster of plinths—shoulder-rolled into the hall—and landed in a crouch between the guards and Safia's captor.

Her sudden appearance startled the man holding Safia. His weapon shifted from his captive's ribs. That was all Painter required. He hadn't wanted the curator shot by reflex. That sometimes happened following a head blow.

Painter slipped from the shadows and swung the spade with deft skill. The gunman's head cracked to the side, bone giving way. His form crumpled, dragging Safia to the floor with him.

"Stay down," Painter barked, stepping past to Coral's aid.

It wasn't necessary. His partner was already in motion.

Pivoting on her free arm, Coral kicked out with her legs and struck the closest guard in the knees. His legs went out from under him. At the same time, her other hand threw the dagger with stunning accuracy, striking the second guard at the base of the skull, severing the brain stem. He fell forward with a strangled gasp. Coral continued her spin with fluid grace, a gymnast performing a deadly floor routine. Her boot heels slammed into the first man's face as he attempted to pick himself up.

His head flew back, then rebounded forward, striking the marble floor.

She rolled over to him, ready to deliver more damage, but he was out, unconscious. Still, Coral kept a wary stance. The other gunman lay sprawled facedown. The only movement from him was the spreading pool of blood on the marble. Dead.

Closer, Safia struggled from beneath the arms of her dead captor. Painter went to her aid, dropping to one knee. "Are you hurt?"

She sat up, scooting free from the limp body, from Painter, too. "N-no . . . I don't think so." Her gaze flickered around the carnage, settling nowhere. A keening note entered her voice. "Oh, God, Ryan. He was shot . . . by the door downstairs."

Painter glanced back to the stairwell. "Are there any more gunmen?"

She shook her head, eyes wide. "I . . . I don't know."

Painter moved closer. "Dr. al-Maaz," he said sternly, drawing her scattered attention. She was close to shock. "Listen. Was there *anyone* else?"

She took several deep breaths; her face shone with fear. With a final shudder, she spoke more firmly. "Not downstairs. But Ryan . . ."

"I'll go check on him." Painter turned to Coral. "Stay with Dr. al-Maaz. I'll recon downstairs and see about rousing security."

He bent down and recovered the gunman's abandoned pistol, a Walther P38. Not a weapon he would've chosen. He preferred his Glock. But right now its weight felt perfect in his hand.

Coral stepped closer, freeing a coil of rope from a debris pile to secure their remaining prisoner. "What about our cover?" she whispered to him, casting a glance toward the curator.

"We're both just very resourceful scientists," he answered.

"So in other words, we're sticking to the truth." The barest glint of amusement showed in her eyes as she turned away.

Painter headed to the stairs. He could get used to a partner like her.

Safia watched the man vanish down the stairs. He moved so silently, as if gliding on ice. *Who was he?*

A grunt drew her attention back to the woman. She had a knee planted in the lower back of the last attacker. She had wrenched his arms back, earning a protest from the groggy gunman. She swiftly bound his limbs with rope, moving with deft skill. Either she had a background that included calf-roping, or there was more to this woman than mere physics. Beyond this one observation, Safia's curiosity could not be further piqued.

She concentrated on her own breathing. There still seemed to be a deficient amount of oxygen in the air, even with the blowing fans. Sweat slicked her face and body.

She kept her position by the wall, knees raised tight, arms hugging her chest. She had to restrain herself from rocking. She did not want to appear *that* crazy. The thought helped calm her. She also kept her eyes away from the two bodies. The alarm would be raised. Security would come with batons, lights, and the comforting presence of others.

In the meantime, the hallway remained too empty, too dark, too humid. She found her gaze lingering on the stairwell opening. *Ryan* . . . The attack again played out in her head, reeling like bloody film stock, only silent. They had been after the iron heart, her own discovery, the one she had been so proud to uncover. Ryan had died because of it. Because of her.

Not again . . .

A sob shook through her. She tried to hold it back with her hands and found herself choking.

"Are you all right?" the woman asked from a step away.

Safia curled into herself, shaking.

"You're safe. Dr. Crowe will get security up here any moment."

She kept herself balled up, seeking a place of safety.

"Maybe I'd better get some—" The physicist's voice cut off with a choke.

Safia lifted her face. The woman stood a step away, stiffly straight, arms out at her sides, head thrown back. She seemed to be trembling from crown to toe. Seizure. The choking sound continued.

Safia crabbed away, unsure, on her hands and knees, heading toward the stairwell. What was happening?

The woman's form suddenly slumped, and she toppled forward to the floor. In the gloom of the hallway, a small blue flame crackled at the base of her spine. Smoke rose from her clothing. She lay unmoving.

It made no sense.

But as the blue flame died, Safia spotted a thin wire. It trailed from the prone woman to a figure standing three meters down the hall.

Another masked gunman.

He held a strange pistol in his fist. Safia had seen such a device before . . . in movies, not in real life. *A tazer.* A silent means of dispatch.

Safia continued scrambling backward, her heels slipping on the slick marble. She remembered her initial fright when leaving her office. She had thought she had heard someone, saw a flicker of light in the Byzantine gallery. It hadn't been her anxious imagination.

The figure dropped the discharged tazer and strode after her.

Safia gained her feet with a speed borne of adrenaline and panic. The stairwell lay ahead. If she could reach it, get down to the security area—

Something struck the marble floor to the right of her toes. It hissed and spat blue sparks. A second tazer.

Safia bolted away from it and charged toward the opening. It would take a few moments to reset the tazer . . . unless the gunman had a third weapon. As she reached the stairwell, she expected to be struck by lightning from behind. Or simply shot.

Neither happened. She fell into the stairwell.

Voices greeted her from below, yelling. A gunshot sounded, deafening in the small space. More gunmen were downstairs.

Moving on pure instinct, Safia fled upward. There was no thought besides escape, to keep running. She pounded up, two steps at a time. There was no third level to this section of the museum.

These stairs led to the roof.

She rounded the first flight, grabbing the handrail to sweep herself around. A door appeared at the top of the next flight. An emergency exit. Locked from the outside, it would automatically open from the inside. An alarm would sound, but that was a good thing at the moment. She prayed it wasn't secured after regular public hours.

Footsteps sounded behind her, at the stairwell entrance.

She lunged at the door, arms out, shoving the emergency latch.

It stuck. Locked.

She slammed into the steel door with a sob. *No* . . .

Painter held up his hands, the Walther P38 on the floor at his feet. He had come close to being shot in the head. The bullet had whizzed past his cheek, near enough for him to feel the burn of its passage. Only a quick dodge and roll had saved him.

But then again, he could imagine how it looked. Him kneeling beside Ryan Fleming's body at the exit door, gun in hand. A trio of security men had come upon the scene, and all chaos had broken out. It had taken him a moment of frantic negotiating to reach this standoff— dropping his gun, hands in the air.

"Dr. al-Maaz was attacked," he called over to the guard with the gun. Another checked the body, while the third was on a radio. "Mr. Fleming was shot when she was kidnapped. My partner and I were able to subdue the attackers upstairs."

There was no note of reaction from the armed guard. He could just as well have been deaf. He simply pointed his pistol. Sweat beaded the man's forehead.

The guard by the radio turned and spoke to his mates. "We're to secure him in the nest until the police arrive. They're on their way."

Painter glanced to the stairwell. Concern jangled through him. The shot must have been heard upstairs. Had it sent Coral and the curator into hiding?

"Oi, you," the guard with the pistol said. "Hands on your head. Move along this way."

The guard waved the gun down the hall, away from the stairwell. It was the only firearm among the three, and its bearer seemed poorly acquainted with the weapon. He held it too loosely, too low. Probably the only gun here, one rarely pulled out of mothball storage. But the recent explosion had made everyone jumpy, overly alert.

Painter laced his fingers atop his head and turned where indicated. He had to reestablish control here. With his hands in plain view, he swung around, stepping closer to the inexperienced guard. As he turned, he shifted his weight on his right leg. The guard's eyes flicked away for a half second. Plenty of time. Painter snap-kicked out with his left foot, striking the guard's wrist.

The gun went skittering down the hall.

Sweeping down, Painter snatched the abandoned Walther from the floor and leveled it at the stunned trio. "Now we're doing things my way."

Desperate, Safia shoved the emergency latch to the roof door again. It refused to budge. She pounded a fist weakly against the jamb. Then she spotted a security keypad in the wall beside it. An old one. Not an electronic card scanner. It needed a code. Panic whined like a mosquito in her ear.

Each employee was assigned a default code. They could change it at their leisure. The default code was each employee's birth date. She had never bothered to change hers.

A scuff of heel drew her attention around.

Her pursuer came around the lower flight, standing on the landing. The two eyed each other. The gunman now had a pistol in his grip. Not a tazer.

With her back to the door, Safia fingered the keypad's buttons and punched in her birth date blindly. After years at the museum, she was accustomed to touch-typing entries into an accounting calculator.

Once done, she pushed the emergency latch.

It clicked but failed to budge. Still locked.

"Dead end," the gunman said, his voice muffled. "Come down or die."

Pinned against the door, Safia realized her mistake. The security grid had been upgraded after the millennium. A *year* was no longer defined by two digits, but *four.* Unclenching her fingers, she rapidly typed in the eight numbers: two for day, two for month, and *four* for her birth year.

The gunman took a step toward her, pistol stretching closer.

Safia rammed her back into the emergency latch. The door flung open. Cold air whipped over her as she tumbled out and darted to the side. A shot ricocheted off the steel door. Driven by desperation, she swung the door shut, slamming it into the masked face of the gunman as he lunged.

She didn't wait, unsure if the door would relock, and fled around the corner of the rooftop exit hut. The night was too bright. Where was London's fog when you needed it? She searched for a place to hide.

Small metal outcroppings offered some shelter: hooded vents, exhaust flumes, electrical conduits. But they were isolated and offered scant protection. The remainder of the roof of the British Museum looked like the parapet of a castle, surrounding a glass-roofed central courtyard.

A muffled shot blasted behind her. A door slammed open with a crash.

Her pursuer had broken through.

Safia sprinted for the closest cover. A low wall lipped the central courtyard, outlining the edges of the Grand Court's glass-and-steel roof. She climbed over the parapet and ducked down.

Her feet rested on the metal rim of the two-acre geodesic roof. It spread out from her position in a vast plain of glass, broken into individual triangular panes. A few were missing, knocked loose by the blast last night and patched with plastic sheeting. The remaining panes shone like mirrors in the starlight, all pointing toward the middle, to where the bright copper dome of the central Reading Room rose from the middle of the courtyard, like an island in a sea of safety glass.

Safia remained crouched, realizing how exposed she was.

If the gunman searched over the wall, there was nowhere to run.

Footsteps sounded, crunching on the graveled roof. They circled around for a few moments, stopped for a long breath, then continued. Eventually they would head here.

Safia had no choice. She crawled out onto the roof, scuttling like a crab across the panes of glass, praying they would hold her weight. The forty-foot fall to the hard marble below would prove just as deadly as a slug in the head.

If she could only make it to the domed island of the Reading Room, get behind it . . .

One of the panes splintered under her knee like brittle ice. It must have been stressed by the blast. She rolled to the side as it gave way beneath her, cracking and falling through its steel frame. A moment later, a loud ringing crash echoed up as the pane struck marble.

Safia crouched only halfway across the vast roof, a fly stuck on a mirrored web. And the spider was surely coming, drawn by the crash.

She needed to hide, a hole to crawl into.

Safia glanced to the right. There was only one hole.

She rolled back to the empty steel frame, and without much more thought than *hide*, she swung her legs down through the frame, then wiggled on her belly. As her fingers grabbed the steel edge, she let herself drop, hanging now by her hands over the forty-foot fall.

She swung in place, facing back toward her initial hiding place by the wall. Through the glass, the starlit night was clear and bright. She watched a masked head peer over the low wall, searching the geodesic roof.

Safia held her breath. Viewed from outside, the roof was mirrored by the silvery starlight. She should be invisible. But already her arm muscles cramped, and the sharp steel cut into her fingers. And she would still need some strength to pull herself back up.

She searched down to the dark courtyard. A mistake. She was so high. The only light came from a handful of red-glowing security lamps near the wall. Still, she spotted the shattered pane of glass under her feet. The same would happen to her bones if she fell. Her fingers gripped tighter, her heart pounded harder.

She tore her gaze from the drop, glancing back up in time to see the gunman climbing over the wall. What was he doing? Once over the wall, he started across the roof, keeping his weight mostly on the steel-framed structure. He was coming straight at her. How did he know?

Then it dawned on her. She had noted the plastic-sheeted gaps in the roof. They were like missing teeth in a bright smile. There was only one such gap that was still uncapped. The gunman must have guessed that his target had fallen through and come to make certain. He moved swiftly, so unlike her own panicked crawl. He swept down on her hiding spot, pistol in hand.

What could she do? There was nowhere else to run. She considered simply letting go. At least she'd have control over her death. Tears rose in her eyes. Her fingers ached. All she had to do was let go. But her fingers refused to unlatch. Panic held her clenched. She hung there as the man crossed the final pane.

Finally spotting her, he started back a step, then stared down at her.

Laughter flowed, low and dark.

In that moment, Safia realized her mistake.

A gun pointed at Safia's forehead. "Tell me the combination—"

The *crack* of a pistol erupted. Glass shattered.

Safia screamed, losing the grip of one hand, hanging by the other. Her shoulder and fingers wrenched. Only then did she spot the shooter on the floor below. A familiar figure. The American.

He stood with his feet planted wide on the marble, aiming up at her.

She turned her face upward.

The pane of glass her attacker had been standing on had crackled into a thousand pieces, held together only by the safety coating. The thief stumbled backward, fumbling and losing the pistol. It flew high, then landed hard upon the shattered pane. The weapon fell through the broken glass and tumbled all the way to the floor below.

The thief sprinted across the roof, fleeing, aiming back toward the wall.

Below, the American fired and fired, blasting out panes of glass, following from below. But the thief was always a step ahead. Finally reaching the wall, the figure vanished over it. Gone.

The American swore loudly. He hurried back to where Safia hung by one arm, like a bat in the rafters. But she had no wings.

Safia struggled to get her other hand up on the support. She had to swing slightly, but finally her fingers gripped steel.

"Can you hold on?" he asked below her, concerned.

"I don't seem to have much choice," she called down hotly. "Now do I?"

"If you swing your legs," he offered, "you might be able to hook them over the next frame."

She saw what he meant. He had shot out the neighboring pane, leaving an open support bar between them. She took a deep breath—then with a small cry of effort, she swung her legs, tucked her knees, and hooked them over the bar.

Immediately, the ache in her hands lessened as the weight eased. She had to force herself not to cry with relief.

"Security's already heading up there."

Safia craned down to the American. She found herself speaking to keep herself from wailing. "Your partner . . . is she . . . ?"

"Fine. Took a jolt, ruined a nice blouse, but she'll be up and around."

She closed her eyes with relief. *Thank God . . .* She couldn't have handled another death. Not after Ryan. She took several more breaths.

"Are you all right?" the American asked, staring up at her.

"Yes. But, Dr. Crowe—"

"Call me Painter . . . I think we've passed formalities here."

"It seems I owe you my life for the second time this night."

"That's what you get for hanging around with me." Though she couldn't see it, she could imagine his wry smile.

"That's not very funny."

"It will be later." He crossed and recovered the thief's gun from the floor.

That reminded Safia. "The one you were shooting at. It was a *woman*."

He continued his study of the weapon. "I know . . ."

Painter inspected the weapon in his hand. It was a Sig Sauer, 45mm, with a Hogue rubberized grip. *It* *couldn't be . . .* He held his breath as he turned the weapon on its side. The thumb catch for the magazine release was on the right side. A custom feature for that rare left-handed shooter.

He knew this gun. He knew the shooter.

He stared up at the path of shattered glass.

Cassandra.

PART TWO

Sand and Sea

6

Homecoming

ᚤ○᚛ᚼ○᚛ᚤᚔᚷ°ᚤ

December 2, 06:42 A.M.
Heathrow International Airport

Kara met him at the foot of the steps leading up to the open door of the Learjet. She stood, blocking the way and pointing a stiff finger at the focus of her anger.

Her voice sharpened. "I want it stated clearly, Dr. Crowe, that you have no authority once you board this jet. You may have wrangled your way into this expedition, but it certainly wasn't by my invitation."

"I got that from the warm reception your pack of corporate lawyers gave me," the American answered, hitching his duffel higher on his shoulder. "Who would've guessed so many suits could put up such a determined fight?"

"Little good it did. You're still here."

He offered a crooked smile as response, then shrugged.

As before, he offered no explanation as to why the U.S. government wanted him and his partner to accompany the expedition into Oman. But insurmountable blocks had appeared: financial, legal, even diplomatic. All this was further complicated by the media circus surrounding the attempted theft.

Kara had always considered her influence to be significant—but it paled beside the pressure placed upon the expedition by Washington. The United States had significant interests in Oman. She'd spent weeks trying to find a way around their roadblocks, but the trip was hung up unless she cooperated.

Still, that didn't mean she hadn't won concessions.

"From here on out," she said firmly, "you will be under our leadership."

"Understood."

The single word irritated Kara further. With no choice, she stepped aside.

He stood his ground on the tarmac. "It doesn't have to be this way. We aren't at cross-purposes here, Lady Kensington. We both seek the same thing."

She pinched her brows. "And what might that be?"

"Answers . . . answers to mysteries." He stared at her with those piercing blue eyes, unreadable, yet not cold. For the first time, she noted how handsome he was. Not model handsome, more a weary masculinity that he carried easily. He wore his hair lanky, a five-o'clock shadow at six in the morning. She could smell his aftershave, musky with a trace of balsam. Or was that just him?

Kara kept her face fixed, her voice flatlined. "And what *mystery* are you seeking to answer, Dr. Crowe?"

He did not blink. "I might ask the same of you, Lady Kensington. What mystery do you seek? It's surely something more than academic interest in old tombs."

Kara's frown deepened, eyes flashing. Presidents of multinational corporations withered under such inspection. Painter Crowe remained unfazed.

He finally stepped forward and mounted the Lear's stairs—but not before adding one last cryptic comment. "It seems we both have secrets we wish to keep . . . at least for now."

She watched him climb.

Painter Crowe was followed by his companion: Dr. Coral Novak. She was tall, firmly toned, wearing a snug gray suit. She carried a matching duffel of personal items. The scientists' trunks and equipment had already been loaded. The woman's eyes searched down the length of the jet, studious.

Kara's frown tracked them as they disappeared inside. Though they claimed to be merely physicists contracted by the U.S. government, she recognized the stamp of the military all over them: the wiry athleticism, the hard eyes, the sharp creases in their suits. They moved together, in unison, casually, one on point, the other watching their backs. They probably weren't even aware of it.

And then there was the battle in the museum to consider. Kara had heard the detailed report: the murder of Ryan Fleming, the attempted theft of the iron heart. If not for this pair's intervention, all would have been lost. Despite Dr. Crowe's clear dissembling, Kara owed him—and for more than just the security of the artifact. She stared across the tarmac as the terminal door swung open.

Safia hurried toward the Lear, dragging a piece of luggage behind her. If the two Americans hadn't been present in the museum, Safia surely would not have survived.

Still, her friend had not passed the night unscathed. The terror, the bloodshed, the death had broken something in Safia. Her protests against joining the expedition had ended. Safia seemed reticent to talk about her change of mind. Her only explanation was a terse response: *It no longer matters.*

Safia crossed to the jet. "Am I the last one here?"

"Everyone's aboard." Kara reached toward her luggage.

Safia snapped down the tote's handle and lifted it herself. "I have it."

Kara didn't argue. She knew what the luggage contained. The iron heart, nestled in a molded, rubberized cocoon. Safia refused to let anyone near it—not to protect it, but as if it was a burden she must bear. Its blood debt was hers alone. Her discovery, her responsibility.

Guilt shadowed her friend like a mourning shroud. Ryan Fleming had been her friend. Murdered before her eyes. All for a chunk of iron, something Safia had unearthed.

Kara sighed as she followed Safia up the stairs.

It was Tel Aviv all over again.

No one could console Safia then . . . and now was no different.

Kara stopped at the top of the stairs and glanced one last time over toward the misty heights of London in the distance as the sun crested the Thames. She searched her heart for some sense of loss. But all she found was sand. This was not her true home. It never had been.

She turned her back on London and climbed inside the jet.

A man in uniform leaned out the cockpit door. "Ma'am, we have clearance from the tower. Ready when you are."

She nodded. "Very good, Benjamin."

She stepped into the main cabin as the door was secured behind her. The Lear had been customized to suit her needs. The cabin's interior was furnished in leather and burled walnut, describing four intimate seating groups. Fresh flowers sprouted from Waterford crystal vases secured to seatside tables. A long mahogany bar, an antique out of Liverpool, stood stocked near the rear of the cabin. Beyond the bar, a set of folding doors marked the entry to Kara's private study and bedroom.

She allowed herself a self-satisfied smile upon seeing Painter Crowe's cocked eyebrow as he surveyed the space. Clearly he was not accustomed to such luxuries on a physicist's salary, even one supplemented by government work. The plane's butler handed him a drink. Soda water and ice, it appeared. His glass clinked as he turned.

"What . . . no honey-roasted peanuts?" he mumbled as he passed. "I thought we were traveling first class."

Her smile grew stale as he crossed and took a seat beside Dr. Novak. *Flippant bastard . . .*

Everyone else began to find their seats as the pilot announced their departure. Safia settled off by herself.

Her graduate student, Clay Bishop, was already buckled across the cabin, face pressed to a window. He wore earphones attached to an iPod resting on his lap, lost to everyone else.

With all in readiness, Kara crossed to the bar. Her usual was waiting for her: a chilled glass of Chardonnay. It came from St. Sebastian, a French winery. Kara had been allowed her first sip on her sixteenth birthday, on the morning of the hunt. Since then, she lifted one glass each morning in honor of her father. She swirled the wineglass and inhaled its crisp bouquet, a hint of peach and oak. Even after so many years, the smell drew her immediately back to that morning, so full of promise. She could hear her father's laughter, the baying of camels in the distance, the whisper of wind with the dawning sun.

So close now . . . after so very long . . .

She sipped slowly, drowning the nagging dryness in her mouth. Her head buzzed with the sharpness of the two pills she had taken upon waking two hours earlier. Through her lips, she felt the minor tremor in her fingertips as they held up the glass. One wasn't supposed to mix alcohol with prescription drugs. But it was only the one glass of Chardonnay. And she owed it to her father.

She lowered the glass and found Safia studying her. Her face was unreadable, but her eyes glowed with concern. Kara met her gaze, unflinching, holding it steady. Safia finally broke away to stare out the window.

Neither had the words to comfort the other. Not any longer . . .

The desert had stolen a part of their lives, a part of their hearts. And only out in the sands could it be recovered.

11:42 A.M.
Muscat, Oman

Omaha slammed through the door to the Ministry of National Heritage.

The door swinging back almost struck his brother, Danny, in the face as he followed. "Omaha, calm down."

"Damn bureaucrats . . . ." He continued his tirade out in the street. "You need a friggin' permit to wipe your ass here."

"You got what you wanted," Danny said in a conciliatory tone.

"It took all goddamn morning. And the only reason we finally got the permit to carry gasoline aboard the Rovers—to carry friggin gasoline!—was because Adolf bin Asshole wanted his damn lunch."

"Calm down." Danny grabbed his elbow and dragged him to the curb. Faces turned in their direction.

"And Safia . . . Kara's plane is landing in"—Omaha checked his watch. "In just over an hour."

Danny waved for a cab. A white Mercedes sedan pulled away from a nearby taxi stand and slid up to the curb. Danny opened the door and shoved Omaha inside. It was gloriously air-conditioned. Noon in Muscat and it was already over a hundred degrees.

The cool interior washed the edge from his irritation. He leaned and tapped at the Plexiglas between the backseat and the front. "Seeb Airport."

The driver nodded and cut into traffic without signaling, simply barging his way into the lunchtime flow.

Omaha fell back into his seat beside his brother.

"I've never seen you this nervous," Danny said.

"What are you talking about? Nervous? I'm pissed."

Danny stared out the window. "Right . . . like meeting your ex-fiancée, face-to-face, hasn't trimmed your fuse a tad short this morning."

"Safia has nothing to do with this."

"Uh-huh."

"I have no reason to be nervous."

"Keep tellin' yourself that, Omaha."

"Shut up."

"You shut up."

Omaha shook his head. Both of them had had too little sleep since arriving two weeks ago. There were a thousand and one details to attend to when putting together an expedition in such a short time: permits; paperwork; hiring guards, manual labor, and trucks; clearing access from Thumrait Air Base; buying potable water, petrol, guns, salt, dry chemical toilets; organizing personnel. And all of it fell squarely upon the Dunn brothers' shoulders.

The trouble back in London had delayed Kara's arrival. If Kara had been here as planned, preparations for the expedition would've gone much more smoothly. Lady Kensington was revered in Oman, the Mother Teresa of philanthropy. Throughout the country, museums, hospitals, schools, and orphanages all bore plaques with her name on them. Her corporation helped win many lucrative contracts—oil, mineral, and fresh water—for the country and its people.

But after the museum incident, Kara had asked the brothers to maintain a low profile, keep her involvement on a need-to-know basis only.

So Omaha chewed a lot of aspirin.

The taxi crossed out of the business district of Muscat and wended through the narrow streets that bordered the stone walls of the old city. They followed a truck loaded with pines, weeping a path of dry needles behind it.

Christmas trees. In Oman.

Such was the country's openness to the West, a Muslim country that celebrated Christ's birth. Oman's attitude could be attributed to the monarchy's head of the state, Sultan Qaboos bin Said. Educated in England, the sultan had opened his country to the wider world, brought extensive civil rights to his people, and modernized his country's infrastructure.

The taxi driver turned on the radio. Strains of Bach floated through the Bose speakers. The sultan's favorite. By royal decree, only classical music could be played at noon. Omaha checked his watch. High noon.

He stared out the window. It must be good to be king.

Danny spoke up. "I think we're being followed."

Omaha glanced at his brother to see if he was joking.

Danny was craning over a shoulder. "The gray BMW, four cars back."

"Are you sure?"

"It's a BMW," Danny said more firmly. His brother—a yuppie wannabe, fascinated by all things

German-engineered—knew cars. "I spotted the same car parked down the street from our hotel, then again at the entrance to the parking lot for the natural history museum."

Omaha squinted. "Could be coincidence . . . same make, different car."

"Five-forty-i. Custom chrome wheels. Tinted privacy glass. Even—"

Omaha cut him off. "Enough of the sales pitch. I believe you."

But if they were truly being followed, only one question stood out.

Why?

He flashed back to the bloodshed and violence at the British Museum. Even the newspapers here reported on it. Kara had warned him to be as cautious as possible, to maintain a low profile. He leaned forward. "Take the next right," he said in Arabic, hoping either to lose or confirm their tail.

The driver ignored him and continued straight.

Omaha felt a sudden twinge of panic. He tried the door. Locked.

They passed the turnoff for the airport.

Bach continued to stream from the speakers.

He yanked at the door handle again.

Crap.

12:04 P.M.
Airborne Over the Mediterranean

Safia stared at the book in her lap, blind to the words. She had not turned a page in the last half hour. Tension stripped her nerves raw. Her shoulder muscles knotted, and a dull headache made her teeth hurt.

She glanced out at the sunlit blue skies. Cloudless. A vast blank canvas. It was as if she were leaving one life and sweeping toward another.

Which in many ways she was.

She was abandoning London, her flat, the stone walls of the British Museum, all that she had thought safe these past years. But that safety had proved to be an illusion, so fragile it shattered in a single night.

Blood once again stained her hands. Because of *her* work.

Ryan . . .

Safia could not erase the momentary glint of surprise in his eyes as the bullet sliced him from this world. Even weeks later, she felt the need to wash her face repeatedly, sometimes even in the middle of the night. Brown soap and cold water. Nothing washed away the memory of the blood.

And even though Safia recognized the illusory nature of London's security, the city had become her home. She had friends, colleagues, a favorite book-store, a theater that played old movies, a coffeehouse that served the perfect caramel cappuccino. Her life had become defined by the streets and trains of London.

And then there was Billie. Safia had been forced to foster her cat with Julia, a Pakistani botanist who rented the flat under hers. Before leaving, Safia had whispered promises in the tomcat's ears, promises she hoped to keep.

Still, Safia worried, deeply, down to the marrow of her bones. Some of the anxiety was inexplicable, just an overwhelming sense of doom. But most was not. She stared around the cabin. What if they all ended up like Ryan, laid out in the city morgue, then buried in a cold cemetery as the first winter snow fell.

She simply could not handle that.

Even the possibility turned her intestines to ice. Her breathing grew pained at the thought. Her hands trembled. Safia fought the wave of panic, sensing its familiar roll. She concentrated on her breathing, focusing outward, away from her own frightened center.

Across the breadth of the cabin, the drone of the engines had driven everyone else to recline their seat backs, to catch what little sleep they could as they winged south. Even Kara had retreated to her private quarters—but not to nap. Muffled whispers reached to her through the door. Kara was preparing for their arrival, handling the niggling details. Did she ever even sleep anymore?

A noise drew Safia's attention back around. Painter Crowe stood beside her chair, appearing as if by magic. He bore a tall tumbler of ice water in one hand and held out a tiny crystal snifter brimming with auburn liquid. Bourbon from the smell of it. "Drink this."

"I don't—"

"Just drink it. Don't sip. Down it all."

Her hand rose and she accepted the glass, more afraid it was going to spill than from any desire to accept his offering. They hadn't spoken since that bloody night, except for a brief thank-you after her rescue.

He lowered into the seat next to her and motioned to the drink. "Go on."

Rather than arguing, she lifted the glass and poured the contents down her throat. It burned all the way down, filling her nostrils, then settled with a fiery glow in her belly. She passed the glass back to him.

He traded it for the glass of water. "Soda water and lemon. Sip it."

She did, holding the cup with both hands.

"Better?"

She nodded. "I'm fine."

He stared at her, half leaning on one shoulder to face her. She kept her gaze averted, focusing on the length of his outstretched legs. He crossed his ankles, exposing his socks. Black argyles.

"It's not your fault," he said.

She stiffened. Was her guilt so plain? She felt a flush of embarrassment.

"It's not," he repeated. His tone of voice lacked the reassurance of the others who had sought to comfort her with platitudes: colleagues, friends, even the police psychologist. Instead, Painter's voice was simply matter-of-fact.

"Ryan Fleming. He was at the wrong place, wrong time. Nothing more."

Her eyes flicked to him, then away again. She felt the heat of him, like the bourbon, whiskey-warm and masculine. She found the strength to speak, to argue. "Ryan wouldn't have been there . . . . if . . . if I hadn't been working so late."

"Bullshit."

The profanity from him startled her.

Painter continued, "Mr. Fleming was at the museum to supervise *us*. Coral and me. His presence that night had nothing to do with you or your discovery of the artifact. Do you blame us?"

A small part of her did. Still, Safia shook her head, knowing who was ultimately to blame. "The thieves were after the heart, my discovery."

"And I'm sure it wasn't the first attempted theft from the museum. I seem to recall a midnight burglary of an Etruscan bust just four months ago. The thieves cut through the roof."

Safia kept her head bowed.

"Ryan was head of security, doing his job. He knew the risks."

Though she was not entirely convinced, the tight knot in Safia's gut loosened a bit. Then again, maybe it was just the alcohol.

His hand touched hers.

She flinched, but the American did not retreat. He cupped her hand between his palms, his touch warm after the cold glass of soda water. "Lady Kensington may not welcome our presence on this expedition, but I just wanted you to know that you aren't alone. We're in this together."

Safia slowly nodded, then slid her hand from between his, uncomfortable by the intimacy, by the attentions of a man she hardly knew. Still, she slipped her hand into her other, preserving the warmth.

He leaned back, perhaps sensing her discomfort. His eyes glinted with easy amusement. "You just hang in there . . . I know from experience you're darned good at that."

Safia pictured herself dangling from the museum's rooftop. How she must have looked! And unbidden, a smile traced the edges of her lips, the first since the horrible night.

Painter studied her, his expression seeming to say, *There you go.* He stood up. "I should try to get some sleep . . . so should you."

Thinking such a thing might be possible now, she watched him stride silently across the carpeted cabin, returning to his seat. She lifted a finger and touched her cheek as her smile faded away. The warmth of the bourbon still glowed deep within her, helping her find her center. How could something so simple have brought her so much relief?

But Safia sensed it wasn't truly the alcohol so much as the kindness. She had forgotten what that was like. It had been too long. Not since . . . not since . . . .

12:13 P.M.

Omaha hunched low in his seat and kicked again at the divider that separated him from the taxi driver. His heels struck with no effect. It was like kicking steel. Bulletproof glass. He slammed an elbow against the side window in frustration.

Trapped. Kidnapped.

"They're still following us," Danny said, nodding behind them to the trailing BWM sedan, fifty yards back. Shadowy figures could be seen filling the front and rear seats.

The taxi rode through a residential area of stucco-and-stone homes, all painted in various shades of white. The sun's reflection was blinding.

The other car kept pace behind them.

Omaha faced forward again. *"Leyh?"* he spat out in Arabic. "Why?"

The driver continued to ignore them, stoic and silent, wending his way through the narrow streets with deft skill.

"We need to get out of here," Omaha said. "Take our chances in the streets."

Danny had turned his attention to his door, staring at the side panel. *"Ton coupe-ongles?* Omaha." His brother was speaking French—clearly attempting to keep the driver from eavesdropping. Danny held out his hand, low, away from the direct view of the driver.

Omaha fished in a pocket. What did Danny think to accomplish with his *coupe-ongles?* Fingernail clippers? He asked in French, "You planning on clipping your way out of here?"

Danny did not look back, only cocked his head forward. "That bastard up there has us locked in by using the child protection feature of the car. Meant to keep kids from opening the back door."

"So?"

"So we're going to use the same safety features to get us out."

Omaha pulled out the fingernail clipper from his pocket. It hung from his keys. He passed it to Danny, who palmed it.

"What are you—"

Danny shushed him, flipped open the clippers, and extracted the tiny nail file. "Magazines reported on the sensitivity of the Mercedes's safety systems. Had to be careful even when removing the access panel."

Access panel?

Before he could ask aloud, Danny turned to him. "How soon do you want to make a break for it?"

Right now would be good, Omaha thought. But then up ahead, a large open-air souk, or market, appeared. He motioned low. "Up there would be perfect. We could get lost in the shops. Shake loose the others following in the BMW."

Danny nodded. "Be ready." He leaned back, straightening. The nail file poised under three imprinted letters on the sill of the passenger window: SRS.

Safety restraint system.

"Air bags?" Omaha asked, forgetting to speak in French this time.

"Side air bags," Danny concurred. "When any of the bags deploy, as a safety feature, all the locks disengage to allow outside emergency rescuers access to the vehicle."

"So you're going to—"

"We're almost at the souk," Danny hissed.

The driver slowed the Mercedes as it passed the entrance to the market, cautious of the bustle of midday shoppers.

"Now," Omaha murmured.

Danny jabbed the nail file under the SRS panel and savagely dug around, like a dentist struggling with a stubborn molar.

Nothing happened.

The sedan slid past the souk, picking up speed.

Danny leaned in closer, swearing under his breath. A mistake. With a pop of a firecracker, the side air bag ejected, smacking Danny in the face and knocking his head back with its sucker punch.

An alarm sounded in the car. The driver braked.

Danny blinked, holding his nose. Blood dripped from under his fingers.

Omaha did not have time to check further. He reached past his brother and yanked the door handle.

It fell open, the lock releasing. Thank God for fine German engineering.

Omaha shoved. "Out!" he yelled.

Dazed, Danny half rolled and half fell out of the backseat, Omaha pushing from behind. They landed on the pavement and tumbled a few feet. The slowing car slipped on ahead, then slammed to a stop.

Omaha scrambled to his feet, hauling Danny up with one arm, his strength fueled by fear. They were only steps from the market's entrance.

But the BMW sped forward—then fishtailed as it braked at the market.

Omaha sprinted, Danny in tow.

Three doors popped open. Dark figures, masks pulled over their heads, jammed out. Pistols appeared in flashes of polished platinum. One rifle swung through the air.

Omaha reached the edge of the souk and bounced aside a woman bearing a basket full of bread and fruit. Loaves and dates flew high.

"Sorry," he mumbled, and danced into the market. Danny kept to his heels, his face bloody from the nose down. Broken?

They fled down the center aisle. The souk spread out in a labyrinthine maze. Reed roofs sheltered carts and booths, laden with bolts of silk and Kashmiri cotton, bushels of pomegranates and pistachio nuts, iced bins of crab and whitefish, barrels of pickles and coffee beans, swaths of fresh-cut flowers, flats of breads, slabs of dried meats. The air steamed from grease stoves, sizzling with spices that burned the eyes. Alleyways reeked of goat and sweat. Others were redolent with a cloying sweetness. Incense and honey.

And crowded within this maze pressed throngs of folk from throughout Arabia and beyond. Faces of every shade flashed past, eyes wide, some behind veils, most not. Voices chased them in dialects of Arabic, Hindu, and English.

Omaha fled with Danny through the rainbow and the noise, darting right and left, serpentine, then straight. Were the pursuers behind them? In front? He had no way of knowing. All he could do was keep moving.

In the distance, the *ah-woo, ah-woo* of the Omani police force crested over the cacophony of the crowd. Help was coming . . . but could they last long enough to take advantage?

Omaha glanced behind him as they danced down a long straight narrow bazaar. At the other end, a masked gunman appeared, head radar-dishing around. He was easy to spot as folk fled in all directions, opening space around him. He seemed to hear the police. Time was running out for him, too.

Omaha was not going to make it easy. He dragged Danny, flowing with the rush of the crowd. They rounded a corner and ducked into a booth selling reed baskets and clay pots. The robed proprietor took one look at Danny's bloody face and waved them out, barking in Arabic.

It would take some skill in communication to gain sanctuary here.

Omaha yanked out his wallet and laid out a row of fifty-rial bills. Ten in all. The salesman glanced down the line, one eye squinted. To barter or not to barter? Omaha reached to gather the bills back up, but a hand stopped him.

"Khalas!" the old man declared, waving them down. Deal done!

Omaha crouched behind a stack of baskets. Danny took a position in the shadow of a large red earthenware pot. It was large enough for his brother to hide *inside* of. Danny pinched his nose, trying to stop the bleeding.

Omaha peered out into the alleyway. The patter of sandals and swish of robes ebbed after a few breaths. A man stepped to the corner, his masked face hurriedly searching all four points of the compass. The police sirens closed toward the souk. The gunman's head cocked, tracking them. He would have to abandon the search or risk being caught.

Omaha felt a surge of confidence.

Until his brother sneezed.

12:45 P.M.
Final Approach

The Lear circled over the water, preparing for its descent into Seeb International Airport. Safia stared out the small window.

The city of Muscat spread out below her. It was really three cities, separated by hills into distinct districts.

The oldest section, called, cleverly enough, Old Town, appeared as the jet banked to the right. Stone walls and ancient buildings lay nestled up against a sweeping crescent bay of blue water, its white sand shoreline dotted by date palms. Surrounded by the old gated city walls, the town housed the Alam Palace and the dramatic towering stone forts of Mirani and Jalai.

Memories overlay all she saw, as tenuous as the reflections in the smooth waters of the bay. Events long forgotten came alive: running the narrows with Kara, her first kiss in the shadow of the city walls, the taste of cardamon candy, visiting the sultan's palace, all atremble and in a new *thob* dress.

Safia felt a chill that had nothing to do with the cabin's air-conditioning. Home and homeland blurred in her mind. Tragedy and joy.

Then as the plane angled toward the airport, Old Town vanished, replaced by the Matrah section of Muscat—and the city's port. One side of the docks moored modern hulking ships, the other the slender single-masted dhows, the ancient sailing ships of Arabia.

Safia stared at the proud line of wooden masts and folded sails, in stark contrast to the behemoths of steel and diesel. More than anything else, this typified her homeland: the ancient and the modern, mixed together, but forever separate.

The third section of Muscat was the least interesting. Inland from the old town and port, stacked against the hills, rose Ruwi, the modern business center, the commercial headquarters of Oman. Kara's corporate offices were there.

The plane's course had mapped out Safia and Kara's life, from Old Town to Ruwi, from riotous children playing in the streets to lives confined by corporate offices and dusty museums.

Now the present.

The jet dropped toward the airport, aiming for the stretch of tarmac. Safia leaned back into her seat. The other passengers gaped out the windows.

Clay Bishop sat across the cabin. The grad student bobbed his head in sync with the current digitalized tract on his iPod. His black glasses kept slipping down his nose, requiring him to push them back up repeatedly. He wore his typical uniform: jeans and a T-shirt.

Ahead of Clay, Painter and Coral leaned together, staring out a single window. They spoke in hushed tones. She pointed, and he nodded, fiddling with a tiny cowlick atop his head that had formed while he napped.

Kara folded back the door to her private suite and stood in the threshold.

"We're landing," Safia said. "You should sit down."

Fingers flicked away her concern, but Kara crossed to the empty seat beside her and dropped heavily into it. She didn't buckle her seat belt.

"I can't ring up Omaha," she said as introduction.

"What?"

"He's not answering his mobile. Probably doing it on purpose."

That wasn't like Omaha, Safia thought. He could be dodgy sometimes, but he was all business when it came to the job. "He's surely just busy. You left him hanging out to dry. You know how touchy and territorial the cultural attachés can be in Muscat."

Kara huffed out her irritation. "He'd better be waiting at the airport."

Safia noted how large her pupils were in the bright light. She looked both exhausted and wired at the same time. "If he said he'd be there, he will be."

Kara cocked a questioning eyebrow at her. "Mr. Reliable?"

Safia felt a pang, her gut wrung in two different directions. Reflex made her want to defend him, as she had done in the past. But memory of the ring she had placed back in his palm constricted her throat. He had not understood the depth of her pain.

Then again, who could?

She had to force her eyes not to glance at Painter.

"You'd better buckle up," she warned Kara.

12:53 P.M.

Danny's sneeze was as loud as a gunshot, startling a pair of caged doves in a neighboring shop. Wings fluttered against bamboo bars.

Omaha watched the masked gunman turn toward their booth, stepping toward them. A yard away, Danny covered his nose and mouth and sank lower behind the tall earthenware urn. Blood ran freely down his chin. Omaha pushed to the balls of his feet, tensing, ready to leap. Their only hope lay in surprise.

The police sirens wailed, piercing now from their proximity to the market. If only Danny could have held back for another minute . . .

The gunman held his rifle shouldered, pointed forward, moving in a crouched stance, experienced. Omaha clenched his fists. He'd have to knock the rifle up, then dive low.

Before he could move, the robed proprietor of the shop shambled forward, into plain view. He waved a fan in one hand and wiped his nose with the other.

"*Hasaseeya,*" he mumbled as he straightened some baskets over Omaha's head, cursing his hay fever. He feigned surprise at seeing the gunman, threw up his hands, fan flying, and fell back.

The gunman gave a muffled curse, waving the old man back with his rifle.

He obeyed, retreating to a low counter, covering his head with his hands.

Off in the direction of the souk's entrance, the squeal of brakes announced the arrival of the Omani police. Sirens whined.

The gunman glanced in their direction, then did the only thing he could. He stepped to the large urn sheltering Danny and shoved his rifle inside. And after a check around, he ripped off the mask and tossed it in, too. Then, with a swirl of a sand-colored cloak, the figure disappeared into the depths of the market, clearly planning on simply joining the mass of humanity.

Anonymous.

Except Omaha had stared hard. He saw *her* face.

Mocha skin, deep brown eyes, a tattoo of a tear under the left eye.

Bedouin.

After a safe stretch, Omaha stepped out of hiding. Danny crawled to join him. Omaha helped his brother up.

The proprietor appeared, straightening his robe with pats of his hands.

"Shuk ran," Danny mumbled around his bloodied nose, thanking the man.

With the typical self-effacing custom of the Omani people, the man shrugged.

Omaha stripped off another fifty-rial bill and held it out.

The shopkeeper crossed his arms, palms facedown. *"Khalas."* The deal had already been struck. It would be an insult to renegotiate. Instead, the old man crossed to the stack of baskets and picked one up. "For you," he said. "Gift for pretty woman."

"Bi kam?" Omaha asked. How much?

The man smiled. "For you? Fifty rial."

Omaha returned his smile, knowing he was being swindled, but he handed over the bill. *"Khalas."*

As they left the market and headed toward the entrance, Danny asked nasally. "Why the hell were those guys trying to kidnap us?"

Omaha shrugged. He had no idea. Apparently Danny hadn't gotten a look at their assailant like he had. Not guys . . . *gals.* Now that he thought back on it—the way the others had moved—they might all have been women.

Omaha pictured the riflewoman's face again. Skin aglow in the sunshine.

The resemblance was unmistakable.

She could've been Safia's sister.

7

Old Town

○１ＨＩＸ○⊙４

December 2, 05:34 P.M.
Seeb International Airport

Painter kept pace behind the trundling cart of gear and equipment. The heat off the tarmac seemed to boil the oxygen right out of the air, leaving only a heavy dampness to sear the lungs. Painter fanned a hand in front of his face. Not to cool himself, an impossibility here, but simply to stir the air enough to catch his breath.

At least they were finally moving again. They had been delayed over four hours, confined to the jet as a result of the heightened security measures after the attempted abduction of one of Kara Kensington's associates. Apparently the matter had been resolved enough to allow them to disembark.

Coral marched beside him, eyes scanning everywhere, wary. The only sign that the late-afternoon heat
had any effect on his partner were the tiny beads of
sweat on her smooth brow. She had covered her white-
blond hair with a fold of beige cloth supplied by Safia,
an Omani headdress called a *lihaf.*

Painter squinted ahead.

The low sun cast shimmering mirages across the airfield and reflected off every surface, even the drab gray
building toward which their group paraded. Omani
customs officials in blue uniforms escorted the party,
while a small delegation sent by the sultan flanked their
sides.

These last were resplendent in the national dress of
Omani men: a white collarless robe with long sleeves,
called a *dishdasha,* covered by a black cloak trimmed
in gold and silver embroidery. They also wore cotton
turbans of varied patterns and hues and leather belts
adorned in silver. On these belts, each man wore a
sheathed *khanjar,* the traditional dagger. In this case,
they were Saidi daggers, pure silver or gold, a mark of
rank, the Rolexes of Omani cutlery.

Kara, trailed by Safia and her graduate student,
remained in a heated discussion with these men.
It seemed the expedition's advance men here, Dr.
Omaha Dunn and his brother, were being held by the

police. Details on the thwarted kidnapping were still sketchy.

"And is Danny all right?" Safia asked in Arabic.

"Fine, fine, my lady," one of the escorts assured. "Bloodied nose, nothing more. He has already been attended to, let me assure you."

Kara spoke to the head official. "And how soon can we be under way?"

"His majesty, Sultan Qaboos, has personally arranged for your transportation to Salalah. There will be no further mishaps. If we had only known sooner . . . that you personally would be accompanying—"

Kara waved his statement aside. *"Kif, kif,"* she dismissed in Arabic. "It is of no matter. As long as we won't be delayed."

A half bow answered her. The official's lack of offense at her tart response spoke volumes concerning Lady Kensington's influence in Oman.

So much for the low profile, Painter thought.

He turned his attention to Kara's companion. Concern crinkled the corners of Safia's eyes. Her momentary peace at the end of the flight had vanished when she heard of the trouble here. She clutched her carry-on luggage in both hands, refusing to load it and its ancient cargo onto the luggage cart.

Still, a determined glint shone in her emerald eyes, or maybe it was just the reflection of gold flecks in them. Painter remembered her hanging from the museum's glass roof. He sensed a well of strength in her, hidden deep but still present. Even the land seemed to recognize this. The sun, glaring harshly off everything else in Oman, glowed upon her skin, as if welcoming her, casting her features in bronze. Her beauty, muted before, shone brighter, like a jewel enhanced by a perfect setting.

At last, the party reached the private terminal building, and doors opened into a cool oasis of air-conditioned comfort. It was the VIP lounge. Their stay at this oasis, however, proved brief. Customs routines were hastily dispatched upon the authority of the sultan's retinue. Passports were glanced at, visas stamped—then the five of them were split between two black limousines: Safia, her grad student, and Kara in one, Coral and Painter in the other.

"It seems our company is not appreciated," Painter commented as he boarded the stretch limo with his partner.

He settled into a seat. Coral joined him.

Up front, beside the limo's driver, a beefy Irishman ran shotgun. He carried a prominent sidearm in a shoulder holster. Painter also noted a pair of escort vehicles—one in front of Kara's limousine, the other trailing. Clearly, after the kidnapping, security was not to be neglected.

Painter slipped a cell phone from a pocket. The phone contained a scrambled satellite chip with access to the DOD computer net and housed a sixteen-megapixel digital camera with flash uploading and downloading.

Never leave home without it.

He drew out the small earpiece and fixed it in place. A small microphone dangled from the line at his lips. He waited as the sat phone transmitted a coded handshake signal that crossed the globe and zeroed in on one person.

"*Commander Crowe,*" a voice finally answered. It was Dr. Sean McKnight, his immediate superior, the head of Sigma.

"Sir, we've landed in Muscat and are headed to the Kensington compound. I was reporting in to see if you've received any intel on the attack on the advance team."

"*We have the preliminary police report already. They were snatched off the street. Fake taxi. Sounds like a typical attempted kidnapping for ransom. Common form of raising capital out there.*"

Still, Painter heard the suspicion in McKnight's voice. First the trouble at the museum . . . now this. "Do you think this could be related to London?"

"Too early to say."

Painter pictured the lithe figure vanishing over the museum wall. He could still feel the weight of Cassandra's Sig Sauer in his hand. Two days after her arrest in Connecticut, she had vanished from custody. The police van transferring her to the airport had been ambushed, two men died, and Cassandra Sanchez had disappeared. Painter had never thought to see her again. How was she connected to all this? And why?

McKnight continued, *"Admiral Rector has coordinated with the NSA in gathering intel. We'll have more in a couple hours."*

"Very good, sir."

"Commander, is Dr. Novak with you?"

Painter stared over at Coral, who watched the scenery flash past. Her eyes were unreadable, but he was sure she was memorizing her surroundings. Just in case. "Yes, sir. She's here."

"Let her know that the researchers over at Los Alamos were able to discover decaying uranium particles in that meteoric iron sample you found at the museum."

Painter recalled her concern over the scanner's readings on the sample.

"They also support her hypothesis that the radiation from the uranium's decay may indeed be acting

*like some sort of nuclear timer, slowly destabiliz-
ing the antimatter until it is susceptible to electrical
shock."*

Painter sat straighter and spoke into the phone receiver. "Dr. Novak also proposed that the same de-
stabilization could be happening at the antimatter's
primary source, if it exists."

*"Exactly. The Los Alamos researchers have inde-
pendently expressed the same concern. As such, your
mission has become time critical. Additional resources
have been allocated. If there is a primary source, it
must be discovered quickly or all may be lost."*

"Understood, sir." Painter pictured the blasted
ruins of the museum gallery, the bones of the guard
melted into the steel grate. If there was a mother lode
of this antimatter, the loss could be more than just
scientific.

*"Which brings me to my last item, Commander. We
do have pressing information that concerns your operation. From NOAA. They report a major storm system
developing in southern Iraq, blowing south."*

"Thunderstorm?"

*"Sand. Winds clocked at sixty miles per hour. A
real barn buster. It's been shutting down city after city,
shifting dunes across roads. NASA confirms its path
toward Oman."*

Painter blinked. "NASA confirms? How big is—"

"Big enough to be seen from space. I'll forward satellite feed."

Painter glanced at the digital screen on the phone. The screen filled in line by line from the top. It was a real-time weather map of the Middle East and the Arabian Peninsula. The detail was amazing: the coastline, blue seas scudded with clouds, tiny cities. Except where a large, hazy blotch skirted the Persian Gulf. It looked like a hurricane, but one on land. A vast reddish brown wave even extended out over the gulf.

"Meteorological predictions expect the storm to amplify in severity and size as it travels south," McKnight narrated as the image refreshed the screen. The blotch of sandstorm swept over a coastal city, obliterating it. *"There's chatter of a storm of the century brewing out there. A high-pressure system in the Arabian Sea is producing vicious monsoon winds, drawn into a low trough over the Empty Quarter. The sandstorm will hit the southern deserts like a freight train, then be whipped up and fed by the monsoon tidals, creating a mega storm system."*

"Jesus."

"It'll be hell out there for a while."

"What's the timetable?"

"The storm should reach the Omani border by the day after tomorrow. And current estimates expect the storm system to last two or three days."

"Delaying the expedition."

"For as short as possible."

Painter heard the command behind the director's words. He raised his head and glanced toward the other limo. A delay. Kara Kensington was not going to be pleased.

7:48 P.M.

"Calm down," Safia urged.

They had all gathered in the garden courtyard of the Kensington estate. High limestone walls of crumbling plaster dated to the sixteenth century, as did the idyllic frescoes of climbing vines that framed off arched land-scapes and seascapes. Three years ago, restoration work had returned the frescoes to their full glory. This was the first time Safia had seen the finished product with her own eyes. Artisans from the British Museum had overseen the details here, while Safia had supervised from London via digital cameras and the Internet.

The pixilated photos failed to do justice to the richness of the colors. The blue pigments came from crushed mollusk shells, the reds from pressed rose madder, as had been originally done in the sixteenth century.

Safia took in the rest of the gardens, a place she had once played in as a child. Baked red tiles lined the grounds, amid raised beds of roses, trimmed hedges, and artfully arranged perennials. An English garden, a bit of Britain in the center of Muscat. In contrast, though, four large date palms dotted each corner, arched and shading a good portion of the garden.

Memories overlapped reality, triggered by the perfume of climbing jasmine and a deeper sandy scent of the old town. Ghosts shifted amid the dappled tiles, shadow plays of the past.

In the center of the courtyard, a traditional Omani tiled fountain with an octagonal reflecting basin tinkled brightly. Safia and Kara used to swim and float in the fountain's pool on especially hot and dusty days, a practice frowned upon by Kara's father. Safia could still hear his amused bluster, echoing off the garden walls, as he returned from a board meeting to find them lounging in the fountain. *You two look like a pair of beached seals.* Still, sometimes he would take off his shoes and wade in with them.

Kara stalked past the fountain with hardly a glance. The bitterness in her words brought the present back in focus. "First Omaha's adventure . . . now the bloody weather. By the time we're under way, half of Arabia will know of our excursion, and we'll not have a moment's peace."

Safia followed, leaving the unloading of the limos to the others. Painter Crowe had announced the dire meteorological news upon his arrival. He'd kept his face neutral. "It's a shame you can't buy good weather," he had finished glibly. He seemed to so enjoy goading Kara. Still, after all the roadblocks Kara had erected to keep the two Americans from this expedition, Safia could hardly blame him.

Safia caught up with Kara at the arched entry to the old palace, a three-story structure of carved and tiled limestone. The upper levels were adorned by shaded balconies, supported on ornate columns. Sea blue tiles lined all inner surfaces of the balconies, calmingly cool to the eye after the blinding glare.

Kara seemed to find no comfort in coming home, her face tight, the muscles of her jaw tense.

Safia touched her arm, wondering how much of her shortness of temper was true frustration and how much was chemically induced. "The storm's not a problem," she assured her friend. "We were planning to travel to Salalah to examine Nabi Imran's tomb first. It's on the coast, away from any sandstorms. I'm sure we'll be there at least a week anyway."

Kara took a deep breath. "Still, this mess with Omaha. I'd hoped to avoid too much notice—"

A commotion at the gate interrupted. Both women turned.

An Omani police car, lights silently flashing, pulled to a stop alongside the pair of limousines. The rear doors opened and two men climbed out.

"Speak of the devil . . ." Kara mumbled.

Safia found it suddenly difficult to breathe, the air gone heavy.

Omaha . . .

Time slipped slower, paced by the dull beat of her heart in her ears. She had thought she'd have more time to prepare, to settle in, to steel herself for the meeting. She felt an urge to flee and took a step back.

Kara placed a hand on the small of her back, supporting her. "You'll be fine," she whispered.

Omaha waited for his brother—then the two of them crossed between the black limos. Danny's face bore two black eyes, his nose bridged by a bandaged splint. Omaha had an arm on his brother's elbow. He wore a blue suit, jacket tucked in the crook of his free arm, white shirt rolled up at the elbows, stained with dirt and dried blood. His gaze lingered a moment on Painter Crowe, eyes traveling up and down his form. Omaha nodded in wary greeting.

Then he turned in Safia's direction. His eyes widened, and his feet slowed. His face froze for a breath, then a slow smile faltered, then firmed. He wiped a few lanky locks of sandy hair from his eyes, as if disbelieving the sight.

His lips mouthed her name, and on the second attempt he spoke aloud. "Safia . . . my God." He cleared his throat and hurried forward, abandoning his brother for the moment.

Before she could stop him, he reached out and embraced her, falling into her. He smelled of salt and sweat, familiar as the desert. He squeezed her hard. "It's good to see you," he whispered in her ear.

Her arms hesitated in returning his hug.

He straightened and stepped back before she could decide. A bit of color had risen to his cheeks.

Safia found language beyond her at the moment. Her eyes flicked to movement over Omaha's shoulder.

Stepping around, Danny offered a wincing smile. He looked like he'd been mugged.

Safia's hand waved at her own nose, glad for the distraction. "I . . . I thought it wasn't broken?"

"Greenstick fracture only," he assured her, a hint of Nebraskan accent in his voice, fresh from the family farm. "Splint's only for support." His gaze wavered between Omaha and Safia, stalling his own smile.

A stretch of awkwardness grew wild and weedy.

Painter appeared, arm out. He introduced himself, shaking hands with the two brothers. Only for a moment did his eyes flick toward Safia, making sure she was okay. She realized he was buying her time to collect herself.

"This is my partner, Dr. Coral Novak, physicist out of Columbia."

Danny straightened, visibly swallowing as he surreptitiously took in her figure. He spoke too quickly. "That's where I graduated. Columbia, that is."

Coral glanced at Painter, as if seeking permission to speak. There was no outward confirmation, but she spoke anyway. "Small world."

Danny opened his mouth, thought better of it, and closed it again. His eyes followed the physicist as she stepped to the side.

Clay Bishop joined them. Safia made the introductions, finding solace in the routines of etiquette. "And this is my graduate student, Clay Bishop."

He grasped Omaha's hand in both of his, shaking rapidly. "Sir, I've read your treatise on Persian trade routes during the time of Alexander the Great. I hope to have a chance to discuss some of your explorations along the Iran-Afghani border."

Omaha turned to Safia and Kara. "Did he just call me 'sir'?"

Kara broke up the introductions, waving everyone to the arched entrance of the palace. "There are rooms assigned to each of you, so you can freshen up before supper and relax afterward." She led the way into the palace, her fashionable Fendi heels tapping on the ancient tiles. "But don't get too comfortable here. We'll be leaving in four hours."

"Another plane trip?" Clay Bishop asked, hiding a groan.

Omaha clapped him on the shoulder. "Not exactly. At least one good thing came from the mess this afternoon." He nodded to Kara. "It's nice to have friends in high places, especially friends with nice toys."

Kara frowned back at him. "Have all the arrangements been made?"

"Supplies and equipment have already been rerouted."

Safia stared between them. On the way here, Kara had made furious calls to Omaha, the British consulate, and Sultan Qaboos's staff. Whatever the result, it did not seem to please Kara as much as it did Omaha.

"What about the Phantoms?" Kara asked.

"They know to meet us there," Omaha said with a nod.

"Phantoms?" Clay asked.

Before anyone could answer, they reached a hall leading into the south wing, the guest wing.

Kara nodded to a waiting butler, oiled gray hair, hands behind his back, dressed in black and white, pure British. "Henry, could you please show our guests to their rooms?"

A stiff nod. "Yes, madam." His eyes twinkled a bit as they swept over to Safia, but he kept his face passive. Henry had been head butler here at the estate since Safia was a child. "This way, please."

The group followed.

Kara called after them. "Supper will be served on the upper terrace in thirty minutes." It sounded more like a command than an invitation.

Safia stepped to follow the others.

"What are you doing?" Kara asked, taking her by the arm. "Your old rooms have been aired and readied for you." She turned her toward the main house.

Safia stared around her as they walked. Little had changed. In many ways, the estate was as much a museum as a residence. Oil paintings hung on the walls, Kensington ancestry dating back to the fourteenth century. In the room's center stood a massive antique mahogany dining table, imported from France, as was the six-tiered Baccarat chandelier that hung above it. Safia had her twelfth birthday party here. She remembered candles, music, a blur of festivity. And laughter. There had always been laughter. Her footsteps echoed hollowly as she circled the long room.

Kara led her to the private family wing.

When she was five, Safia had moved from the orphanage to the estate, to act as playmate for young Kara. It was the first room she had ever had to herself . . . and a private bath. Still, most of her nights were spent nestled with Kara in her room, the two of them whispering of futures that never came.

They stopped outside the door.

Suddenly Kara hugged her tight. "It's so good to have you home again."

Returning the genuinely warm embrace, Safia felt the girl behind the woman, her dearest and oldest friend. *Home.* And at this very moment, she almost believed it.

Kara shifted. Her eyes were bright in the reflected glow of the wall sconces. "Omaha . . ."

Safia took a deep breath. "I'm fine. I thought I was ready. But to see him. He hasn't changed."

"That's so true," Kara said with a scowl.

Safia smiled and returned a quick hug. "I'm fine . . . honestly."

Kara opened the door. "I've had a bath drawn, and there are fresh clothes in the wardrobe. I'll see you at dinner." She stepped away and continued down the hall. She passed her old room and continued toward the double set of carved walnut doors at the end of the hall, the suite belonging to the master of the estate, her father's old rooms.

Safia turned away and pushed through the door to her own chamber. Beyond lay a small but high-ceilinged entry hall, a greeting chamber once used as a playroom but now a private study. She had studied for her Ph.D. oral exams in this room. It smelled freshly of jasmine, her favorite flower and scent.

She crossed through the room to the bedchamber beyond. The silk canopied bed looked as if it had not been disturbed since she had left here to go to Tel Aviv so long ago. That painful memory smoothed as her fingers trailed down a fold of Kashmiri silk. A wardrobe stood on the far side, near the windows that opened upon a shadowed side garden, gloomy with the setting sun. The planted beds had grown a bit hedgy since last she had stared out from here. There were even a few weeds, which touched a well of loss she hadn't known was so deep.

Why had she come back? Why had she left?

She could not seem to connect the past to the present.

A tinkling drip of water drew her attention away, to the neighboring bathing chamber. There was not much time until dinner. She shed her clothes, letting them drop to the floor behind her. The bath was a sunken tile tub, deep but narrow. Water steamed into the air with a whisper that could almost be heard. Or maybe it was the shifting layer of white jasmine petals floating on the surface, the source of the room's perfume.

The sight drew a tired smile.

She crossed to the tub, and though she couldn't see the step hidden beneath the waters, she entered without hesitation, instincts from a past perhaps not entirely misplaced. She settled into the steamy warmth, sinking to her chin, leaning back against the tile, hair spreading over the water and petals.

Something deeper than sore muscles loosened and relaxed.

She closed her eyes.

Home . . .

8:02 P.M.

The guard patrolled the alleyway, flashlight in hand, the beam pointed at the cobbled path. His other hand scraped a match against the limestone outer wall of the Kensington estate. The tiny flame flared with a hiss. He failed to notice the black-cloaked figure hanging in the deeper shadows cast by the wide leaves of the date palm that hung over the top of the wall.

The light ate away the shadows, threatening to expose the climber. Cassandra pressed the trigger on her grappling gun's winch. The slight noise of its oiled mechanism was covered by the bark of a stray dog, one of many that ran the streets of Muscat. Her feet, muffled in slippers, fled up the wall as her body was hauled upward, drawn by the thin steel-alloy grappling cable as it rewound back into the handheld pistol. Reaching the top, she used her momentum to fling her body atop the wall, then lay flat.

Razor-sharp glass shards were embedded along the top of the wall, planted to deter interlopers. But they failed to penetrate her lightweight black Kevlar bodysuit and gloves. Still, she felt one shard pressing near her right temple. Her mask hid and protected the rest of her face, except for a strip open across her eyes. Nonreflective night-vision goggles rested atop her forehead, ready for use. The lenses were capable of taking an hour of digital footage and were hooked up to a microparabolic receiver for eavesdropping.

Painter Crowe's own design.

This thought drew a thin smile. She loved the irony. *To use the bastard's own tools against him . . .*

Cassandra watched the guard vanish around the corner of the estate. She freed her grappling hook and resecured it to the muzzle of her compact gun. She rolled onto her back, ejected the spent compressed-air cartridge from the pistol's grip, grabbed a fresh cylinder from her belt, and slapped it in place. Ready, she swung around and crawled along the jagged parapet of the palace wall, aiming for the main building.

The outer wall did not merge with the palace, but surrounded the structure from a distance of ten meters. Smaller gardens filled the narrow space, some separated into private, hedge-lined shade gardens, dotted with fountains. The tinkling of dancing water echoed up to her as she continued along the parapet.

Earlier, she had scoped the estate, ensuring the security schematics supplied to her by the Guild were accurate. She knew better than to trust ink and paper. She had personally checked each camera's position, the schedule of the guards, the layout of the palace.

Ducking beneath the overhanging leaves of another palm, she crept more slowly toward a section of the palace ablaze with light. A tiny columned court framed arched windows that looked in upon a long dining hall. Candles, carved into delicate flowers and afloat in silver basins, flickered atop the table, while others tapered out of elaborate candelabras. Crystal and fine porcelain reflected the firelight. Figures mingled before the silk-draped table. Servants bustled among them, filling water goblets and offering wine.

Lying flat to hide her silhouette, Cassandra lowered her digital goggles over her eyes. She did not activate the night-vision mode, only toggled the magnification, telescoping closer to the action. Her earpiece buzzed with the amplified conversation, sounding tinny from its digitalization. She had to keep her head very still to fix the parabolic receiver on the conversation.

She knew all the players present.

The lanky graduate student, Clay Bishop, stood by one of the windows, ill at ease. A young serving girl offered to fill his wineglass. He shook his head. *"La, shuk-ran,"* he mumbled. No, thank you.

Behind him, two men sampled a tray of varied hors d'oeuvres, traditional dishes of Oman, bits of braised meat, goat cheese, olives, and slivered dates. Dr. Omaha Dunn and his brother, Daniel. Cassandra knew all about their narrow escape earlier. Sloppy work on the part of the kidnappers.

Still, she eyed the pair. She knew better than to underestimate an opponent. Defeat lay along that path. There could be strengths to this pair that bore watching.

Omaha chewed around an olive pit. "While you were in the shower," he said, sucking on the pit, "I checked the weather report on the local news. The sandstorm shut down Kuwait City, shoved a dune right down Main Street."

The younger brother made a noncommittal noise. He did not seem to be paying attention. His gaze followed a tall blonde as she entered on the far side of the room.

Coral Novak, Sigma operative, her replacement.

Cassandra turned her attention to her adversary. The woman's coolness seemed too practiced, especially considering how easily she had been taken down at the museum, caught off guard. Cassandra's eyes narrowed with distaste. *This is who they thought to take my place at Painter's side? Someone green to Sigma?* No wonder things had to change.

On the heels of the woman, Painter appeared. Tall, dressed in black slacks and black shirt, formal, yet casual. Even from her perch on the wall, Cassandra recognized his study of the room, circumspect, out of the corner of his eye. He was taking in all sights, analyzing, calculating.

Her fingers tightened on the wall's shards of glass.

He had exposed her, threatened her position with the Guild, brought her low. She had been perfectly poised, spent years cultivating her role as a lead operative, earning her partner's trust . . . and at the end, maybe even something beyond simple loyalty.

Anger built in her chest, stirring bile. He had cost her everything, driven her out of the limelight, limiting her role to ops that required total anonymity. She rose from her spot and continued along the wall. She had a mission. One thwarted before by Painter, at the museum. She knew the stakes involved.

She would not fail this night.

Nothing would stop her.

Cassandra worked around to the far wing of the palace, toward a lone light in the darkness at the rear of the building. She rose up on her toes and ran the last distance. She could not risk missing her target.

At last, she settled before a window that looked down upon an unkempt garden. Through the steamy window, a lone woman reclined in a sunken bath. Cassandra scanned the remaining rooms. Empty. She listened. Not a sound.

Satisfied, Cassandra aimed her grappling gun toward an upper balcony. In her left ear, she heard the woman mumble. It sounded groggy, a dream, a choked cry: "*No . . . not again . . .*"

Cassandra pulled the gun's release trigger. The hooks snapped wide and sailed through the air, spiraling a thin cable of steel behind. A tight zipping noise accompanied it. The grappling hooks sailed over the balustrade of the third-story balcony.

Securing the hooks with a snug pull, Cassandra swung from the wall toward the garden below. Wind whistled. Dogs barked in a neighboring alley. She landed without breaking a twig and leaned against the wall beside the window, one ear cocked for the sound of alarm.

Silence.

She checked the window. It had been left cracked open a finger's breadth. Beyond, the woman mumbled in her dreams.

Perfect.

8:18 P.M.

Safia stands in the waiting room of a large hospital. She knows what is going to happen. Across the way, she spots the bent woman walking with the limp, entering the ward. Face and form covered in a berka. The bulge under the woman's cloak evident now.

. . . not like before.

Safia lunges to cross the waiting room, frantic to stop what is going to happen next. But children crowd around her feet, clambering at her legs, snatching at her arms. She struggles to push them away, but they cry out.

She slows, unsure whether to console or push forward.

Ahead, the woman disappears into the mass of people by the desk. Safia can no longer see her. But the station nurse raises her arm, points in Safia's direction. Her name is called.

. . . like before.

The crowd parts. The woman is spotlit in her own light, angelic, cloak swelling out like wings.

No, Safia mouths. She has no air to speak, to warn.

Then a blinding explosion, all light, no noise.

Sight returns in an instant—but not hearing.

She is on her back, staring as silent flames race along the ceiling. She hides her face from the heat, but it's everywhere. With her head turned, she sees children sprawled, some aflame, others crushed under stone. One sits with her back to an overturned table. The child's face is missing. Another reaches toward her, but there is no hand, only blood.

Safia now realizes why she can't hear. The world has become one scream stretched to infinity. The scream comes not from the children, but from her own mouth.

Then something . . .

. . . touched her.

Safia startled awake in the tub, choking on the same scream. It was always inside her, trying to get out. She covered her mouth, shaking out a sob, holding every-thing else inside. She trembled in the cooling water, arms hugged around her breasts. Tight. Waiting for the echo of the panic attack to subside.

Only a dream . . .

She wished she could believe it. It had been too forceful, too vivid. She still tasted the blood in her mouth. She wiped her brow but continued to tremble. She wanted to blame her reaction, the dream, on her exhaustion—but that was a lie. It was this place, this land, home again. And Omaha . . .

She closed her eyes, but the dream waited, only a breath away. It was no mere nightmare. All of it *had* happened. All of it was her fault. The local imam, a holy Muslim leader, had tried to deter her from excavating the tombs in the hills outside of Qumran. She had not listened. Too confident in the shield of pure research.

The year before, Safia had spent six months deciphering a single clay tablet. It suggested a cache of scrolls might be buried at the location, possibly another sepulcher of the famous Dead Sea Scrolls. Two months of digging proved her right. She uncovered forty urns containing a vast library of Aramaic writings, the discovery of the year.

But it came with a high price.

A fanatical fundamentalist group took offense at the defilement of a Muslim holy place. Especially by a woman, one of mixed blood, one with close ties to the West. Unknown to her at the time, Safia was targeted.

Only it was the blood and lives of innocent children that paid the price for her hubris and gall.

She was one of only three survivors. A miracle, it was described in newspapers, a miracle she had survived.

Safia prayed for no other such miracles in her life.

They came at too high a price.

Safia opened her eyes, fingers clenched. Anger warmed past grief and guilt. Her therapist had told her this was a perfectly natural response. She should allow herself to feel this fury. Still, she felt ashamed of her anger, undeserving.

She sat straighter. Water splashed over the tub's edge and washed across the tiles, leaving a trail of jasmine petals on the floor. The remaining petals sloshed around her bare midsection.

Under the water, something brushed against her knee, something as soft as a flower, but with more weight. Safia tensed, a rabbit in headlights.

The waters settled. The slick of jasmine petals hid the depths of the tub. Then slowly a lazy S-curve disturbed the layer from beneath.

Safia froze.

The snake's head surfaced through the petals, a few clinging to its mud brown head. Gray eyes turned black as the protective inner eyelid pulled down. It seemed to be staring right at her.

Safia knew the snake on sight, spotting the telltale white cross atop its crown. *Echis pyramidum.* Carpet viper. All Omani children knew to watch for its mark. The sign of the cross meant death here, not Christian salvation. The snake was ubiquitous in the region, frequenting shady spots, found hanging from limbs of trees. Its venom was both hemotoxic and neurotoxic, a fatal combination, from bite to death in less than ten minutes. Its ability to strike was so broad and swift that it was once thought to be capable of flight.

The meter-long viper swam through the tub, aiming for Safia. She dared not move or risk provoking it. It must have slipped into the water after she fell asleep, seeking moisture to aid in the shedding of its skin.

The snake reached her belly, rising a bit from the water, tongue flicking the air. Safia felt the tickle on her skin as it sidled even closer. Goose bumps traced down her arms. She fought not to shiver.

Sensing no danger, the viper beached onto her belly, slithered upward, and slowly crested her left breast. It paused to flick its tongue again. Scaled skin was warm on her own, not cold. Its movements were muscular, hard.

Safia kept her own muscles tight, rigid. She dared not breathe. But how long could she hold her breath?

The snake seemed to enjoy its perch, unmoving, settling atop her breast. Its behavior was so odd. Why didn't it sense her, hear her heartbeat?

Move . . . she willed it with all her might. If only it would retreat across the room, find some corner to hide, give her a chance to climb from the bath . . .

She found the need for air growing into a sharp pain in her chest, a pressure behind her eyes.

Please, go . . .

The viper sampled the air again with its red tongue. Whatever it sensed seemed to content it. It settled in for a rest.

Tiny stars danced across Safia's vision, birthed by the lack of oxygen and the tension. If she moved, she died. If she even breathed . . .

Then a shift of shadows drew her eye to the window. Condensation steamed the glass, making the view murky. But there was no doubt.

Someone was out there.

8
Snakes and Ladders

ᚷᚻᚻᚾᛉᚷᛁᚻᛉᚻᛁᛁᚻᚻᚻᛉᛞᚷ

December 2, 08:24 P.M.
Old Town, Muscat

"Where the hell's Safia?" Omaha asked, checking his watch.

It was ten minutes past the time they were all supposed to gather for dinner. The woman he had known in the past was painfully punctual, something drilled into her at Oxford. It was her attention to detail that made her such an accomplished curator.

"Shouldn't she be here by now?" he said.

"I had a bath drawn for her," Kara announced as she stepped into the room. "A maid just went up with fresh clothes."

Kara entered, resplendent in a traditional Omani *thob* gown of flowing red silk with gold filigree embroidered along the hems. She abandoned any headdress, leaving her auburn hair free, and wore Prada sandals. As always, to Kara, a line had to be drawn between the traditional and the fashionable.

"A bath?" Omaha groaned. "Then we'll never see her this evening."

Safia loved water in all its forms: showers, fountains, flowing taps, dips in streams and lakes, but especially baths. He used to tease her, attributing her fixation to her desert past. *You can take the girl out of the desert, but never the desert out of the girl.*

With this thought, other uninvited memories intruded, of long baths shared, limbs entwined, laughter, soft moans, steam off water and skin.

"She'll be along when she's ready," Kara warned, protective, drawing him back to the room. She nodded to the household butler. "We'll be serving a light Omani dinner before we head out in a few hours. Please sit."

Everyone found seats, dividing into party lines. Painter and Coral sat on one side, along with Safia's graduate student, Clay. Danny and Omaha took seats on the other. Lastly, Kara settled on the lone chair at the head of the table.

Upon some unseen signal, servants paraded through a set of swinging doors from the kitchen hallway. They bore aloft covered trays, some held above their heads on a single palm. Others carried wider trays in both arms.

As each platter was lowered to the table, the servant stepped deftly back, lifting the lids to expose what lay beneath. It was all clearly choreographed.

Kara named each dish as it was revealed. "*Maqbous* . . . saffron rice over lamb. *Shuwa* . . . pork cooked in clay ovens. *Mashuai* . . . spit-fired kingfish served with lemon rice." She named a handful of other curried dishes. Amid the feast were plates of thin, oval breads. They were familiar to Omaha. The ubiquitous *rukhal* bread of Oman, baked over burning palm leaves.

Kara finally finished her introductions. "And lastly, honeycakes, one of my favorites, flavored with the syrup from the native elb tree."

"What . . . no sheep's eyes?" Omaha mumbled.

Kara heard him. "That delicacy can be arranged."

He held up a conciliatory palm. "I'll pass this time."

Kara waved a hand over the spread. "Tradition among the Omani is to serve oneself. Please enjoy."

The group took her at her word and proceeded to spoon, spear, ladle, and grab. Omaha filled a cup from the tall pot. *Kahwa.* Omani coffee. Deadly strong. Arabs might shun alcohol, but they had no qualms about caffeine addiction. He took a deep sip and sighed. The bitter tang of the thick coffee was softened by cardamom, a distinct and welcome aftertaste.

Conversation centered initially on the quality of the fare. Mostly murmurs of surprise at the tenderness of the meat or the fire of the spices. Clay seemed content to fill his plate with honeycakes. Kara merely picked at her food, keeping a watch on the servants, guiding with a nod or turn of her head.

Omaha studied her while sipping his *kahwa*.

She was thinner, more wasted than when last he saw her. Kara's eyes still shone, but now appeared more fevered. Omaha knew how much effort she had invested in this trip. And he knew why. Safia and he had kept few secrets . . . at least back then. He knew all about Reginald Kensington. His portrait stared down at Kara from the wall behind her. Did she still feel those eyes?

Omaha imagined he'd be no better if his own father had vanished into the desert, sucked out of this world. But thank God, it *required* his imagination to fathom such a loss. His father, at eighty-two, still worked the family farm back in Nebraska. He ate four eggs, a rasher of bacon, and a pile of buttered toast each breakfast and smoked a cigar each night. Omaha's mother was even more fit. *Solid stock,* his father used to brag. *Just like my boys.*

As Omaha thought of his family, his brother's sharp voice drew his attention from Kara. Danny was elaborating on the escapade of the midday abduction, using his fork as much as his voice to tell the story. Omaha recognized the flush of excitement as he relived the day's events. He shook his head, hearing the bluster and swagger in his younger brother. Omaha had once been the same. Immortal. Armored in youth.

No longer.

He stared down at his own hands. They were lined and scarred, his father's hands. He listened to Danny's story. It had not been the grand adventure his brother related. It had been deadly serious business.

A new voice interrupted. "A woman?" Painter Crowe asked with a frown. "One of your kidnappers was a woman?"

Danny nodded. "I didn't see her, but my brother did."

Omaha found the other man's eyes turning to him, a piercing blue. His brow furrowed, his gaze concentrating attention like a well-focused laser.

"Is this true?" Crowe asked.

Omaha shrugged, taken aback by his intensity.

"What did she look like?"

This last was spoken too quickly. Omaha answered slowly, watching the pair. "She was tall. My height. From the way she handled herself, I'd say she had military training."

Painter glanced at his partner. A silent message seemed to pass between them. They knew something they weren't telling. The scientist faced Omaha again. "And her appearance?"

"Black hair and green eyes. Bedouin descent. And oh, a small red teardrop tattoo by one eye . . . her left."

"Bedouin," Painter repeated. "Are you sure?"

"I've worked this region for the past fifteen years. I can tell individual tribe members and clans apart."

"Which tribe was the woman from?"

"Hard to say. I didn't get a long enough look at her."

Painter leaned back, clearly the thread of tension in him broken. His partner reached for one of the honeycakes, placed it on her plate, and ignored it. Neither exchanged a glance this time, but something had been resolved.

"Why the interest?" Kara asked, voicing Omaha's own thought.

Painter shrugged. "If it was a random abduction for profit, then it probably doesn't matter. But if not . . . if it was connected to the museum heist in some manner, I think we should all know who to keep an eye out for."

His words sounded reasonable enough, practical and scientific, but Omaha sensed something deeper lay behind his expressed interest.

Kara let it drop. She glanced to her diamond Rolex. "Where is Safia? Surely she's not still in the bath?"

09:12 P.M.

Safia kept her breathing shallow.

She had no phobia of snakes, but she had learned to respect them while exploring dusty ruins. They were as much a part of the desert as the sand and wind. She sat perfectly still in the bath. The waters cooled as she waited . . . or maybe it was the fear chilling her.

The carpet viper draped over her left breast seemed to have settled in for a good long soak. Safia recognized the roughness of its outer skin. It was an old specimen, making the shedding of its skin especially difficult.

Again movement caught her eye, beyond the window. But as she searched, the darkness lay still and quiet.

Paranoia often preceded a panic attack, an all-consuming anxiety that saw threat and danger where none existed. Her attacks were more commonly triggered by emotional stress or tension, not physical threats. In fact, the surge of adrenaline from immediate danger was a good buffer against the electric cascade of a panic episode. Still, the strain of outwaiting the viper had begun to wear thin the veneer of Safia's buffer.

The symptoms of a carpet-viper bite were immediate and severe: blackened skin, fire in the blood, convulsions that broke bones. There was no known antidote.

A small tremor began in her hands.

No known antidote . . .

She forced herself to calm.

Safia slowly exhaled, again watching the snake. She inhaled even more slowly, savoring the sweetness of fresh air. The scent of jasmine, a pleasure earlier, was now cloying.

A knock at her door startled her.

She jumped slightly. Water rippled around her.

The viper lifted its head. She felt the rest of the snake's body harden against her bare belly, tensing, wary.

"Mistress al-Maaz," a voice called from the hall.

She did not answer.

The snake sampled the air with its tongue. Its body slid higher up, pushing its triangular head toward her throat.

"Mistress?"

It was Henry, the household butler. He must have come to see if she had fallen asleep. The others would be in the dining hall. There was no clock in the room, but it felt like the entire night had passed.

In the deadly silence, the sound of a key scraping in the old lock reached her. The creak of the outer door followed.

"Mistress al-Maaz . . . ?" Less muffled now. "I'm sending Liza in."

For Henry, ever the efficient English butler, it would be unseemly to enter a lady's apartment, especially when the lady was in her bath. Tiny, hurried footsteps crossed the rooms, aiming for the back bathroom.

All the commotion agitated the snake. It rose up between her breasts like her venomous champion. Carpet vipers were notoriously aggressive, known to chase a man a full kilometer if threatened.

But this viper, lethargic from its soaking, made no move to strike.

"Hello," a timid voice called just outside the door.

Safia had no way to warn the maid off.

A young girl kept her head bowed shyly as she crept into the doorway, her dark hair braided under a lace cap. From two steps away, she mumbled, "I'm sorry to disturb your bath, mistress."

She finally glanced up, met Safia's eyes—then the snake's as it rose higher, hissing in threat, coiling in anticipation. Wet scales sawed together with a sound like sandpaper.

The maid's hand flew to her mouth, but it failed to stifle her scream.

Drawn by the noise and movement, the snake surged from the water, flying bodily over the wide tiled lip of the tub, aiming for the girl.

The maid was too frightened to move.

Safia was not.

She instinctively grabbed for the viper's tail as it leaped, catching it up in midstrike. She yanked it back from the maid and swung its length wide. But it was no limp piece of rope.

Muscles writhed in her hand, hard under her fingers. She felt more than saw the snake coil around upon itself, ready to strike at what had snatched it. Safia kicked her feet, trying to gain purchase to stand, to get some advantage. The slippery tiles kept betraying her. Water slopped across the floor.

The viper struck at her wrist. Only a quick twist and whip of her arm kept fangs from flesh. But like a skilled combatant, the old snake contorted for another attempt.

Safia finally gained her legs. She spun around in the tub, swinging her arm wide, using centrifugal force to keep the snake's head from reaching her. Instinct made her want to fling it away. But that didn't ensure the end of the battle. The bathroom was small, the aggression of the viper notorious.

Instead, she cracked out her arm. She had used a bullwhip before, having given one to Omaha as a silly Christmas gift, playing off Kara's persistence in referring to him as Indiana. She used the same technique now, snapping her wrist with a well-practiced twist.

The viper, dazed from the spin, failed to react in time. Its length responded to age-old physics and whipped outward. Its head struck the tiled wall with enough impact to chip ceramic.

Blood spurted in a spray of crimson.

The body convulsed a beat in her hand, then dropped limply, splashing back into the bathwater around her thighs.

"Mistress al-Maaz!"

Safia turned her head and found the butler, Henry, in the doorway, drawn by the maid's scream. He had a hand on the terrified girl's shoulder.

Safia stared down at the limp snake, at her own nakedness. She should have felt shame and tried to cover herself, but instead she let the scaled body slip from her fingers and stepped from the bath.

Only the trembling of her fingers betrayed her.

Henry collected a large cotton towel from a warming rack. He held it open. Safia stepped forward, and Henry folded her into its embrace.

Tears began to flow, her breath shortened painfully.

Through the window, the moon had risen, peeking over the palace wall. For half a breath, something darker fluttered over its surface. Safia startled, but then it was gone.

Just a bat, the nocturnal predator of the desert.

Still, her trembling grew worse while Henry's arms grew stronger, holding her up, carrying her to the bed in the next room.

"You're safe," he whispered in a fatherly fashion.

She knew his words could not be further from the truth.

09:22 P.M.

Outside the window, Cassandra crouched in the bushes. She had watched the museum curator deal with the snake, moving lithely, dispatching it with alacrity. She had hoped to wait until the woman was gone, then quickly abscond with the luggage that housed the iron heart. The viper had turned out to be an unwelcome visitor for the both of them.

But unlike the curator, Cassandra knew the presence of the snake was deliberate, planted, planned.

She had caught the barest reflection in the window, mirrored silver in the moonlight. Another presence. Climbing the wall.

Cassandra had dropped down and away, her back to the palace, a pistol in each hand, twin black matte Glocks, pulled from shoulder holsters. She caught the sight of the cloaked figure sailing over the outer wall.

Gone.

An assassin?

Someone had shared the garden with her . . . and she'd been unaware.

Damn foolish . . .

Anger quickened her thoughts as she recalculated the night's plan. With the commotion in the curator's room, the likelihood of absconding with the artifact dimmed.

But the cloaked thief . . . that was another matter entirely.

She had already obtained the intelligence on the attempted abduction of Omaha and Daniel Dunn. It was unclear if the attack was mere unlucky chance: wrong time, wrong place. Or if it was something more meaningful, a calculated attack, an attempt at collecting ransom from the Kensington estate.

And now this threat to the curator's life.

It could not be pure chance. There must be a connection, something unknown to the Guild, a third party involved in all this. But how and why?

All this ran through her head in a heartbeat.

Cassandra tightened her grip on her pistols.

Answers could come from only one place.

Crossing her arms, Cassandra holstered both pistols and unhooked the grappling gun from her belt. She aimed, pulled the trigger, and heard the zip of the steel cord sailing upward. She was on the move when the grappling hook clunked against the wall's lip. She squeezed the retracting winch. In the time it took to reach the wall, the steel cable had drawn taut and hauled her weight upward. Her soft-heeled shoes scaled the wall as the grappling motor whined.

Reaching the top, she straddled the parapet and resecured the grappling gun. Searching below, she snapped down her night-vision goggles. The dark alleyway bloomed into crisp greens and whites.

Across the way, a cloaked figure slunk along the far wall, aiming for the neighboring street.

The assassin.

Cassandra gained her feet atop the glass-strewn parapet and ran in the direction of the cloaked thief. Her footfalls must have been heard. Her target sped faster with a swirl of shadow.

Damn it.

Cassandra reached a spot along the wall where another date palm rose from within the walled compound.

Its fronded leaves fanned wide, shading both sides of the wall, blocking her run.

Without slowing, Cassandra kept one eye on her quarry. As she reached the tree, she lunged out, grabbed a handful of leaves, and leaped off the twenty-foot wall. Her purchase gave way under her weight. Leaves ripped from between her gloved fingers, but the temporary support helped break her fall. She landed in the alley, her knees absorbing the impact.

She shot after her quarry, who vanished down a cross street.

Cassandra subvocalized into her controls. An overlay map of the immediate cityscape appeared within her goggles. It took a practiced eye to interpret the mishmash of imagery.

Here in Old Town, there was no rhyme or reason to the layout. The surrounding environment was a labyrinth of alleys and cobbled streets.

If the thief escaped into that twisted maze . . .

Cassandra sped faster. The other had to be slowed. Her digital overlay showed the side street to be less than thirty yards long before it crisscrossed more alleys.

Cassandra had only one chance.

She dove for the corner, yanking her grappling gun free. As she slid into the street, she quickly tracked and locked her quarry, thirty yards away.

She pulled the trigger.

The zip of cable hissed. The grappling hook shot in a low arc down the alley, passing over the shoulder of her mark.

Cassandra squeezed the retractor, reversing the winch, while yanking back with her own arm. Like fly-fishing.

The hooks dug into the other's shoulder, spinning the figure, legs flailing.

Cassandra allowed herself a grim smile of satisfaction.

She savored her victory too soon.

Her adversary continued the spin, unwinding a fan of cloak, pulling free of the garment with a skill that would have astounded Houdini. Moonlight cast the figure as bright as midday through the night-vision goggles.

A woman.

She landed with feline grace upon one hand, springing back to her toes. With a sweep of dark hair, she sped down the street.

Cassandra swore and gave pursuit. A part of her appreciated her target's skill and the challenge. Another wanted to shoot the woman in the back for making her night that much longer. But she needed answers.

She dogged the woman, whose movement was lithe and surefooted. Cassandra had been a champion sprinter in high school and only got faster during her rigorous Special Forces training. Being one of the first women in the Army Rangers, she needed to be fast.

Her target fled around another corner.

By this time at night, the streets were empty, except for a few crouched dogs and scurrying cats. After sundown, Old Town locked itself up and shuttered its windows, leaving the streets dark. Occasional bits of music or laughter echoed from inner courtyards. A few lights shone from upper balconies, but even these were barred against intrusion.

Cassandra checked her digital overlay. A smile stretched her lips thin. The warren of alleys into which her quarry had fled was circuitous but ultimately a dead end, terminating against the towering flank of the ancient fort of Jalai. The walled fortress had no entrance on this side.

Cassandra kept pace. In her head, she planned her assault. She freed one of her Glocks. With her other hand, she tapped her radio. "I'll need evac in ten," she subvocalized. "Fix on my GPS."

The response was terse. *"We copy. Evac in ten."*

As planned, the team subcommander would send out a trio of modified dirt bikes with silenced mufflers, solid rubber tires, and jacked engines. Automobiles had limited mobility in Old Town's narrow passages. The bikes suited the region better. Cassandra's expertise: fitting the right tool to the right job. By the time she had her target cornered, backup would be riding at her heels. She would only have to hold the woman at bay. If there was any resistance, a bullet to a knee should dampen the other's spirit.

Ahead, a flash of white limb on her night-vision scope alerted Cassandra that her target was slowing, the distances closing. She must be realizing the trap she had run into.

Cassandra paced the other, keeping her in sight.

Finally, a last twist of narrow alley revealed the towering Jalai fort. The storefronts to either side ran up against the structure, creating a box canyon.

The woman, stripped of her cloak, wore only a loose white shift. She stood at the base of the fort's sheer sandstone wall, staring upward. The closest purchase or opening was thirty feet up. If the woman attempted to scale the neighboring storefront rooftops, Cassandra would discourage her with a few well-placed shots from her Glock.

Cassandra stepped into the alley, blocking any escape.

The woman sensed her and turned from the fort wall to face her.

Cassandra flipped up her night-vision scope. The moon illuminated the alley well enough. She preferred her natural vision in close quarters.

With her Glock conspicuously pointed forward, Cassandra closed the distance. "Don't move," she said in Arabic.

Ignoring her, the woman shrugged a shoulder. Her shift dropped from her form and pooled around her ankles, leaving her naked in the street. Long of limb, bearing apple-size breasts, and bending a shapely long neck, she seemed unabashed by her nakedness, a rarity in Arabia. There was a measure of nobility to her pose, a Greek statue of an Arab princess. Her only jewelry was a small ruby tattoo by her left eye. A teardrop.

The woman spoke for the first time, slowly, warning in her voice. Her words, though, were not Arabic. With a background in linguistics, Cassandra was fluent in a dozen languages, efficient in a score of others. She bent an ear to the words, sensing a familiarity but unable to pin it down.

Before Cassandra could discern anything else, the naked woman stepped barefoot from her clothes and backed into the shadow of the towering wall. Moving from moonlight into darkness, her form vanished for a breath.

Cassandra stepped forward, maintaining the distance between them.

She stared harder.

No.

She flipped down her night-vision goggles. Shadows dissolved. The sandstone cliff of the fort sharpened into focus. She searched right and left.

The woman was nowhere in sight.

Cassandra rushed forward, pistol raised. She reached the wall in seven steps. One hand went out, touching the stone to ensure it was real, solid. With her back to the wall, she scanned the alley with her night-vision goggles. No movement, no sign of the woman.

Impossible.

It was as if she had turned to shadow and vanished.

A veritable djinn, a ghost of the desert.

Cassandra only had to stare at the pile of discarded clothes to know better. Since when did ghosts wear cloaks?

A crunch of gravel and a low growl drew her attention to the entrance to the alley. A small motorbike rounded the bend, flanked by two others. Her backup.

With a final check around, Cassandra crossed to them. She spun in circles twice more. When she reached the lead bike, she asked, "Did you see a naked woman in the alley on your way here?"

The rider's face was masked, but confusion shone in his eyes. "Naked?"

Cassandra heard the negation in his voice. "Never mind."

She climbed onto the bike behind the rider. The night had been a bust. Something strange was afoot out here. She needed time to sort it out.

She tapped the man's shoulder. He swung the bike around and the trio fled back the way they had come, aiming for the empty warehouse they had rented at the docks for their base of operations in Muscat. It was time to finish the mission assigned her. It would have been easier with the iron heart in her hands. But contingencies were already in place. By midnight, they would move forward with the plans to eliminate Crowe's expeditionary force.

Her mind ran over the final details that needed to be arranged, but she had a hard time concentrating. What had happened to the woman? Had there been a secret door into the fort? One unknown to her intel. It was the only explanation.

As she pondered the strangeness, the woman's words echoed in her head.

The muffled rev of the bikes helped her focus.

Where had she heard that language?

She glanced back at the ancient fort of Jalai, its towers thrust up into moonlight above the lower buildings. An ancient structure, from a lost era.

Then it struck her. The familiarity of the language. Not modern. *Ancient.*

In her head, the words played out again, thick with warning. Though she still didn't understand, she knew what she was hearing. A dead language.

Aramaic.

The language of Jesus Christ.

10:28 P.M.

"How did it get in there?" Painter asked. He stood by the entrance to the bath, staring at the floating length of dead snake among the jasmine petals.

The entire dining party had heard the maid's scream and come running. They had been held at bay by the butler until Kara could help Safia into a robe.

Kara answered his question from her seat beside her friend on the bed, "Bloody buggers are always turning up, even in the plumbing. Safia's rooms had been closed off for years. It could've been nesting anywhere in here. When we aired out her rooms and cleaned the place, it must have been disturbed, then was drawn out by the water in the tub."

"Shedding," Safia whispered hoarsely.

Kara had given her a pill. Its effect had lazed the woman's tongue, but she seemed calmer than when the group first arrived. Her wet hair hung damply to her skin. Color slowly returned. "Shedding snakes seek water."

"Then more likely it came from outside," Omaha added. The archaeologist stood by the arch into the study. The others waited out in the hall.

Kara patted Safia's knee and stood up. "Either way, the matter's over. It's best that we get ready for our departure."

"Surely it can be put off a day," Omaha said, glancing at Safia.

"No." Safia pushed past the sedative haze. "I can manage."

Kara nodded. "We're due to rendezvous at the port at midnight."

Painter held up a hand. "You never did tell us how we'd be traveling."

Kara waved away his words like a foul smell. "You'll all see when we get there. I have a thousand last-minute details to attend to." She strode past Omaha and out of the rooms. Her words carried back as she addressed the others in the hall. "Gather in the courtyard in an hour."

Omaha and Painter stood across the room from each other, on either side of Safia. Neither man moved, both equally unsure if it was appropriate to comfort Safia.

The matter was settled by Henry stepping through the archway, the butler's arms full of folded clothing.

Henry nodded to the two men. "Sirs, I've rung for a maid to help Mistress al-Maaz dress and gather her things. If you would be so kind . . ." He nodded toward the door, dismissing them.

Painter stepped closer to Safia. "Are you sure you're okay to travel?"

She nodded, an effort. "Thank you. I'll be fine."

"Just the same, I'll wait outside in the hall for you."

This earned him the smallest smile. He found himself matching it.

"That won't be necessary," she said.

He turned. "I know, but I'll be there anyway."

Painter found Omaha studying him, his eyes slightly more narrowed than a moment before. The man's expression was tight. He was clearly suspicious, but also a trace of anger lay under the surface.

As Painter crossed toward the door, Omaha made no room to allow him to pass. He had to turn sideways to get by.

As he did so, Omaha addressed Safia. "You did good in there, babe."

"It was just a snake," she answered, standing to accept the clothes from the butler. "And I have a lot to do before we leave."

Omaha sighed. "All right. I hear you." He followed Painter out the door.

The others had all cleared, leaving the hallway empty.

Painter moved to take a post beside the door. Omaha started to march past him, but Painter cleared his throat. "Dr. Dunn . . ."

The archaeologist stopped, glancing sidelong at him.

"That snake," Painter said, following a thread left untied earlier. "You said you thought it came from outside. Why?"

Omaha shrugged, stepping back a bit. "Can't say for sure. But carpet vipers like the afternoon sun, especially when shedding. So I can't imagine it was holed up in there all day."

Painter stared over at the closed door. Safia's room had an eastern exposure. Morning sunlight only. If the archaeologist was correct, the snake would've had to travel a long way from a sunny roost to the tub.

Omaha read his thoughts. "You don't think someone put it there?"

"Maybe I'm just being too paranoid. But didn't some militant group once try to kill Safia?"

The man scowled, an expression worn into the lines of his face. "That was five years ago. Way up in Tel

Aviv. Besides, if someone planted that snake, it couldn't have been those bastards."

"Why's that?"

Omaha shook his head. "The extremist group was rooted out by Israeli commandos a year later. *Wiped out*, actually."

Painter knew the details. It was Dr. Dunn who had helped the Israelis hunt the extremists down, using his contacts in the area.

Omaha mumbled, more to himself than Painter, a bitter tone. "Afterward, I thought Safia would be relieved . . . would return here . . ."

It's not that easy, guy. Painter already had a good fix on Omaha. The man tackled problems head-on, bulled through them without looking back. It wasn't what Safia needed. He doubted Omaha would ever understand. Still, Painter sensed a well of loss in the man, one that had been filled by the sand of passing years. So he tried to help. "Trauma like that is not overcome by—"

Omaha cut him off sharply. "Yeah, I've heard it all before. Thanks, but you're not my goddamn therapist. Or *hers*." He stalked off down the hall, calling back derisively, "And sometimes, doc, a snake is just a snake."

Painter sighed.

A figure moved from the shadows of a neighboring archway. It was Coral Novak. "That man has issues."

"Don't we all."

"I overheard your conversation," she said. "Were you just chatting with him, or do you really think another party is involved?"

"There's definitely someone stirring the pot."

"Cassandra?"

He slowly shook his head. "No, some unknown variable."

Coral scowled, which consisted of the barest downturn of the corner of her lips. "That's not good."

"No . . . no, it's not."

"And this curator," Coral persisted, nodding to the door. "You've really got the role of the attentive *civilian* scientist down pat."

Painter sensed a subtle warning in her voice, a cloaked concern that he might be crossing the line between professionalism and something more personal.

Coral continued, "If there's another party sniffing around, shouldn't we be searching the grounds for evidence?"

"Definitely. That's why you're going out there now."

Coral raised an eyebrow.

"I have a door to guard," he said, answering her unspoken question.

"I understand." Coral began to turn away. "But are you staying here to safeguard the woman or the mission?"

Painter let command harden his voice. "In this particular case, they're one and the same."

11:35 P.M.

Safia stared out at the passing scenery. The two tablets of diazepam kept her head muzzy. Lights from passing streetlamps were phosphorous blurs, smudges of light across the midnight landscape. The buildings were all dark. But ahead, a blaze of light marked the port of Muscat. The commercial harbor was active twenty-four hours a day, kept bright with floodlights and sodium-lit warehouses.

As they rounded a tight turn, the harbor came into view. The bay was mostly empty, most of the oil barges and container ships having docked before sunset. During the night, their cargo would be off-loaded and reloaded. Even now, H-cranes and trundling train-car-size containers swung through the air, like giant toy blocks. Farther out, near the horizon, a behemoth of a cruise liner floated on the dark waters like some candlelit birthday cake, backdropped against a spray of stars.

The limo aimed away from the commotion toward the far side of the harbor, where the more traditional dhow sailing vessels of Arabia stood docked. For thousands of years, Omanis had plied the seas, from Africa to India. The dhows were simple wooden-planked shells with a distinctive triangular sail. They varied in size from the shallow draft of the *badan* form to the deep-sea *baghlah*. The proud array of old ships lined the far harbor, stacked close together, sails furled, masts poking high amid tangles of ropes.

"We're almost there," Kara mumbled to Safia from the other side of the limo. The only other occupant, besides the driver and a bodyguard, was Safia's student, Clay Bishop. He snorted a bit when Kara spoke, half drowsing.

Behind them trailed the other limo with all the Americans: Painter and his partner, Omaha and his brother.

Safia sat straighter now. Kara had yet to tell her how they were getting to Salalah, only that they were heading to the harbor. So she guessed they would be traveling by boat. Salalah was a coastal city, like Muscat, and travel between the two cities was almost easier by sea than by air. Transports, both cargo and passenger, left throughout the day and night. They varied from diesel-engine ferries to a pair of lightning-fast hydrofoils. Considering Kara's urgency to be under way, Safia guessed they'd be taking the fastest vessel possible.

The limo turned through the gated entry, followed by its twin. Both continued down the pier, passing rows and rows of docked dhows. Safia was familiar with the regular passenger terminal. This wasn't it. They were heading down the wrong pier.

"Kara . . . ?" she began.

The limo cleared the last harbor office at the end of the pier. Parked beyond, lit by lights and crowded with clusters of line-haulers and dockworkers, stood a magnificent sight. From the commotion and the unfurled sails, there could be no doubt this was their transportation.

"No," Safia mumbled.

"Yes," Kara answered, sounding none too pleased.

"Holy Christ," Clay said, leaning forward, the better to see.

Kara checked her watch. "I couldn't refuse the sultan when he offered us its use."

The limo pulled athwart the pier's end. Doors opened. Safia climbed to her feet, swaying a bit as she stared at the top of the hundred-foot masts. The ship's length was almost twice that.

"The *Shabab Oman*," she whispered in awe.

The high-masted clipper ship was the sultan's pride, the country's maritime ambassador to the world, a reminder of its nautical history. It had the traditional English design of a square-rigged foremast, the main and aft masts bearing both square and sloop sails. Built in 1971 from Scottish oak and Uruguayan pine, it was the largest vessel of its era in the world that was still seaworthy and in active service. For the past thirty years, it had traveled throughout the world, participating in races and regattas.

Presidents and premiers, kings and queens, had strode its deck. And now it was being lent to Kara for her personal transportation to Salalah. This, more than anything, demonstrated the sultan's esteem for the Kensington family. Safia now understood why Kara could not refuse.

Safia had to suppress a small bit of glee, surprised by the burbling feeling. Worries of snakes and nagging doubts dimmed. Maybe it was just the drugs, but she preferred to believe it was the fresh salt of the sea breeze, clearing her head and her heart. How long had it been since she'd felt this way?

By now, the other limo had drawn up and parked. The Americans climbed out, all eyes wide on the ship.

Only Omaha seemed unimpressed, having already been informed of the change in transportation. Still, to see the ship in person clearly affected him. Though, of course, he tried to hide it. "Great, this whole expedition is turning into a great big Sinbad movie."

"When in Rome . . ." Kara mumbled.

11:48 P.M.

Cassandra watched the ship from across the harbor. The Guild had secured this warehouse through contacts with a trafficker in black-market pirated videos. The back half of the rusted structure was stacked with crates of bootlegged DVDs and VHS videos.

The remainder of the warehouse, though, met her requirements. Formerly a mechanics shop, it had its own enclosed dry dock and berth. Water slapped in a continual rhythm against the nearby pilings, disturbed by the wake of a passing trawler heading out to sea.

The motion jostled the group of attack vessels brought in last week. Some had arrived disassembled in crates, then reassembled on-site; others were brought in by sea in the dead of night. Rocking in the berth were three Boston whalers, each tethering a rack of sleek, black Jet Skis, modified by the Guild with swivel-mounted assault rifles. In addition, the dock housed Cassandra's command boat, a hydrofoil capable of rocketing to speeds in excess of a hundred knots.

Her twelve-man team bustled about with final preparations. They were all ex–Special Forces, like herself, but these hard men had never been recruited by Sigma. Not that they weren't intelligent enough. Drummed out of the Forces, most had gone into various mercenary and paramilitary groups around the world, learning new skills, growing harder and more cunning. From these men, the Guild had handpicked those with the best adaptability, the keenest intelligence, those who demonstrated the fiercest loyalty to their team, traits even Sigma would have appreciated. Only in the Guild's case, one criterion was paramount: These men had no qualms about killing, no matter the target.

Her second-in-command approached. "Captain Sanchez, sir."

She kept her attention on the video feed from the exterior cameras. She counted as Painter's party climbed aboard the ship and were greeted by Omani officials. Everyone was aboard. She finally straightened. "Yes, Kane."

John Kane was the only non-American in the group. He had served in the elite Australian SAS, Special Air Services. The Guild did not limit its talent search to U.S. borders, especially as it operated internationally. Standing over six and a half feet, Kane was solidly muscled. He kept his head shaved smooth, except for a patch of black hair under his chin.

The team here was actually Kane's own men, positioned in the Gulf until called to duty by the Guild. The organization had teams planted throughout the world, independent cells who knew nothing about the others, each ready at a moment's notice to do the Guild's bidding.

Cassandra had been sent to activate this particular cell and lead the mission, gaining the assignment because of her knowledge of Sigma Force, the Guild's adversary on this op. She knew how Sigma operated, their strategies and procedures. She also had intimate knowledge of their op leader—Painter Crowe.

"We're locked and loaded," Kane said.

Cassandra nodded, checked her watch. The *Shabab Oman* was due to disembark at the stroke of midnight. They would wait a full hour, then set off in pursuit. She stared again at the video monitor and calculated in her head.

"The *Argus*?" she asked.

"Radioed in a few minutes ago. She's already in position, patrolling our attack zone to ensure no trespassers."

The *Argus* was a four-man submersible, capable of off-loading divers without surfacing. Its peroxide-propellant engines and ordnance of minitor-pedoes made it as fast as it was deadly.

Cassandra nodded again. All was in place.

None aboard the *Shabab* would live to see the dawn.

Midnight

Henry stood in the center of the bathroom as the draining tub gurgled. His butler's jacket lay on the bed outside. He rolled up his sleeves and pulled on a pair of yellow rubber gloves.

He sighed. A maid could have easily handled this chore, but the girls were already put off by the commotion, and he felt it his duty to rid the house of the viper's remains. Ultimately the well-being of the palace's guests fell upon his shoulders, a duty he felt he had failed in this evening. And though Lady Kensington's group had departed, he still felt it a personal responsibility to cast the snake out, to correct his mistake.

Stepping forward, he leaned down and gingerly reached for the body. It floated in a lazy S-shape upon the water, even seeming to writhe slightly, bobbled by the tidal pull of the drain.

Henry's finger hesitated. The bloody thing looked alive.

He squeezed his gloved hand. "Get a grip on yourself, old man."

Taking a deep breath, he grabbed the snake by the middle. His face clenched in distaste, teeth grinding. "Bloody piece of shite," he muttered, reverting to the language of his Dublin youth. He cast a silent prayer of thanks to Saint Patrick for driving these buggers out of Ireland.

He dragged the limp form out of the tub. A plastic-lined pail awaited his catch. Turning, holding the snake at arm's length, he positioned the snake's tail over the bucket and wound its body down into it, coiling it into place.

As he settled its head atop the pile, he was again amazed at the lifelike appearance of the creature. Only its slack mouth ruined the image.

Henry began to straighten, then cocked his head, seeing something that made no sense. "What's this, then?"

He turned and collected a plastic comb from the vanity. Gingerly grabbing the snake behind its skull, he used the comb to pry the mouth open farther, confirming what he had noticed.

"How odd," he mumbled. He probed with the comb to make sure.

The snake had no fangs.

9
Blood on the Water

⊓1∘∘◢|∘५|XY⋝|ϕꙮX⋝)

December 3, 1:02 A.M.
Arabian Sea

Safia stood at the rail, staring at the dark coastline as it floated past. The ship creaked and groaned around her. Sails snapped as the winds twisted over the midnight seas.

It was as if they had been transported to another time, when the world was just wind, sand, and water. The smell of the salt and the whisper of waves sliding along the boat's sides erased the bustle of Muscat. Stars shone above but clouds were blowing in. They would have rain before they reached Salalah.

The ship's captain had already relayed the weather reports. A squall was raising swells to ten feet. "Nothing the *Shabab* can't handle," he had said with a grin, "but it'll make for a bit of a roll and yaw. Best stick to your cabins when the rains hit."

So Safia had decided to take advantage of the clear skies while they lasted. After the excitement of the day, she found it too confining in the cabin. Especially now that the sedatives were wearing thin.

She watched the dark coastline glide past, so quiet, so smooth. The last oasis of light, an industrial complex on the very outskirts of Muscat, began to disappear around a spur of land.

A voice spoke behind her, sounding intentionally indifferent. "There goes the last vestige of civilization as we know it."

Clay Bishop stepped to the rail, gripped it with one hand, and raised a cigarette to his lips. He still wore his Levi's and a black T-shirt emblazoned with the words GOT MILK. For the two years he had served as her grad student, he never wore anything but T-shirts, usually advertising rock bands in garish colors. The black-and-white one he wore now was clearly his formal wear.

Slightly irritated at the intrusion, she kept her voice stiff and scholarly. "Those lights," she said, nodding to the fading complex, "mark the city's most important industrial site. Can you tell me what it is, Mr. Bishop?"

He shrugged, and after a moment's hesitation, guessed, "An oil refinery?"

It was an answer she expected, but it was also wrong. "No, it's the desalination facility that produces the city's freshwater supply."

"Water?"

"Oil may be the wealth of Arabia, but water is its lifeblood."

She allowed her student to dwell on this fact. Few in the West knew of the importance of such desalination projects here in Arabia. Water rights and freshwater resources were already replacing oil as the hotbed of contention in the Middle East and North Africa. Some of the fiercest conflicts between Israel and its neighbors—Lebanon, Jordan, and Syria—were not over ideology or religion, but over control of the Jordan Valley's water supply.

Clay finally spoke up. "Whiskey is for drinkin', water is for fightin'."

She frowned.

"Mark Twain," he said.

Once again, she was surprised by his astute intuitiveness and nodded to him. "Very good."

Despite his slacker appearance, there was a sharp intelligence behind those thick black glasses. It was one of the reasons she had allowed the young man to join this expedition. He would make a fine researcher one day.

Clay raised his cigarette again. Studying him, she noted the slight waver in its lit end and, for the first time, his white-knuckled grip on the ship's rail.

"Are you all right?" she asked.

"Not a big fan of the open sea. If God had meant for man to sail, He wouldn't have ground the dinosaurs into jet fuel."

She reached over and patted his hand. "Go to bed, Mr. Bishop."

The desalination plant finally vanished around the spit of land. All went dark, except for the ship's lights, reflected in the waters.

Behind Safia, solitary lanterns and strings of electric lights lit the decks, aiding the crew in working lines and rigging, preparing for the rougher seas of the approaching storm. The crew was mostly trainees, young men from the Royal Navy of Oman, practicing while the ship was home, running short trips up and down the coastline. The *Shabab* was due in another two months to compete in the President's Cup regatta.

The murmur of the young men was interrupted by a sudden shout from the middle of the deck, a flurry of Arabic cursing. A crash erupted. Safia turned to see a middeck cargo hatch thrown wide, knocking a sailor back. Another man came flying out the open doorway, flinging himself to the side.

The reason for the sailor's mad flight appeared at his heels, hooves smashing down onto the planks. A white stallion galloped up the hold's ramp and out onto the deck. Tossing his mane, he stood silvery in the moonlight, his eyes two pieces of smoldering coal. Shouts now echoed all around.

"Jesus!" Clay blurted beside her.

The horse reared up, neighing threateningly, then crashed back, hooves dancing on the planking. It was haltered, but the rope end was frayed.

Men ran in circles, waving arms, trying to corral the stallion back down the hatch. It refused to budge, kicking out with a hoof, butting with its head, or snapping with its teeth.

Safia knew the horse was one of four stalled below—two stallions, two mares—all headed to the royal stud farm outside Salalah. Someone must have been careless in securing the animal.

Fixed at the rail, Safia watched the crew battle the stallion. Someone had freed a length of rope and attempted to lasso the horse. The roper earned himself a broken foot, hopping backward with a sharp cry.

The stallion crashed through a tangle of rigging, ripping bodily through. A line of electric lights struck the deck. Glass bulbs popped and shattered.

New shouts arose.

Finally, a rifle appeared in one of the sailor's hands.

The stallion's rampage risked life and damage to the ship.

"*La!* No!"

A flash of bare skin drew Safia's eye in the other direction. Amid the clothed sailors, a half-naked figure ran from a foredeck door. Wearing only a pair of boxers, Painter stood out like some wild savage. His hair was a mess, as though he had just woken. The cries and crashing of the horse had plainly roused him from his cabin.

He snatched a tarp from atop a coil of rope and sprinted barefoot through the others. "*Wa-ra!*" he shouted in Arabic. "Get back!"

Clearing the ring of sailors, Painter fluttered the tarp. The motion caught the attention of the stallion. It reared up and pounded back down, a threatening, warning stance. But its coal black eyes remained fixed on the tarp and man. A matador and a bull.

"Ye-ahh!" Painter yelled, waving an arm.

The stallion backed a step, lowering its head.

The American swept forward—not straight at the horse, but to its side. He tossed the tarp over the horse's head, covering it completely.

The stallion bucked once, thrashed its head, but the drape of tarp was too large for the beast to shake free.

The horse settled back to the planks and stood still, blinded by the tarp, unsure. It shivered, sweat gleaming in the moonlight.

Painter kept a step away. He spoke too softly for Safia to hear. But she recognized the tone. She'd heard it on the airplane. Simple reassurance.

Finally, he walked cautiously forward and placed a palm on the stallion's heaving side. The horse nickered and tossed its head, but more gently this time.

Moving closer, Painter patted the stallion's neck, continuing to murmur. With his other hand, he reached to the frayed rope attached to the halter. Slowly, he guided the stallion around.

Unable to see, the horse responded to the familiar signals, having to trust the man at the end of the rope.

Safia watched him. Painter's skin gleamed as much as the horse's flank. He combed a hand through his hair. Was there a tremble in the gesture?

He spoke to one of the sailors, who nodded. The sailor led him down into the hold, horse in tow.

"Very cool," Clay said approvingly, stamping out his cigarette.

With the excitement over, the crew slowly returned to their duties. Safia stared around her. She noted that most of Kara's party had gathered on the deck by now: Painter's partner in a belted robe, Danny in a T-shirt and shorts. Kara and Omaha hadn't changed their clothes. They must have still been going over last-minute arrangements. At their shoulders stood four tall, hard-looking men dressed in military fatigues. Safia did not recognize them.

From the hatch, Painter returned, rolling the tarp in his hands.

A small cheer rose from the crew. A few palms slapped his back. He winced from the attention and ran a hand again through his hair, a gesture of modesty.

Safia found herself crossing to him. "Well done," she said as she reached Painter. "If they'd had to shoot the horse—"

"I couldn't let that happen. It was just spooked."

Kara appeared, arms crossed over her chest. Her face was unreadable but missing its usual scowl. "That was the sultan's champion stud. What happened here will reach his ears. You've just made yourself a good friend."

Painter shrugged. "I did it for the welfare of the horse."

Omaha stood at Kara's shoulder. His face reddened, plainly irritated. "Where did you learn that horsemanship, Tonto?"

"Omaha . . ." Safia warned.

Painter ignored the insult. "Claremont Stables in New York City. I cleaned stalls when I was a kid." The man finally seemed to note his undressed state, staring down at himself. "I should be getting back to my cabin."

Kara spoke up, stiffly. "Dr. Crowe, before you retire, I'd appreciate your stopping by my cabin. I'd like to go over the itinerary once we reach port."

His eyes widened in surprise at the offer. "Certainly."

It was Kara's first sign of cooperation. Safia was not surprised. She knew of Kara's deep affection for horses, a tenderness that she felt for no man. Kara had been a champion rider in dressage. Painter's timely intervention to protect the stallion had won him more than just the sultan's appreciation.

Painter nodded to Safia, his eyes glinting in the lantern light. She found her breath catching before she could choke out a good-night.

He departed, passing through the four men standing behind Kara. Others slowly followed, dispersing to their respective cabins.

Omaha remained at Safia's side.

Kara turned and spoke in Arabic to one of the men, a tall black-haired fellow, wearing an Omani *shamag* headcloth and military khakis. Bedouin. All were outfitted similarly. Safia noted the sidearms holstered at their belts. The man bending an ear to Kara also bore a curved dagger tucked into his belt. It was not a ceremonial knife, but a wicked weapon that looked like it had been well used. Clearly he was the leader, distinguished from his men by a pale, ropy scar across this throat. He nodded at whatever Kara said, then spoke to his men. The group marched off.

"Who was that?" Safia asked.

"Captain al-Haffi," Kara said. "From the Omani military border patrol."

"Desert Phantoms," Omaha mumbled, using the border patrol's nickname.

The Phantoms were the Special Forces of Oman. They waged an ongoing war with smugglers and drug runners in the deep desert, spending years out in the sands. There were no harder men in all the world. British and American Special Forces teams were taught desert warfare and survival by ex-Phantoms.

Kara spoke. "He and his squad have volunteered as bodyguards for the expedition. With the permission of Sultan Qaboos."

Safia watched the men head below.

Omaha stretched and yawned. "I'm off to crash for a few hours before sunrise." He glanced back at Safia. His eyes were hooded under his brows. "You should try to get some sleep. We have a long day ahead of us."

Safia shrugged, noncommittal. She hated to agree with him on even such a simple suggestion.

His gaze fell from her. For the first time, she noted the passing of years on his face, deeper and longer sun crinkles at the corners of his eyes, a bruising under them. He bore a few more threadlike scars. She could not deny his rugged handsomeness. Sandy-blond hair, hard planes to his face, dusky blue eyes. But the boyish charm had faded. He looked tired now, sun-bleached.

Still . . . something stirred inside her as his eyes fell away, an old ache that was as familiar as it was warm. As he turned away, she caught a hint of his musky scent, a reminder of the man who once lay beside her, snoring in a tent. She had to force herself not to reach out to him, to hold him back a moment longer. But what was the use? They had no words left between them, just uncomfortable silences.

He left.

She turned to find Kara staring at her.

Kara shook her head. "Let the dead rest in peace."

1:38 A.M.

The video monitor displayed the dive team. Cassandra hunched at the screen, as if trying to hear over the whine of the hydrofoil's engines. The feed came from the team's submersible, the *Argus,* five miles away and sunk to twenty fathoms.

The *Argus* was designed with two chambers. Aft housed the vessel's pilot and copilot. The stern chamber, filling now with seawater, held the two assault divers. As the water swamped over the two men, equalizing pressure inside and out, the stern canopy opened like a clamshell. The two divers pushed out into the waters, illuminated by the sub's lights. Strapped to each of their waists hung maneuvering pulse jets. The DARPA-engineered devices were capable of propelling the divers to astounding speeds. Slung below them in pocket nets, the pair dragged an arsenal of demolition gear.

Tinny words whispered in her ear. "Sonar contact established on target," the pilot of the *Argus* reported. "Deploying force team. Estimate contact in seven minutes."

"Very good," she answered under her breath. Then sensing someone at her shoulder, she glanced back. It was John Kane. She held up a hand.

"Mine deployment at zero two hundred," the pilot finished.

"Roger that," Cassandra said, repeating the time and signing off.

She straightened and turned.

Kane lifted a satellite phone. "Scrambled line. Your ears only."

Cassandra accepted the phone. *Your ears only.* That could mean one of her superiors. By now, they would have received the report on her failure in Muscat. She had left out the details of the strange bedouin woman who had vanished. Her report had been damning enough. For a second time, she had failed to secure the artifact.

A mechanical voice answered, synthesized for anonymity. Though its inflection and tone were masked, she knew who spoke. The head of the Guild, simply code-named "The Minister," as in "prime minister." It seemed a foolish precaution, cartoonish, but the Guild patterned its organization on terrorist cells. Information passed among teams on a need-to-know basis, each under independent authority, accountable only to the upper echelon. She had never met the Minister; only three people ever had, the three lieutenants who ran the overseer's board. She hoped to gain such a position someday.

"*Gray leader,*" the eerily synthesized voice said, using her op designation. "*Mission parameters have been changed.*"

Cassandra stiffened. She had the time schedule tattooed in her head. Nothing would go wrong. The

Shabab's diesel engines would be blown, signaling a strafing run by the Jet Ski gunboats. An assault team would follow, mopping up, cutting off communication. Once the iron heart was in hand, the ship would be blasted apart and sunk. "Sir? Deployment's under way. Everything's in motion."

"*Improvise,*" the mechanical voice intoned. "*Secure the museum curator along with the artifact. Is that understood?*"

Cassandra bit back her surprise. It was not a simple request. The original objective—acquiring the iron artifact—required no parameters for preserving the lives of those on board the *Shabab Oman*. As planned, it was a brutal grab-and-run. Blunt, bloody, and swift. She already began revising in her head. "May I ask why we need the curator?"

"*She may prove useful to stage two. Our original expert in Arabian antiquity has proven . . . uncooperative. And expediency is paramount to success if we hope to discover and secure the source of this power. Delay equals defeat. We must not waste the talent conveniently at hand.*"

"Yes, sir."

"*Report when you're successful.*" A hint of threat lingered in these last words as the line went dead.

She lowered the phone.

John Kane waited a few steps away.

Cassandra turned to him. "Change of plans. Alert your men. We're going in first ourselves." She stared beyond the window of the hydrofoil's bridge. Off in the distance, the lantern-rigged sailing ship shone like a scatter of fiery jewels on the dark seas.

"When do we deploy?"

"Now."

1:42 A.M.

Painter knocked on the cabin door. He knew the layout of the rooms beyond the ornately carved Scottish oak door. It was the Presidential Suite, reserved for potentates and magnates of industry, and now the domicile of Lady Kara Kensington. Upon boarding the ship earlier, Painter had downloaded information and schematics on the *Shabab Oman*.

Best to know the lay of the land . . . even if it was at sea.

A cabin steward opened the door. The older man, standing just shy of five feet, carried himself with the dignity of a much taller man. He was dressed all in white, from small brimless cap to sandals. "Dr. Crowe," he greeted with a small bow of his head. "Lady Kensington has been expecting you."

The man turned from the door, motioning him to follow. Past the antechamber, Painter was led to the main living space. The wide room was decorated simply, but elegantly. A large antique Moroccan desk marked off a study, lined with barrister bookshelves. The center of the room contained a pair of overstuffed sofas, upholstered in British Royal Navy blue, flanked by a pair of high-backed chairs, pillowed in Omani fashion, striped in red, green, and white, the colors of the Omani flag. In all, the room held a mix of British and Omani appointments, acknowledgment of their shared histories.

Still, the most dramatic feature of the room was the wide row of windows that overlooked the dark ocean.

Kara stood framed against the backdrop of the starry sky and moonlit waters. She had changed out of her clothes into a thick cotton robe. Her feet were bare. She turned as he entered, catching his reflection in the window.

"That will be all, Yanni," she said, dismissing the steward.

Once he'd vacated the suite, she raised a hand, vaguely pointing at the sofa. "I'd offer you a nightcap, but this bloody boat's as dry as all Arabia."

Painter crossed and settled in the seat as Kara shifted to one of the chairs and sat down. "Not a problem. I don't drink, myself."

"AA?" she asked.

"Personal preference," he said with a deep frown. It seemed the stereotype of the drunken Indian persisted even in Britain—not that it didn't have some truth. His own father had found more solace within a bottle of Jack Daniel's than in family and friends.

She shrugged.

Painter cleared his throat. "You mentioned updating me on the itinerary?"

"It'll be printed up and under your door before sunrise."

One eye narrowed. "Then why the late-night meeting?" He found himself staring at her bare ankles as she crossed her legs. Had she asked him up here for more personal reasons? He knew from his briefing that Kara Kensington went through men as often as she changed hairstyles.

"Safia," she said simply, surprising him.

Painter blinked back up at her.

"I can tell by the way she looks at you." There was a long pause. "She's more fragile than she appears."

And tougher than you all think she is, he added to himself.

"If you're using her, then you'd best find some forgotten corner of the world to hide in afterward. If it's just sex, you'd best keep your pants zipped or you'll be missing a significant part of your anatomy. So which is it?"

Painter shook his head. For the second time in a matter of hours, he was being questioned about his affection for Safia: first by his partner, now by this woman. "It's neither," he said more harshly than he intended.

"Then explain it."

Painter kept his face unreadable. He could not dismiss Kara as easily as he had Coral earlier. In fact, his mission would fare better with her cooperation than with her present hostility. But he remained silent. He couldn't even come up with a good lie. The best lies were those closest to the truth—but what was the truth? How *did* he feel about Safia?

For the first time, he considered it more fully. Without a doubt, he found Safia attractive: her emerald eyes, her coffee-smooth skin, the way even a shy smile lit up her face. But he had encountered many beautiful women over the course of his life. So what was it about this particular woman? Safia was smart, accomplished, and there was certainly a strength in her to which the others seemed blind, a core of granite that could not be broken.

Yet, as he looked back, Cassandra had been just as strong, resourceful, and beautiful, and it had taken him years to respond to her. So what was it about Safia that should stir him so quickly?

He had a suspicion, but one he was reluctant to admit . . . even to himself.

Staring toward the ship's windows, Painter pictured Safia's eyes, the soft wound behind the emerald shine. He remembered her arms around his shoulders as she was lowered down from the museum roof, squeezing tight to him, the whisper of relief, the tears. Even then, there had been something about her that begged the hand to touch, something that called to the man in him. Unlike Cassandra, Safia was not just granite. She was a well of strength *and* vulnerability, the hard and the soft.

Deep in his heart, he knew it was this contradiction that fascinated him more than anything else. Something he wanted to explore in more depth.

"Well?" Kara pressed after his long silence.

He was saved from answering by the first explosion.

1:55 A.M.

Omaha awoke with thunder in his ears. He sat up, startled, feeling the vibration in his gut, hearing the rattle of the tiny porthole window. He had known they were headed into a squall. He checked his watch. Less than ten minutes had passed. *Too soon for the storm . . .*

Danny slipped from the upper bunk, landing in a tumble, catching himself with one hand, hiking up his boxers with the other. "Damn! What was that?"

The chatter of gunfire erupted over their heads. Shouts followed.

Omaha threw back his covers. They had sailed into a storm all right . . . just not the one predicted by any weatherman. "We're under attack!"

Danny grabbed his eyeglasses from the top drawer of a small desk. "Who's attacking? Why?"

"How the hell should I know?"

Omaha leaped to his feet and pulled a shirt over his head, feeling less exposed. He cursed himself for leaving his shotgun and pistols crated in the hold. He knew how treacherous the Arabian seas could be, plied by modern-day pirates and paramilitary factions tied to terrorist organizations. It seemed the high seas were still ripe with bounty to plunder. But he had never suspected anyone would attack the flagship of the Omani navy.

Omaha creaked the door open an inch and peered out into the dark passageway. A single wall sconce cast a pool of light near the stairwell that led to the upper two levels and the open deck. As usual, Kara had assigned Omaha and his brother the worst berths, one floor above the bilge, a crew cabin versus the more luxurious passenger accommodations. Across the passage, another door peeked open.

Omaha and his brother were not the only ones granted the lowliest cabins. "Crowe," he called out.

The far door pushed wider to reveal Crowe's partner instead. Coral Novak crept out barefoot, in sweatpants and a sports bra, her white-blond hair loose past her shoulders. She waved him silent. She carried a dagger in her right hand, a wicked length of polished stainless steel with a black carbonized handle. Military design. She held it low, deadly steady, even with the barrage of gunfire breaking out in spats above their heads.

She was alone.

"Where's Crowe?" he hissed.

She cocked a thumb up. "Gone to meet Kara twenty minutes ago."

Where the gunfire seemed to concentrate, Omaha added. Fear narrowed his vision as he stared toward the stairs. Safia and her student had private cabins below Kara's suite, both close to the fighting. His heart clutched with every burst of rifle fire. He had to get to her. He stepped toward the stairway.

A new spate of gunplay erupted, sounding from the top of the stairs.

Booted footsteps pounded, coming their way.

"Weapons?" Coral whispered.

Omaha turned and showed his empty palms. They had been forced to abandon all personal arms before boarding the ship.

She scowled and hurried to the foot of the narrow stairs. She used the hilt of her knife to shatter the single bulb that lit the corridor. Darkness fell.

The footsteps rushed toward them. A shadow appeared first.

Coral seemed to read something in the shadow, subtly changing her position, widening her stance, lowering her arm.

A dark figure stumbled down the last of the stairs.

Coral kicked out a leg, cracking the man in the knee. He fell headlong into the corridor with a cry. It was only one of the crew. The ship's galley cook. His face struck the planks with a crack, snapping his head back. He groaned but lay still, stunned, dazed.

Coral crouched over him with her knife, unsure.

Spatters of gunfire continued above, but only sporadically now, sounding more deadly, purposeful.

Omaha pushed forward, eyeing the stairs. "We have to get to the others."

To Safia.

Coral stood up and blocked him with an arm. "We need weapons."

A rifle blast sounded above, loud in the tight space.

Everyone took a step back.

Coral met Omaha's eye. He stared up, caught between rushing to Safia's rooms and proceeding cautiously. Caution was not at the top of his core values. Still, the woman was right. Fists against bullets was not a good rescue plan.

He swung around. "There are rifles and ammo stored in the hold," he said, and pointed to the floor hatch that led down into the bilge compartment. "We should be able to crawl through there and get to the main hold."

Coral tightened her grip on her knife and nodded. They crossed to the hatch, threw it open, and climbed down the short ladder to the low-ceilinged bilge. It smelled of algae, salt, and oak resins. Omaha was the last through.

A fresh barrage of gunfire erupted, punctuated by a sharp scream. A man, not a woman. Still, Omaha cringed and prayed for Safia to keep her head low.

Hating himself, he closed the hatch. Darkness fell over them. Blind, he dropped down the short ladder, landing with a tiny splash in the bilge.

"Anyone bring a flashlight?" he asked.

No one answered.

"Great," Omaha muttered, "just great."

Something scurried over his foot and disappeared with the sound of tiny splashes. Rats.

1:58 A.M.

Painter leaned out one of the ship's windows. A two-man Jet Ski buzzed below, sweeping under the overhang of the protruding forecastle. It fled past with barely a whine, exhaust muffled, leaving a V-shaped wake across the waves. Even in the darkness, he recognized the design.

DARPA-engineered, experimental prototype for covert ops.

The pilot crouched low behind the windshield. His passenger sat higher, manning a swivel-mounted assault rifle in the rear, gyroscopically stabilized. Both men wore night-vision goggles.

The patrol whined past. So far he counted four. Probably more circling outward. Across the dark sea, he saw no evidence of the main attack ship, the one that had surely off-loaded the assault team. Most likely it had moored to one of the ship's flanks, then raced away afterward, maintaining a safe distance until it was time to recollect the team.

He ducked back inside.

Kara crouched behind a sofa, looking more angry than scared.

As soon as the first explosion rocked the ship, Painter had checked outside the cabin. Through the deck hatch, he'd spotted a curl of smoke and an ominous crimson glow from the back of the ship.

An incendiary grenade.

Even that brief glimpse almost got him killed. A man in black camouflage gear suddenly appeared in the doorway, steps away. Painter ducked back inside as the man strafed the opening. If it hadn't been for the metal reinforcement of the Presidential Suite door, Painter would've been chopped in half. After bolting the door, he gave Kara his assessment.

"They took out the radio room."

"Who?"

"Don't know . . . paramilitary group from the looks of them."

Painter abandoned his post by the window and crouched beside Kara. He knew with certainty who led the team. There was no doubt. *Cassandra.* The Jet Skis were stolen DARPA prototypes. She had to be out there somewhere. Possibly even on board, leading the assault team. He pictured the determined glint in Cassandra's eyes, the double furrow between her brows as she concentrated. He shoved this thought

away, surprised by the sudden pang, something between fury and loss.

"What are we going to do?" Kara asked.

"Stay put . . . for now."

Barricaded in the Presidential Suite, the two of them
were safe from immediate harm, but the others were at
risk. The Omani sailors had been trained well, responding quickly to the threat, putting up a fierce firefight.
But the sailors aboard the ship were mostly young, only
moderately armed, and Cassandra would know all their
weaknesses. The ship would soon be hers.

But was that her goal?

Painter crouched beside Kara. He closed his eyes and
took a deep breath. He needed a moment to stop reacting and to think, to concentrate. His father had taught
him a few Pequot chants, his weak attempt to imbue
his one son with tribal tradition, usually done while
his breath reeked of tequila and beer. Still, Painter had
learned the chants, whispering them in the dark when
his parents fought, yelling, cursing in the neighboring
room. He found comfort and focus in the repetition,
not knowing the meaning—then or now.

His lips moved silently, meditatively. He shut out
the spates of gunfire.

Again, he pictured Cassandra. He could guess the
purpose of her attack. To obtain what she had been

after from the start. The iron heart. The only solid clue to the mystery of the antimatter explosion. It still lay in the curator's cabin. His mind ran along various attack scenarios, mission parameters—

In midchant, it struck him.

He bolted back to his feet.

From the start, he had been nagged by the sloppiness of the assault. Why blow up the radio room and alert the crew prematurely? If it was an ordinary mercenary group, he could blame the lack of planning and precision on inexperience, but if Cassandra was behind it . . .

A sinking feeling hollowed out his gut.

"What?" Kara asked, pushing up with him.

The gunfire beyond the cabin had gone deathly quiet. In the silence, he heard a telltale whine.

He crossed to the window and ducked his head out.

Four Jet Skis came sweeping in out of the darkness— but each was manned only by the pilot. No passengers. The rear assault seats were empty.

"Damn it . . ."

"What?" Kara asked again, fear entering her voice.

"We're too late."

He knew with certainty that the grenade explosion hadn't marked the *start* of the mission, but its *end*.

He silently cursed his stupidity. This was all the endgame. And he hadn't even been playing. He had been caught totally off guard. He allowed himself this moment of anger, then focused on the situation.

An endgame was not necessarily the end itself.

He stared as the four Jet Skis swooped toward the boat. Come to collect the last members of the assault team, the rear guard, the demolition team assigned to blow the radio shack. One of the Omani sailors must have stumbled upon these men, leading to the firefight on the deck.

More gunfire erupted, sounding farther away, more determined, near the stern of the boat. They were attempting to retreat.

Out the window, Painter watched the last of the Jet Skis circle wide, wary of the gunfire. The other Jet Skis, those with men manning the mounted assault rifles, were nowhere in sight. He also heard no sign of their engagement. They were gone. Along with the point team, Painter imagined. Along with the prize.

But to where?

Again he searched the water for the main assault ship. It was out there somewhere. But only dark waters lay beyond. Storm clouds now obliterated both moon and stars, turning the world black. His fingers clenched on the sill of the wide window.

As he searched, a flicker of light drew his eye—not *out* across the waters, but *down* below it.

He leaned farther and stared into the depths.

Deep in the midnight waters, a glow glided out from under the ship. It slowly slipped off to starboard and floated determinedly away. Painter's brow crinkled. He recognized what he saw. A submersible. Why?

The answer came immediately with the question.

With the mission over, the sub and the main assault team were bugging out. All that was left was the cleanup. To leave no witnesses.

He knew the purpose of the sub's presence. To come in baffled and silent, too small to detect . . .

"They've mined the ship," he said aloud. He calculated in his head how long it would take for a sub to clear the blast zone.

Kara said something, but he had gone deaf to her.

Painter swung from the window and hurried to the door. The firefight seemed to have settled to a stalemate of sporadic shots. He listened at the door. Nothing sounded close. He slid back the bolt.

"What are you doing?" Kara asked at his shoulder, sticking close but clearly irritated by her own need to do so.

"We must get off this boat."

He cracked the door open. A few steps away lay the opening to the middeck. The winds had kicked up as the edge of the coming storm brushed over the *Shabab Oman.* Sails snapped like whips. Ropes rattled in stanchions.

He studied the deck, reading it like a chessboard.

The crew had no opportunity to reef and secure the mainsails. The Omani sailors were pinned down by a pair—no, *three* gunmen—hidden behind a pile of barrels stacked at the far end of the middeck. The masked men had the perfect vantage point to guard the forward sections of the ship. One of the pair kept his rifle pointed toward the raised stern deck, protecting their rear.

Closer, a fourth masked gunman lay sprawled on the deck, facedown, blood pooled around his head, the body only a few steps from Painter.

He took in the situation with a glance. Similarly ensconced behind crates on this side of the middeck were the four Omani border-patrol agents, the Desert Phantoms. They lay on their bellies, rifles pointed toward the gunmen. It was a standoff. It must have been the Phantoms who had waylaid the assault team's rear guard, pinned them down, kept them from escaping over rails.

"C'mon," Painter said, and took Kara by the elbow. He dragged her out the suite's door and toward the lower stairs.

"Where're we going?" she asked. "What about getting off the boat?"

He didn't answer. He was too late, but he had to be sure. He clambered down the stairs to the next landing. A short passage led to the guest quarters.

In the middle of the hall, bathed in the light from the single overhead lamp, a body draped across the floor. Facedown like the masked man above. But this was not one of the attackers.

He wore only boxers and a white T-shirt. A tiny dark stain marred the center of his back. Shot from behind as he attempted to flee.

"It's Clay . . ." Kara mumbled in shock, hurrying forward with Painter.

She knelt near the boy's body, but Painter stepped over him. He had no time for mourning. He hurried to the door toward which the graduate student had been heading, seeking a place to hide or to warn others. Too late.

They'd all been too late.

Painter stopped outside the door. It was cracked half open. Lamplight flowed into the hall. Painter listened intently. Silence. He steeled himself against what he would find.

Kara called to him, knowing what he feared. "Safia?"

2:02 A.M.

Omaha shoved out an arm as the ship rolled beneath him. The darkness of the bilge threw off his sense of balance. Water sloshed over his shoes, chilling his ankles.

A crash sounded behind him . . . and a curse. Danny was faring no better.

"Do you know where you're going?" Coral asked Omaha, her voice frosty, echoing a bit in the dank bilge.

"Yes," he snapped back. It was a lie. He kept trailing one hand along the sloped wall to the left, praying he'd find a ladder leading back up. The next one should lead to the main storage hold under the middeck. Or so he hoped.

They continued in silence.

Rats squeaked in sharp protest, sounding larger in the darkness, as big as wet bulldogs. Their numbers multiplied in the imagination. Omaha heard their bodies splashing through the bilge waters, running ahead of them, likely piling into an angry mass at the stern of the ship. In an alley in Calcutta, he had seen a rat-gnawed corpse. The eyes gone, the genitals eaten away, all soft places gnashed. He did not like rats.

But fear for Safia drove him onward, his anxiety heightened by the darkness, the spates of gunfire.

Bloody images flashed across his mind's eye, too terrible to dwell upon. Why had he put off telling her how he still felt about her? He would gladly drop on his knees now to have her safe and sound.

His outstretched hand struck something solid. He reached out and discovered rungs and nail heads. A ladder.

"Here it is," he said with more confidence than he felt. He didn't care if he was right or wrong or where the hell the ladder led. He was climbing out.

As Danny and Coral moved closer, he mounted the rungs.

"Be careful," Coral warned.

The gunfire continued above. Close. That was warning enough.

Reaching the topmost rung, he searched until he found the inner handle to the hatch. Praying it wasn't locked or weighted down with cargo, he shoved up.

The hatch flew open with ease, swinging back and crashing against a wooden support pillar.

Coral hissed at him. No words, just protest.

Blessed light flowed over him, blindingly bright after the gloom below. The smell was also refreshing after the salt and mold of the ship's bilge.

Fresh-cut hay.

A large shadow shifted to his right.

He turned and found himself facing a huge horse, looming over him. The same Arabian stallion that had broken free earlier. It threw its head and huffed at him. Eyes white with terror, it raised a hoof in threat, ready to stamp out the sudden intruder into its shipboard stables.

Omaha ducked back, cursing their luck. The bilge hatch had opened into the stallion's stall. He spotted other horses in neighboring stanchions.

He turned his attention to the stallion. The horse tugged at the lead tethering him in place. The spooked Arabian was better than any armed guard. But they had to get out and reach the crated weapons in the neighboring hold.

Fear for Safia fired his blood. He had come this far . . .

Trusting the ropes held the horse, he dove out of the hatch, rolled flat across the planks, and passed under the fence that closed off the stall.

Gaining his feet, he dusted off his bare knees. "Move quick!"

He found a horse blanket, brightly colored in reds and yellows. He waved it at the stallion, keeping it distracted so the others could climb to safety. The horse whinnied at his motions, but rather than growing more perturbed at the additional intruders, the stallion pulled at the ropes that secured it, drawn to the saddle blanket.

Omaha realized it must recognize its own blanket, a promising sign that someone was about to take it for a ride, to let it out of the stalls. Alarm heightened the stallion's desire to break free.

With regret, he lowered the blanket back over the fence once Danny and Coral reached his side. The stallion's large eyes met his, scared, full of the need for reassurance.

"Where are the guns?" Coral asked.

Omaha turned from the stall. "Should be over there." He pointed past the ramp that led to the upper deck. A stack of crates, three high, stood along the back wall. A Kensington crest marked each one.

As Omaha led them across the hold, he kept his head low with each new burst of gunfire. A repeated exchange of gunfire, a volley back and forth. The deadly match sounded like it was coming from outside the double doors at the top of the ramp.

He remembered Danny's earlier question. Who was attacking? This was no mere band of pirates. This was too sustained, too organized, too damn bold.

Reaching the crates, he searched the stapled manifests. Having organized the supplies himself, he knew there should be a crate of rifles and handguns. He found the right box. Using a crowbar, he broke it open.

Danny took out one of the rifles. "What are we going to do?"

"*You're* going to stay low," Omaha said, grabbing a Desert Eagle pistol.

"What about you?" Danny asked.

Omaha cocked an ear to the fighting as he loaded the pistol on the floor. "I have to get to the others. Make sure they're safe."

But in truth, he pictured only Safia, smiling, younger.

He had failed her before—not again.

Coral finally rose from her own search of the crate's contents with a single pistol. She quickly and efficiently loaded its magazine with .357 rounds, then slammed it home. Armed now, she seemed more relaxed, a lioness loosened up and ready for the hunt.

She met his eyes. "We should return forward through the bilge. Join the others from there."

More gunfire spat just outside the double doors.

"We'd lose too much time." Omaha glanced to the ramp that led directly to the heart of the gunfire. "There may be another way."

Coral frowned at him as he outlined his plan.

"You've got to be kidding," Danny muttered.

But Coral nodded as Omaha finished. "It's worth a shot."

"Then let's go," he said. "Before we're too late."

10

Storm Surge

⟨𝙓⟩⟨⟩◁⟨⟩◁⟨𝙓⟩⟨𝙓⟩

December 3, 2:07 A.M.
Arabian Sea

They were too late.

Painter approached the open door to Safia's cabin.
A lamp glowed from within. Despite the urgency, the
certain knowledge that the ship had been mined, he
hesitated a breath.

Behind him, Kara remained with Clay Bishop's
body. Painter feared finding Safia in the same condition. Dead on the floor. But knew he had to face the
truth. She had trusted him. The deaths were all his
fault. He'd not been vigilant enough. The mission had
taken place under his nose, on his watch.

Standing to the side, he pushed the door wider.
Unblinking, he searched the cabin. Empty.

Disbelieving, he stepped cautiously over the threshold. A scent of jasmine lingered in the room. But that was all that was left of the woman who had once occupied it. There was no sign of violence. Yet the metal suitcase that housed the museum artifact was nowhere in sight.

He stood, momentarily paralyzed between concern and confusion.

A moan sounded behind him.

He turned.

"Clay's still alive!" Kara called from the passageway.

Painter stumbled back into the hall.

Kara knelt over the young man's body. She held something pinched between her fingers. "I found this in his back."

As he crossed to her, Painter noted the boy's chest moving shallowly up and down. How had he missed that? But he knew the answer. He had been too rushed, too certain of their doom.

Kara offered what she held. A small bloody dart.

"Tranquilizer," he confirmed.

He glanced back toward the open doorway. *Tranquilizers*. So they had wanted Safia alive. This was all a kidnapping. He shook his head, biting back a laugh—half in appreciation for Cassandra's cleverness, half in relief.

Safia was still alive. For now.

"We can't leave him," Kara said.

He nodded, picturing the glow of the submersible in the dark waters, waking again to the urgency. *How much time did they have?* "Stay with him."

"Where are—"

He didn't explain. He rushed down to the lower deck and searched the rooms for the other members of the party: the Dunn brothers and his partner. Like Safia's room, their cabins were empty. Were they all taken?

Below he discovered a cowering crewman, one of the galley workers, with a bloody nose. He tried to encourage the man to follow him back up, but fright kept the fellow paralyzed.

Painter did not have time to persuade him and pounded back up the stairs.

Kara had managed to get the student to sit up. He was groggy, head lolling. Unintelligible words mumbled from his mouth.

"C'mon." Painter scooped Clay under one arm, drawing him to his feet. It was like maneuvering a wet sack of cement.

Kara collected his eyeglasses from the floor. "Where are we going?"

"We have to get off this ship."

"What about the others?"

"They're all gone. Safia and the others."

Painter led the way up the stairs.

As they reached the last landing, a figure swept down toward them. He spoke rapidly in Arabic, too fast for Painter to follow.

"Captain al-Haffi," Kara said quickly in introduction.

Painter had intel on the man. He was the leader of the Desert Phantoms.

"We need more ammunition from the stockpiles in the hold," the captain said rapidly. "You must all go into hiding."

Painter blocked him. "How long can you last with what you have?"

A shrug. "Minutes only."

"You *must* keep them pinned down. They mustn't leave the ship." Painter thought quickly. He imagined the only reason the *Shabab Oman* hadn't been blasted apart already was that the demolition team was still on board. Once they were gone, nothing would stop Cassandra from detonating the mines.

Painter spotted a slumped form by the doorway. It was one of the masked gunmen, the one he had seen sprawled on the deck. He lowered Clay to the floor and crept next to the man. Perhaps he could find something on the gunman that would help. A radio or something.

Captain al-Haffi joined him. "I dragged him back here, hoping he had extra ammunition on him. Or a grenade." He said this last with thick bitterness. A single grenade would have ended the stalemate on the deck.

Painter patted the body down, ripping away the mask. The man wore a subvocalizing radio. He tugged it free and pushed the earpiece in place. Nothing. Not even static. The team had gone silent.

As he searched further, he pocketed the man's night-vision gear and discovered a thick strap around the man's chest. An EKG monitor.

"Damn it."

"What?" Kara asked.

"Lucky you never discovered that grenade," he said. "The men are rigged with status monitors. Killing them would be as good as letting them escape. Once they're gone—overboard or dead—the others will blow the ship."

"Blow the ship?" al-Haffi repeated, eyes narrowing, speaking English.

Painter quickly explained what he had spied and the implication. "We must get off this ship before the rear guard does. I saw a motorized skiff stowed behind the stern."

"It's the ship's gig," the captain confirmed.

Painter nodded. An aluminum runabout.

"But the infidels stand between us and the launch," al-Haffi argued. "We could perhaps try to go under them, through the ship's bowels, but once my men stop shooting, the others will escape."

Painter abandoned his search of the gunman and peered outside the doorway to the open deck. The fire-fight had slowed, both sides running low on ammunition, needing to make each round count.

The Phantoms were at a disadvantage. They couldn't let the gunmen escape—but neither could they kill them.

Another form of stalemate.

Or was it?

He swung around, having a sudden idea.

Before he could speak, a thunderous crash erupted from the aft deck. He glanced back outside. The lower hold's hatch had been thrown violently open, shoved under the weight of a trio of horses. The Arabians galloped and bucked out onto the windy deck, smashing into crates and tangling through rigging. Chaos ensued. Lights shattered. Night fell darker across the ship.

One of the horses, a mare, trampled directly through the gunmen's barricade. Shots were fired. A horse screamed.

Amid the confusion, a fourth horse appeared from the hold, galloping under a head of steam. The white

Arabian stallion. It flew up the lower ramp and onto the deck, hooves pounding the planks.

But this time it was not wild and unguided.

Astride the stallion's back, Omaha rose from the saddle, pistols in both hands. He aimed toward the nearest masked men and fired both guns, emptying them without mercy at almost point-blank range.

Two men fell as he rode past.

"No!" Painter called out, pushing out the door.

The barrage deafened his words.

Movement by the aft hatch revealed Coral sneaking into a sniper's post. She had a rifle on her shoulder. She took aim at the only standing gunman. The man dove for the starboard rail, intending to leap overboard.

A single rifle blast exploded with a muzzle flash.

The gunman jolted in midair as if kicked by a phantom horse. The left side of his head exploded away. His body slid across the deck, coming to rest against the rails.

Painter bit back a groan. The stalemate had finally ended. With the rear guard dead, nothing would stop Cassandra from blowing the ship.

2:10 A.M.

Cassandra checked her watch as she climbed from the Zodiac pontoon boat and back aboard the hovercraft.

The mission timetable was behind by ten minutes. Clambering onto the deck, she was met by her second.

John Kane crossed to her. He barked for two men to help haul the prone form of the museum curator aboard. The seas were getting choppy as the winds kicked up, making climbing aboard an exercise in balance and timing. Cassandra dragged up the suitcase with the artifact.

Despite the setback, they had completed their mission.

Kane stepped to her side. He was more shadow than man, dressed in black, from boots to a knit black cap. "The *Argus* radioed their all clear eight minutes ago. They await your order to detonate the mines."

"What about the demolition team?" Cassandra had heard the firefight aboard the *Shabab*. While she was racing back, sporadic gunfire had echoed over the waters. But for the past minute, there had been only silence.

He shook his head. "Status monitors just went tits up."

Dead. Cassandra pictured the men's faces. Skilled mercenaries.

Footfalls pounded across the deck from the pilot-house. "Captain Sanchez!" It was the team's radioman. He skidded to a stop on the slick surface. "We're picking up the signals again. All three!"

"From the demolition squad?" Cassandra glanced across the sea. As if noting her attention, a new barrage of gunfire erupted from the *Shabab Oman*. She glanced to Kane, who shrugged.

"We lost contact a short time," the radioman reported. "Maybe interference from the storm. But the signal's back, strong and solid."

Cassandra continued to stare across the seas toward the lights of the other ship. Her eyes narrowed, picturing the men again.

Kane stood at her shoulder. "Orders?"

She glared across the seas as a stiff rain began to pelt the deck. She barely felt its sting on her cheek. "Detonate the mines."

The radioman startled but knew better than to question. He glanced at Kane, who nodded. The man clenched a fist and ran back toward the pilothouse.

Cassandra rankled at the delay in snapping to her orders. She had noted the radioman seeking confirmation from her second. Though Cassandra had been assigned to lead this operation, these were Kane's men. And she had just condemned three of them to death.

Though Kane's face remained stoic, his eyes glass, she elaborated. "They're already dead," she said. "The new signal is false."

Kane's brows drew together. "How can you be so—"

She cut him off. "Because Painter Crowe is over there."

2:12 A.M.

Crouched with the others, Painter checked the straps snugged around the bare chests of Omaha and Danny. The dead men's heart monitors seemed to be functioning fine. The device on his own chest blinked regularly, transmitting his pulse to the hidden assault ship out there.

Danny wiped the rain from his glasses. "These things won't electrocute us if they get wet?"

"No," Painter assured him.

Everyone gathered on the stern deck: Kara, the Dunn brothers, Coral. Clay had been revived enough to stand. But the steep rolling of the ship in the higher seas kept him weaving and needing support. Steps away, the four Omani border patrol fired off rifles periodically, mimicking a continued standoff.

He didn't know how long the ruse would hold. Hopefully long enough for them to abandon ship. Captain al-Haffi had rallied the crew. The ship's motorized launch had been untied and was ready for boarding.

The other lifeboat was being swung out, ready to drop. The fifteen-man crew was now ten. With no time to spare, the dead would have to be left behind.

Painter watched the ever-growing seas from a shadowy vantage, not wanting to be spotted by the patrolling Jet Skis. Waves had climbed to twelve feet. Winds snapped sails while rain swept in bursts over the deck. The aluminum launch knocked against the stern as it hung free now.

And the full brunt of squall had yet to strike.

Painter spotted one of the black Jet Skis fly over a tall wave, hang in the air, then race down the far face. He instinctively ducked lower, but there was no need. The pilot of the Jet Ski was angling away.

Painter stood. The Jet Ski was heading *away*.

She knows . . .

Painter spun around. "To the boats!" he screamed. "Now!"

2:14 A.M.

Safia woke out of blackness to the crack of thunder. Cold rain spattered her face. She was on her back, soaked to the skin. She sat up. The world spun. Voices. Legs. Another burst of thunder. She cringed at the noise, sinking back.

She felt rocking, heaving. *I'm on a boat.*

"Tranq's wearing off," someone said behind her.

"Get her below."

Safia's head rolled to stare at the speaker. A woman. She stood a yard away, staring across the seas, some strange scope fixed to her face. She was dressed in black, wore her long ebony hair braided away from her face.

She knew the woman. Memory came flooding back. A shout from Clay, followed by a knock at her door. *Clay?* She had refused to answer, sensing something wrong. She had spent too many years at the edge of panic not to have built up a thick layer of paranoia. But it made no difference. The lock was picked as easily as if they had a key.

The woman standing before her now had been the first through the door. Something had stung Safia's neck. She reached fingers now and felt a tender spot below the angle of her chin. She had scrambled to the far side of the cabin, choking, panic narrowing her vision to a laser point. Then even this sight vanished. She had felt herself slumping but never felt herself hit the floor. The world had slipped away.

"Get her some dry clothes," the woman said.

With shock, Safia recognized the voice, the disdain, the sharp consonant strikes. The rooftop of the British Museum. *Tell me the combination.* It was the thief from London.

Safia shook her head. She was in a waking nightmare.

Before she could respond, two men hauled her to her feet. She tried to find her legs, but her toes slipped on the wet deck. Her knees were warm butter. Even holding her chin up took all her will.

Safia stared beyond the metal rail of the boat. The storm had struck. Seas rose and fell in dark hummocks, like the backs of whales, slick and smooth. A few white-caps flashed silver in the meager light. But what drew her eye, kept her head strained up, was the fiery ruin a short distance away.

All strength left her.

A ship burned atop the rough seas, masts now torches. Sailcloth fanned out in swirls of fiery ash, car-ried by the gusting winds. The hull lay gutted. All around bits of flaming flotsam decorated the seas like so many campfires.

She knew the ship. The *Shabab Oman.*

All air squeezed from her lungs. She strangled be-tween a scream and despair. The roll of the seas sud-denly sickened her. She vomited across the deck, splattering the shoes of her guards.

"Fucking Christ, man . . ." one of them cursed, yanking her cruelly.

Still, Safia's eyes remained fixed across the sea. Her throat burned.

Not again . . . not everyone I love . . .

But a part of her knew she deserved this pain, this loss. Since Tel Aviv, she had expected everything would be taken from her. Life was cruelty and sudden tragedy. There was no permanence, no safety.

Tears ran hotly down her cheeks.

Safia stared at the fiery ruin of the *Shabab Oman*. She held little hope of survivors—and even this hope was dashed with her captor's next words.

"Send back the patrol," the woman said. "Kill anything that moves."

2:22 A.M.

Painter wiped the blood from the cut above his left eye. He kicked his feet to keep himself above water as the seas heaved up and down. Rain fell heavily out of low skies, flashing with lightning. Thunder grumbled.

He glanced back to the overturned launch as it rose and fell in sync with him. Around his waist, a length of towline secured him to the skiff's bow. Immediately around him, the seas remained dark, as if he were floating in oil. But farther out, fires sputtered in the rolling seas, appearing and disappearing. And in the center, the fiery bulk of the *Shabab Oman* loomed, half sunk, burning down to the waterline.

Swiping blood and rain from his eyes, Painter searched the waters for any threat. A vague worry about sharks fluttered across his mind. Especially with the blood. He hoped the squall would keep such predators deep.

But Painter watched for other predators.

He didn't have long to wait.

Lit by the many fires, a Jet Ski hoved into view, circling wide.

Painter reached up and slipped the night-vision goggles over his eyes. He sank lower, minimizing his silhouette. The world dissolved to greens and whites. Fires appeared as blindingly bright glows, while the seas took on a silvery aquamarine sheen. He focused on the Jet Ski. Through the scope, the ski now shone starkly, its shaded headlamp as bright as the fires. He toggled the magnification feature. A pilot hunched in front. Behind him, his passenger manned the mounted assault rifle, capable of firing a hundred rounds a minute.

With the goggles in place, Painter easily spotted two other Jet Skis circling the debris field. They were starting wide and circling inward. Somewhere beyond the bulk of the fiery ship, the rattle of gunfire erupted. A scream accompanied it, but it ended immediately; the gunfire did not.

The purpose of these scavengers was plain.

No survivors. No witnesses.

Painter swam back to his overturned launch, a cork in the rough seas. Once near the skiff, he dove down and under it. The night-vision goggles were watertight. It was strange how bright the seas were through the scope. He spotted the many legs dangling from beneath the capsized skiff.

Maneuvering up through them, he surfaced under the runabout. Even with the night-vision scope, details were blurry. Figures clung to gunwales and bolted aluminum seats. Eight in all. Hidden beneath the launch. The air had already staled with their fear.

Kara and the Dunn brothers helped keep Clay Bishop in place. The grad student seemed mostly recovered. Captain al-Haffi took a position near the launch's windshield. Like his two men, he had stripped out of his desert cloak and wore only a loincloth. The fate of the fourth Phantom remained unknown.

The explosion had occurred just as the launch had hit the water. The concussive force had tossed them away, toppling the small runabout. All bore minor injuries. Afterward, amid the confusion, Painter and Coral had herded the others under the launch as debris rained down. It also offered good cover from searching eyes.

Coral whispered at his ear, "Did she send a cleanup crew?"

Painter nodded. "We'll have to hope the storm shortens their search."

A whine drew nearer, waning and ebbing as the launch and its hidden passengers rose and fell with the waves. Finally, the noise sharpened. The ski must have angled into the trough with them.

Painter had a bad feeling.

"Everyone underwater!" he warned. "For a count of thirty!"

He waited to make sure everyone obeyed. Coral was the last to vanish. Painter took a deep breath, then—

Gunfire rattled against the launch's aluminum side. Deafening. Golf-ball-size hail on a tin roof. But it wasn't hail. At such close range, a few rounds perforated the double hull of the runabout.

Painter dove down. A pair of stray bullets sizzled through the water. He watched the others holding themselves beneath the skiff, arms extended upward, hands clutching. Painter hoped the speed of the bullets would be dulled by the launch's double hull and impact with the water.

Painter watched one of the trajectories slam past his shoulder.

He held his breath clenched until the barrage stopped, then rose up. The whine of the Jet Ski still sounded near. Thunder caused the aluminum hull to reverberate like a struck bell.

Omaha popped up beside him, followed by the others as their need for air overwhelmed them. No one spoke. They all listened to the nearby puttering engine. Everyone prepared themselves to dive again if necessary.

The Jet Ski whined closer, bumping against the side of the skiff.

If they tried to turn it over . . . used a grenade . . .

A large swell lifted the boat and its hidden passengers. The Jet Ski bumped harder, jostled by the storm surge. A loud curse erupted from outside. The engine whined louder and began to pull away.

"We could commandeer that Jet Ski," Omaha whispered at him, nose to nose. "The two of us. We've still got a couple pistols between us."

Painter frowned at him. "And then what? You don't think they'd miss one of their skis? There's a main boat out there, something fast. They'd be upon us in a heartbeat."

"You're not getting it," Omaha pressed. "I wasn't talkin' about leaving. I'm talking about taking the damn thing back to where it came from. Going in undercover. To rescue Safia."

Painter had to grant the man had balls. Too bad he didn't have the brains to go with them. "These aren't amateurs," he snapped. "You're going in blind. All the advantage is theirs."

"Who gives a damn about the odds? It's Safia's life we're talking about."

Painter shook his head. "You wouldn't get within a hundred yards of the main boat before you were discovered and blown away."

Omaha refused to back down. "If you won't go, I'll take my brother."

Painter made to grab for him, but Omaha shoved his hand away.

"I'm not leaving her." Omaha turned his back and swam to Danny.

Painter recognized the pain in the other's voice, the fury. He felt the same. Safia's kidnapping was his fault, his responsibility. A part of him wanted to lash out, to charge in, to risk all.

But it was also a futile course. He knew this.

Omaha had his pistol out.

Painter could not stop him—but he knew who could. He turned and grabbed another person's arm. "I care for her," he said sharply.

Kara tried to free her arm, but Painter held tight. "What are you talking about?" she asked.

"Your question earlier . . . in your cabin. I *care* about Safia." It was hard to admit aloud, but he had no choice but to recognize the truth. He did indeed care. While maybe it was not love . . . not yet . . . he was willing to see where it would lead. This surprised him as much as it seemed to surprise Kara.

"I do," Painter pressed. "And I'll get her back—but not this way." He nodded toward Omaha. "Not *his* way. He's more likely to get her killed. She's safe right now. Safer than we are. We need to survive for her sake. All of us. If there's to be any hope of a *real* rescue for her."

Kara listened. Ever the consummate corporate leader, she did not delay her decision. She swung to Omaha. "Put the bloody gun away, Indiana."

Beyond the aluminum hull, the predatory Jet Ski suddenly screamed, its engine Dopplering up. It was heading off.

Omaha glanced in its direction—then swore and shoved the pistol away.

"We'll find her," Painter said, but he doubted the other man heard. And perhaps it was just as well. As much as he had blustered, he didn't know if it was a promise he could keep. He was still shaken from the assault, the defeat. From the outset, Cassandra had been a step ahead of him.

He needed to clear his head.

"I'm going to keep watch. Make sure they leave."

He dove back down and kicked free of the launch. His thoughts remained on Cassandra's skill at anticipating their moves. How had she managed that? A worry had seeded in his chest. Was there a traitor among them?

2:45 A.M.

Omaha clung to the launch's gunwale, rising and falling with the waves. He hated waiting in the dark. He heard the others' breathing. No one spoke. All remained lost in their own worries.

His grip tightened on the aluminum frame as the launch climbed another wave, taking them all up with it. All but one. *Safia.*

Why had he listened to Painter? He should have tried to commandeer the Jet Ski. To hell with what anyone thought. Pressure built in his throat, tightening his breath. He clamped it down, unsure if he let it loose whether it would come out as a sob or a scream. In the dark, the past came rolling up out of the depths of the sea.

He had walked away from her.

After Tel Aviv, something had died in Safia, taking all love with it. She had retreated to London. He had tried to stay with her, but his career, his passion, lay elsewhere. Each time he returned, more and more of her was gone. She was wasting away inside. He found himself dreading the return to London from the lost corners of the world. He felt trapped. Soon his visits grew fewer and fewer. She didn't notice or complain. That hurt the most.

When did it end, when did love become dust and sand?

He couldn't say. It was well before he finally admitted defeat and asked for his grandmother's ring back. It had been over a long, cold dinner. Neither had spoken. Both knew. Their silence said more than his faltering attempt to explain.

Ultimately she had only nodded and removed the ring. It came off easily. She placed it in his palm, then looked into his eyes. There was no sorrow, only relief.

That's when he walked away.

The others stirred as Painter splashed up to them. He rose among them with a sigh of breath. "I think we're clear. There's been no sign of the Jet Skis for the past ten minutes."

Relief murmured among the others.

"We should strike for shore. We're too exposed out here."

In the dark, Omaha noted the man's slight Brooklyn accent. He hadn't noticed it before. It grated with each word now. Painter's instructions sounded too much like commands. Military background. Officer training.

"There are two oars secured in oarlocks on either side of the boat. We'll need them to overturn the launch." He sidled among them and showed them how to free the oars.

Omaha found one oar shoved into his hand.

"We'll need to split into two groups. One group to heave weight down on the port side, the others to use the oars to prop up the starboard. We should be able to flip it. But first I'm going to detach the outboard. It was strafed, shot, and now's leaking oil."

After a final few coordinations, everyone ducked down and out.

Rain spattered out of the dark skies. The winds had died to faltering gusts. After the time he'd spent hiding under the launch, the night seemed brighter to Omaha. Lightning flickered among the clouds, illuminating patches of ocean. A few fires still floated atop the water. There was no sign of the *Shabab Oman*.

Omaha spun around a bit, searching. Painter swam to the stern of the launch and fought to free the engine. Omaha considered going to help, but instead simply watched the man's struggle with the locking pin.

After a few tugs, Painter finally freed the engine. It dropped into the sea. His eyes found Omaha. "Let's get this baby flipped."

It wasn't as easy as Painter had described. It took four attempts until they put everyone on one side, leaning their weight down. Painter and Omaha, each armed with an oar, levered the starboard side up. They also timed the maneuver with the roll of a wave. But finally the launch flipped back upright, half filled with water.

They climbed aboard and bailed the craft. Omaha fit the oars into place.

"It's still filling with water," Kara said as the water level inside the launch began to rise again under all their weight.

"Bullet holes," Danny said, feeling through the water.

"Keep bailing," Painter said, again with that bite of command. "We'll alternate between rowing and bailing. It's a long haul to shore."

"Be warned," Captain al-Haffi said, bare-chested but unabashed. "The currents here are treacherous. We must watch for reefs and rocks."

Painter nodded and waved Coral toward the prow.

Omaha stared at the few burning bits of flotsam, then back the other way. The coast was barely discernible, a slightly darker bank of cloud. Flashes of lightning revealed how far they had drifted.

Painter also stared around the boat. But it wasn't sharks or coastline that concerned him. The worry was plain in the set of his lips. Somewhere out there lurked the murderous men who had kidnapped Safia. But did he fear for her safety or his own skin?

Painter's earlier words repeated in Omaha's head.

I care for her . . . for Safia.

Omaha felt a burst of anger warm the chill from his wet clothes. Was he lying? Omaha clenched both fists on the two oars and set his back. He began to row. Painter, at the stern, glanced over to him. Cold eyes, the glass of the night-vision goggles, studied him. What did they know about the man? He had much to account for, much to explain.

The muscles of Omaha's jaw ached from clenching too long.

I care for her.

As he rowed, Omaha wasn't sure what made him more angry.

If the man was lying . . . or telling the truth.

3:47 A.M.

An hour later, Painter waded through the waist-high water, dragging the towline over his shoulder. The beach stretched silvery before him, framed in tumbled rocky cliffs. The rest of the coastline was dark, except for a few meager lights to the far north. A small village. The immediate vicinity seemed deserted. Still, he kept a wary eye. He had given Coral the night-vision goggles to keep a watch from the launch.

As he continued forward, his shoes dug deep into the rocky sand. His thighs burned from the effort. His shoulders ached from his shift at the oars. Waves helped push him toward the waiting shore.

Only a little farther . . .

At least the rain had stopped.

He leaned his shoulder into the line and hauled the trailing boat toward solid ground. Behind him, Danny worked the oars while Painter guided the boat around the rocks. At last, the beach opened up ahead, a clear shot.

"Pull hard!" Painter called back to Danny.

Slack grew in the line as Danny obeyed. The launch leaped forward with a sweep of oars. Painter fought the water, climbing out of the waves, knee-deep. He slogged forward and to the side.

The launch surfed a final wave and passed to Painter's right. He ducked to avoid being hit. "Sorry!" Danny called to him, dragging in the oars.

The boat's prow ground into the sand with a screech of aluminum. The wave receded, leaving the boat beached.

Painter crawled and kicked out of the water, gaining his feet.

The eight men and women clambered from the launch. Coral helped Kara, while Danny, Omaha, and Clay half fell out of the boat. Only the three Desert Phantoms—Captain al-Haffi and his two men—remained on their feet, scanning the beach.

Painter lumbered farther out of the lapping water, sodden, limbs heavy. He crossed beyond the tide line in the sand. Winded, he turned to see how the others were faring with the launch. They'd have to hide the boat, drag it somewhere, or sink it.

A shadow loomed behind him. He failed to see the raised fist. He was struck in the face. Too weak, he simply fell backward onto his rear.

"Omaha!" Kara called out.

Painter now recognized his attacker. Omaha stood over him.

"What are you—" Before Painter could finish, the man was on him, shoving him back into the sand, one hand on his throat, the other going for another punch.

"You goddamn son of a bitch!"

Before the fist could land, hands grabbed Omaha's shoulder, shirt. He was tugged backward. He fought, twisting, but Coral had a fistful of the man's collar. She was strong. Cotton ripped along the neckline.

Painter took the opportunity to scramble backward. His left eye wept from the first punch.

"Let me go!" Omaha bellowed.

Coral threw him bodily into the sand.

Kara circled to his other side. "Omaha! What the hell are you doing?"

He sat up, red-faced. "That bastard knows more than he's been telling us." He jerked a thumb at Coral. "Him and his Amazon sidekick."

Even his brother tried to calm him. "Omaha, this isn't the time to be—"

Omaha shoved up to his knees, panting, spittle flying. "Goddamn right it's time! We followed the bastard this far. I want answers before we move one step further." He heaved to his feet, swaying a bit.

Painter gained his feet with an arm from Coral.

The others all faced them, a line drawn in the sand between them.

Kara stood in the center, glancing at each group. She held up a hand, seeming to settle on a side. She faced Painter. "You said you had a plan. Let's start there."

Painter took a deep breath and nodded. "Salalah. That's where they'll be taking Safia. Where we have to go next."

Omaha called out, "How do you know that? Why are you so sure? They could be taking her anywhere

. . . for ransom, to sell the artifact. Who the hell knows where?"

"I know," Painter said coolly. He let silence stretch before speaking again. "This was no random raiding party that attacked us. They were focused, purposeful in their assault. They whisked in and grabbed Safia *and* the iron heart. They knew what they were going after and who knew the most about it."

"Why?" asked Kara, clipping some outburst from Omaha with a thrust of an arm. "What do they want?"

Painter stepped forward. "What we wanted. Some clue to the true location of the lost city of Ubar."

Omaha swore under his breath. The others simply stared.

Kara shook her head. "You haven't answered my question." Her tone darkened. "*What do they want? What do they seek to gain by finding Ubar?*"

Painter licked his lips.

"This is bullshit!" Omaha growled. He shoved past Kara, fast.

Painter stood his ground, holding Coral back with a hand signal. He would not be punched again.

Omaha lifted his arm. Metal glinted in the meager light. A pistol pointed at Painter's head. "You've been yanking our chains long enough. Answer the woman's question. What the hell's going on?"

"Omaha," Kara warned, but there was not much energy in her voice.

Coral sidled to the side, positioning to go for Omaha's flank. Painter again signaled her to hold.

Omaha punched the gun at him harder. "Answer me! What goddamn game is going on here? Who do you really work for?"

Painter had no choice but to come clean. He needed the group's cooperation. If there was to be any hope of stopping Cassandra, of rescuing Safia, he would need their help. He couldn't do it with Coral alone.

"I work for the U.S. Department of Defense," he finally admitted. "Specifically DARPA. The research-and-development arm of the DOD."

Omaha shook his head. "Fucking great. The military? What does any of this have to do with them? We're an archaeological expedition."

Kara answered before Painter could. "The explosion at the museum."

Omaha glanced at her, then back at Painter.

He nodded. "She's right. It was no ordinary blast. Residual radiation pointed to an extraordinary possibility." All eyes were on him, except Coral's, who still had her full attention on Omaha and the gun. "There is a high probability that the exploded meteorite contained some form of antimatter."

Omaha let out an explosive sound of derision, as if he had been holding it all along. "*Antimatter* . . . what a load of bullshit! Who do you take us for?"

Coral spoke at his side, matter-of-fact, professional. "Dr. Dunn, he is telling you the truth. We tested the blast zone ourselves, detecting Z-bozons and gluons, decay particles from an antimatter/matter interaction."

Omaha frowned, less sure.

"I know it sounds preposterous," Painter said. "But if you'll lower your gun, I'll explain."

Omaha steadied the pistol instead. "So far this is all that's kept you talking."

Painter sighed. *It was worth the try.* "Have it your way, then."

With the gun pointed at his face, he gave a brief overview: of the Tunguska explosion in Russia in 1908, of the unique gamma radiation found both there and at the British Museum, of the plasma characteristics of the explosion, and how evidence hinted that somewhere out in the deserts of Oman lay a possible source of antimatter, preserved in some unknown fashion to make it stable and unreactive while in the presence of matter.

"Though now it may be destabilizing," Painter finished. "That may be why the meteor exploded at the museum. And it may happen here, too. Time is critical.

Now may be the only time we can discover and preserve this source of unlimited power."

Kara frowned. "And what does the United States government plan on doing with such a limitless source of power?"

Painter read the suspicion in her eyes. "Safeguard it for now. That's the immediate and primary goal. To protect it from those who would abuse it. If this power should fall into the wrong hands . . ."

Silence lingered as his words died away. They all knew borders no longer divided the world so much as ideologies. Though it was undeclared, there was a new world war being waged, where fundamental decency and respect for human rights were under assault by forces of intolerance, despotism, and blind fervor. And while its battles were sometimes waged in plain sight—in New York City, in Iraq—its greater struggle was carried on invisibly, fought in secret, its heroes unknown, its villains hidden.

Willing or not, the group assembled here on the beach had been drafted into this war.

Kara finally spoke. "And this other group. Safia's kidnappers. They're the same ones who broke into the British Museum."

Painter nodded. "I believe so."

"Who are they?" Omaha still held the pistol at him.

"I don't know . . . not for sure."

"Bullshit!"

Painter held up a hand. "All I know for certain is who leads the team. A partner I once worked with, a mole planted in DARPA." He was too exhausted to hide his anger. "Her name is Cassandra Sanchez. I never discovered who she worked for. A foreign power. Terrorists. A black-market group. All I know is that they are well funded, organized, and cold-blooded in their methods."

Omaha scoffed, "And you and your partner are the warm, fuzzy types."

"We don't kill innocent people."

"No, you're fucking *worse!*" he spat. "You let others do your dirty work. You knew we were walking into a possible shitstorm but kept your mouths closed. If we had known before now, we might've been better prepared. We might have stopped Safia's abduction."

Painter had no comeback. The man was right. He'd been caught off guard, jeopardizing the mission and their lives.

Distracted by his own guilt, he failed to respond in time. Omaha lunged and pressed the pistol's barrel against his forehead, knocking him back a step. "You bastard . . . this is all your fault!"

He heard the pain and anguish in Omaha's voice. The man was beyond reason. Anger built in Painter's chest. He was cold, sore, and tired of having a gun waved in his face. He didn't know if he'd have to take Omaha out.

Coral waited, tense.

Support came from an unlikely source.

A thunder of hooves suddenly broke across the beach. All eyes turned, even Omaha's. He stepped back and finally lowered the gun.

"Goddamn . . ." he muttered.

Across the sand, an amazing sight galloped. A white stallion, mane flying, hooves casting up gouts of sand. It was the horse from the *Shabab Oman*.

The stallion raced toward them, perhaps drawn by their raised voices. It must have swum to shore after the explosion. It slammed to a stop a few yards from them, huffing white into the cool night air, heated. It tossed its head.

"I can't believe it got away," Omaha said.

"Horses are excellent swimmers," Kara scolded, but she couldn't keep the awe from her voice.

One of the Desert Phantoms slowly approached the horse, palm out, whispering in Arabic. It shivered but allowed the approach. Exhausted, frightened, needing reassurance.

The sudden arrival of the horse cut the tension. Omaha stared down at his gun as if unsure how it had gotten into his fist.

Kara stepped forward and faced Painter. "I think it's time we stopped arguing. Casting blame. We all had our reasons for coming out here. Hidden agendas." She glanced back to Omaha, who would not meet her eye. Painter could guess the man's agenda. It was plain from the way he'd been looking at Safia, his furious anger a moment ago. He was still in love.

"From here," Kara continued, "we must figure out what we're going to do to save Safia. That's the priority." She turned to Painter. "What do we do?"

Painter nodded. His left eye ached with the motion. "The others think we're dead. That gives us an advantage we'd best keep. We also know where they're heading. We have to reach Salalah as quickly as possible. That means crossing almost three hundred miles."

Kara stared toward the lights of the distant village. "If I could reach a phone, I'm sure I could get the sultan to—"

"No," he cut her off. "No one must know we're alive. Not even the Omani government. Any word, anywhere, that we're still alive jeopardizes our thin advantage. Cassandra's group managed to abduct Safia through their advantage of surprise. We can win her back the same way."

"But with the sultan's help, Salalah could be locked down and searched."

"Cassandra's group has already proven too damn resourceful. They've brought in significant manpower and weapons. That couldn't have happened without resources in the government."

"And if we come out of hiding, word would reach the kidnappers," Omaha mumbled. He had holstered the pistol in his waistband and rubbed his knuckles. His angry outburst seemed to have steadied the man. "The kidnappers would be gone before any action could be taken. We'd lose Safia."

"Exactly."

"Then what do we do?" Kara asked.

"We find transportation."

Captain al-Haffi stepped forward. Painter was unsure how the man would feel about deceiving his own government, keeping them in the dark, but then again, when out in the field, the Desert Phantoms acted with full independence. He nodded to Painter. "I'll send one of my men over to the village. They won't arouse suspicion."

The captain must have read something in Painter's face, some question about why he was so readily

helping the team. "They killed one of my men. Kalil.
He was my wife's cousin."

Painter nodded with sympathy. "May Allah carry
him home." He knew there was no stronger loyalty
than that to the members of one's own tribe and
family.

With a half bow of thanks, Captain al-Haffi waved to
the taller of his two men, a true giant of a man, named
Barak. They spoke rapidly in Arabic. Barak nodded
and began to step away.

Kara stopped him. "How are you going to get a
truck with no money?"

Barak answered her in English, "Allah helps those
who help themselves."

"You're going to steal one?"

"Borrow. It is tradition among our desert tribes. A
man may borrow what he needs. Stealing is a crime."

With this little bit of wisdom, the man headed out
toward the distant lights at a steady jog, disappearing
into the night like a true phantom.

"Barak will not fail us," Captain al-Haffi assured
them. "He will find a vehicle large enough to carry all
of us . . . and the horse."

Painter glanced back along the rocky shore. The remaining Phantom, a taciturn young man named Sharif,
led the stallion with a length of towline.

"Why bring the horse?" Painter asked, concerned about the exposure of a large vehicle. "There's good grazing here, and someone would find it."

Captain al-Haffi answered, "We have little money. And the horse may be bartered, sold. Used as transportation if needed. It is also a cover for us to be traveling to Salalah. The horse farms there are well known. It will lessen suspicion if we bring the stallion along on our journey. And besides, white is good luck." This last was said with deadly seriousness. Luck among the folks of Arabia was as important as a roof over one's head.

They made a brief camp. While Omaha and Painter beached the launch behind some rocks to hide it, the others built a fire out of driftwood, sheltering it within the lee of a tumbled section of cliff. Hidden, the tiny pyre would be hard to spot, and they all needed its warmth and light.

Forty minutes later, the grinding of gears announced the arrival of their transportation. Headlights rounded a bend in the coastal road. A flatbed truck rolled up. It was an old International 4900, painted yellow, scarred with rust. Its bed was framed in wooden fencing with a drop gate behind.

Barak hopped out.

"I see you found something to *borrow*," Kara said.

He shrugged.

They put out the fire. Barak had also managed to *borrow* some clothes: robes and cloaks. They quickly dressed, concealing their Western wear.

Once ready, Captain al-Haffi and his men took the truck's cab, in case they were stopped. The others clambered into the back. It took blindfolding the horse to get it to walk up the drop gate into the flatbed. They tied the Arabian near the front cab. Then Painter and the others huddled near the back.

As the truck bounced onto the coastal road, Painter studied the stallion. *White is good luck.* Painter hoped so . . . they would need every bit of it.

PART THREE

Tombs

ᚷᛟᛒᚢᚷ

11
Marooned

ᛒᛡ)∘∘ᚺᛢᚻ

December 3, 12:22 P.M.
Salalah

Safia woke in a cell, disoriented and nauseated. The dark room spun and jittered as she moved her head. A groan bubbled up from her core. A high barred window let in stabbing shafts of light. Too bright, searing.

A wave of queasiness rolled over her.

She turned on her side and dragged her head, too heavy for her shoulders, over the edge of the cot. Her stomach clenched, then clenched again. Nothing. Still, she tasted bile as she collapsed back down.

She took deep breaths, and slowly the walls stopped their spin.

She became aware of the sweat covering her body, pasting the thin cotton shift to her legs and chest. The heat stifled. Her lips felt cracked, parched. How long had she been drugged? She remembered the man with the needle. Cold, tall, dressed in black. He had forced her to change out of her wet clothes aboard the boat and into the khaki shift.

Carefully, Safia stared around her. The room was stone walls, plank flooring. It stank of fried onions and dirty feet. The cot was the only furnishing. A single door of stout oak stood closed. No doubt locked.

She lay unmoving for several more minutes. Her mind floated, half deadened by the aftereffects of the drug they had given her. Still, deep inside her, panic coiled around her heart. She was alone, captured. The others dead. She pictured flames in the night, reflecting off storm-swept water. The memory had burned into her like a camera flash in the dark. All red, painful, too bright to blink away. Her breathing tightened, throat closed down. She wanted to cry but couldn't. If she started, she would never stop.

Finally, she pushed up and rolled her feet to the floor. It was not with any determination beyond the heavy pressure in her bladder. Biological need, a reminder that she lived. She stood, unsteady, a hand against the wall. The stones were welcoming cool.

She stared up at the barred window. From the heat, the angle of the sun, it had to be close to midday. But which day? Where was she? She smelled the sea and the sand. Still in Arabia, she was sure. She crossed the room. The burning in her bladder sharpened.

She hobbled to the door, lifted an arm. Would they merely drug her again? She fingered the purple bruise at the angle of her left arm, where the needle had dug in. She had no choice. Need outweighed caution. She pounded on the door and called out hoarsely, "Hello! Can anyone hear me?" She repeated her words in Arabic.

No one answered.

She knocked harder, stinging her knuckles, an ache flaring between her shoulder blades. She was weak, dehydrated. Had they left her here to die?

Finally, footsteps responded. A heavy bar scraped against wood. The door swung open. She found herself facing the same man as before. He stood a half a foot taller than she, looming in a black shirt and scuffed, faded jeans. She was surprised to find his head shaved. She didn't remember that. No, he had been wearing a black cap then. The only hair on his head were his dark eyebrows and a small tuft at his chin. But she did not forget those eyes, blue and cold, unreadable, passionless. A shark's eyes.

She shivered as he stared at her, the heat suddenly gone from the room.

"You're up," he said. "Come with me."

She heard a trace of an Aussie accent, but one blunted by years away from home. "Where . . . I have to use the lavatory."

He frowned at her and strode away. "Follow me."

He led her to a small hall bath. It had a squat toilet, curtainless shower, and a small stained washbasin with a leaking tap. Safia ducked inside. She reached a hand to the door, unsure if she would be allowed privacy.

"Don't be long," he said, pulling the door the rest of the way shut.

Alone, she searched the room for some weapon, some means of escape. Again the lone window was barred. But she could at least see out of this one. She hurried forward and stared out at the small township below, nestled against the sea. Palm trees and white buildings spread between her and the water. Off to the left, a flutter of rainbow-colored tarps and awnings marked off a market souk. And in the distance, green patches beyond the city defined banana, coconut, sugarcane, and papaya plantations.

She knew this place.

The Garden City of Oman.

Salalah.

It was the capital city of the Dhofar Province, the original destination of the *Shabab Oman*. It was a lush region, green, with waterfalls and rivers feeding the pastures. Only in this section of Oman did the monsoon winds bless the land with sweeps of rain, a regular light drizzle, and an almost continual mist over the nearby coastal mountains. It was a weather system like no other in the Gulf, one that allowed for the growth of the rare frankincense tree, a source of great wealth in ancient times. The riches here had led to the founding of the legendary cities of Sumharam, Al-Balid, and lastly, the lost city of Ubar.

Why had her kidnappers taken her here?

She crossed to the toilet and quickly relieved herself. Afterward she washed her hands and stared at her reflection in the mirror. She appeared a shadow of herself, gaunt, tense, hollow-eyed.

But she was alive.

A knock on the door. " 'Bout done in there?"

With no other recourse, Safia stepped back to the door and opened it.

The man nodded. "This way."

He strode off, not even glancing back, so sure of his control of the situation. Safia followed. She had no other choice, but her legs dragged, leaden with despair.

She was marched down a short flight of stairs, along another hall. Other men, hard-eyed, rifles over shoulders, lounged behind doorways or stood guard. They finally reached a tall door.

The man knocked and pushed open the door.

Safia found a room furnished spartanly: a threadbare rug with the color long bleached out of it by the sun, a single sofa, two stiff wooden chairs. A pair of fans buzzed, stirring the air. A table to the side was weighted down by an array of weapons, electronic equipment, and a laptop computer. A cable trailed out the neighboring window to a palm-size satellite dish pointed at the sky.

"That'll be all, Kane," the woman said, stepping away from the computer.

"Captain." The man nodded and left, closing the door.

Safia considered lunging for one of the guns on the table, but knew she would not get within a step of them. She was too weak, still wobbly.

The woman turned to her. She wore black slacks, a gray T-shirt, and over that, a loose long-sleeved shirt, unbuttoned, cuffs rolled to elbows. Safia noted the black butt of a holstered pistol at her side.

"Please sit," she instructed, and pointed to one of the wooden chairs.

Safia moved slowly, but obeyed.

The woman remained standing, pacing behind the sofa. "Dr. al-Maaz, it seems your reputation as an expert in the antiquities of the region has come to the attention of my superiors."

Safia barely understood her words. She found herself staring at the woman's face, her black hair, her lips. This was the woman who had tried to kill her in the British Museum, orchestrated the death of Ryan Fleming, murdered all her friends last night. Faces, images shuffled through her mind, distracting her from the woman's words.

"Are you listening, Dr. al-Maaz?"

She couldn't answer. She searched for evil in the woman, for the capability for such cruelty and savagery. Some mark, some scar, some understanding. There was nothing. How could that be?

A heavy sigh escaped the woman. She crossed around the sofa and sat down, leaning forward, elbows on her knees. "Painter Crowe," she said.

The unexpected name startled Safia, a flash of anger burning through her.

"Painter . . . he was my partner."

Shock and disbelief rattled Safia. *No* . . .

"I see I have your attention." The smallest smile of satisfaction shadowed her lips. "You should know the truth. Painter Crowe was using you. All of you. Needlessly putting you in harm's way. Keeping secrets."

"You're lying," she finally croaked out past her parched lips.

The woman lounged back into the sofa. "I have no need to lie. Unlike Painter, I'll tell you the truth. What you stumbled into, discovered by misfortune and chance, holds the possible key to untold power."

"I don't know what you're talking about."

"I'm talking about *antimatter*."

Safia frowned at the impossibility of what she was hearing. The woman continued explaining about the explosion at the museum, radiation signatures, the search for the primary source of some stable form of antimatter. Despite her wish to deny it all, much of it began to make sense. Certain statements by Painter, some of his gear, the pressure by the U.S. government.

"The meteor fragment that exploded at the museum," the woman continued. "It was said to guard the true gates of the lost city of Ubar. It is there that you will lead us."

She shook her head, more in denial. "This is all preposterous."

The woman stared a moment longer, stood, and walked across the room. She dragged something from under the table and grabbed a device from among the stacked equipment. As she returned, Safia recognized her own suitcase.

The woman flipped the trunk's clasps and swung open the lid. The iron heart lay nestled within molded black Styrofoam. It glowed ruddy in the bright sunlight. "This is the artifact you discovered. Inside a statue dating back to 200 B.C. With the name of Ubar written on its surface."

Safia slowly nodded, surprised at the woman's intimate knowledge. She seemed to know everything about her.

The woman leaned down and passed the handheld device over the artifact. The device crackled and popped, sounding not unlike a Geiger counter. "It gives off an extremely low-level radiation signature. Barely detectable. But it's the same as the exploded meteor. Did Painter ever tell you that?"

Safia remembered Painter testing the artifact with a similar device. Could it be true? Again despair settled to the pit of her stomach, a cold stone.

"We need you to continue your work for us," the woman said, resealing the trunk. "To guide us to the lost gates of Ubar."

Safia stared at the closed trunk. All the bloodshed, all the deaths . . . all tied to her discovery. Again. "I won't," she mumbled.

"You will, or you will die."

Safia shook her head and shrugged. She didn't care. All that she loved had been taken from her. By this woman. She would never help.

"We will proceed with or without you. There are other experts in your field. And I can make your last hours *very* unpleasant if you refuse."

This actually drew a weak laugh from her. *Unpleasant?* After all she had been through . . . Safia lifted her head and fully met the woman's eyes for the first time, a place she had feared staring into until now. They weren't cold like those of the man who had led her here. They sparked with a deep-seated anger . . . but also confusion. A frown thinned the woman's lips.

"Do what you have to," Safia said, realizing the power in her own despair. This woman could not touch her, harm her. They had taken too much last night. Left nothing that could threaten her. Both of them knew this truth at the same moment.

A flash of worry showed in the pinch of the other's eyebrows.

She needs me, Safia knew with certainty. The woman had lied about having access to some other expert. She *can't* get someone else. Steel flowed through Safia, firming her resolve, firing away the last of her drug-induced lassitude.

Once before, a woman had walked out of nowhere and into her life, a bomb strapped to her chest, passionate with religious fervor, ending lives without mercy. All aimed at Safia.

That woman had died in the explosion back in Tel Aviv. Afterward, Safia had never been able to confront her, to hold her responsible. Instead, she took the guilt upon herself. But it was even more than that. Safia had never been able to exact revenge for the deaths laid at her feet, to purge her guilt.

That was no longer true.

She faced her captor, never breaking eye contact.

She remembered wishing she could've stopped that woman in Tel Aviv, met her earlier, somehow prevented the explosion, the deaths. Could it be true about a source of antimatter? She pictured the explosion at the British Museum, the aftermath. What would someone like this woman do with such power? How many more would die?

Safia could not let that happen. "What is your name?"

The question startled her captor. The reaction caused a flash of pleasure to erupt in Safia, as bright as the sun, painful but satisfying.

"You said you'd tell me the truth."

The woman frowned, but answered slowly. "Cassandra Sanchez."

"What will you have me do, *Cassandra*?" Safia enjoyed the look of irritation in the other at the informal use of her name. "If I cooperate."

The woman stood, anger flashing. "In an hour, we will leave for the tomb of Imran. Where the heart's statue was found. Where you were planning to head with the others. That's where we'll start."

Safia stood. "One last question."

The woman stared at her quizzically.

"Who do you work for? Tell me that and I'll cooperate."

Before answering, the woman crossed to the door, opened it, and waved for her man Kane to collect the prisoner. She spoke from the doorway.

"I work for the U.S. government."

1:01 P.M.

Cassandra waited until the museum curator had left and the door had been closed. She kicked a palm-frond-woven wastepaper basket across the room, scattering its contents across the plank floor. A Pepsi can rattled and rolled to a stop by the sofa. *Fucking bitch . . .*

She had to restrain herself from further outbursts, bottling back her anger. The woman had seemed broken. Cassandra had never imagined her to be so cunning there at the end. She had seen the shift in the other's eyes, a glacial slide of power from her over to her prisoner. She had been unable to stop it. How had that happened?

She clenched her hands into fists, then forced her fingers to relax and shook her arms. "Bitch . . ." she mumbled to the room. But at least the prisoner was going to cooperate. It was a victory with which she would have to be satisfied. The Minister would be pleased.

Still, bile churned in her stomach, keeping her mood sour. The curator had more strength in her than Cassandra had imagined. She began to understand Painter's interest in the woman.

Painter . . .

Cassandra heaved out a perturbed sigh. His body had never been found. It left her feeling unmoored. If only—

A knock at the door interrupted her thoughts. John Kane pushed inside before she could even turn. Irritation flashed at his blatant invasion of her privacy, his lack of respect.

"Lunch was brought up to the prisoner," he said. "She'll be ready at fourteen hundred."

Cassandra crossed to the table of electronic gear. "How did the subdermal function?"

"Registering perfectly. A good, strong tracking signal."

Last night, after the prisoner had been drugged, they had implanted a subdermal microtransceiver between her shoulder blades. The same device Cassandra was supposed to have implanted on Zhang back in the States. Cassandra found it especially gratifying to use Painter's own design in this matter. The microtransceiver would act as an electronic leash on the prisoner when they were on the streets. They would be able to track the curator for a ten-mile radius. Any attempt at escape would be quashed.

"Very good," she said. "See that your men are all ready."

"They are." Kane bristled at her command, but his neck was also on the line if this mission failed.

"Any word from local authorities about the ship's explosion last night?"

"CNN is blaming it on unknown terrorists." He snorted at this last.

"What about survivors? Bodies?"

"Definitely no survivors. Salvage is just beginning to determine cause and body count."

She nodded. "Okay, get your men ready. You're dismissed."

Rolling his eyes a bit, he swung away and left the room, pushing the door behind him, but he didn't close it completely. She had to cross over and shove it the rest of the way. The latch clicked.

Just keep needling, Kane . . . payback's a bitch.

Sighing her frustration, she moved back to the sofa. She sat down, on the edge. *No survivors.* She pictured Painter, remembering the first time he had succumbed to her subtle advances, her carefully orchestrated seduction. Their first kiss. He had tasted sweet, of the wine they'd had at dinner. His arms around her. His lips . . . his hands slowly sliding up the curve of her hip.

She touched herself where his palm had come to a rest and leaned back into the sofa, less resolved than a moment ago. She felt more anger than satisfaction after the night's mission. More edgy. And she knew why. Until she saw Painter's drowned corpse, his name on the list of the dead dragged from the sea, she would never know with certainty.

Her hand moved down along her hip, remembering. Could things have turned out differently between them? She closed her eyes, fingers clenching on her belly, hating herself for even pondering the possibility.

Damn you, Painter . . .

No matter what she might fantasize, it would've ended badly. That's what the past had taught her. First her father . . . sneaking into her bed at night, starting when she was eleven, high on crack, promising, threatening. Cassandra had retreated to books, erecting a wall between her and the world. In books, she learned how potassium stops the heart. Undetectable. On her seventeenth birthday, her father was found dead in his La-Z-Boy. No one paid attention to one needle puncture among the others. Her mother suspected and feared her.

With no reason to stay at home, she joined the army at eighteen, finding pleasure in hardening herself, testing herself. Then the offer, to enter a Special Forces marksman program. It was an honor, but not everyone thought of it that way. At Fort Bragg, an enlisted man pushed her into an alley, intending to correct her. He held her down, ripped open her shirt. "Who's your daddy now, bitch?" A mistake. Both the man's legs were broken. They were never able to repair his genitalia. She was allowed to leave the service as long as she kept her mouth shut.

She was good at secrets.

Afterward, Sigma came calling, and the Guild. It became all about power. Another way to harden herself. She had accepted.

Then Painter . . . his smile, his calm . . .

Pain flowed into her. Dead or alive?

She had to know. While she knew better than to make any assumptions, she could make contingency arrangements. She shoved off the sofa and stalked to the equipment table. The laptop was open. She checked the feed from the microtransceiver planted on the prisoner and clicked the GPS mapping feature. A three-dimensional grid appeared. The tracking device, depicted by a rotating blue ring, showed her in her cell.

If Painter was out there, he'd come for her.

She stared at the screen. Her prisoner might think she had gained an upper hand earlier, but Cassandra took the longer view.

She had modified Painter's subdermal transceiver, paired it with one designed by the Guild. It required amplifying the power cell, but once this was done, the modifications allowed Cassandra at any time to ignite an embedded pellet of C4, to take out the woman's spine, killing her with a keystroke.

So if Painter was still out there, let him come.

She was ready to end all uncertainty.

1:32 P.M.

Everyone collapsed on the sand, bone-tired. The stolen flatbed truck steamed on the narrow coastal road behind them, its hood open. The stretch of white sand spread in an arc, bordered by rocky limestone cliffs that tumbled into the sea on either end. It was deserted, isolated from any village.

Painter stared south, trying to pierce the fifty or so miles that lay between him and Salalah. *Safia had to be there.* He prayed he wasn't already too late.

Behind him, Omaha and the three Desert Phantoms argued in Arabic over the engine compartment of the truck.

The others sought the shade of the cliffs, collapsing, spent from the long night of rugged travel. The steel bed of the truck offered no cushioning against the bumps and ruts in the coastal road. Painter had caught snippets of sleep, but managed no real rest, just restless dreams.

He touched his left eye, half swollen shut now. The pain focused him on their situation. The journey, while steady, had been slow, limited by the terrain and the condition of the old road. And now a radiator hose had burst.

The delay risked all.

A crunch of sand drew his attention around to Coral. She wore a loose fitting robe, a bit too short, showing her bare ankles. Her hair and face were smudged with the oil from the bed of the truck.

"We're late," she said.

He nodded. "But how late?"

Coral glanced at her watch, a Breitlinger diver's chronograph. She was rated one of the best logisticians and strategists in the organization. "I estimate Cassandra's assault team made landfall at Salalah no later than midmorning. They'll delay only long enough to make sure no one marked them for the *Shabab*'s bombing and to secure a fallback position in the city."

"Best- and worst-case scenarios?"

"Worst. They reached the tomb two hours ago. Best. They're heading there right now."

Painter shook his head. "Not much of a window."

"No, it's not. We shouldn't fool ourselves otherwise." She eyed him. "The assault team demonstrated their drive and focus. With their victory at sea, they'll proceed with a renewed determination. But there may be one hope."

"What's that?"

"Though determined, they'll proceed with extra caution."

He frowned at this.

Coral explained, "You mentioned earlier the element of surprise. That's not truly where our best strength lies. From the profile I received on Captain Sanchez, she's not one to take risks. She'll proceed as if she *expects* pursuit."

"And this is to our advantage? How?"

"When someone is always looking over their shoulder, they're more likely to trip."

"How very Zen of you, Novak."

She shrugged. "My mother was a Buddhist."

He glanced at her. Her statement was said so deadpan that he couldn't tell if she was joking or not.

"Okay!" Omaha called as the engine choked, caught, and grumbled. More roughly than before, but it was running. "Mount up, everybody!"

A few wordless protests erupted as the others pushed from the sand.

Painter climbed in ahead of Kara, helping her up. He noted a tremble in her hands. "Are you all right?"

She freed her hand, clasping it in her other. She would not meet his eyes. "Fine. Just worried about Safia." She found a shady spot in the back corner.

The others did the same. The sun had begun to heat up the flatbed.

Omaha leaped into the back as the giant Barak closed the drop gate. He was covered with oil and grease from his elbows to fingertips.

"You got it running," Danny said, squinting at his brother, not so much from the sun's glare as nearsightedness. He'd lost his glasses during the explosion. It had been a very tough introduction to Arabia for the young man, but he seemed to be holding up well. "Will the engine last to Salalah?"

Omaha shrugged, collapsing on the bed next to his brother. "We jerry-rigged something. Stoppered the bad hose to keep it from leaking. The engine may overheat, but we only have another fifty or so miles to go. We'll make it."

Painter wished he could share the man's enthusiasm. He settled into a seat between Coral and Clay. The truck jerked forward, jostling them all, earning a worried whinny from the stallion. Its hooves clattered on the knobby bed. Wafts of diesel exhaust smoked up as the truck lurched back onto the road and set off again toward Salalah.

As the sun reflected off of every surface, Painter closed his eyes against the glare. With no hope of sleep, he found himself thinking about Cassandra. He rolled his past experience with his ex-partner through his head: strategy sessions, interoffice meetings, various operations in the field. In all such matters, Cassandra had proven his equal. But he'd been blind to her subterfuge, her streak of cold-bloodedness, her calculated ruthlessness. Here she surpassed him, making her a better field operative.

He pondered Coral's words from a moment ago: *When someone is always looking over their shoulder, they're more likely to trip.* Had he done that himself? Since the museum's foiled heist, he had been too conscious of his past with Cassandra, his focus on her too muddled, unable to balance past with present. Even in his heart. Was that what had allowed him to let his guard down aboard the *Shabab Oman*? Some belief in Cassandra's ultimate goodness? If he had fallen for her, there must have been something true between them.

Now he knew better.

A grunt of protest drew his attention across the truck bed. Clay yanked his cloak to cover his knees. He made for a poor Arab, what with his pale skin, shaved red hair, and studded ears. He caught Painter's eye. "So what do you think? Will we get there in time?"

Painter knew honesty was best from here on out. "I don't know."

2:13 P.M.

Safia rode in the backseat of the four-wheel-drive Mitsubishi. Three other identical vehicles trailed behind. They composed a small funeral parade headed to the tomb of the Virgin Mary's father, Nabi Imran.

Safia sat stiffly. The SUV smelled new. The crispness of the interior—charcoal leather, titanium trim, blue accent lights—all belied the ragged state of its passenger. And she could not blame all the red-rimmed fogginess on the aftereffects of the sedatives. Instead, her mind spun on her earlier conversation with Cassandra.

Painter . . .

Who was he? How could he have once been part-nered with Cassandra? What did that mean? She felt bruised inside, sore to the touch, as she pictured his wry smile, the way his hand touched so lightly on hers, reassuring. What else had he kept hidden? Safia pushed her confusion down deep, unable to face it yet, not sure even why it affected her so much. They barely knew each other.

She turned her focus instead on the other disturbing comment by Cassandra. How she worked for the U.S. government. Was that possible? Though Safia was well aware of the occasionally ruthless nature of American foreign policy, she could not fathom U.S. policymakers advocating this attack. Even the men under Cassandra had a raw, mercenary flare about them. Their nearness prickled her skin. These were no ordinary American soldiers.

And then there was the man named Kane, always dressed in black. She recognized his Queensland accent. An Aussie. He drove their vehicle, a little heavy-footed.

Corners taken too sharply, almost angrily. What was his story?

The truck's remaining occupant sat beside Safia. Cassandra watched the passing scenery, her hands in her lap. Like any tourist. Except she carried three guns. Cassandra had showed them to Safia. A warning. One in a shoulder holster, another at the base of her back, and the last strapped to her ankle. Safia suspected there was a hidden fourth weapon.

Trapped, she had no choice but to sit still.

As they traversed central Salalah, Safia watched the built-in navigation track the vehicle. They rounded past a beachside resort, the Hilton Salalah, then cut across traffic and aimed for the inner municipal district, the Al-Quaf area, where the tomb of Nabi Imran awaited them.

It was not much farther. Salalah was a small town, taking minutes to cross from one side to the other. The city's chief attractions lay beyond the municipality, in the natural wonders of the surrounding landscape: the magnificent sandy beach of Mughsal, the ancient ruins of Sumhurran, the myriad plantations that prospered under the monsoon rains. And a bit farther inland, the green mountains of Dhofar loomed as a backdrop, one of the few places on Earth where the rare frankincense trees grew.

Safia gazed toward the misted mountains, a place of eternal mystery and wealth. Though oil had replaced frankincense as Oman's main source of riches, incense still drove the local economy of Salalah. The traditional open-air markets scented the township with samplings of rosewater, ambergris, sandalwood, and myrrh. It was the perfume center of the world. All the top designers flew here to sample wares.

Still, in the past, frankincense was the true treasure of the country, surpassing even gold. Trade in the precious incense fueled Omani commerce, drove its seafaring dhows to as far north as Jordan and Turkey and as far west as Africa. But it was the overland route, the Incense Road, that became the true stuff of legend. Ancient ruins dotted its course, cryptic and mysterious, their histories mingled with the religions of Judaism, Christianity, and Islam. The most famous was Ubar, the thousand-pillared city, founded by the descendants of Noah, a city that grew rich through the pivotal role it played as a major watering hole for caravans passing through the desert.

Now, millennia later, Ubar had become the focus of power again. Blood had been shed to discover its secret, to expose its heart.

Safia had to resist glancing over her shoulder to the silver case in back. The iron heart had come from

Salalah, a bread crumb left behind, a trail marker to the true wealth of Ubar.

Antimatter.

Could it be possible?

Their Mitsubishi slowed and turned down an unpaved side street. They passed a line of roadside stands, sheltered under palm trees, selling dates, coconuts, and grapes. Their truck idled slowly past. Safia considered jumping for it, fleeing away. But she'd been buckled in place. Any move toward the belt's release and she'd be stopped.

And then there were the trailing vehicles, full of armed men. One truck made the turn behind them, the other continued, perhaps circling around to cordon off the other end of the alley. Safia wondered at such extra measures. Kane and Cassandra seemed more than enough to handle the prisoner. Safia knew there was no escape.

It would be her death to attempt it.

A surge of fiery heat, a long-suppressed anger, burned through her. She would not sacrifice herself needlessly. She would play their game but wait for her chance. She glanced sidelong at Cassandra. She would have her revenge . . . for her friends, for herself. This thought sustained her as their truck pulled to a stop outside a set of wrought-iron gates.

The entrance to the tomb of Nabi Imran.

"Don't try anything," Cassandra warned, as if reading her mind.

John Kane spoke to a gate attendant, half leaning out the window. A few Omani rials passed hands. The gate guard pressed a button, and the gate swung open, allowing the vehicle to pass inside. Kane pulled in slowly and parked.

The other truck took a position by the roadside stands.

Kane hopped out and came back to open her door. It could be taken as a chivalrous act in any normal circumstance. At the present time it was merely a precaution. He offered a hand to help her out.

Safia refused, climbing free herself.

Cassandra came around the back of the truck. She carried the silver case. "What now?"

Safia searched around her. Where to begin?

They stood in the middle of a flagstone courtyard, walled and bordered by small orderly gardens. Across the courtyard, a small mosque rose. Its whitewashed minaret climbed blindingly into the midday glare, topped by a brownish gold dome. A small circular balcony at the top marked the place for the muezzin to sing the *adhan,* the Muslim call to prayer, five times a day.

Safia offered her own prayer. Silence was her only answer, but it still gave her comfort. Within the courtyard, the sounds of the surrounding town were muted, hushed, as if the very air had stilled at the holiness of the shrine. A few worshipers moved discreetly through the grounds, respectful of the burial tomb that stretched along one side: a long, low building, framed in arches, painted white, trimmed in green. Within the building stood the gravesite of Nabi Imran, the father of the Virgin Mary.

Cassandra stepped in front of her. The woman's impatience, her pent-up energy, stirred the air, leaving a wake behind her that was almost palpable. "So where do we begin?"

"At the beginning," Safia mumbled, and strode forward. They needed her. Though a prisoner, she would not be rushed. Knowledge was her shield.

Cassandra strode after her.

Safia walked toward the entrance to the burial sanctuary. A robed man, one of the tomb's attendants, strode out to meet their party.

"*Salam alaikum,*" he greeted.

"*Alaikum as salam,*" Safia responded.

"*As fa,*" he apologized, and pointed to his head. "Women are not allowed into the tomb with their hair uncovered." He pulled free a pair of green scarves.

"*Shuk ran.*" Safia thanked him and quickly donned the apparel. Her fingers moved with a skill she long thought lost. She found not a small degree of satisfaction when the man had to help Cassandra.

The caretaker stepped away. "Peace be with you," he offered as he retreated to the shaded gallery, back to his post.

"We'll have to take off our shoes and sandals, too," Safia said, nodding to the row of abandoned footwear outside the door.

Soon barefoot, they entered the tomb.

The sanctuary was simply one long hall, encompassing the length of the building. At one end was a raised brown marble headstone the size of a small altar. Incense burned atop the marble in a pair of matching bronze braziers, giving the room a medicinal scent. But it was the grave below the headstone that captured the immediate attention. Down the middle of the hall stretched a thirty-meter-long sepulcher, raised a half meter above the floor and draped in a rainbow of cloths imprinted with phrases from the Koran. Flanking the grave, the floor was draped with prayer rugs.

"That's a big grave," Kane said softly.

A single worshiper rose from his rug, glanced at the newcomers, and silently exited the room. They had the space to themselves.

Safia paced the thirty-meter length of the shrouded tomb. It was said that if you measured the length along one side of the sepulcher, you'd never get the same measurement on the other. She had never tested this bit of folklore.

Cassandra followed at her shoulder, gazing around. "What do you know about this place?"

Safia shrugged as she circled the end of the tomb and began the return journey toward the marble headstone. "The tomb has been revered since the Middle Ages, but all these trappings . . ." She waved her hand to encompass the vault and courtyard. "All of this is relatively new."

Safia strode forward to the marble headstone. She placed a hand on its surface. "This was the spot where Reginald Kensington excavated the sandstone statue that hid the iron heart. Some forty years ago."

Cassandra stepped forward with the small case. She circled the stone altar. The floating snakes of incense from the pair of braziers stirred in her passage, an angry, writhing motion.

Kane spoke up. "So the Virgin Mary's father is really buried here?"

"There's some controversy surrounding that claim."

Cassandra glanced at her. "How so?"

"Most major Christian groups—Catholics, Byzantines, Nestorians, Jacobites—believe Mary's father was a man named Joachim. But this is contested. The Koran claims she descended from a highly respected family, that of Imran. As does the Jewish faith. According to their stories, Imran and his wife desired a child, but his wife was barren. Imran prayed for a male child, one whom he would dedicate to the temple in Jerusalem. His prayer was answered, his wife became pregnant—but with a *female* child. Mary. Joyous still, her parents devoted her to live a life of piety in honor of God's miracle."

"Until she got knocked up by an angel."

"Yes, that's when things get sticky between the religions."

"What about the statue, the one at the head of the grave?" Cassandra asked, drawing the conversation back to their goal. "Why was it placed here?"

Safia stood before the marble headstone and pondered the same question herself, as she had on the whole journey from London. Why would someone place a clue to Ubar in a place tied to the Virgin Mary, a figure revered by all three religious faiths—Judaism, Christianity, and Islam? Was it because they knew the site would be protected throughout the ages? Each religion had an interest in preserving the tomb. No one could've anticipated Reginald Kensington excavating the statue and adding it to his collection back in England.

But who originally brought the statue to the shrine and why? Was it because Salalah marked the beginning of the Incense Road? Was the statue the first signpost, the first trail marker leading into the heart of Arabia?

Safia's mind spun with various scenarios: the age of the statue, the mysteries surrounding the tomb, the multifaith veneration of the site.

She turned to Cassandra. "I need to see the heart."

"Why?"

"Because you're right. The statue must've been placed here for a reason."

Cassandra stared at her for a long moment, then knelt atop one of the prayer rugs, snapped open the case. The iron heart shone dully within its black rubberized cushioning.

Safia joined her and lifted the heart free. Again she was surprised by its weight. It felt too dense for plain iron. As she stood, she felt the vague sloshing from within, heavy, as if some molten lead filled the heart's iron chambers.

She carried it over to the marble altar. "The statue was said to be propped up here." As she swung around, a few bits of frankincense dribbled from the end of one of the heart's vessels and scattered like salt atop the marble altar.

Safia held the heart up to her own chest, positioning it anatomically—ventricles down, the aortic arch passing on the left—as it would lie in her own body. She stood above the long narrow tomb and pictured the museum statue before the explosion had blasted it apart.

It had stood almost seven feet, a draped figure, wearing a headdress and face scarf, typical of the bedouin today. The figure had borne aloft a long funerary incense burner, on the shoulder, as if aiming a rifle.

Safia stared down at the grains of ancient frankincense. Was the same incense once burned here? She cradled the fist of cold iron in the crook of one arm, and picked up a few crystalline grains and tossed them in a neighboring brazier, sending up a prayer for her friends. They sizzled and gave off a fresh whiff of sweetness to the air.

Closing her eyes, she inhaled. The air was redolent with frankincense. The scent of the ancient past. As she breathed, she traveled back in time, to before the birth of Christ.

She pictured the long-dead frankincense tree that produced this incense. A scraggly, scrubby tree with tiny gray-green leaves. She imagined the ancients who harvested the sap. They were a reclusive tribe in the mountains, so isolated and old that their language predated modern Arabian. Only a handful of tribesmen still survived in isolation up in their mountains, eking out a meager living. She heard their language in her head, a singsong sibilance that was compared to birdsong. These people, the Shahra, claimed to be the last surviving descendants of Ubar, tracing their lineage to its founding fathers.

Had such a people harvested this incense themselves?

As she drew the past into her with each breath, she felt herself swoon, the room spinning beneath her. Momentarily unable to discern up from down, she caught herself on the edge of the altar, her knees losing strength.

John Kane grabbed her elbow, the elbow cradling the heart.

It bobbled in her grip . . . and fell.

The heart struck the altar with a dull clank and rolled across the slick marble, spinning on its iron surface, slightly wobbly, as if whatever liquid was inside had thrown it off balance.

Cassandra lunged for it.

"No!" Safia warned. "Leave it be!"

The heart spun a final time and came to rest. As it settled, it seemed to rock and swing slightly contrary, then stopped completely.

"Don't touch it." Safia knelt down, eyes even with the edge of the altar stone. The incense cloyed the air.

The heart rested in the exact position she had been holding it a moment before: ventricles down, aortic arch up and to the left.

Safia stood. She adjusted her body to match the position of the heart, again as if it were residing in her own chest. Once in position, she corrected the placement of her feet and lifted her arms, pretending to hold an invisible rifle in her hands—or a funerary incense burner.

Frozen in the pose of the ancient statue, Safia sighted down the length of her raised arm. It pointed straight along the long axis of the tomb, perfectly aligned. Safia lowered her arms and stared at the iron heart.

What were the odds that the heart would by pure chance settle into this exact position? She remembered the sloshing inside the heart, pictured its jittery spin, its final wobble at the end.

Like a compass.

She stared down the long length of tomb, raising her arm to sight along it. Her gaze traveled past the walls, out over the city, and beyond. Away from the coast. Out toward the distant green mountains.

Then she knew.

She had to be sure. "I need a map."

"Why?" Cassandra asked.

"Because I know where we have to go next."

12
Safety First

ᚷᚺᛟᛉᛪᛈᛁᛟᛃᛞᛇᚷ

December 3, 3:02 P.M.
Salalah

Omaha, half drowsing in the truck's bed, felt the telltale rattle under the seat of his pants. *Damn it* . . . The vibration in the flatbed grew worse, jarring. Those who had been dozing, heads lolling in the heat, glanced up, faces creased with strained worry.

From the front of the truck, the engine coughed a final time and died with a sighing gasp of smoke. Black clouds billowed over the truck, issuing from under the hood. A reek of burned oil accompanied it. The flatbed coasted to the side of the road, bumped into the sandy shoulder, and braked to a stop.

"End of the line," Omaha said.

The Arabian stallion stamped a hoof in protest.

You and me both, Omaha thought. He stood along with the others, dusted off his cloak, and crossed to the drop gate. He yanked the release. The gate fell away and crashed with a clatter into the sand.

They all clambered down as Captain al-Haffi and his two men, Barak and Sharif, vacated the cab. Smoke still billowed, smudging into the sky.

"Where are we?" Kara asked, shielding her eyes and staring down the winding road. To either side, sugarcane fields climbed in swaths of dense fronds, obscuring distances. "How far are we from Salalah?"

"No more than a couple of miles," Omaha said, punctuating with a shrug. He was unsure. It could be twice that.

Captain al-Haffi approached the group. "We should go now." He waved an arm toward the smoke. "People will come to see."

Omaha nodded. It wouldn't be good to be found loitering around a stolen truck. Or even a *borrowed* one.

"We'll have to walk the rest of the way," Painter said. He was the last out of the flatbed. He had the stallion in tow on a rope lead. He led the skittish horse down the dropped gate. It shook and danced a bit once on solid ground.

As Painter consoled it, Omaha noted the man's left eye had begun to purple but appeared less swollen. He glanced away, balanced between shame for his earlier outburst and the residual anger he still felt.

With no gear, they were soon under way, trekking along the road's shoulder. They moved like a small caravan, in twos. Captain al-Haffi led them. Painter and Coral trailed last with the horse.

Omaha heard the pair speaking in whispers, strategizing. He slowed to drop beside them. He refused to be left out of the discussion. Kara noted this, too, and joined them.

"What's the plan once we get into Salalah?" Omaha asked.

Painter frowned. "We keep low. Coral and I will go to—"

"Wait." Omaha cut him off. "You're not leaving me behind. I'm not going to hide away in some hotel while you two go traipsing about."

His angry outburst was heard by all.

"We can't all go to the tomb," Painter said. "We'll be spotted. Coral and I are trained in surveillance and intelligence gathering. We'll need to reconnoiter the area, search for Safia, stake it out if she's not arrived there yet."

"And what if she's already been there and gone?" Omaha asked.

"We can find that out. Ask some discreet questions."

Kara spoke up. "If she's gone, we won't know where they've taken her."

Painter stared. Omaha noted the worry shadowing the man's eyes, as dark as the bruise under the left one.

"You think we're already too late," Omaha said.

"We can't know for certain."

Omaha stared off into the distance. A few buildings could be seen near the horizon. The city's edge. Too far. Too late.

"Someone has to go on ahead," Omaha said.

"How?" Kara asked.

Not turning around, Omaha pointed a thumb back over his shoulder. "The horse. One of us . . . maybe two . . . could ride the horse into town. Go straight to the tomb. Check it out. Keep hidden. Watch for Safia. Trail her if she leaves."

Silence answered him.

Coral met his eyes. "Painter and I were just discussing that."

"I should go," Painter said.

Omaha stopped, turning to face the man fully. "And why the hell's that? I know the city. I know its back alleys."

Painter stared him down. "You haven't the experience in surveillance. This is no time for amateurs. You'll be spotted. Give away our advantage."

"Like hell I will. I may not've had any formal training, but I've had years of fieldwork in places where it's best not to be seen. I can blend in if I have to."

Painter spoke bluntly, no bravado. "But I'm better. This is what I do."

Omaha clenched a fist. He heard the certainty in the other's voice. A part of him wanted to pound it out of the man, but another part believed him. He didn't have Painter's experience. What was the best choice? How could he walk when he wanted to run to Safia? A cord of pain wrapped around his heart.

"And what will you do if you find her?"

"Nothing." Painter continued, "I will study their manpower. Find a weakness. Wait for the proper moment."

Kara spoke up, hands on her hips. "And what about us?"

Coral answered her as Omaha and Painter continued their standoff. "We have a safe house prearranged as backup in Salalah. Cash and supplies."

Of course they would, Omaha thought.

"Guns?" Kara asked.

Coral nodded. "We'll go there first. Load up. I'll make contact with Washington. Debrief them on our status. Arrange for additional—"

"No," Painter interrupted. "No communication. I'll contact you all as soon as I can. We'll move forward from there on our own. No outside help."

Omaha read the silent discourse that passed between Painter and his partner. It seemed it was not only the Omani government that Painter suspected of leaks, but also their own government. This woman, Cassandra Sanchez, had been one step ahead of them all along. She must be getting inside information.

Painter's eyes settled back to Omaha. "Are we straight with this plan?"

Omaha slowly nodded, though it was like iron bars had been rammed down the back of his neck. Painter began to turn away, but Omaha stopped him, moving in closer. Omaha pulled free the pistol from inside his cloak and passed Painter the gun. "If you have a chance . . . any chance . . ."

"I'll take it," he said, accepting the weapon.

Omaha stepped back, and Painter mounted the stallion. He rode bareback, using a makeshift rein of towline. "I'll see you all in Salalah," he mumbled, and kicked the horse into a trot, then a full gallop, crouched low.

"I hope he's as good a spy as he is a rider," Kara said.

Omaha watched Painter vanish around a bend in the road. Then the group set off again, moving slowly, too slowly, toward the waiting city.

3:42 P.M.

Safia leaned over the topographical map of the Dhofar region. It lay spread over the hood of their truck. She had a digital compass resting in the center, along with a straight-edged plastic ruler. She made a subtle alteration in the ruler's position on the map, aligning it exactly along the same axis as the tomb of Nabi Imran. Before leaving the vault, she had spent several minutes using the laser-calibrated compass to get the precise measurement.

"What are you doing?" Cassandra asked at her shoulder for the fifth time.

Still ignoring her, Safia bent closer, nose almost to the paper. *This is the best I can do without computers.* She held out a hand. "Pen."

Kane reached into an inside jacket pocket and passed her a ballpoint. Glancing up, she caught a brief glimpse of a gun holstered at his shoulder. She took the pen cautiously from his fingers. She refused to meet his eyes. More than Cassandra, the man made her edgy, shook her resolve.

Safia concentrated on the map, focusing her full attention on the mystery. The next clue to the secret heart of Ubar.

She drew a line along the edge of the ruler, then pulled it away. A blue line arrowed straight out from Nabi Imran's tomb and shot across the countryside.

She followed the line with her finger, noting the terrain it crossed, searching for a specific name.

She had a good idea what she would find.

As her finger followed beyond the city of Salalah, the lines of the topographic map began to multiply as the landscape rippled up into foothills, then mountains. She followed the line of blue ink until it crossed a small black dot atop a steep-sided mount. Her finger came to rest and tapped the spot.

Cassandra leaned closer and read the name printed beneath her finger. "Jebal Eitteen." She glanced to Safia.

"*Mount* Eitteen," Safia said, and studied the small black dot that marked the small mountain. "Atop there lies another tomb. And like the one here, this spot is also revered across all faiths—Christianity, Judaism, and Islam."

"Whose tomb is it?"

"Another prophet. Ayoub. Or in English: Job."

Cassandra simply frowned at her.

Safia elaborated. "Job appears in both the Bible and the Koran. He was a man rich in wealth and family, who remained steadfast in his devotion to God. As a test, all was stripped from him: wealth, children, even his own health. So horrible were his afflictions that he was shunned and forced to live in isolation here." She tapped the map. "On Mount Eitteen. Still, despite the hardships, Job continued in his faith and devotion.

For his loyalty, God told Job to 'strike the ground with your foot.' A spring was called forth from which Job drank and bathed. His afflictions were cured, and he became a young man again. He lived the rest of his life on Mount Eitteen and was eventually buried there."

"And you think this tomb is the next spot on the road to Ubar?"

"If the *first* signpost was erected at this tomb, it only follows that the next would be in a similar location. Another gravesite of a holy personage revered by all the religions of the region."

"Then that's where we must go next."

Cassandra reached to the map.

Safia slapped a hand atop the paper, stopping her. "There's no way I can be certain what, if anything, we'll find there. I've been to Job's tomb before. I saw nothing significant related to Ubar. And we have no clue where to begin to search. Not even an iron heart." She again pictured the way the heart had wobbled atop the marble altar, aligning itself like a compass. "It could take years to discover the next piece to the puzzle."

"That is why you're here," Cassandra said, snatching up the map and waving for Kane to get the prisoner back into the SUV. "To solve this riddle."

Safia shook her head. It seemed an impossible task. Or so Safia wanted Cassandra to believe. Despite her protests, she had a distinct idea of how to proceed, but she was unsure how to use this knowledge to her advantage.

She climbed into the back again with Cassandra and settled into her seat as the truck angled through the entry gate. Out in the street, the vendors were beginning to load up their wares as the afternoon waned. A lone stray dog, all ribs and leg bones, wandered listlessly among the strip of stands and carts. It lifted its nose as a horse passed slowly along behind the row of makeshift shops, led by a man draped from head to toe in a bedouin desert cloak.

The truck continued down the lane, aiming for another Mitsubishi parked at the end. The procession would continue into the foothills.

Safia stared at the GPS navigation system on the dashboard. Streets radiated outward. The countryside awaited.

And another tomb.

She hoped it wasn't her own.

4:42 P.M.
Mount Eitteen

Damned scorpions . . .

Dr. Jacques Bertrand crushed the black-armored intruder under his heel before settling to the rug that cushioned his workspace. He had been gone only minutes to fetch more water from his Land Rover, and the scorpions had already invaded his shaded alcove in the cliff. In this harsh landscape of hardscrabble, bitterbrush, and stone, nothing went to waste. Not even a spot in the shade.

Jacques sprawled on his back in the niche, faceup. An inscription in Epigraphic South Arabian had been carved into the roof of the niche, an ancient burial crypt. The surrounding landscape was littered with them, all overshadowed by Job's tomb atop the mount where he labored. The entire region had become a cemetery. This was the third crypt he had documented today. The last for this long, interminably hot day.

He already dreamed of his hotel suite at the Salalah Hilton, a dip in the pool, a glass of Chardonnay.

With this thought firming him to his task, he set to work. Running a camel-hair brush over the inscription, he cleaned it a final time. As an archaeologist specializing in ancient languages, Jacques was currently on a grant to road-map early Semitic scripts, tracing their lineage from past to present. Aramaic, Elymaic, Palmyrene, Nabataean, Samaritan, Hebrew. Gravesites were great sources of the written word, immortalizing prayers, praises, and epitaphs.

With a prickly shiver, Jacques lowered his brush. He suddenly had an intense feeling of being watched. It welled over him, some primeval sense of danger.

Raising up on an elbow, he stared down past his legs. The region was rife with bandits and thieves. But in the shadow of Job's tomb, a most holy shrine, none would venture to commit a crime. It would be a death sentence. Knowing this, he had left his rifle back in the Rover.

He stared out into the brightness.

Nothing.

Still, he pulled his booted feet fully into the niche. If someone was out there, someone meaning him harm, perhaps he could remain hidden.

A *tick-tick* of a pebble rolling down a rocky slope sounded from the left. His ears strained. He felt trapped.

Then a shape moved across the entrance to the crypt.

It padded past, sauntering, lazy, but confident with power. Its red fur, speckled in shadow, blended with the red rock.

Jacques held his breath, trapped between terror and disbelief.

He had heard tales, been warned of their presence in the wilds of the Dhofar Mountains. *Panthera pardus nimr*. The Arabian leopard. Nearly extinct, but not extinct enough for his tastes.

The large cat moved past.

But it was not alone.

A second leopard strode into view, moving faster, younger, more agitated. Then a third. A male. Huge paws, splaying with each step, yellow claws.

A pack.

He held his breath, praying, near mindless, a caveman huddling against the dangers beyond his hole.

Then another figure strode into view.

Not a cat.

Bare legs, bare feet, moving with the same feline grace.

A woman.

From his vantage point, he could see nothing above her thighs.

She ignored him as surely as the leopards, moving swiftly past, heading higher up the mountain.

Jacques slipped from the crypt, like Lazarus rising from his grave. He could not stop himself. He poked his head out, on his hands and knees. The woman climbed the rock face, following some path known only to her. She was the color of warm mocha, sleek black hair to the waist, naked, unashamed.

She seemed to sense his gaze, though she did not turn around. He felt it in his head, the overwhelming feeling of being watched again. It bubbled through him. Fear prickled, but he could not look away.

She strode among the leopards, continuing upward, toward the tomb at the top. Her form seemed to shimmer, a heat mirage across sunbaked sand.

A scratching sound drew his glance to his hands and knees.

A pair of scorpions scuttled over his fingers. They were not poisonous but dealt a wicked sting. He gasped as more and more boiled out of cracks and crevices, scrabbling down walls, dropping from the roof. Hundreds. A nest. He scrambled from the crypt. He felt stings, sparks of fire on his back, ankles, neck, hands.

He fell out of the opening and rolled across the hard soil. More stings flashed like cigarette burns. He cried out, maddened with pain.

He clambered up, shaking his limbs, stripping his jacket, slapping a hand through his hair. He stamped his feet and stumbled back down the slope. Scorpions still scuttled about the crypt's opening.

He glanced higher, suddenly fearful of drawing the leopards' attention. But the cliff face was empty.

The woman, the cats, had vanished.

It was impossible. But the fire from the scorpion stings had burned all curiosity from him. He fell back and away, retreating for his parked Rover. Still, his eyes quested, moving higher, to the top.

To where the tomb of Job waited.

He pulled open the door to his Rover and climbed into the driver's seat. He had been warned away. He knew it with dread certainty.

Something horrible was going to happen up there.

4:45 P.M.
Salalah

"Safia's still alive," Painter said as soon as he strode through the door of the safe house It was not so much a house as a two-room flat above an import-export shop that bordered the Al-Haffa souk. With such a business fronting the safe house, none would question the comings and goings of strangers. Just a normal part of business. The noise of the neighboring market was a chatter of languages, voices, and bartering. The rooms smelled of curry and old mattresses.

Painter pushed past Coral, who had opened the door upon his knock. He had already noted the two Desert Phantoms posted discreetly out front, watching the approach up to the safe house.

The others were gathered in the front room, exhausted, road-worn. A run of water tinkled from the neighboring bathroom. Painter noted Kara was missing. Danny, Omaha, and Clay all had wet hair. They had been taking turns showering away the trail dust and grime. Captain al-Haffi had found a robe, but it was too tight for his shoulders.

Omaha stood as Painter entered. "Where is she?"

"Safia and the others were leaving the tomb just as I arrived. In a caravan of SUVs. Heavily armed." Painter crossed to the tiny kitchenette. He leaned over the sink, turned the tap, and ran his head under the spigot.

Omaha stood behind him. "Then why aren't you tracking them?"

Painter straightened, sweeping back his sodden hair. Trails of water coursed down his neck and back. "I am." He kept his eyes hard upon Omaha, then stepped past him to Coral. "How are we equipped?"

She nodded to the door leading to the back room. "I thought it best to wait for you. The electronic keypad proved trickier than I had imagined."

"Show me."

She led him to the door. The flat was a CIA safe house, permanently stocked, one of many throughout the world. Sigma had been alerted to its location when the mission was assembled. Backup in case it was needed.

It was.

Painter spotted the electronic keypad hidden under a fold of curtain. Coral had pinned the drape out of the way. A small array of crude tools lay on the floor: fingernail clipper, razor blades, tweezers, nail file.

"From the bathroom," Coral said.

Painter knelt in front of the keypad. Coral had opened the casing, exposing the electronics. He studied the circuits.

Coral leaned beside him, pointing to some clipped wires, red and blue. "I was able to disable the silent alarm. You should be able to key into the equipment locker without alerting anyone. But I thought it best you oversee my work. This is your field of expertise."

Painter nodded. Such lockers were rigged to silently send out an alarm, notifying the CIA when such a safe house was employed. Painter did not want such knowledge sent out. Not yet. Not so broadly. They were dead . . . and he meant to keep them that way for as long as possible.

His eyes ran along the circuits, following the flows of power, the dummy wires, the live ones. All seemed in order. Coral had managed to sever the power to the telephone line while leaving the keypad powered and untampered with. For a physicist, she was proving to be a damn good electrical engineer. "Looks good."

"Then we can enter."

During his premission briefing, Painter had memorized the safe house's code. He reached to the keypad and typed in the first number of the ten-digit code. He would have only one chance to get it right. If he entered the code wrong, the keypad would disable itself, locking down. A failsafe.

He proceeded carefully.

"You have ninety seconds," Coral reminded him.

Another failsafe. The ten-digit sequence had to be punched in within a set time span. He tapped each number with care, proceeding steadily. As he reached the seventh number in the sequence—the number nine—his finger hovered. The illuminated button seemed slightly dimmer than its neighbor, easy to miss. He held his finger. Was he being too paranoid? Jumping at shadows?

"What's wrong?" Coral asked.

By now, Omaha had joined them, along with his brother.

Painter sat back on his heels, thinking. He clenched and unclenched his fingers. He stared at the number-nine button. Surely not . . .

"Painter," Coral whispered under her breath.

If he waited much longer, the system would lock down. He didn't have time to spare—but something was wrong. He could smell it.

Omaha hovered behind him, making him too conscious of the time ticking away. If Painter was to save Safia, he needed what lay behind this door.

Ignoring the keypad, Painter picked up the tweezer and nail file. With a surgeon's skill, he carefully lifted free the number-nine key. It fell into his hand. Too easily. He leaned closer, squinting.

Damn . . .

Behind the key rested a small square chip with a pressure plunger in its center. The chip was wrapped tightly with a thin metal filament. An antenna. It was a microtransmitter. If he had pressed the button, it would have activated. From the crudeness of its integration, this was not a factory installation.

Cassandra had been here.

Sweat rolled into Painter's left eye. He had not even been aware of the amount of moisture that had built up on his brow.

Coral stared over his shoulder. "Shit."

That was an understatement. "Get everyone out of here."

"What's going on?" Omaha asked.

"Booby trap," Painter said, anger firing his words. "Out! Now!"

"Grab Kara!" Coral commanded Omaha, ordering him into the bathroom. She got everyone else moving toward the door.

As they fled, Painter sat before the keypad. A litany of curses rang through his head like a favorite old song. He had been singing this tune too long. Cassandra was always a step ahead.

"Thirty seconds!" Coral warned as she slammed the flat's door. He had half a minute until the keypad locked down.

Alone, he studied the chip.

Just you and me, Cassandra.

Painter set down the nail file and picked up the nail clipper. Wishing he had his tool satchel, he set to work on removing the transmitter, breathing deeply, staying in a calm place. He touched the metal casing to bleed away any static electricity, then set to work. He carefully dissected away the power wire from its ground, then just as carefully filed the plastic coating off the power wire without breaking it. Once the ground wire was exposed, he tweezed it up and touched it to the hot wire. There was a snap and a sizzle. A hint of burned plastic wafted upward.

The transmitter was fried.

Eight seconds . . .

He cut the dead transmitter free and plucked it out. He closed his fingers over it, feeling its sharp edge dig into his palm.

Fuck you, Cassandra.

Painter finished tapping in the final three digits. Beside him, the door's locks tumbled open with a whir of mechanics.

Only then did he sigh in relief.

Straightening, he inspected the door's frame before testing the knob. It all looked untouched. Cassandra had counted on the transmitter doing the job.

Painter twisted and pulled the knob. The door was heavy, reinforced with steel. He said a quick final prayer as he hauled the door open.

From the doorway, he stared inside. A bare bulb illuminated the room.

Damn it . . .

The neighboring room was filled with steel shelves and racks, from floor to ceiling. All empty. Ransacked.

Again, Cassandra had taken no chances, left no crumbs, only her calling card: a pound of C4 explosive, rigged with an electronic detonator. If he had tapped the number-nine button, it would have taken out the entire building. He crossed and pulled free the detonator.

Frustration built into a painful pressure behind his rib cage. He wanted to scream. Instead, he crossed back to the flat's entry door and called the all clear.

Coral's eyes were bright as she climbed the stairs

"She cleaned us out," Painter said as his partner entered.

Omaha frowned, following on Coral's heels. "Who . . . ?"

"Cassandra Sanchez," Painter snapped. "Safia's kidnapper."

"How the hell did she know about the safe house?"

Painter shook his head. How indeed? He led them to the empty locker, stepped inside, and crossed to the bomb.

"What are you doing?" Omaha asked.

"I'm salvaging the explosives. We may need them."

As Painter worked, Omaha entered the locker. Kara followed, her hair wet and tangled from her interrupted shower, her body snugged in a towel.

"What about Safia?" Omaha asked. "You said you could track her."

Painter finished freeing the C4 and motioned them all back out. "I did. Now we have a problem. There should've been a satellite-linked computer here. A way to reach a DOD server."

"I don't understand," Kara said thinly. Her flesh shone pale yellow under the fluorescents. She appeared wasted, leaving Painter to suspect it wasn't drugs that had worn the woman down, but the *lack* of them.

Painter led them back into the main room, revising his plans with one step, cursing Cassandra with the next. She knew about the safe house, obtained the locker code, and booby-trapped it. How did she know their every move? His gaze traveled over the group here.

"Where's Clay?" Painter asked.

"Finishing a cigarette on the stairs," Danny answered. "He found a pack in the kitchen."

As if on command, Clay pushed through the door. All eyes turned to him. He was taken aback by all the attention. "What?" he asked.

Kara turned to Painter. "What's our next step?"

Painter turned to Captain al-Haffi. "I left the sultan's horse with Sharif downstairs. Do you think you could sell the stallion and quickly roust up some weapons and a vehicle that could carry us?"

The captain nodded with assurance. "I have discreet contacts here."

"You have half an hour."

"What about Safia?" Omaha pressed. "We're wasting too much time."

"Safia is safe for the moment. Cassandra still needs her, or Safia would be sharing that tomb with the Virgin Mary's father right now. They took her away for a reason. If we hope to rescue her, the cover of night might be best. We have some time to spare."

"How do you know where they're taking Safia?" Kara asked.

Painter searched the faces around him, unsure how freely to speak.

"Well?" Omaha pressed. "How the hell are we going to find her?"

Painter crossed toward the door. "By finding the best coffee in town."

5:10 P.M.

Omaha led the way across the Al-Haffa souk. Only Painter followed. The others were left at the safe house to rest and await the return of Captain al-Haffi and their transportation. Omaha hoped they had someplace to travel to.

Dull anger throbbed with each step. Painter had seen Safia, been within yards of her . . . and he had let the kidnappers ride off with her. The man's confidence in his ability to track her had been shaken back at the safe house. Omaha saw it in Painter's eyes. *Worry.*

The bastard should've attempted to rescue her when he had the chance. To hell with the odds. The man's insufferable caution was going to get Safia killed. And then all their efforts would be too late.

Omaha stalked among the booths and stalls of the market, deaf to the chatter of voices, the cries of hawkers, the angry burble of heated bartering, the squawk of caged geese, the braying of a mule. It all blended into white noise.

The market was near to closing for the day as the sun sank toward the horizon, stretching shadows. An evening wind had kicked up. Awnings rattled, dust devils danced amid piles of littered refuse, and the air smelled of salt, spice, and the promise of rain.

It was past monsoon season, but the weather reports warned of a December storm, a front moving inland. They would have rain by nightfall. The squall last night had been only the first in a series of storms. There was talk that this weather system would cross the mountains and collide with the sandstorm rolling south, creating the perfect monster storm.

But Omaha had larger concerns than wild weather.

Omaha hurried across the souk. Their goal lay on the far side, where a modern strip of commercial facilities had sprouted, including a Pizza Hut and a minimart. Omaha wound through the last of the stalls, passing shops selling knockoff perfumes, incense burners, bananas, tobacco, handcrafted jewelry, traditional Dhofari dresses made of velvet and covered with beads and sequins.

At last, they reached the street separating the souk from the modern strip mall. Omaha pointed across the way. "There it is. Now how is that place going to help you find Safia?"

Painter headed across. "I'll show you."

Omaha followed. He stared up at the sign: SALALAH INTERNET CAFÉ. The establishment specialized in elaborate coffees, offering an international array of teas, cappuccinos, and espressos. Similar establishments could be found in the most remote places. All it took was a telephone connection, and even the most out-of-the-way corner of the world could be surfing the Web.

Painter headed inside. He approached the counter-person, a blond-haired Englishman by the name of Axe who wore a T-shirt that read FREE WINONA, and gave him his credit card number and expiration date.

"You have that memorized," Omaha asked.

"You never know when you're going to be attacked by pirates at sea."

As the man ran the number, Omaha asked, "I thought you wanted to keep a low profile. Won't using your credit card give away that you're still alive?"

"I don't think it really matters anymore."

The electronic credit card machine chimed. The man gave him a thumbs-up. "How much time do you want?"

"Is it a highspeed connection?"

"DSL, mate. No other way to surf."

"Thirty minutes should be enough."

"Brilliant. Machine in the corner is free."

Painter led Omaha over to the computer, a Gateway Pentium 4. Painter sat down, accessed the Internet connection, and typed in a long IP address.

"I'm accessing a Department of Defense's server," he explained.

"How is that going to help find Safia?"

He continued typing, fingers flying, screens flashed, refreshed, disappeared, changed. "Through the DOD, I can gain access to most proprietary systems under the National Security Act. Here we go."

On the screen appeared a page with the Mitsubishi logo.

Omaha read over his shoulder. "Shopping for a new car?"

Painter used the mouse to maneuver through the site. He seemed to have full access, flashing past password-encrypted screens. "Cassandra's group was traveling in SUVs. Mitsubishis. They did not make much effort to hide their backup vehicles. It didn't take much to get close enough to read the VIN number off one in the alley."

"VIN? The Vehicle Identification Number?"

Painter nodded. "All cars or trucks with GPS navigation systems are in constant contact with the orbiting satellites, keeping track of their location, allowing the driver to know where he is at all times."

Omaha began to understand. "And if you have the VIN number, you can access the vehicle's data remotely. Find out where they are."

"That's what I'm counting on."

A screen appeared, asking for the VIN number. Painter typed it in, not looking at his fingers. He pressed the enter button, then leaned back. His hand had a slight shake in it. He clenched a fist in an attempt to hide it.

Omaha could read his mind. Had he remembered the number correctly? What if the kidnappers had disabled the GPS? So many things could go wrong.

But after a long moment, a digital map of Oman appeared, fed from a pair of geosynchronous satellites orbiting far above. A small box scrolled a series of longitude and latitude designation. The moving location of the SUV.

Painter sighed with relief. Omaha echoed it.

"If we could find where they're holding Safia . . ."

Painter clicked the zoom feature and zeroed in on the map. The city of Salalah appeared. But the tiny blue arrow marking the truck's location was beyond its borders, heading deeper inland.

Painter leaned closer. "No . . ."

"Goddamnit. They're leaving the city!"

"They must've found something at that tomb."

Omaha swung away. "Then we have to go. Now!"

"We don't know *where* they're going," Painter said, remaining at the computer. "I have to track them. Until they stop."

"There is only one highway. The one they're on. We can catch up."

"We don't know if they'll go overland. They were in four-wheel-drives."

Omaha felt pulled in two different directions: to listen to Painter's practical advice, or to steal the first vehicle he could find and race after Safia. But what would he do if he reached her? How could he help her?

Painter grabbed his arm. Omaha balled a fist with the other.

Painter stared hard at him. "I need you to think, Dr. Dunn. Why would they be leaving the city? Where could they be going?"

"How the hell should—"

Painter squeezed his arm. "You're as much an expert in this region as Safia. You know what road they're taking, what lies along the way. Is there anything out there that the tomb here in Salalah might point toward?"

He shook his head, refusing to answer. They were wasting time.

"Goddamnit, Omaha! For once in your life, stop reacting and *think!*"

Omaha yanked his arm away. "Fuck you!" But he didn't leave. He remained trembling in place.

"What is out there? Where are they going?"

Omaha glanced over to the screen, unable to face Painter, afraid he'd blacken the man's other eye. He considered the question, the puzzle. He stared at the blue arrow as it wound away from town, up into the foothills.

What had Safia discovered? Where were they headed?

He ran through all the archaeological possibilities, all the sites peppered across the ancient land: shrines, cemeteries, ruins, caves, sinkholes. There were too many. Turn over any stone here and you discover a piece of history.

But then he had an idea. There was a major tomb near that highway, just a few miles off the road.

Omaha moved back to the computer. He watched the blue arrow coursing along the road. "There's a turnoff about fifteen miles up the highway. If they take that turn, I know where they're headed."

"That'll mean waiting a bit more," Painter said.

Omaha crouched by the computer. "It seems we have no choice."

5:32 P.M.

Painter bought time on another computer. He left Omaha to monitor the SUV's progress. If they could get a lead on where Cassandra was headed with Safia, they could get a head start. It was a slim hope.

Alone with his computer, Painter again accessed the DOD server. There was no reason to feign death any longer. He'd left enough of an electronic trail. Besides, considering the elaborate trap at the safe house, Cassandra knew he was alive . . . or at least, she was acting that way.

That was one of the reasons he needed to log back onto the DOD site.

He entered his private pass code and accessed his mail system. He typed in the address for his superior, Dr. Sean McKnight, head of Sigma. If there was anyone he trusted, it was Sean. He needed to apprise his commander of the events, let him know the status of the operation.

An e-mail window opened, and he typed rapidly, relating a thumbnail sketch of events. He stressed the role of Cassandra, the possibility of a mole in the organization. There was no way Cassandra could have known about the safe house, the electronic code for the equipment locker, without some inside information.

He finished:

I cannot stress enough that matters at your end must be investigated. Success of this mission

will depend on cutting off further flow of intelligence. Trust no one. We will attempt to rescue
Dr. al-Maaz this evening. We believe we know
where Cassandra's group is taking the doctor. It
appears they are headed to

Painter paused, took a deep breath, then continued
typing:

the Yemeni border. We are headed there right
now in an attempt to stop the border crossing.

Painter stared at the letter. Numb at the possibility.
Omaha waved to him from the neighboring computer. "They made the turnoff on the side road!"
Painter hit the send button. The letter vanished, but
not his guilt.
"C'mon." Omaha crossed to the exit. "We can close
the distance."
Painter followed. At the door, he gave one final
glance back to his workstation. He prayed he was
wrong.

13

Footprints of the Prophet

◊∘∘ΧΠ)Υϟ჻Χ჻Ⅰ∘◊ⅠΧΥℨⅠΠ)∘ΠΥℨΧ

December 3, 5:55 P.M.
Dhofar Mountains

Safia stared out the window as the truck wound up a switchback through the mountainous hills. After they left the highway, asphalt had given way to gravel, which in turn disintegrated into a rutted red dirt path. They proceeded slowly, cautious of the deep gorge that shouldered the road to the left.

Below, the valley flowed away in deepening shades of lush green, disappearing into shadows near the bottom as the sun set to the west. A scatter of baobab trees dotted the slope, monstrous trees with tangled, rooted trunks that seemed more prehistoric than specimens of the modern world. Everywhere the land rolled in shades of emerald, striped in shadows. A waterfall glistened between two distant hills, its cataracts sparkling in the last rays of the sun.

If Safia squinted, she could almost imagine she was back in England.

All the lushness of the high country was due to the annual monsoon winds, the *khareef,* that swept the foothills and mountains in a continual misty drizzle from June through September. Even now, as the sun set, a steady wind had begun to blow, buffeting the truck. The sky overhead had darkened to slate gray, canopied with frothy clouds that brushed the higher hills.

The radio had been tuned to a local news channel during the ride up here. Cassandra had been listening for reports on the ongoing salvage operation on the *Shabab Oman.* Still no survivors had been found, and the seas were again kicking up with the approach of a new storm system. But what dominated the weather reports was news of the fierce sandstorm continuing its sweep south across Saudi Arabia, heading like a freight train for the desert of Oman, leaving a swath of destruction.

The wild weather matched Safia's mood: dark, threatening, unpredictable. She felt a force building inside her, below her breastbone, a tempest in a bottle. She remained tense, tingling. It reminded her of an impending anxiety attack, but now there was no fear, only determined certainty. She had nothing, so could lose nothing. She remembered her years in London. It had been the same. She had sought comfort by becoming nothing, cutting herself off, isolating herself. But now she had truly succeeded. She was empty, left with only one purpose: to stop Cassandra. And that was enough.

Cassandra remained lost in her own thoughts, only occasionally leaning forward to speak in hushed tones to John Kane up front. Her cell phone had rung a few minutes ago. She had answered it tersely, turning slightly away, speaking in a whisper. Safia heard Painter's name. She had tried to eavesdrop, but the woman kept her voice too low, blocked by the babble of the radio. Then she had hung up, made two other calls, and sunk into a palpably tense silence. Anger seemed to radiate in waves from the woman.

Since then, Safia kept her attention on the countryside, searching for places where she might hide, mapping the terrain in her head, just in case.

After another ten minutes of slow trekking, a larger hill appeared, its top still bathed in light. The golden bell of a short tower glinted in the sun.

Safia straightened. Job's tomb.

"Is that the place?" Cassandra stirred, eyes still narrowed.

Safia nodded, sensing that now was not the time to provoke her captor.

The SUV coasted down a final slope, circled the base of the mount, and then began a long climb toward the top, crawling up a switchback. A group of camels lounged beside the road as their vehicle neared the hilltop tomb. The beasts were all couched for a rest, kneeling down atop their knobby knees. A few men sat in the shadow of a baobab, tribesmen from the hills. The eyes of both camels and men followed the passage of the three trucks.

After a last switchback, the walled tomb complex appeared, consisting of a small beige building, a tiny whitewashed mosque, and a handsome garden courtyard of native shrubs and flowers. Parking was merely an open stretch of dirt in front, presently empty because of the lateness of the day.

As before, Kane settled the truck to a stop, then came around to open Safia's door. She climbed out, stretching a kink from her neck. Cassandra joined them as the other two SUVs parked and the men unloaded. They were all dressed in civilian clothes: khakis and Levi's, short-sleeved shirts, polos. But all the men wore matching windbreakers with the logo for Sunseeker Tours, all a size too big, hiding their holstered weapons. They quickly dispersed into a loose cordon near the road, feigning interest in the gardens or walls. A pair had binoculars and scanned the immediate area, turning in a slow circle.

Except for the road leading here, the remaining approaches were steep, almost vertical cliff faces. It would not be easy to flee on foot.

John Kane went among his men, nodding, bowing his head in last-minute instructions, then returned. "Where first?"

Safia motioned vaguely to the mosque and vault. *From one tomb to another.* She led the way through the opening in the wall.

"Place looks deserted," Kane commented.

"There must be a caretaker somewhere about," Safia said, and pointed to the steel chain that lay loose beside the entrance. No one had locked the place.

Cassandra signaled to two men. "Search the grounds."

Obeying, the pair took off.

Cassandra led the way after them. Safia followed with Kane at her side. They entered the courtyard between the mosque and small beige vault. The only other feature of the complex was a small set of ancient ruins near the back, neighboring the tomb. An ancient prayer room, supposedly all that was left of Job's original home.

Closer by, the door to the tomb lay open, unlocked like the gate.

Safia stared toward the doorway. "This may take some time. I don't have the slightest idea where to begin to look for the next clue."

"If it takes all night, then it takes all night."

"We're staying here?" Safia could not keep the surprise from her voice.

Cassandra wore a hard-edged expression. "For as long as it takes."

Safia swept the courtyard with her gaze. She prayed the caretaker had been careless in locking the place up and had already left. She feared hearing a gunshot somewhere out there, marking his death. And what if other pilgrims came later? How many more would die?

Safia felt conflicted. The sooner Cassandra had what she wanted, the less chance that other innocent folk would die. But that meant helping her. Something she was loath to do.

With no other choice, she crossed the grounds and entered the crypt. She had an inkling of what needed to be found—but not where it might be hidden.

She stood a moment in the entryway. The crypt here was smaller than Nabi Imran's tomb, a perfect square. The walls were painted white, the floor green. A pair of red Persian prayer rugs flanked the grave mound, which again was draped in silk shawls imprinted with passages from the Koran. Beneath the cloths was the bare dirt in which Job's body was said to have been buried.

Safia made a slow circle around the mound. There was no marble headstone as there had been at Imran's tomb, only a scattering of clay incense burners, scorched black from frequent use, and a small tray for visitors to leave gifts of coins. The room was otherwise unadorned, with the exception of a wall chart listing the names of the prophets: Moses, Abraham, Job, Jesus, and Muhammad. Safia hoped they wouldn't need to track all these men's tombs on the road to Ubar. She ended back at the entrance, none the wiser.

Cassandra spoke at the door. "What about that iron heart? Can we use it here?" As before, she had brought the silver case and had set it outside the door.

Safia shook her head, sensing that the heart would not be significant here. She exited the chamber, slipping between Cassandra and Kane.

As Safia stepped outside, she realized she had walked through the tomb in her shoes. She had also left her hair uncovered. She frowned.

Where was the caretaker?

She eyed the grounds, fearful for the man's safety, again hoping he'd already left. The winds had kicked up, scurrying through the yard, bobbing the heads of a row of daylilies. The place appeared deserted, displaced in time.

Yet Safia sensed something . . . something she could not name, almost an expectation. Maybe it was the light. It cast everything—the neighboring mosque, the edges of the walls, even the hard-packed gravel of the garden path—in stark, flat detail, a silver negative held over a bright light. She sensed if she waited long enough, all would be revealed in full color and clarity.

But she didn't have the time.

"What now?" Cassandra pressed, drawing her back.

Safia turned. Beside the entranceway, a small metal door was affixed to the ground. She bent to the handle, knowing what lay beneath it.

"What are you doing?" Cassandra asked.

"My job." Safia let her disdain shine through, too tired to care if she provoked her captor. She tugged up the door.

Hidden below was a shallow pit, sixteen inches deep, dug from the stone. At the bottom was a pair of petrified prints: a large man's bare footprint and a horse's hoof.

"What's all this?" Kane asked.

Safia explained, "If you remember my story of Job, he was afflicted with disease until God ordered him to strike his foot down and a healing spring was called forth." She pointed into the stone pit, to the footprint. "That is supposedly Job's footprint, where he struck the ground."

She pointed to the hole in the ground. "And there is where the spring bubbled up, fed from a water source at the foot of the hill."

"The water traveled uphill?" Kane asked.

"It wouldn't be a miracle otherwise."

Cassandra stared down. "What does the hoofprint have to do with the miracle?"

Safia's brow crinkled as she stared at the hoof. It was stone, too. "There is no story associated with it," she mumbled.

Still something tweaked her memory.

Petrified prints of a horse and a man.

Why did that sound familiar?

Throughout the region, there were countless stories of men or beasts turning to stone. Some even concerned Ubar. She shuffled through her memories. Two such stories, found in the *Arabian Nights* collection—"The Petrified City" and "The City of Brass"—related the discovery of a lost desert city, a place so evil it was damned and its inhabitants frozen in place for their sins, either petrified or turned to brass, depending on the story. It was a clear reference to Ubar. But in the second story, the treasure hunters hadn't stumbled upon the condemned city by accident. There had been clues and signposts that led them to its gates.

Safia recalled the most significant signpost from this story: a sculpture of brass. It depicted a mounted horseman, who bore aloft a spear with an impaled head atop it. On the head, an inscription had been written. She knew the line from the story by heart, having done extensive research for Kara about Arabian mysteries:

O thou who comest unto me, if thou know not the way that leadeth to the City of Brass, rub the hand of the horseman, and he will turn, and then will stop, and in whatsoever direction he stoppeth, thither proceed, for it will lead thee to the City of Brass.

To Ubar.

Safia pondered the passage. A metallic sculpture turning with a touch to point to the next signpost. She pictured the iron heart, aligning itself like a compass needle atop the marble altar. The similarity was uncanny.

And now this.

She stared into the pit.

A man and a horse. Petrified.

Safia noted how both the foot- and hoofprint pointed in the same direction, as if the man were walking his mount. Was that the next direction? She frowned, sensing the answer was too easy, too obvious.

She lowered the lid and stood.

Cassandra kept at her side. "You're onto something."

Safia shook her head—lost in the mystery. She strode in the direction of the prints, walking where the long-dead prophet would have headed with his horse. She ended up at the entrance to the small archaeological site located behind the main tomb, separated from the newer building by a narrow alley. The ruins were a nondescript structure of four crumbling walls, no roof, outlining a small chamber ten feet across. It seemed once a part of a larger home, long gone. She walked through the threshold and into the interior.

While John Kane guarded the door, Cassandra followed her inside. "What is this place?"

"An ancient prayer room." Safia stared up at the darkening skies as the sun sank away, then stepped over a kneeling rug on the floor.

Safia walked to where two of the walls had crude niches constructed into them, built to orient worshipers about the direction in which to pray. She knew the newer one faced toward Mecca. She crossed to the other, the older niche.

"Here is where the prophet Job prayed," Safia mumbled, more to herself than Cassandra. "Always facing Jerusalem."

To the *northwest*.

Safia stepped into the niche and faced backward, back the way she had come. Through the dimness, she made out the metal lid of the pit. The footsteps led right here.

She studied the niche. It was a solid wall of sandstone, quarried locally. The niche was a tumble of loose stone blocks, long deteriorated by age. She touched the inner wall.

Sandstone . . . like the sculpture where the iron heart had been found.

Cassandra stepped next to her. "What do you know that you're not telling us?" A pistol pressed into Safia's side, under her rib cage. Safia had not even seen the woman pull it free.

Keeping her hand flat against the wall, Safia turned to Cassandra. It was not the pistol that made her speak, but her own curiosity.

"I need a metal detector."

6:40 P.M.

As night fell, Painter turned off the main highway onto the gravel side road. A green sign with Arabic lettering stated JEBAL EITTEEN 9 KM. The truck bounced from the asphalt surface to gravel. Painter didn't slow down, spitting a shower of stones onto the highway. Gravel rattled in the wheel wells, sounding distinctly like automatic fire. It heightened his anxiety.

Omaha sat in the shotgun seat, his window rolled half down.

Danny sat behind his brother in the backseat. "Remember, this piece of crap doesn't have four-wheel drive." His teeth rattled as much as the vehicle.

"I can't risk slowing down," Painter called back. "Once nearer, I'll have to go more cautiously. With the lights off. But for now we have to push it."

Omaha grunted his approval.

Painter punched the accelerator as they reached a steep incline. The vehicle fishtailed. Painter fought it steady. It was not a vehicle suited for backcountry trekking, but they had no other choice.

Upon returning from the Internet Café, Painter had found Captain al-Haffi waiting with a 1988 Volkswagen Eurovan. Coral was examining his other purchases: three Kalashnikov rifles, and a pair of Heckler & Koch 9mm handguns. All traded for the sultan's stallion. And while the weapons were sound, with plenty of extra ammunition, the van would not have been Painter's first choice. The captain hadn't known they'd be leaving the city. And with time running short, they had no time to seek alternate transportation.

Still, at least the van could carry all of them. Danny, Coral, and the two Desert Phantoms sat crammed in the backseat, Kara, Clay, and Captain al-Haffi in the extra third row. Painter had attempted to dissuade them all from accompanying him, but he had little time to state his case. The others wanted to come, and they unfortunately knew too much. Salalah was no longer safe for any of them. Cassandra could dispatch assassins at any time to silence them. There was no telling where she had eyes, and Painter didn't know whom to trust. So they stuck together as a group.

He bounced the van around a tight switchback. His headlights swung about and blinded a large animal standing in the road. The camel stared at the van as Painter slammed on the brakes. They skidded to a stop.

The camel glanced down at the vehicle, eyes shining red, and slowly sauntered the rest of the way across the road. Painter had to creep onto the shoulder in order to edge around it.

Once past, he accelerated—only to brake again in another fifty feet. A dozen more camels filled the road, ambling along in no order, free-roaming.

"Beep your horn," Omaha said.

"And alert Cassandra's group that someone's coming?" Painter said with a scowl. "Someone will have to get out and scatter a path through them."

"I know camels," Barak said, and slid out.

As soon as his feet hit the gravel, a handful of men stepped out from behind boulders and shadowed alcoves. They pointed rifles at the van. Painter caught movement in his rearview mirror. There were another two men back there. They wore dusty ankle-length robes and dark headdresses.

"Bandits," Omaha spat, reaching to his holstered pistol.

Barak stood beside the open van door. He kept his palms bared, away from his weapon. "Not bandits," he whispered. "They're the Bait Kathir."

Bedouin nomads could distinguish various tribes at a distance of a hundred yards: from the way they tied their headcloths, to the colors of robes, to the saddles of their camels, how they carried their rifles. While Painter did not have this ability, he had educated himself on all the local tribes of southern Arabia: Mahra, Rashid, Awamir, Dahm, Saar. He knew the Bait Kathir, too, tribesmen of the mountains and desert, a reclusive, insular group prone to taking affront at the least slight. They could be dangerous if provoked and very protective of their camels.

One of the tribesmen stepped forward, a man worn by sun and sand into just bone and skin. *"Salam alaikum,"* he muttered. Peace be on you. They were strange words coming from someone still holding a weapon aimed at them.

"Alaikum as salam," Barak responded, palms still bared. On you be peace. He continued in Arabic. "What is the news?"

The man lowered his rifle a fraction. "What is the news?" was the standard question all tribesmen asked upon meeting. It could not be left unanswered. A flurry of words passed between Barak and the tribesman: information about the weather, of the sandstorm threatening the desert, of the predicted megastorm to come, of the many bedouin fleeing the *ar-rimal,* the sands, of the hardships along the way, of the camels lost.

Barak introduced Captain al-Haffi. All desert folk knew of the Phantoms. A murmur passed among the remaining men. Rifles were finally slung up.

Painter had vacated the van and stood to the side. An outsider. He waited for the ritual of introductions and news to be shared. It seemed, if he followed the discourse correctly, that Sharif's great-grandmother had worked on the film *Lawrence of Arabia* with the leader of this band's grandfather. With such a bond, an air of celebration began to arise. Voices grew more excited.

Painter sidled to Captain al-Haffi. "Ask them if they saw the SUVs."

The captain nodded, bringing a serious tone to his voice. Nods answered him. Their leader, Sheikh Emir ibn Ravi, reported that three trucks had passed forty minutes ago.

"Did they come back down?" Painter urged, speaking now in Arabic, slowly infiltrating the conversation. Perhaps his own brown skin, ambiguously ethnic, helped alleviate their suspicion of his foreignness.

"No," the sheikh answered, waving a hand toward the rising lands. "They stay at the tomb of Nabi Ayoub."

Painter stared up the dark road. So they were still up there. Omaha stood by the open passenger door. He had heard the exchange.

"Enough already," he urged. "Let's get going,"

The Bait Kathir had begun to round up their camels and shoo them off the road. The beasts protested with gurgles and angry belches.

"Wait," Painter said. He turned to Captain al-Haffi. "How much money do you have left from the sale of the stallion?"

The man shrugged. "Nothing but a handful of rials."

"Enough to buy or rent a few camels?"

The captain's eyes narrowed. "You want the camels. For what? Cover?"

"To get closer to the tomb. A small group of us."

The captain nodded and turned to Sheikh Emir. They spoke rapidly, two leaders conferring.

Omaha stepped to Painter. "The van is faster."

"On these roads, not *much* faster. And with the camels, we should be able to get very close to the tomb without alerting Cassandra's group. I'm sure she noted these tribesmen on her way up. Their presence will not be unexpected. Just a part of the natural landscape."

"And what do we do when we're up there?"

Painter already had a plan in mind. He told Omaha the gist of it. By the time he was done, Captain al-Haffi had reached some agreement with the sheikh.

"He will lend us his camels," the captain said.

"How many?"

"All of them." The captain answered Painter's look of surprise. "It is unseemly for a Bedu to refuse the request of a guest. But there is a condition."

"What is that?"

"I told them of our wish to rescue a woman from the group up at the tomb. They are most agreeable to help. It would be an honor to them."

"Plus they like to shoot their guns," Barak added.

Painter was reluctant to put them in danger.

Omaha did not share his hesitation. "They do have weapons. If your plan is going to work, the more firepower the better."

Painter had to agree.

With Painter's acquiescence, the sheikh broke into a broad grin and rallied his men. Saddles were cinched, camels were dropped into crouched positions for easy mounting, and ammunition was spread around like party favors.

Painter pulled his own group together, pooled in the headlights of the Eurovan. "Kara, I want you to stay behind with the van."

She opened her mouth to protest, but it was a weak effort. Her face shone with a film of sweat, despite the wind and chill of the night.

Painter cut her off. "We'll need someone to hide the van off the road, then bring it forward on my signal. Clay and Danny will stay with you with a rifle and a pistol. If we should fail, and Cassandra flees with Safia, you'll be the only ones able to track them."

Kara frowned, hard lines creasing her face, but she nodded. "You'd better not fail," she said fiercely. But even this outburst seemed to tax her.

To the side, Danny argued with his brother, wanting to come along.

Omaha stood firm. "You don't even have your goddamn eyeglasses. You'll just end up shooting me in the ass by mistake." Still, he placed a hand on his younger brother's shoulder. "And I'm counting on you here. You're the last line against trouble. I can't risk losing her again."

Danny nodded and backed down.

Clay had no objection to being left behind. He stood a step away, a burning cigarette in his fingers. His eyes stared at nothing, almost glazed over. He was nearing the end of his ability to handle all this.

With matters decided, Painter turned to the waiting camels. "Mount up!"

Omaha strode beside him. "Have you ever ridden a camel?"

"No." Painter glanced at him.

For the first time in the past day, Omaha wore a wide grin as he stepped away. "This'll be fun."

7:05 P.M.

Bathed in the beams of two floodlights, Cassandra watched as one of Kane's men waved the metal detector over the back wall of the niche. Just right of center in the wall, the detector buzzed with discovery. She tightened and turned to Safia. "You knew something would be found. How?"

Safia shrugged. "The iron heart had been posted by the coastal tomb of Imran, hidden in a sandstone sculpture. It pointed here. Up into the mountains. It only made sense that the next marker would be something similar. Another piece of iron, like the heart. The only mystery was *where* it was located."

Cassandra stared at the wall. Despite the frustrated anger she felt for the prisoner, the curator had indeed proven her worth. "What now?"

Safia shook her head. "It will have to be dug out. Freed from the stone. Like the iron heart from the statue." She faced Cassandra. "We'll have to proceed with caution. A single misstep and the buried artifact could be damaged. It will take days to extract it."

"Perhaps not." Cassandra turned and strode away, leaving Safia under Kane's watch. Stepping out of the prayer room, she crossed back toward the trucks, following the white gravel path through the dark gardens. As she marched past the entrance to the main tomb, a flicker of shadow caught her eye.

In a fluid motion, Cassandra dropped to a knee, sweeping a pistol from her shoulder holster, fueled by reflex and wariness. She covered the entrance and waited a full two breaths. Winds whispered the fronds of a palmetto bush. Her ears strained to listen.

Nothing. No movement from the tomb.

She rose smoothly, pistol held steady on the opening. She sidled toward the entrance, stepping off the path and onto the bare dirt to avoid the crunch of gravel.

She reached the doorway, covered one side of the room, edged in, and swept the other. The back windows allowed in enough reflected glow from the powerful work lights next door.

The grave mound was a shadowed hummock. There was no furniture. No place to hide. The tomb was empty.

She backed out and holstered her pistol. Just a mirage of shadows and lights. Perhaps someone had stepped in front of one of the work lights.

With a final glance around, she swung back to the path. With determined strides, she marched off toward the waiting trucks and silently scolded herself for jumping at shadows.

Then again, she had a good reason to be jumpy.

She pushed this thought aside as she reached the trucks. The SUVs carried not only Kane's men, but also an array of archaeological gear. Knowing they'd be heading out on a treasure hunt, the Guild had supplied her with an assortment of the usual equipment: spades, picks, jackhammers, brushes, sifting screens. But they had also outfitted her with state-of-the-art electronic tools, including a ground-penetrating radar system and an on-the-fly link to the LANDSAT satellite system. This last was capable of delving up to sixty feet under the sand to produce a detailed topographical map of what lay down below.

Cassandra crossed to where one of the trucks had been off-loaded to free up the metal detector. She knew what tool she needed now.

She used a crowbar to crack open the proper crate. The interior was lined with straw and Styrofoam to protect the piece of equipment, a Guild design based on a DARPA research project. It looked like a shotgun, but was belled at the end of the barrel. And its ceramic stock was extra bulky, wide enough to accept the battery block needed to charge the device.

Digging in the crate, Cassandra freed the battery unit and locked it in place. The device was heavy in her arms. She hefted it to her shoulder and headed back to the prayer room.

Spread along the perimeter, Kane's men remained at full attention. There was no slacking, no joking. Kane had trained them well.

Cassandra followed the garden path back to the prayer room. As she entered, Kane noted what she held in her arms. His eyes glinted.

Safia turned from where she was huddled in front of the wall. She had chalked out a rectangle. A foot wide at the top and about four feet tall.

"We're getting readings all along this area," the curator said, standing up. She frowned as she caught sight of the device in Cassandra's arms.

"A ULS laser," Cassandra explained. "Used to dig through rock."

"But—"

"Get back." Cassandra lifted the unit to her shoulder and pointed the belled barrel of the unit at the wall.

Safia stepped aside.

Cassandra pressed the button near her thumb, the equivalent of a safety. At her touch, tiny beams of crimson light speared outward, like the spray from a shower nozzle. Each beam was a tiny laser gun, focused through alternating crystals of alexandrite and erbium. Cassandra centered her aim on the chalked section of wall. The tiny dots of the idling laser formed a perfect circle.

She pulled the trigger. The device vibrated on her shoulder as the array of tiny lasers began to spin, faster and faster. A sound beyond hearing ached the bones of her ear. She concentrated, staring over the barrel.

Where the crimson beam struck the wall, the stone began to disintegrate in a cloud of dust and silica. For decades, dentists had been using ultrasonics to scale tartar from teeth. The same principle was being employed here, only intensified by the concentrated energy of the lasers. The sandstone continued to dissolve under the twin assault.

Cassandra slowly swept the beam back and forth over the wall, erasing the sandstone layer by layer.

The ULS laser worked only on aggregate material, like sandstone. Harder stone, like granite, was impervious to it. It was even harmless to flesh. The worst it would do was leave a bad sunburn.

She continued to work at the wall. Sand and dust filled the prayer room, but the wind gusting through kept it relatively clear. After three minutes, she had worn a swath about four inches into the wall.

"Stop!" Safia called out, holding up an arm.

Cassandra released the trigger. She shifted the idling gun upward.

Safia waved sand from her face and moved to the wall. Winds scurried the last of the smoky dust out through the roof as she leaned forward.

Cassandra and Kane joined her. Kane shone a flashlight into the cubbyhole worn by the laser. A bit of metal glinted ruddy from the depths of the pocket.

"Iron," Safia said behind her, a trace of awe in her voice, a mix of pride and incredulity. "Like the heart."

Cassandra retreated back and lowered her weapon. "Then let's see what prize is in this fucking Cracker Jack box." She pulled the trigger, now concentrating around the iron artifact.

Spinning lasers again dissolved sandstone to dust, eroding away layers. More and more of the artifact became clear, lit by the crimson glow. From the stone, details emerged: a nose, a heavy brow, an eye, the corner of a lip.

"It's a face," Safia said.

Cassandra continued her careful sweep, wiping stone away as if it were mud, revealing the face beneath. It seemed to be pushing out of the stone toward them.

"My God . . ." Kane muttered, bringing his flash-light to bear, bathing it brightly. The likeness was too remarkable for chance.

Kane glanced over to Safia. "It's you."

7:43 P.M.

Painter sat atop the camel, staring across the dark valley that separated their party from Jebal Eitteen. Atop the far hill, the tomb blazed against the moonless night sky. The brightness was enhanced by the night-vision goggles he wore, turning the tomb into a light-house beacon.

He studied the terrain. It was an easily defensible site. There was only one approach: the dirt road wind-ing up the south face of the mount. He adjusted the magnification on his goggles. He had counted fourteen hostiles but no sign of Safia. She must already be within the tomb complex.

At least he hoped so.

She had to be alive. The alternative was unthinkable.

He pulled off the goggles and attempted to shift into a comfortable position atop his camel. He failed.

Captain al-Haffi sat on a camel to his right, Omaha on his left. They both seemed as relaxed as if they were sitting on lounge chairs. The saddles, double vises of wood over palm thatch, offered little cushioning, positioned on the animals' withers in front of the hump. To Painter, it was a torture device designed by a sadistic Arab. After only a half hour, he felt as if he were being split slowly in half, like some human wishbone.

Grimacing, Painter pointed down the slope. "We'll proceed as a group to the bottom of the valley. Then I'll need ten minutes to get in position. After that time, everyone will slowly climb the road toward the tomb. Make lots of noise. Once you reach that last switchback, stop and settle in, like you're going to overnight there. Set up a fire. It'll blind their night vision. Let the camels graze. The movement will make it easier to get yourselves into sniping positions. Then wait for my signal."

Captain al-Haffi nodded and passed on the instructions as he slowly worked down the line.

Coral took the captain's place at Painter's side. She leaned forward a bit in her saddle, her face tight. It seemed his partner was not any happier about their mode of transportation than he was.

She crossed her arms atop her saddle. "Perhaps I should be the one to take the lead on this op. I've more experience with infiltration than you." She lowered her voice. "And I'm less personally involved."

Painter tightened his grip as the camel shifted under him. "My feelings for Safia will not interfere with my abilities."

"I meant Cassandra, your ex-partner." She lifted one eyebrow. "Are you trying to prove something? Is any of that energy going into this operation?"

Painter glanced to the tomb blazing atop the neighboring hill. When he had been searching the complex, noting terrain and manpower, a part of him had also been watching for some sign of Cassandra. She had orchestrated everything since the British Museum. Still, he had yet to see her face. How would he react? She had betrayed, murdered, kidnapped. All in the name of what cause? What could make her turn against Sigma . . . against him? Just money? Or was it something more?

He had no answers.

He stared at the lights. Was that a part of the reason he insisted on taking point on this mission? To see her for himself? To look in her eyes?

Coral broke the silence. "Don't give her any leeway. No mercy, no hesitation. Play it cold, or you'll lose it all."

He remained silent as the camels continued their slow, painful trek down to the bottom of the valley. The vegetation grew thicker as they descended along the dirt road. Tall baobab trees cast a thick canopy, while massive tamarinds, heavy with yellow flowers, towered like sentinels. Everywhere, ropy liana vines tangled amid wreaths of jasmine.

The party stopped in this patch of dense forest.

Camels began to drop and unload their riders. One of the Bait Kathir approached Painter's camel, helping him couch the beast.

"Farha, krr, krr . . ." the man said as he stepped before the animal. *Farha* was the camel's name, meaning "joy." To Painter, nothing could be further from the truth. The only joy he could imagine would be getting off her hump.

The camel dropped under him, swaying backward and settling to her hindquarters. Painter held tightly, legs clenching. She then sank to her hocks in front, shuffling her knees down, and came to a rest on the ground.

With the camel couched, Painter slid from the saddle. His legs were rubbery, his thighs knotted. He stumbled a few steps away as the tribesman cooed at the camel and kissed her on the nose, earning a soft burble from the beast. It was said the Bait Kathir loved their camels more than their wives. It certainly seemed that way with this fellow.

Shaking his head, Painter crossed to join the others. Captain al-Haffi sat on his haunches beside Sheikh Emir, drawing in the dirt of the road, holding a penlight, outlining how to best distribute the men. Sharif and Barak watched over Omaha and Coral as the two Americans prepped their Kalashnikov rifles. Each of them had an Israeli Desert Eagle pistol as a backup weapon.

Painter took the moment to check his own guns, a pair of Heckler & Koch pistols. In the dark, he slipped out and checked the 9mm magazines, seven rounds apiece. He had two additional magazines loaded and ready in his belt. Satisfied, he holstered the weapons, one at the shoulder, one at the waist.

Omaha and Coral approached him as he cinched the small ditty bag to his belly. He didn't check its contents, having inventoried it all back in Salalah.

"When does the ten-minute clock start running?" Omaha asked, exposing his wristwatch as he stopped, pushing a button to illuminate its face.

Painter coordinated his own watch with Coral's Breitlinger. *"Now."*

Coral caught his gaze, concern in her blue eyes. "Stay cold, Commander."

"As ice," he whispered.

Omaha blocked him as he turned to the road leading up to the hilltop tomb. "Don't come back without her." This was as much a plea as a threat.

Painter nodded, acknowledging both, and headed out.

Ten minutes.

8:05 P.M.

Working under the glow of a pair of floodlights, Safia used a pick and brush to loosen the artifact from the sandstone's embrace. The winds had kicked up, stirring the sand and dust, trapped by the four walls of the roofless prayer room. Safia felt caked in it, a living statue of sandstone.

With the fall of night, the temperature dropped precipitously. Heat lightning flickered to the south, getting closer, accompanied by the occasional bass rumble, a clear promise of rain.

Wearing gloves, Safia brushed grit from the artifact, afraid of scratching it. The life-size iron bust of a woman shone in the sharp lights, eyes open, staring back at her. Safia feared that gaze and concentrated on the work at hand.

Cassandra and Kane whispered behind her. Cassandra had wanted to use her laser gun to finish freeing the iron artifact, but Safia had urged caution, lest it be damaged. She feared the laser might etch the metal, erasing details.

Safia picked away the last of the stone. She attempted not to stare at the features, but found herself glancing at it from the corner of her eye. The face was remarkably similar to her own. It could have been a younger version of herself. Perhaps at eighteen. But this was impossible. It had to be just a racial coincidence. It merely depicted a southern Arabian woman, and as a native of the region, Safia would, of course, bear some resemblance, even with her mixed-blood heritage.

Still, it did unnerve her. It was like staring at her own funereal mask.

Especially as the bust was impaled atop an iron spear, four feet long.

Safia leaned back. The artifact occupied the center of the chalked rectangle on the wall of the prayer niche. The red iron spear stood upright, the bust impaled atop it. All one object. Though the sight disturbed her, Safia was not totally surprised. It made a certain historical sense.

"If this takes any longer," Cassandra interrupted her thoughts, "I'm going to pull out the goddamn ULS laser again."

Safia reached forward and tested the rock's hold on the iron object. It wobbled with her touch. "Another minute." She set to work.

Kane shifted, his shadow dancing on the wall. "Do we need to remove it? Maybe it's facing the right direction already."

"It's facing southeast," Safia answered him. "Back to the coast. That can't be the way. There's another riddle to solve."

With her words, the top-heavy artifact broke free of the rock and fell face forward. Safia caught it on her shoulder.

"About time," Cassandra mumbled.

Safia stood, cradling the bust. She held the spear haft in both of her gloved hands. It was heavy. With the iron head resting near her ear, she heard the slight sloshing sound coming from inside. *Like the heart.* A molten heaviness lay at its core.

Kane took the artifact from her, lifting it like it was a stalk of corn. "So what do we do with it?"

Cassandra pointed a flashlight. "Back to the tomb, like in Salalah."

"No," Safia said. "Not this time."

She slipped past Cassandra and led the way. She thought about delaying the search, dragging it out. But she had heard the jingle of camel bells, echoing up from the valley. There was an encampment of bedouin nearby. If any of them should wander up here . . .

Safia hurried forward and crossed to the covered pit near the entrance to the tomb. She knelt down and hauled it open. Cassandra shone her light down into the hole, illuminating the pair of footprints. Safia remembered the story that had made her follow those footsteps: the tale of the brass horseman who had borne a spear in his hand, a spear impaled with a head.

Safia glanced past Cassandra's shoulder to Kane and the artifact. After untold centuries, she had found that spear.

"What now?" Cassandra asked.

There was only one other feature in the pit, one that had yet to yield a clue: the hole in the center of the pit.

According to the Bible and the Koran, through this hole, a magical spring had gushed forth, one that led to miracles. Safia prayed for her own miracle.

She pointed to the hole. "Plant it there."

Kane straddled the pit, positioned the haft end of the spear, and settled it into the hole. "Tight fit."

He stood back. The spear remained standing, firmly rooted. The bust atop it stared out over the valley.

Safia walked around the impaled spear. As she inspected it, rain spattered out of the dark skies, tapping the packed dirt and stone with a sullen beat.

Kane grumbled. "Bloody brilliant." He pulled out a ball cap and tugged it over his shaved head.

In moments, the rain began to fall more heavily.

Safia circled the spear a second time, frowning now.

Cassandra shared her concern. "Nothing's happening."

"We're simply missing something. Pass me the torch." Safia took off her dirty work gloves and held out a palm for the flashlight. Cassandra relinquished it with clear reluctance.

Safia shone it over the length of the spear. Its shaft was striated at regular intervals. Was it decoration or something significant? With no idea, Safia straightened from a crouch and stood behind the bust. Kane had planted the spear with the face still pointing south, toward the sea. Clearly the wrong way.

Her eyes drifted to the bust. Staring at the back of the head, she spotted tiny writing on the base of the neck, shadowed by the hairline. She brought the flashlight closer. The lettering must have been partially obscured by the residual dust, but the rain was washing it clean. Four letters became clear.

Cassandra noted her attention and the script. "What does it mean?"

Safia translated, her frown deepening. "A woman's name. *Biliqis.*"

"Is it the woman sculpted here?"

Safia didn't answer, too astounded. *Could it be?* She stepped around and studied the woman's face. "If true, then this is a find of phenomenal significance. Biliqis was a woman revered across all faiths. A woman lost in mystery and myth. Said to be half human, half spirit of the desert."

"I never heard of her."

Safia cleared her throat, still stunned by the discovery. "Biliqis is better known by her title: the Queen of Sheba."

"As in the story of King Solomon?"

"Among countless other tales."

As rain pattered down and ran in rivulets over the iron face, the statue appeared to be crying.

Safia reached and wiped the tears from the queen's cheek.

With her touch, the bust moved as if pivoting on slippery ice, swinging from her fingertips. It spun once fully around, then slowed and wavered to a stop, staring in the opposite direction.

To the northeast.

Safia glanced back to Cassandra.

"The map," Cassandra ordered Kane. "Get the map."

14

Tomb Raider

ⵝⵁⵙⵏⵉⵁⵂⵖⵂ

December 3, 8:07 P.M.
Jebal Eitteen

Painter checked his watch. One more minute.

He lay flat on his belly at the base of a fig tree, sheltered behind an acacia bush. Rain pitter-pattered against the canopy of leaves overhead. He had positioned himself far to the right of the road, carefully picking his way up a nearly sheer cliff face to reach this spot. He had a clear view of the parking lot.

With the night-vision goggles fixed to his face, the guards were easy to spot in the darkness, all in their blue windbreakers, now with hoods pulled up against the rain. Most were posted near the road leading here, but a few others slowly circled wider. It had taken precious minutes to creep into position, moving forward as the guards shifted past.

Painter took slow steady breaths, preparing himself. It was a thirty-yard dash to the nearest SUV. He fixed the plan, visualizing it, refining it. Once things began to roll, he would have no time to think, only react.

He glanced at his watch. Time was up.

He slowly raised himself into a crouched position, staying small, compact. He strained to listen, tuning out the rain. Nothing. He glanced at his watch again. Ten minutes had passed. Where were—

Then he heard it. A song, being sung by a handful of voices, rose from the valley behind him. He glanced over a shoulder. Through his night-vision lenses, the world was cast in shades of green, but sharp shards of brilliance bloomed below. Torches and flashlights. He watched the Bait Kathir begin a slow, steady climb up the road, singing as they proceeded.

Painter swung his attention back to the tomb complex.

The guards had noted the stirring of the tribesmen and had slowly shifted positions to concentrate on the road. Two men fled into the brush flanking the road and continued down the switchback.

With the forces pulled away from the parked SUVs, Painter made his move. He swept from his hiding place, staying low, and raced across the thirty yards to the nearest truck. He held his breath as he ran, avoiding the noisy splash of puddles. No alarm was raised.

Reaching the first SUV, he ducked behind it while pulling open the oiled zipper of his ditty bag. He removed the prewired C4 packages, each wrapped in cellophane, and tucked one into the truck's wheel well, near the gas tank.

Painter silently thanked Cassandra for the gift of the explosives. It was only fitting that he return what was hers.

Staying low, he hurried forward to the next SUV and planted the second package. He left the third truck untouched, only checked to make sure the keys had been left in the ignition. Such a precaution was a common practice in an ops situation. When the shit hit the fan, you didn't want to have to hunt down the driver with the keys.

Satisfied, he checked the lot. The guards remained focused on the approaching band of camels and men.

Swinging around, he darted toward the low wall that enclosed the tomb complex. He kept the line of SUVs between him and the guards. Behind, he heard shouts rising from below . . . in Arabic . . . jovial arguing. The singing had ceased. A pair of camels bleated forlornly, accompanied by the jingle of harness bells. The bedouin were halfway up the hill.

He had to hurry.

Painter vaulted the low wall. It was only four feet high. He had chosen an isolated spot, behind the mosque. He landed with more of a thud than he intended, but the rain covered the noise with a grumble of thunder.

He paused. Light flowed down either side of the mosque, coming from the courtyard in front of the building. It shone blindingly bright through his night-vision goggles. He heard mumbled voices, but the rain drummed away any distinction. He had no clue how many were out there.

Crouching to keep his silhouette below the wall, he fled along the back of the mosque, keeping to the shadows. He came to a back door, checked the knob. Locked. He could force the door, but it would make too much noise. He continued on, looking for a window or another way inside. He would be too exposed if he attempted to reach the central courtyard directly from either side of the building. There was no shelter and too much light. He needed a way through the mosque, a way to get closer. To abduct Safia from under Cassandra's nose, he would need to be close to the action.

He reached the far corner of the mosque. Still no windows. Who built a place with no windows in back? He stood in a small weedy vegetable garden. Two date palms guarded over it.

Painter stared up. One of the palms grew close to the mosque's wall, shadowing the roof's edge. The mosque's roof was flat. If he could scale the palm . . . reach the roof . . .

He stared at the clumps of dates hanging beneath the fronds.

It would not be an easy climb, but he'd have to risk it.

With a deep breath, he jumped as high as he could, straddling his arms around the trunk, hitching his feet up on it. The bark offered no purchase. He promptly slid down, landing on his backside in the mud.

As he began to push back up, he spotted two things, both hidden behind a hedgerow flanking the back wall: an aluminum ladder . . . and a pale hand.

Painter tensed.

The hand did not move.

He crawled forward, parting the bushes. A ladder leaned against the back wall, along with a pair of clipping shears. Of course, there had to be a way to reach those hanging dates. He should have known to search for a ladder.

He moved to the figure stretched out on the ground.

It was an older Arab man, in a *dishdasha* robe embroidered with gold thread. He was most likely a member of the tomb's staff, a caretaker of some sort. He lay in the dirt, unmoving. Painter pressed fingers to the man's throat. He was still warm. A slow pulse beat under Painter's fingers. Alive. Unconscious.

Painter straightened. Had Cassandra darted the man, as she had done to Clay? But why drag him back here and hide him? It made no sense, but he had no time to ponder the mystery.

He hauled out the ladder, checked to make sure he was still hidden from the guards, and propped it against the back wall of the mosque. The ladder reached just shy of the roofline.

Good enough.

He quickly scaled the rungs. As he climbed, he glanced over his shoulder. He saw that the guards had moved to block the road completely. Downslope, he spotted the lights and torches of the Bait Kathir clan as they clustered a short way down. They had stopped and begun to make camp. He heard occasional snatches of loud voices, all in Arabic, as the men kept up the pretext of nomadic travelers bunking down for the night.

Reaching the top of the ladder, Painter grabbed the edge of the roof and hauled himself up, hooking a leg over the lip and rolling out of sight.

Staying low, he hurried across the roof, aiming for the minaret near the front. Just a few feet above the roofline, an open balcony encircled the tower, where the call to prayer would be sung for the local worshipers.

It was easy to grab the railing and vault over the balustrade.

Painter crouched and edged around the balcony. He had a bird's-eye view of the courtyard. It was too bright for his night-vision gear, so he pushed the goggles up and studied the layout.

Across the way, the small set of ruins blazed with light.

A flashlight lay abandoned near the entrance to the neighboring tomb. Its shine illuminated a metal pole planted in the ground. It appeared to be surmounted by some sculpture, a bust by the looks of it.

Voices rose from below . . . coming from the squat tomb. Its door to the courtyard lay open. Lights glowed from inside.

He heard a familiar voice. "Show us on the map."

It was Cassandra. Painter's gut clenched, fiery and determined.

Then Safia answered her. "It makes no sense. It could be anywhere."

Painter crouched lower. Thank God she was still alive. A surge of relief and renewed concern swept through him. How many people were with her? He spent a few minutes studying the shadows across the frosted windows. It was hard to say, but it didn't appear that more than four were in the room. He watched the courtyard for additional guards. It remained quiet. Everyone seemed to be in the one building, out of the rain.

If he moved quickly . . .

As he began to swing away, a figure stepped out of the tomb doorway, a tall muscular man dressed in black. Painter froze, afraid of being spotted.

The man tucked the brim of a ball cap farther over his eyes and shoved into the rain. He crossed and knelt beside the pole.

Painter spied as the man reached to the bottom of the pole and ran his fingers slowly up its length. *What the hell was he doing?* Reaching the top of the shaft, the man stood and hurried back to the tomb, shaking out his ball cap.

"Sixty-nine," he said as he disappeared inside.

"Are you sure?" Cassandra again.

"Yes, I'm bloody damned sure."

Painter dared wait no longer. He ducked through the archway to reach the tower stairs that spiraled down into the mosque. He flipped his night-vision goggles in place and inspected the dark staircase.

It seemed quiet.

He pulled free his pistol and thumbed off the safety.

Wary of guards, he proceeded with one shoulder near the wall, gun pointed forward. He continued down the short spiral, sweeping the mosque's prayer room as he descended. Highlighted in green, the room was empty, prayer mats stacked in back. He stepped out and moved toward the entryway in front.

The outer doors were open. He pushed the goggles back up and sidled to the entrance. He crouched to one side. A covered porch spread along the front. Directly ahead, three steps led down to the courtyard. To either side, a short stucco wall framed the porch, topped by arched openings.

Painter waited and checked the immediate area.

The courtyard remained empty. Voices murmured across the way.

If he dashed across to the tomb, hid outside the doorway . . .

Painter calculated in his head, unblinking. For this to work, speed was essential. He straightened, pistol held steady.

A slight noise froze him in place. It came from behind.

An electric thrill of terror lanced through him.

He wasn't alone.

He swept around in a crouch, pistol pointing into the depths of the mosque. Out of the gloom, a pair of dark shadows stalked toward him, eyes glowing in the reflected light of the courtyard. Feral and hungry.

Leopards.

As silent as the night, the two cats closed in on him.

8:18 P.M.

"Show me on the map," Cassandra said.

The curator knelt on the floor of the tomb. She had spread out the same map as before. A straight blue line led from the first tomb on the coast to this one in the mountains. Now a second line, this one in red, branched away, heading northeast, crossing out of the mountains and into a great blank expanse of the desert, the Rub' al-Khali, the vast Empty Quarter of Arabia.

Safia shook her head, running a finger along the line out into the sands. "It makes no sense. It could be anywhere."

Cassandra stared down at the map for several breaths. They were looking for a lost city in the desert. It had to be somewhere along that line, but where? The line crossed through the center of the vast expanse. It could be anywhere.

"We're still missing something," Safia said, leaning back on her heels. She rubbed her temples.

Kane's radio buzzed, interrupting them. He spoke into his throat mike. "How many?" A long pause.

"Okay, just keep a bloody close eye on them. Keep them away. Let me know if anything changes."

Cassandra eyed him as he finished.

He shrugged. "Those sand rats we saw on the side of the road have returned. They're setting up camp where we spotted them earlier."

Cassandra noted the concern in Safia's face. The woman feared for her countrymen's safety. *Good.* "Order your men to shoot anyone who gets close."

Safia tensed at her words.

Cassandra pointed to the map. "The sooner we solve this mystery, the sooner we're out of here." That should light a fire under the curator.

Safia stared sullenly at the map. "There must be some distance marker built into the artifact. Something we missed. A way to determine how far down this red line we must travel."

Safia closed her eyes, rocking a bit. Then she suddenly stopped.

"What?" Cassandra asked.

"The spear," she said, glancing to the door. "I noticed striations along its shaft, marks scored into it. I thought them merely decoration. But back in the ancient past, measurements were often recorded as notches on a stick."

"So you think the number of marks could signify a distance?"

Safia nodded and began to stand. "I have to count them."

Cassandra distrusted the woman. It would be easy to lie and lead them astray. She needed accuracy. "Kane, go out and count the number of marks."

He grimaced but obeyed, slapping on his sodden ball cap.

After he left, Cassandra crouched by the map. "This has to be the final location. First the coast, then the mountain, now the desert."

Safia shrugged. "You're probably right. The number three is significant to ancient faiths. Whether it's the trinity of the Christian God—the Father, the Son, and the Holy Spirit—or the ancient celestial trinity: the moon, the sun, and the morning star."

Kane appeared in the doorway, shaking rain from his cap. "Sixty-nine."

"Are you sure?"

He scowled at her. "Yes, I'm bloody damned sure."

"Sixty-nine," Safia said. "That has to be right."

"Why?" Cassandra asked, turning her attention back to the curator as she bent over the map.

"Six and nine," Safia explained to the map. "Multiples of three. Just like we were talking about. Sequential, too. A very magical number."

"And here I always thought 'sixty-nine' meant something else," Kane said.

Seemingly deaf to the man, Safia continued to work, measuring with a protractor and tapping a calculator. Cassandra watched over her.

"This is sixty-nine miles along the red line." Safia circled the spot. "It ends up here in the desert."

Cassandra knelt down, took the protractor, and re-checked her measurements. She stared at the red circle, noting the longitude and latitude in her head. "So this may be the location of the lost city?"

Safia nodded. She continued to stare at the map. "As best I can tell."

Cassandra's brow crinkled, sensing the woman was keeping something from her. She could almost see the woman calculating something in her head.

She grabbed Safia's wrist. "What are you holding back—"

A shot rang out nearby, clipping away any further words.

It could be a misfire. It could be one of the bedouin shooting off his rifle. But Cassandra knew better. She swung around. "Painter . . ."

8:32 P.M.

Painter's first shot went wild as he fell backward out the mosque's doorway and onto the porch. A corner of a wall blasted away in a shower of plaster. Inside, the leopards parted, vanishing into the shadows of the mosque.

Painter flung himself to the side, sheltering behind the half wall of the porch. *Stupid.* He shouldn't have shot. He had reacted out of instinct, self-preservation. That wasn't like him. But some terror beyond the leopards had gripped him, as if something had jangled the deepest root of his brain.

And now he had given away the element of surprise.

"Painter!" The shout came from the direction of the tomb.

It was Cassandra.

Painter dared not move. Leopards prowled on the inside, Cassandra on the outside. The lady or the tiger? In this case, both meant death.

"I know you came for the woman!" Cassandra shouted into the rain. A rumble of thunder punctuated her words.

Painter remained quiet. Cassandra couldn't know for sure in which direction his gunshot had come from. Sound traveled oddly among these mountainous hills. He imagined her hiding in the tomb, calling out from the doorway. She dared not move into the open. She knew he was armed, but she didn't know where he was.

How could he use that to his advantage?

"If you don't show yourself—arms up, hands empty—in the next ten seconds, I'm going to shoot the prisoner."

He had to think quickly. To reveal himself now would only mean his death, along with Safia's.

"I knew you'd come, Crowe! Did you really think that I'd believe you were heading to the border of Yemen?"

Painter flinched. He had sent out the e-mail only hours ago, planted with false information, delivered through a secure server to his boss. It had been a test balloon. As he feared, word had reached Cassandra intact. A sense of despair settled over him. That could only mean one thing. The betrayal of Sigma started at the very top.

Sean McKnight . . . his own boss . . .

Was that why Sean had paired him with Cassandra to begin with?

It seemed impossible.

Painter closed his eyes and took a deep breath, sensing his isolation.

He was now alone out here, cut off. He had no one to contact, no one to trust. Oddly, this thought only helped energize him. He felt a giddy sense of freedom. He had to rely on himself and his immediate resources.

That would have to be enough.

Painter reached into his ditty bag and palmed the radio transmitter.

Thunder growled, throatier, guttural. Rain fell harder.

"Five seconds, Crowe."

All the time in the world . . .

He stabbed the transmitter's button and rolled toward the stairs.

8:34 P.M.

From seventy yards away, Omaha jolted as the twin explosions rocketed the two SUVs into the air, as bright as lightning strikes. The dark night went brilliant. The concussion squeezed his ears, thundered in his rib cage.

It was Painter's signal. He had secured Safia.

A moment ago, Omaha had heard a single gunshot, terrifying him. Now flames and debris rained down across the parking lot. Men lay sprawled in the dirt. Two were on fire, bathed in burning gasoline.

It was time to move.

"Now!" Omaha shouted, but his yell sounded tinny in his own ears.

Still, rifle fire spat out of the forest to either side of Omaha. Additionally, a few flashes of muzzle fire sparked from a high shoulder that overlooked the parking lot, coming from a pair of Bait Kathir snipers.

Up at the tomb, two guards had been picking themselves off the ground. They suddenly jerked, bodies thrown backward. Shot.

Other guards sought cover, reacting with well-honed skill. These were no amateurs. They retreated over the compound walls, seeking fast cover.

Omaha lifted his binoculars.

Atop the hill's plateau, the two burning SUVs lit the parking lot. The third vehicle had been shoved a few feet by the concussion. Pools of flaming gasoline dotted the dirt and hood, steaming in the rain. Painter was supposed to use the vehicle as an escape vehicle. He should've been there by now.

Where was he? What was he waiting for?

An ululating cry rose to Omaha's right. Bells jangled. A dozen camels scattered uphill. Amid them ran more of the Bait Kathir. Cover fire rained from out of the tree line.

A few shots now answered. A camel bellowed, dropping to one knee, skidding in the dirt. An explosion ripped into the hillside off to Omaha's left. A flash of fire and torn tree limbs, smoking leaves, and dirt flumed upward.

A grenade.

And then a new sound.

It came from the deep gorge to the right.

Shit . . .

Five small helicopters rose into view, as swift as gnats and as tiny. One-man vehicles. Just blades, engine, and pilot. They looked like flying sleds. Spotlights swept the grounds, peppering the area with automatic gunfire.

Camels and men fled in all directions.

Omaha clenched a fist. The bitch had been expecting them. She'd had a backup force lying in wait, an ambush. How had she known?

Coral and Barak appeared at Omaha's elbow. "Painter's going to need help," Coral hissed. "He can't reach the escape vehicle now. It's too exposed."

Omaha glanced up to the lot, now a bloodbath of bodies and camels. From the forest, shots fired up at the helicopters, driving them higher. But they continued a zigzagging pattern over the compound, guarding it tightly.

The entire plan had fallen to shit.

But Safia was up there. Omaha was not leaving her again.

Coral freed her pistol. "I'm going in."

Omaha grabbed her arm. Her muscles were cords of steel. He held tight, brooking no argument. "This time, we're all going in."

8:35 P.M.

Kara stared down at the Kalashnikov rifle on her lap. Fingers twitching uncontrollably on the stock, she found it hard to concentrate. Her eyes felt too large for her head, threatening a migraine, while nausea lapped at her belly.

She dreamed of a little orange pill.

To her side, Clay fought to get the engine started. He cranked it again, but it failed to turn over. Danny sat in the backseat with the lone pistol.

The explosion had lit up the northern hills like a rising sun. It was Painter's signal. Across the intervening two valleys, echoing spatters of gunfire sounded like fireworks.

"Piece of shit!" Clay swore, and struck his hand on the steering wheel.

"You've flooded it," Danny said sourly from the back.

Kara stared out the passenger window. A ruddy glow persisted to the north. It had started. If all went well, the others would be racing downhill in one of the kidnappers' SUVs. The remainder of the party would scatter into the hills. The Bait Kathir knew many paths through the forested mountains.

But something felt wrong.

Maybe it was just the edgy frazzle in Kara's head. It grew more acute with each breath. Pain lanced behind her eyes. Even the light of the dashboard stabbed pain-fully bright.

"You're going to wear the battery down," Danny warned as Clay engaged the engine again. "Let it rest. Five minutes at least."

A buzzing filled Kara's skull, as if her body were an antenna, tuning in on static. She had to move. She could no longer sit still. She pulled open the latch and half fell out the door, bobbling her rifle.

"What are you doing?" Clay called to her, fright-ened.

She didn't answer. She stepped into the road. The van had been pulled under the branches of a tamarind tree. She crossed out into the open and wandered a short distance up the road, out of sight of the van.

Gunfire continued to echo.

Kara ignored it, her attention focused closer at hand.

An old woman stood in the roadway, facing Kara, as if waiting for her. She was dressed in a long desert cloak, her face hidden behind a black veil. In her bony fingers, she carried a staff of gnarled wood, worn smooth and shiny.

Kara's head throbbed. Then the static in her head fi-nally tuned to a proper station. Pain and nausea drained from her. She felt momentarily weightless, unburdened.

The woman merely stared.

Numbness filled the empty spaces inside her. She didn't fight it. The rifle dropped from Kara's limp fingers.

"She will need you," the woman finally said, turning away.

Kara followed after the stranger, moving as if in a dream.

Back by the tamarind tree, she heard the van's engine crank and fail.

Kara continued walking, leaving the road behind and heading down into the forested valley. Kara did not resist, even if she had been able to.

She knew who needed her.

8:36 P.M.

Safia had been forced to her knees, hands on top of her head. Cassandra crouched behind her, a pistol pressed at the base of her skull, another pointed toward the entrance. They both faced the doorway, poised tensely on the far side of the chamber. The grave mound stood between them and the exit.

With the explosion, Cassandra had extinguished the lights and sent Kane out a back window. To circle around. To hunt down Painter.

Safia clenched her fingers together. Could it be true? Could Painter still be alive, be somewhere out there? If that was so, had the others survived? Tears welled. No matter what, she was not alone. Painter had to be out there.

Gunfire still rattled from beyond the compound.

Fires cast the night in crimson and shadow.

She heard the beat of helicopters, spatters of automatic fire.

"Just let us go," Safia pleaded. "You have Ubar's location."

Cassandra remained silent in the dark, her full attention on the door and windows. Safia didn't know if she had even heard her plea.

From beyond the door, a shuffling sound reached them.

Someone was coming. Painter or Kane?

Across the doorway, a large shadow passed, lit momentarily by the lone flashlight still out in the courtyard.

A camel.

It was a surreal sight as it sauntered past, soaked by the rain. In its wake, a woman stood framed in the doorway, naked. She seemed to shimmer in the crimson glow of the nearby fires.

"You!" Cassandra gasped.

In one hand, the stranger carried the silver case containing the iron heart. It had been resting just outside the door.

"No you don't, bitch!" Cassandra fired her pistol, two rounds, deafeningly close to Safia's left ear.

Crying out from the painful sound of the blast, Safia fell forward onto one of the prayer rugs. She rolled a step away, toward the grave mound.

Cassandra followed, still firing at the door.

Safia craned up, her head ringing. The doorway was empty again. She glanced sidelong to Cassandra, who'd assumed a shooter's stance, both pistols pointed toward the open door.

Safia saw her chance. She grabbed the edge of the prayer rug, which she now shared with Cassandra. In a swift motion, she lunged up, dragging the rug with her.

Caught by surprise, Cassandra toppled, her feet going out from under her.

A pistol fired.

Plaster shattered from the ceiling.

As Cassandra fell backward, Safia dove over the grave mound and rolled toward the door. At the entrance, she leaped headlong over the threshold.

Another blast.

In midair, Safia felt a kick in her shoulder, shoving her around. She hit the ground and skidded in the mud. Her shoulder burned. Shot. Panicked, reacting on pure instinct, she rolled to the side, away from the doorway.

Rain washed over her.

She scrambled around the corner, pushing through a hedgerow to enter the narrow alley between the tomb and the ruins of the prayer room.

As she reached cover, a hand from behind reached out of the darkness and clamped over her mouth hard, bruising her lips.

8:39 P.M.

Painter held tight to Safia, clinging to her. "Stay quiet," he whispered in her ear, leaning against the wall of the ruins.

She quaked in his grip.

He had been hiding here for the past few minutes, watching the courtyard, attempting to ascertain some way to draw Cassandra out. But his ex-partner seemed entrenched, patient, letting her team do the work for her while she guarded the prize. Spotlights from the hovering helicopters crisscrossed the yard, keeping him pinned down. Again Cassandra had outwitted him, hiding an aerial force, probably sent here in advance.

All seemed hopeless.

Then a moment ago, he had watched a camel stroll by through the rain, seemingly unconcerned by the gunfire, moving with steady determination to pass his hiding place and disappear in front of the tomb. Next, a spatter of shots and Safia came tumbling out.

"We have to reach the back wall of the complex," he whispered, motioning down the alleyway. There was too much gunfire coming from out front. They'd have to take their chances on the steep slopes out back, try to reach cover. He released his grip on her, but she still clung to him.

"Keep behind me," he urged.

Twisting around, Painter led the way in a low crouch, heading back toward the rear of the complex. The shadows lay thicker there. He kept a keen watch through his night-vision glasses, wary and tense. Pistol pointed forward. Nothing moved. The world was defined in shades of green. If they could reach the far wall that encircled the complex . . .

Taking another step, he saw the alleyway bloom with light, blindingly bright through the goggles, burning the back of his eye sockets. He tore away the scopes.

"Don't move."

Painter froze. A man lay flat atop the wall of the ruins. He held a flashlight in one hand, a pistol in the other, both aimed at Painter.

"Don't even twitch," the man warned.

"Kane," Safia moaned behind him.

Painter cursed silently. The man had been lying in wait atop the wall, spying from on high, waiting until they had moved into his line of sight.

"Drop your weapon."

Painter had no choice. If he refused, he'd be shot where he stood. He let the pistol fall from his fingers.

A new voice called sharply from behind him, coming from the entrance to the alleyway. Cassandra. "Just shoot him."

8:40 P.M.

Omaha crouched beside Coral as she finished checking the body on the ground. Barak covered them with his rifle. They were hidden at the edge of the parking lot, awaiting a chance to make a run across the open space.

Clutching his Desert Eagle, Omaha fought to keep his heart from hammering out of his chest. He seemed incapable of getting enough oxygen. A minute ago, he had heard pistol blasts from within the complex.

Safia . . .

Ahead, the parking lot was still lit by flaming pools of gasoline. A pair of helicopters swept by overhead, searchlights crisscrossing in a deadly pattern. Both sides had settled into a standoff. Only occasional spates of gunfire shattered the stillness.

"Let's go," Coral said, standing up, still shadowed by the limbs of the wild fig tree. Her eyes were on the skies. She watched a second pair of helicopters swoop overhead. "Be ready to run."

Omaha frowned—then saw the grenade resting in her palm, taken from the dead guard at her feet.

She pulled the pin and stepped out into the open, her full attention on the skies. She pulled her arm back, leaning like a pitcher onto one leg. She held that stance for a breath.

"What are you doing?" Omaha asked.

"Physics," she answered. "Vector analysis, timing, angle of ascent." She threw the grenade with a wicked fling of her entire body.

Omaha immediately lost sight of it in the darkness.

"Run!" Coral dove ahead, following the momentum of her toss.

Before Omaha could even move, the grenade exploded overhead in a brilliant flash, lighting up the underbelly of the one-man craft. Its spotlight swung wildly as the concussion hit it. Shrapnel ripped into the belly. A piece must have struck its fuel tank. The copter blew up in a fiery bloom.

"Run!" Coral called again, urging Omaha to move.

Barak was already on Coral's heels.

Omaha ran. Debris rained down off to the right. A piece of rotor impacted the ground with a thunking twang. Then the flaming bulk smashed into the tree line, casting up backwash of fire and black smoke.

He continued his flight across the lot. The other helicopters had swung away, scattering like a flock of startled crows.

Ahead, Coral reached the lone SUV. She flew into the driver's seat. Barak hauled open the back door, leaving the front passenger seat to Omaha.

As his fingers closed on the door, the truck's engine roared to life. Omaha had barely gotten the door open when Coral shifted into gear and hit the accelerator. Omaha's arm was wrenched. He had to run and leap inside.

Coral had no time for stragglers.

He fell into the seat as a rifle blast exploded.

Omaha ducked, but the shot was not from the enemy.

From the backseat, Barak had shot out the truck's moonroof. He used an elbow to crack away the shattered safety glass, then shoved his body up through the opening along with his rifle. He immediately began firing as Coral fought the steering wheel, spinning tires in the mud.

The truck slipped as she made a sharp turn toward the open gate in the compound wall. Wheels mired. The SUV struggled to move.

Another helicopter hove into view, blades angled steeply. Automatic fire flashed from its nose, chattering and digging a trough toward their mud-bogged vehicle. It would slice them in half.

Coral grabbed the stick, shoved the SUV into reverse, and jammed the accelerator. The SUV found traction again, barreled backward as the guillotine of bullets sliced just inches in front of the bumper.

A second helicopter dove toward them.

Barak opened fire skyward. The copter's searchlight shattered away. But it kept coming.

Still going in reverse, Coral spun the wheel. The car fishtailed in the mud. "Omaha, your left!"

While Barak was busy with the helicopter, one of the guards had decided to take advantage of his inattention. The man rose with his rifle on his shoulder. Omaha leaned back in his seat. The SUV swung to face the man. No choice, Omaha fired his Desert Eagle through the windshield. He squeezed two more shots. The safety glass held, but fractured into spiderwebs.

The guard ducked away.

The SUV caught traction in the fresh mud and sped across the lot, still in reverse. Craned around, Coral expertly maneuvered the vehicle, aiming for the gate to the compound, going in ass backward, pursued by the helicopters.

"Hold on!"

8:44 P.M.

Pinned in the alley, Safia stood between Painter and Cassandra. Ahead, Kane pointed his gun. Everyone had frozen for half a breath as the helicopter exploded behind them.

"Shoot him," Cassandra repeated, staying focused.

"No!" Safia attempted to step around Painter, to shield him. Every movement flamed her shoulder. Blood ran down her arm. "Kill him and I won't help you! You'll never discover the secret at Ubar!"

Painter held her back, protecting her from Kane.

Cassandra pushed through the hedge. "Kane, you have your order."

Safia glanced between the two armed assailants. She spotted a shift of shadows behind the man. Something rose from a crouch, sharing the crest of the wall. Eyes shone a feral red.

Painter tensed beside her.

With a growled roar, the leopard pounced on Kane. His pistol fired. Safia felt the shot whistle past her ear and strike the dirt with a thud. Man and cat tumbled off the wall, into the prayer room beyond.

Painter ducked, grabbed Safia's arm, and swung her behind him as he turned to face Cassandra. He had a second pistol in his free hand.

He fired.

Cassandra leaped backward, crashing through the bushes. The bullet missed, clipping the corner of the tomb. She ducked to the side.

Next door, screams arose—bloody and sharp. It was impossible to discern man from beast.

Bullets ricocheted off the sandstone walls as Cassandra returned fire, staying low around the corner, shooting through the bushes. Painter pushed Safia against the tomb's wall, out of direct line of fire . . . at least for the moment.

"Make for the outer wall," he urged, and shoved her down the alley.

"What about you?"

"She'll follow us. The slope's too exposed." He intended to hold Cassandra at bay.

"But you—"

"Goddamnit, *go!*" He pushed her harder.

Safia stumbled down the alley. The sooner she reached safety, the sooner Painter could make his own escape. So she justified it in her head. But a part of her knew she was simply running for her own life. With each step, her shoulder throbbed, protesting her cowardly flight. Still, she kept going.

The exchange of gunfire continued.

In the neighboring ruins of the prayer room, all had gone deathly quiet, the fate of Kane unknown. More gunfire erupted from the parking lot. A helicopter flashed low overhead, whipping up the rain with its rotor wash.

Reaching the end of the alleyway, Safia lunged across the wet gardens toward the far wall. It was only four feet high, but with her wounded shoulder, she feared she'd never make it over. Blood soaked through the shirt.

From beneath a baobab tree, a camel appeared on the far side of the wall. It moved to meet her. It seemed to be the same camel that had sauntered past the tomb's door earlier. In fact, it had the same companion: the naked woman.

Only now she rode atop the camel.

Safia didn't know whether to trust the stranger or not, but if Cassandra shot at her, then the woman had to be on her side. *The enemy of my enemy . . . .*

The stranger offered her arm as Safia reached the wall—then spoke. It wasn't Arabic or English. Yet Safia understood it—not because she had studied the language, which she had, but because it seemed to translate through her skull on its own.

"Welcome, sister," the stranger said in Aramaic, the dead language of this land. "Be at peace."

Safia reached for the woman's hand. Fingers gripped hers, hard and strong. She felt herself pulled up effortlessly. Pain lanced out, shooting down her wounded arm. A cry escaped her. Blackness closed her vision to a pinpoint.

"Peace," the woman repeated softly.

Safia felt the word wash over her, through her, taking pain and the world with it. She slumped and slipped away.

8:47 P.M.

Painter pulled the screen off the window beside his head. It was a flimsy affair. With his back pressed against the tomb's wall, he fired his pistol twice, keeping Cassandra at bay.

He used his palm to slide open the window. Thankfully it was unlocked. He glanced down the alleyway and watched Safia vanish around the corner.

Dropping to a knee, Painter fired another shot, ejected his clip, grabbed another from his belt, and slammed it home.

Cassandra fired again. The slug struck the wall by his leg.

Where was another goddamn leopard when you needed one?

Painter returned a shot, then holstered his weapon. Without a second glance, he leaped up, boosted himself through the window, and fell in an undignified tumble into the tomb.

Inside, he rolled to his feet. His eyes discerned a central shrouded mound. He kept to the wall and circled the gravesite, his pistol back in his hand, aimed at the door. Crossing past the back window, he felt a wet breeze through it.

So that was how that bastard got the jump on me.

Painter glanced through the window, noting movement outside.

Beyond the wall, a camel turned away, heading down the far slope. A naked woman sat astride it, seemingly guiding it with her knees. In her arms, she cradled another woman. Limp, unmoving.

"Safia . . ."

The camel and its riders descended out of sight. A pair of leopards bounded from the dark gardens to the wall, then away, following the camel.

Before he could decide to pursue or not, Painter heard a scuff by the door. He dropped and turned. A shadow lay draped across the entry.

"This isn't over, Crowe!" Cassandra called in to him.

Painter kept his pistol trained.

A new roar reached his ears. A truck. Barreling his way.

Shots fired. He recognized the retort of a Kalashnikov. Someone from his own group. Cassandra's shadow vanished, sweeping out of sight, retreating.

Painter hurried to the door, keeping his weapon ready. He spotted a discarded map on the floor. He reached down and crumpled it in a fist.

Out in the courtyard, one of the Mitsubishi trucks bounced through the gardens, digging ragged furrows. A figure protruded through the moonroof. A muzzle, pointed skyward, flashed. Barak.

Painter checked the rest of the yard. It appeared empty. Cassandra had retreated into hiding, outgunned for the brief moment. He stepped out of the tomb and waved the crumpled map.

Spotting him, the driver of the Mitsubishi swung sharply. Its back bumper aimed for him. He fell back inside to avoid getting hit. The SUV skidded to a stop, scraping paint off its side panels. Its backseat door landed abreast of the tomb.

He spotted Coral in the driver's seat.

"Get in!" Barak called.

Painter glanced back to the tomb's back window. *Safia . . .*

Whoever had taken her, they had at least been heading away, out of immediate harm. That would have to do for now.

Turning back, he popped the handle, dove inside, and slammed the door. "Go!" he called to the front.

Coral jostled the SUV into forward gear, and the truck sped away.

A pair of helicopters gave chase. Barak shot at them from his topside vantage. The SUV raced toward the open gate. Coral leaned forward to peer through the cracked windshield.

They swept out of the complex, bounced over a muddy rut, momentarily airborne, then jammed back down. Wheels spun, caught, and the SUV sped toward the road and the cover of the heavy forest.

From the front, Omaha stared back at him, eyes lost. "Where's Safia?"

"Gone." Painter shook his head, unblinking. "She's gone."

15
Mountain Trek

ᛒ∘◫�528ᛉ��⟨Ⅹ⟩�

December 4, 12:18 A.M.
Dhofar Mountains

Safia woke from slumber, falling. She threw her arms out, panic racking her body, as familiar as her own breath. Agony speared her shoulder.

"Calm yourself, sister," someone said near her ear. "I have you."

The world swirled into focus, midnight dark. She was propped against a couched camel, who chewed its cud with indifference. A woman loomed at her side, an arm under her good shoulder, holding her up.

"Where . . . ?" she mumbled, but her lips seemed glued together. She tried to find her legs, but failed. Memory slowly returned. The fight at the tomb.

Gunfire filled her head. Flashes of images. One face. Painter. She shuddered in the woman's arms. What had happened? Where was she?

She finally found enough strength to stand, leaning heavily on the camel. Safia noted that her wounded shoulder had been crudely bandaged, wrapped to slow the bleeding. It ached with every movement.

The woman at her side, shadowy in the gloom, appeared to be the one who had rescued her; only now she wore a desert cloak.

"Help comes," the other whispered.

"Who are you?" she forced out, suddenly noting the cold of the night. She was in some jungle grotto. The rain had stopped, but drops still wept from the canopy overhead. Palm and tamarind trees rose all around her. Tangles of lianas and hanging gardens of jasmine draped everywhere, perfuming the air.

The woman remained silent. She pointed an arm.

A bit of fiery light pierced the jungle ahead, glowing brightly through the ropy vines. Someone was coming, bearing aloft a torch or lamp.

Safia had an urge to flee, but her body was too weak to obey.

The arm around her shoulder squeezed as if the woman had heard her heart, but it didn't feel like she was attempting to hold Safia captive, only to reassure her.

In moments, Safia's eyes acclimated to the gloom enough to recognize that the jungle immediately before her hid a rocky limestone cliff, thick with vines, creepers, and small bushes. The approaching light came from a tunnel in the face of the cliff. Such caverns and passages riddled the Dhofar Mountains, formed from the trickles of monsoon flows melting through the limestone.

As the light reached the tunnel entrance, Safia spotted three figures: an old woman, a child of perhaps twelve, and a second young woman who could've been the twin of the one beside her. All were identically dressed in desert cloaks, hoods thrown back.

Additionally, each bore an identical bit of decoration: a ruby tattoo at the outer corner of the left eye. A single teardrop.

Even the child who carried the glass oil lantern.

"She who was lost," the woman at her side intoned.

"Has come home," the elder said, leaning on a cane. Her hair was gray, tied in a braid, but her face, though lined, looked vital.

Safia found it hard to meet those eyes, but also impossible to turn away.

"Be welcome," the elder said, speaking English, stepping aside.

Safia was assisted through the entrance, supported by the woman. Once she was through, the child led the way, lantern held high. The elderly woman kept behind them, thudding with a walking stick. The third woman left the tunnel and strode to the couched camel.

Safia was led onward.

No one spoke for several steps.

Safia, edgy with questions, could not hold her tongue. "Who are you? What do you want with me?" Her voice sounded petulant even to her own ears.

"Be at peace," the elderly woman whispered behind her. "You are safe."

For now, Safai added silently. She had noted the long dagger carried in the belt of the woman who had left the tunnel behind them.

"All answers will be given by our *hodja.*"

Safia startled. A *hodja* was a tribal shaman, always female. They were the keepers of knowledge, healers, oracles. *Who were these people?* As she continued, she noted a continual wisp of jasmine in the air. The scent calmed her, reminding her of home, of mother, of security.

Still, the pain in her wounded shoulder kept her focused. Blood had begun to flow anew, through the bandage and down her arm.

She heard a scuffing sound behind her. She glanced over her shoulder. The third woman had returned. She bore two burdens, collected from the camel. In one hand, she carried the silver suitcase, battered now, that held the iron heart. And on her shoulder leaned the iron spear with its bust of the Queen of Sheba.

They had stolen the two artifacts from Cassandra.

Safia's heart thudded louder, vision tightening.

Were they thieves? Had she been rescued or been kidnapped again?

The tunnel stretched ahead, continuing deep under the mountain. They had passed side tunnels and caves, angling this way and that. She was quickly lost. Where were they taking her?

Finally the air seemed to freshen, growing stronger, the scent of jasmine richer. The passage lightened ahead. She was led forward. A wind flowed down the throat of the tunnel, coming from up ahead.

As they rounded a bend, the tunnel dumped into a large cavern.

Safia stepped into it.

No, not a cavern, but a great bowl of an amphitheater, the roof of which, high overhead, bore a small opening to the sky. Water flowed through the hole in a long, trickling waterfall, draining into a small pond below. Five tiny campfires circled the pool, like the points of a star, illuminating the flowering vines that wreathed the room and hung in long tangles from the roof, some reaching the shallow bowl of the floor.

Safia recognized the geology. It was one of the countless sinkholes that peppered the region. Some of the deepest were found in Oman.

Safia gaped.

More cloaked figures moved or sat about the chamber. Some thirty or so. Faces turned toward her as the party entered. The illuminated cavern reminded Safia of the thieves' cave from the story of Ali Baba.

Only these forty thieves were all *women.*

All ages.

Safia stumbled into the room, suddenly weak from the trek, blood running hot down one arm, the rest of her body shivering.

A figure rose by one of the fires. "Safia?"

She focused on the speaker. The woman was not dressed like the others. Safia could make no sense of her presence here. "Kara?"

1:02 A.M.
Thumrait Air Base, Oman

Cassandra leaned over the chart table in the captain's office. Using a satellite map of the region, she had re-created the curator's map. With a blue Sharpie marker, she had drawn a line from the tomb in Salalah to the one in the mountains, and with a red marker, a line from Job's tomb to the open desert. She had circled their destination in red, the location of the lost city.

Her present position, Thumrait Air Base, lay only thirty miles away.

"How quickly can you have the supplies ready?" she asked.

The young captain licked his lips. He was the leader of the Harvest Falcon depot, the USAF's source of supplies and war materials for its bases and troops throughout the region. He carried a clipboard and tapped items off with the tip of a ballpoint pen. "Tents, shelters, equipment, rations, fuel, water, medical supplies, and generators are already being loaded into transport helicopters. You'll be supplied on-site at zero seven hundred as instructed."

She nodded.

The man still wore a frown as he studied their place of deployment. "This is the middle of the desert. Refugees are funneling into the air base hourly. I don't see how placing an advance camp out there will help."

A gust of wind rattled the asphalt shingles atop the building.

"You have your orders, Captain Garrison."

"Yes, sir." But his eyes looked little settled, especially when he glanced out the window to the hundred men lounging on packs, checking weapons, wearing dun-colored sand fatigues, no insignia.

Cassandra let him have his doubts as she headed to the door. The captain had received his orders, passed through the chain of command from Washington. He was to aid her in outfitting her team. Guild command had orchestrated the cover story. Cassandra's team was a search-and-rescue unit sent to help refugees fleeing the coming sandstorm and to aid in any rescue during the storm itself. They had five all-terrain trucks with giant sand tires, an eighteen-ton M4 high-speed desert tractor, a pair of transport Hueys, and six of the one-man VTOL copter sleds, each fitted and lashed to open-bed four-wheel-drive trucks. The overland team would leave within the half hour. She would be accompanying them.

Exiting the command depot for Harvest Falcon, Cassandra checked her watch. The sandstorm was due to slam into the region in another eight hours. Reports were coming in of winds gusting to eighty mph. Already the winds here, where the mountains met the desert, were kicking up.

And they were heading into the teeth of the storm. They had no choice. Word had come from Guild command, some hint that the source of the antimatter could be destabilizing, that it could self-destruct before it was discovered. That must not happen. Timetables had been accelerated.

Cassandra searched the dark airfield. She watched a lumbering British VC10 tanker touch ground off in the distance, illuminated by landing lights. Guild command had shipped in the men and additional equipment yesterday. The Minister had coordinated with her personally after the firefight last night. It was damn lucky she had learned the location of the lost city before losing Safia. With such a significant discovery, the Minister had been grudgingly satisfied with her performance.

She was not.

She pictured Painter crouched in the alley between the ruins and the tomb. The sharpness of his eyes, the crinkles of concentration, the way he moved so swiftly, pivoting on one leg, sweeping out his gun. She should have shot him in the back when she had the chance. She risked hitting Safia, but she had lost the woman anyway. Still, Cassandra hadn't shot. Even when Painter swung on her, she had paused a fraction of a second, falling back instead of pushing forward.

She clenched a fist. She had hesitated. She cursed herself as much as she cursed Painter. She would not make that mistake a second time. She stared across the acres of tarmac and gravel.

Would he come?

She had noted that he had stolen her map during his escape, along with one of the vehicles, her own truck. They found it abandoned and stripped of gear, buried in the forest a few miles down the road.

But Painter had the map. He would definitely come.

Yet not before she was ready for him. She had plenty of manpower and firepower to hold off an army out there. Let him try.

She would not hesitate a second time.

A figure appeared from a small outbuilding near the parked trucks, her temporary command center. John Kane strode toward her, his left leg stiff in a splint. He scowled as he stomped to her side. The left side of his face was sealed with surgical glue, giving his features a bluish tint. Beneath the glue, claw marks slashed across his cheek and throat, blackened with iodine. His eyes glinted brighter than usual in the sodium lights. A slight morphine haze.

He refused to be left behind.

"Cleanup was completed an hour ago," he said, tucking back his radio mike. "Assets have all been cleared out."

She nodded. All evidence of their involvement with the firefight at the tomb had been removed: bodies, weapons, even the wreckage of the VTOL copter sled. "Any word on Crowe's crew?"

"Vanished into the mountains. Scattered. There are side roads and camel trails throughout the mountains. And heavy patches of forest in all the deep valleys. He and those sand rats have tucked their tails and gone into hiding."

Cassandra had expected as much. The firefight had left her team with limited manpower for a proper pursuit and search. They had to take care of their own wounded and clear the site before local authorities responded to the fiery attack. She had evacuated in the first airlift, radioing Guild command of the operation, playing down the chaos, highlighting their discovery of the true site of Ubar.

The information had bought her life.

And she knew to whom she was indebted for that.

"What about the museum curator?" she asked.

"I have men patrolling the mountains. Still no trace of her signal."

Cassandra frowned. The microtransceiver she had implanted on the woman had a range of ten miles. How was it possible that they hadn't picked up her signal? Maybe interference from the mountains. Maybe it was the storm system. Either way, she'd eventually expose herself. She'd be found.

Cassandra pictured the small pellet of C4 incorporated into the transceiver. Safia might have escaped . . . but she was dead already.

"Let's move out," she said.

1:32 A.M.
Dhofar Mountains

"Good girl, Saff," Omaha mumbled.

Painter stirred from his post by the road. What had the man discovered? With his night-vision glasses, he had been watching the dirt track. The Volkswagen Eurovan stood parked under a stand of trees.

Omaha and the others gathered at the back of the van, the tailgate ajar. Omaha and Danny were bent over the map he had stolen from the tomb site.

Next to them, Coral had been inventorying their supplies, pilfered from the back of Cassandra's SUV.

Downslope from the tomb, they had run into Clay and Danny, frantic about Kara's disappearance. They had found her rifle in the road, but no sign of the woman herself. They had called and called for her, but no answer. And with Cassandra on their tail and helicopters in the air, they could not wait long. While Painter and Omaha searched for Kara, the others had hurriedly shoved all the supplies from the SUV into the Eurovan, then drove the SUV over a steep slope. Painter feared Cassandra would track them with its GPS feature, just as he had.

Additionally, the Eurovan was unknown to her. A small advantage.

So they had taken off, hoping Kara had kept her head low.

Painter paced the road now, less settled with his decision. They had found no body. Where had Kara gone? Did her disappearance have something to do with her withdrawal from the drug? He took a deep breath. Maybe it was best. Away from them, Kara might have a better chance of surviving. Still, Painter paced.

Off to the side, Barak shared a smoke with Clay, the two men a contrast in size, form, and philosophy bonded by the lure of tobacco. Barak knew the mountains and had led them through a series of rutted roads, well camouflaged. They ran with their lights off, going as fast as safety allowed, stopping at times whenever the sound of helicopters approached.

It was just six of them now: he and Coral, Omaha and Danny, Barak and Clay. The fate of Captain al-Haffi and Sharif remained unknown, scattered to the winds with the fleeing Bait Kathir. They could only hope for the best.

After three hours of harried driving, they had stopped to rest, regroup, plan what to do next. All they had to guide them from here were the inked marks on the map.

At the van, Omaha straightened a kink in his back with a pop that was heard all the way to the road. "She tricked the bitch."

With the mountain valley quiet and dark, Painter walked back to join the others. "What are you talking about?"

Omaha waved him over. "Come see this."

Painter joined him. At least, Omaha's belligerence toward him had lessened. En route, Painter had related his story of the leopards, the firefight, the intervention of the strange woman. Omaha finally seemed to settle on the belief that as long as Safia was away from Cassandra, it was an improvement.

Omaha pointed to the map. "See these lines. The blue one clearly leads from the tomb in Salalah to Job's tomb here in the mountains. Safia must've found some clue at the first tomb to lead to the second."

Painter nodded. "Okay, what about the red line?"

"Safia found some clue at Job's tomb, too."

"The metal post with a bust on it?"

"I suppose. It doesn't matter any longer. See here. She's marked a circle along this red line. Out in the desert. Like this is where to go next."

"The location of Ubar." Painter felt a sick, sinking feeling. If Cassandra already knew where it was . . .

"No, it's not the location," Danny said.

Omaha nodded. "I measured it. The circle is marked sixty-nine miles from Job's tomb, along this red line."

Painter had debriefed them on all the details, including overhearing the tall man call out the number sixty-nine, measuring something along the pole.

"So it matches the number I heard," Painter said.

"But they figured miles," Omaha said. "*Our* miles."

"So?"

Omaha gave him a look as if it were obvious. "If that artifact they found at Job's tomb was dated the same as the iron heart—and why wouldn't it be?—then it goes back to sometime around 200 B.C."

"Okay," Painter said, accepting the fact.

"Back then, a mile was defined by the Romans. A mile was calculated as five thousand Roman feet. And a Roman foot is only eleven and a half inches. Safia would know this! She let Cassandra believe it was modern miles. She sent the bitch on a wild-goose chase."

"So what's the real distance?" Painter asked, moving closer to the map.

At his side, Omaha chewed the edge of his thumb, clearly doing a calculation in his head. After a moment, he spoke. "Sixty-nine *Roman* miles is equivalent to just over sixty-three modern miles."

"He's right," Coral said. She had been doing her own calculation.

"So Safia sent Cassandra six miles past the true location." Painter frowned. "That's not too far."

"In the desert," Omaha countered, "six miles is more like six hundred."

Painter didn't squash the man's pride in Safia, but he knew the ruse would not fool Cassandra for long. As soon as she realized that nothing was at that false site, she'd start consulting. Someone would solve the mystery. Painter estimated Safia's ruse bought them a day or two at most.

"So where on the map is the true location?" Painter asked.

Omaha bobbed his head, excited. "Let's find out." He quickly adjusted his strings and pins, measuring and rechecking. A frown crinkled his brow. "That doesn't make sense." He stuck a pin in the map.

Painter leaned over and read the name pinned there. "Shisur."

Omaha shook his head, dismay in his voice. "It's been a goddamn wild-goose chase all along."

"What do you mean?"

Omaha continued to frown at the map, as if it were to blame.

Danny answered for him. "Shisur is where the old ruins of Ubar were originally discovered. Back in 1992, by Nicolas Clapp and a few others." Danny glanced to Painter. "There's nothing there. All this running around just leads to a place that's already been discovered and scoured."

Painter could not accept that. "There has to be something."

Omaha slammed a fist on the map. "I've been there myself. It's a dead end. All this danger and bloodshed . . . for nothing!"

"There has to be something everyone has missed," Painter persisted. "Everyone thought those two tombs we were at before had been thoroughly examined, but in a matter of days, new discoveries were made."

"Discoveries made by Safia," Omaha said sourly.

No one spoke for a long stretch.

Painter focused on Omaha's words. Realization slowly dawned. "She'll go there."

Omaha turned to him. "What are you talking about?"

"Safia. She lied to Cassandra to stop her from getting to Ubar. But like us, she knows where the clues truly pointed."

"To Shisur. To the old ruins."

"Exactly."

Omaha frowned. "But like we said, there's nothing there."

"And like you said, Safia discovered clues where no one found them before. She'll think she can do the same at Ubar. She'll go there for no other reason but to keep whatever might be there from Cassandra's grasp."

Omaha took a deep begrudging breath. "You're right."

"That's if she's allowed to go," Coral said from the side. "What about the woman who took her away? The one with the leopards."

Barak answered her, his voice somewhat embarrassed. "I've heard tales of such women, spoken around campfires out in the desert. Spoken among all tribes of the sands. Warriors of the desert. More djinn than flesh. Able to speak to animals. Vanish on command."

"Yeah, right," Omaha said.

"There was indeed something strange about that woman," Painter conceded. "And I don't think this is the first time we've had a run-in with her."

"What do you mean?"

Painter nodded to Omaha. "Your kidnappers. In Muscat. It was a woman you saw in the market."

"What? You think she's the same woman?"

Painter shrugged. "Or perhaps one of the same group. There's another party involved in all this. I know it. I don't know if it's Barak's warrior women or just some group looking to make a buck. Either way, they've taken Safia for a reason. In fact, they may have even attempted to kidnap you, Omaha, because of Safia's affection for you. To use you as leverage."

"Leverage for what?"

"To get Safia to help them. I also spotted the silver case tied on the camel's back. Why take the artifact unless there's a good reason? Everything keeps pointing back to Ubar."

Omaha pondered his words, nodding his head. "Then that's where we'll go. With that bitch distracted, we'll wait and see if Safia shows up."

"And search the place in the meantime," Coral said. She nodded to the stacked gear. "There's a ground-penetrating radar unit in here, good for looking under sand. And we've a box of grenades, additional rifles, and I don't know what this is." She held up a weapon that looked like a shotgun with a belled end to it. From the glint in her eyes, she was dying to try it out.

Everyone turned to Painter, as if waiting for his agreement.

"Of course we're going," he said.

Omaha clapped him on the shoulder. "Finally something we agree on."

1:55 A.M.

Safia hugged Kara. "What are you doing here?"

"I'm not sure." Kara trembled in her grip. Her skin felt clammy, moist.

"The others? I saw Painter . . . what about Omaha, his brother . . . ?"

"As far as I know, everyone's okay. But I was away from the fighting."

Safia had to sit down, her legs weak, knees rubbery. The cavern swam a bit around her. The tinkling of the waterfall through the hole in the roof sounded like silver bells. Firelight from the five campfires dazzled her eyes.

She sank to a rumpled blanket by the fire. She couldn't feel the heat of the flames.

Kara followed her down. "Your shoulder! You're bleeding."

Shot. Safia didn't know if she'd spoken aloud or not.

Three women approached, arms full. They carried a steaming basin, folded cloths, a covered brazier, and oddly out of place, a box with the red cross of an emergency medical kit. An elderly woman, not the same as the one who had led her here, followed with a tall walking stick, fiery in the glow of the campfire. She was ancient, shoulders hunched, hair white but neatly combed and braided back over her ears. Rubies adorned her lobes, matching her teardrop tattoo.

"Lie down, daughter," the old woman intoned. English again. "Let us see to your injuries."

Safia had no energy to resist, but Kara guarded over her. She had to trust that her friend would protect her if necessary.

Safia's blouse was stripped from her. The soiled bandage was then soaked in a steaming poultice of aloe and mint and slowly peeled back. It felt as if they were flaying the skin off her shoulder. She gasped, and her vision darkened.

"You're hurting her," Kara warned.

One of the three women had knelt and opened the emergency medical kit. "I have one ampoule of morphine, *hodja*," the woman said.

"Let me see the wound." The elder leaned down, supported by her staff.

Safia shifted so her shoulder was bared.

"The bullet passed cleanly through. Shallow. Good. We'll not have to operate. Sweet myrrh tea will ease her pain. Also two tablets of Tylenol with codeine. Hook an IV to her good arm. Run in a liter of warmed LRS."

"What of the wound?" the other woman asked.

"We'll cauterize, pack, and wrap the shoulder, then sling the arm."

"Yes, *hodja*."

Safia was propped up. The third woman poured a steaming mug of tea and handed it to Kara. "Help her drink. It will give her strength."

Kara obeyed, accepting the mug with both hands.

"You'd best sip, too," the old woman told Kara. "To clear your head."

"I doubt this is strong enough."

"Doubt will not serve you here."

Kara sipped the tea, grimaced, then offered it to Safia. "You should drink. You look like hell."

Safia allowed a bit to be dribbled between her lips. The warmth flowed down into the cold pit that was her stomach. She accepted more. Two pills were held in front of her.

"For the pain," the youngest of the three women whispered. All three looked like sisters, only a few years apart.

"Take them, Saffie," Kara urged. "Or I'll take them myself."

Safia opened her mouth, accepted the medication, and swallowed them down with a bit more of the tea.

"Now lie back while we minister to your wounds," the *hodja* said.

Safia collapsed to the blankets, warmer now.

The *hodja* slowly lowered to the blanket beside her, moving with a grace that belied her age. She rested her walking stick over her knees.

"Rest, daughter. Be at peace." She placed one hand atop Safia's.

A gentle bleary feeling swelled through her, fading all the ache from her body, leaving her floating. Safia smelled the jasmine wreathed about the cavern.

"Who . . . who are you?" Safia asked.

"We're your mother, dear."

Safia flinched, denying the possibility, offended. Her mother was dead. This woman was too old. She must be speaking metaphorically. Before she could scold, all sight dissolved. Only a few words followed her away.

"All of us. We're *all* your mother."

2:32 A.M.

Kara watched the group of women attend to Safia as her friend lolled on the blankets. A catheter was inserted into a vein in her right hand and hooked to an intravenous drip attached to a warm bag of saline, held aloft by one of Safia's nurses. The other two rinsed and daubed the bullet wound in Safia's shoulder. The injury was smaller than a dime. A cauterizing powder was sprinkled generously over the site, which was then painted with iodine, packed with cotton gauze, and expertly wrapped.

Safia thrashed slightly, but remained asleep.

"Make sure she keeps her arm in a sling," the older woman said, watching the work of the others. "When she is awake, make sure she drinks a cup of the tea."

The *hodja* lifted her staff, posted it on the ground, and pulled herself up. She faced Kara. "Come. Let my daughters care for your sister."

"I won't leave her." Kara moved closer to Safia.

"She will be well cared for. Come. It is time for you to find what you have sought."

"What are you talking about?"

"Answers to your life. Come or stay. It makes no matter to me." The old woman thumped off. "I will not argue with you."

Kara glanced to Safia, then to the elder. *Answers to your life.*

Kara slowly rose. "If anything happens . . ." But she didn't know whom she was threatening. The nurses seemed to be taking good care of her friend.

With a shake of her head, Kara set off after the *hodja*.

"Where are we going?"

Ignoring Kara, the *hodja* continued. They left the trickling waterfall and fires behind and crossed into the deeper gloom that rimmed the chamber.

Kara stared around. She barely remembered entering this cavern. She had been conscious of it, but it was as if she had moved in a pleasant fog, plodding behind a similarly clad older tribeswoman. After leaving the van, they had walked for well over an hour, through a shadowy forest, to an ancient dry well, accessed via a narrow cut in the rock. They had spiraled down into a mountainside, walking for some time. Once they reached the cavern here, Kara had been abandoned by the fire, told to wait, the fog lifting from her. With its dissipation, her headache, tremors, and nausea had returned like a leaden blanket. She felt barely able to move, let alone find her way out of this warren of tunnels. Questions she asked were ignored.

And she had many.

She stared at the back of the elder ahead of her now. *Who were these women? What did they want with her and Safia?*

They reached a tunnel opening in the wall. A child waited at the entrance, bearing a silver oil lamp, like something you'd rub to raise a genie. A tiny flame lapped the tip of the lamp. The girl, no more than eight, wore a desert cloak that appeared too large for her, the hem bunching slightly at her toes. Her eyes were huge upon Kara, as if she were staring at some alien being. But there was no fright, only curiosity.

The *hodja* nodded the child forward. "Go, Yaqut."

The child turned and shuffled forward down the tunnel. *Yaqut* was Arabic for "ruby." It was the first time she had heard a name spoken here.

She stared at the *hodja* at her side. "What is your name?"

The old woman finally glanced at her. Green eyes flashed brightly in the lamp's flame. "I am called many names, but my given name is Lu'lu. I believe in your language that means 'pearl.'"

Kara nodded. "Are all your women named after jewels?"

There was no answer as they continued walking behind the child in silence, but Kara sensed the woman's acknowledgment. In Arabic tradition, such jeweled names were given to only one caste of folk.

Slaves.

Why did these women pick such names? They certainly seemed freer than most Arab women.

The child turned off the tunnel into a limestone chamber. It was cold, the walls damp, scintillating in the lamplight. A prayer rug lay on the cave's floor, cushioned by a bed of straw. Beyond it stood a low altar of black stone.

Kara felt a thrill of fear ice through her. Why had they brought her here?

Yaqut walked to the altar, circled behind it, and bent out of sight.

Suddenly flames crackled brighter behind the stone. Yaqut had used her oil lamp to light a small stack of wood. Kara smelled incense and kerosene from the pile, scented and oiled for easy lighting. The kerosene burned away quickly, leaving only the sweet fragrance of frankincense.

As the flames licked higher, Kara saw her mistake. The dark altar was not opaque but crystalline, like a chunk of black obsidian, only more translucent. The glow of the flames shone through the stone.

"Come," Lu'lu intoned, and led Kara to the prayer rug. "Kneel."

Kara, exhausted from lack of sleep and shaky from the drain of adrenaline from her system, both naturally and artificially induced, gratefully sank to the soft rug.

The *hodja* stood behind her. "This is what you have come so far and searched so long to find." She pointed her stick toward the altar.

Kara stared at the block of translucent stone. Her eyes widened as the stack of wood blazed behind the altar, shining through it.

Not opaque stone . . . *raw glass.*

Flames lit the interior, illuminating the heart of the glass block. Inside, embedded like a fly in amber, rested a figure, plainly human, blackened to bone, legs curled fetally but arms out in agony. Kara had seen a similar stricken figure. In the ruins of Pompeii. A form turned to stone, buried and petrified under hot ash from the ancient eruption of Vesuvius. The same posture of tortured death.

But worst of all, Kara knew why she had been brought here, shown this.

Answers to her life.

She collapsed to her hands on the rug, her body suddenly too heavy. *No . . .* Tears burst to her eyes. She knew who lay buried in the heart of the glass, preserved in agony.

A cry escaped her, wrenching everything from her body: strength, sight, hope, even the will to live, leaving her empty.

"Papa . . ."

3:12 A.M.

Safia woke to music and warmth. She lay on a soft blanket, instantly awake, but she languished in the moment. She listened to the soft stringed cords from a lute, accompanied by the soft piping from a reed instrument, haunting and lonely. Firelight danced across the roof overhead, limning the drapes of vines and flowers. The tinkling water added counterpoint to the music.

She knew where she was. There was no slow waking back to the present, only a vague muzzy-headedness from the codeine she had ingested. She heard voices speaking softly, occasional dazzling flashes of laughter, a child playing.

She slowly sat up, earning a grumpy complaint from her shoulder. But the pain was dull, more a deep ache than a sharp twinge. She felt inordinately rested. She checked her watch. She had been asleep only a little more than an hour, but she felt as if she had slept for days. Relaxed and rested.

A young woman stepped toward her, kneeling down, a mug warmed between her hands. "The *hodja* wishes you to drink this."

Safia accepted the tea with her good arm. The other lay in a sling across her belly. She sipped gratefully and noticed a conspicuous absence. "Kara? My friend?"

"When you finish your tea, I'm to take you to the *hodja*. She waits with your sister."

Safia nodded. She sipped her tea as quickly as its steaming heat would allow. The sweet tea warmed through her. She placed the mug on the ground and crawled to her feet.

Her escort offered a hand to help, but Safia declined, feeling steady enough.

"This way."

Safia was led to the far side of the sinkhole cavern and down another tunnel. With a lantern in one hand, her guide walked her assuredly through the maze of passages.

Safia addressed her guide. "Who are you all?"

"We are the Rahim," she answered stiffly.

Safia translated. *Rahim* was the Arabic word for "womb." Were they some bedouin tribe of women, Amazons of the desert? She pondered the name. It also held an undercurrent of divinity, of rebirth and continuity.

Who were these women?

Ahead a light appeared, glowing from a side cavern.

Her escort stopped a few steps away and nodded Safia forward.

She continued, feeling for the first time since waking a tingle of unease. The air seemed to grow thicker, harder to breathe. She concentrated on inhaling and exhaling, riding through the moment of anxiety. As she stepped nearer, she heard sobbing, heart-deep, broken.

Kara . . .

Safia pushed aside her fears and hurried to the cavern. She found Kara collapsed on a rug in the cavern. The elder *hodja* knelt at her side, cradling Kara. The old woman's green eyes met Safia's.

Safia rushed over. "Kara, what's wrong?"

Kara lifted her face, eyes swollen, damp-cheeked. She was beyond words. She pointed an arm toward a large stone with a fire behind it. Safia recognized the chunk as slag glass, molten sand that had hardened. She had found such pieces around lightning strikes. They were revered by ancient peoples, used as jewelry, sacred objects, prayer stones.

She didn't understand until she spotted the figure in the glass. "Oh, no . . ."

Kara croaked, "It's . . . it's my father."

"Oh, Kara." Tears welled up in Safia's eyes. She knelt on Kara's other side. Reginald Kensington had been like a father to Safia, too. She understood her friend's grief, but confusion shattered through. "How? Why . . . ?"

Kara glanced at the old woman, too overwhelmed to speak.

The *hodja* patted Kara's hand. "As I've already explained to your friend, Lord Kensington is not unknown to our people. His story leads here as much as the story of you two. He had entered sands forbidden on the day he died. He had been warned, but chose to dismiss it. And it was not chance that brought him to those sands. He sought Ubar, like his daughter. He knew those same sands were near its heart and could not stay away."

"What happened to him?"

"To tread the sands around Ubar is to risk the wrath of a power that has lain hidden for millennia. A power and place we women guard. He heard of the place, was drawn to it. It was his doom."

Kara sat up, clearly having heard all this already. "What is this power?"

The *hodja* shook her head. "That we don't know. The Gates of Ubar have been closed to us for two millennia. What lies beyond those gates has been lost to the ages. We are the Rahim, the last of its guardians. Knowledge passed from mouth to ear, from one generation to another, but two secrets were never spoken after Ubar was destroyed, never passed to our line by the surviving queen of Ubar. So great was the tragedy that she sealed the city, and with her death, those two secrets died: where the gates' keys were hidden and what power lies under the sand, at the heart of Ubar."

Each word spoken by the old woman raised a thousand questions in Safia's mind. *The Gates of Ubar. The last of its guardians. The heart of the lost city. Hidden keys.* But some inkling reached through to her.

"The keys . . ." she muttered. "The iron heart."

The *hodja* nodded. "To lead to Ubar's heart."

"And the spear with the bust of Biliqis, the Queen of Sheba."

The elder bowed her head. "She who was the mother of us all. The first of the royal house of Ubar. It is only right she adorns the second key."

Safia reviewed the known history of Ubar. The city had indeed been founded around 900 B.C., the same period during which the historical Queen of Sheba lived. Ubar prospered until the collapse of a sinkhole destroyed the city around A.D. 300. It had a long reign. But the existence of the ruling house was well documented.

Safia questioned this fact. "I thought King Shaddad was the first ruler of Ubar, the great-grandchild of Noah." There was even a reclusive clan of bedouin, the Shahra, who claimed to be descendants of this same king.

The old woman shook her head. "The line of Shaddad were administrators only. The line of Biliqis were the true rulers, a secret hidden from all but the most trusted. Ubar gave its powers to the queen, chose her, allowed her to birth her line strong and sure. A line that continues to this day."

Safia remembered the visage on the bust. The young women here bore a striking resemblance. Could such a line remain pure for over two millennia?

Safia shook her head, incredulous. "Are you saying your tribe can trace their lineage all the way back to the Queen of Sheba?"

The *hodja* bowed her head. "It is more than that . . . much more." She lifted her eyes. "We *are* the Queen of Sheba."

3:28 P.M.

Kara felt sick, nauseous—but not from withdrawal. In fact, since her arrival here in these caves, she felt less jagged, the shakes slowly subsiding, as if something had been done to her head. But what she now suffered was a thousandfold worse than the lack of amphetamines. She felt crushed, heartsick, worn thin, devastated. All this talk of secret cities, mysterious powers, ancient lineages meant nothing to her. Her eyes stared at the remains of her father, his mouth frozen in a rictus of agony.

Words of the *hodja* had locked up her brain.

He had sought Ubar, like his daughter.

Kara recalled the day of her father's death, the hunt on her sixteenth birthday. She had always wondered why they had traveled all the way out to that section of the desert. There was good hunting much closer to Muscat, why fly out to Thumrait Air Base, travel overland in Rovers, then start their pursuit on sand cycles. Had he used her birthday as an excuse to hunt those lands?

Anger built in her chest, shining out of her like the flames behind the chunk of glass. But it had no focus. She was angry at these women who had held this secret for so long, at her father for throwing his life away on a deadly quest, at herself for following in his footsteps . . . even at Safia for never making her stop, even when the search was destroying Kara from the inside. The fire of her fury burned away the dregs of her sickness.

Kara sat back and turned to the old *hodja*. She interrupted her history lesson with Safia, her words bitter. "Why was my father searching for Ubar?"

"Kara . . ." Safia said in a consoling tone. "I think that can wait."

"No." Anger put command in her voice. "I want to know now."

The *hodja* remained unimpressed, bowing before Kara's fury like a reed in the wind. "You are right to ask. That is why you are both here."

Kara frowned from lips to brow.

The woman glanced between Kara and Safia. "What the desert takes, it also gives back."

"What does that mean?" Kara snapped.

The *hodja* sighed. "The desert took your father." She waved toward the gruesome stone. "But it gave you a sister." She nodded to Safia.

"Safia has always been my dearest friend." Despite her anger, Kara's voice flared with emotion. The truth and depth of her words, spoken aloud, struck her bruised heart with more impact than she would have imagined. She tried to shake them away, but she was too raw.

"She is more than your friend. She is your sister in both spirit . . . and flesh." The *hodja* raised her staff and pointed it at the body entombed in glass. "There lies your father . . . and *Safia's*."

The *hodja* faced the two stunned women.

"You are sisters."

3:33 A.M.

Safia's mind could not grasp what the woman was saying.

"Impossible," Kara said. "My mother died when I was born."

"You share a father, not a mother," the *hodja* clarified. "Safia was born from a woman of our people."

Safia shook her head. They were half sisters. The peace she had experienced upon waking moments ago had shattered. For ages, she had known nothing about her mother, only that she had died in a bus accident when Safia was four. Nothing was known about her father. Even among the vague memories of her childhood before the orphanage—foggy glimpses, scents, a whisper in the ear—there had never been a male figure, a father. All she had left from her mother was her name, al-Maaz.

"Calm yourself, both of you." The woman raised her hands, one palm toward each. "This is a gift, not a curse."

Her words drained some of the wild beating in Safia's heart, like a palm placed on a thrumming tuning fork. Still, she could not bring herself to glance toward Kara, too ashamed, as if her presence somehow fouled the good memory of Lord Kensington. Safia's mind went back to the day she was taken from the orphanage, a terrifying, hopeful day. Reginald Kensington had chosen her above all the other girls, a mixed-blood child, taken her home, put her in her own room. Kara and Safia had instantly bonded. Had they, even at that young age, recognized a secret bond, an easy comfort of family? Why hadn't Reginald Kensington ever told them of their secret sisterhood?

"If only I'd known . . ." Kara gasped out, reaching out to Safia.

Safia looked up. She read no blame in her friend's eye; the anger of a moment ago had been snuffed. All she saw was relief, hope, and love.

"Maybe we did know . . ." Safia mumbled, and leaned into her sister's embrace. "Maybe we always knew down deep."

Tears flowed. And just like that, they were no longer just friends—they were *family*.

They hugged for a long moment, but questions eventually pulled them apart. Kara kept Safia's hand in her own.

The *hodja* finally spoke. "Your shared story goes back to Lord Kensington's discovery of the statue at the tomb of Nabi Imran. His remarkable find was significant to us. The statue dated from the founding of Ubar, buried at a tomb tied to a woman of miracles."

"The Virgin Mary?" Safia asked.

A nod answered her. "As guardians, one of our number had to get close, to examine the funerary object. It was said that the keys to the Gates of Ubar would reveal themselves when the time was right. So Almaaz was sent."

"Al-Maaz," Safia said, noting the pronunciation was slightly off.

"*Almaaz*," the *hodja* repeated more firmly.

Kara squeezed her hand. "All the women here are named after jewels. The *hodja*'s name is Lu'lu. Pearl."

Safia's eyes widened. "*Almaaz*. My mother's name was Diamond. The orphanage thought it was her family name, al-Maaz. So what happened to her?"

The *hodja*, Lu'lu, shook her head with a weary frown. "Like many of our women, your mother fell in love. In investigating the discovery of the statue, she allowed herself to get too close to Lord Kensington . . . and he to her. They both were lost to each other. And after a few months, a child grew in her womb, seeded the natural way of all women."

Safia frowned at the strange choice of words but didn't interrupt.

"The pregnancy panicked your mother. It was forbidden for one of us to bear a child from a man's loins. She fled Lord Kensington. Back to us. We cared for her until she gave birth. But after you were born, she had to leave. Almaaz had broken our rule. And you, a child of mixed blood, were not pure Rahim." The old woman touched her teardrop tattoo, the ruby symbol of the tribe. Safia had no tattoo. "Your mother raised you as best she could in Khaluf on the Omani coast, not far from Muscat. But the accident left you an orphan.

"During all this time, Lord Kensington never gave up his search for your mother . . . and the possible child she carried. He scoured Oman, spent fortunes, but when one of our women wish to be unseen, we are not found. The blood of Biliqis has blessed us in many ways."

The old woman glanced down to her staff. "When we learned you were orphaned, we could not abandon you. We found where you were taken and passed the information to Lord Kensington. He was heartsick to hear of Almaaz, but as the desert takes, it also returns. It gave him back a daughter. He collected you and pulled you into his family. I suspect he planned on waiting until you both were old enough to understand the complexities of the heart before revealing your shared blood."

Kara stirred. "On the morning of the hunt . . . my father told me that he had something important to tell me. Something that, on my sixteenth birthday, I was woman enough to hear." She swallowed hard, voice cracking. "I thought it was only something about school or university. Not . . . not . . ."

Safia squeezed her hand. "It's all right. Now we know."

Kara glanced up, her eyes full of confusion. "But why did he still pursue Ubar? I don't understand."

The *hodja* sighed. "It is one of many reasons we are forbidden from men. Perhaps it was a whisper across a pillow. A bit of history shared between lovers. But your father learned of Ubar. He sought the lost city, maybe as a way of being closer to the woman he lost. But Ubar is dangerous. The burden of its guardianship is a heavy one."

As if demonstrating, the old woman hauled herself up with considerable effort.

"And what of us now?" Safia asked, standing with Kara.

"I will tell you along the way," she said. "We have far to travel."

"Where are we going?" Safia asked.

The question seemed to surprise the *hodja*. "You are one of us, Safia. You brought us the keys."

"The heart and the spear?"

A nod. She turned away. "After two millennia, we go to unlock the Gates of Ubar."

PART FOUR

The Gates of Ubar

16

Crossroads

H) ∘ ⴵ ⴵ) ∘ ⱶ ⴵ Ⴈ

December 4, 5:55 A.M.
Dhofar Mountains

As the skies brightened to the east, Omaha slowed the van at the top of the pass. The road continued down the far side . . . if the rutted, stone-plagued track could be called a *road*. His lower back ached from the constant bump and rattle of the last ten miles.

Omaha braked to a halt. Here the road crested the last pass through the mountains. Ahead, the highlands dropped to salt flats and gravel plains. In the rearview mirror, fields of green heather spread, dotted with grazing cattle. The transition was abrupt.

To either side of the van lay a moonscape of red rock, interrupted by patches of straggly, red-barked trees, bent by the winds flowing over the pass. *Boswellia sacra.* The rare and precious frankincense trees. The source of wealth in ages past.

As Omaha braked, Painter's head snapped up from a light drowse. "What is it?" he asked blearily. One hand rested on the pistol in his lap.

Omaha pointed ahead. The road descended through a dry riverbed, a wadi. It was a rocky, treacherous course, meant for four-wheel-drive vehicles.

"It's all downhill from here," Omaha said.

"I know this place," Barak said behind them. The fellow never seemed to sleep, whispering directions to Omaha as they wound through the mountains. "This is Wadi Dhikur, the Vale of Remembrance. The cliffs to either side are an ancient graveyard."

Omaha popped the van into gear. "Let's hope it doesn't become ours."

"Why did we come this way?" Painter asked.

In the third row of seats, Coral and Danny stirred, slumped against each other. They sat straighter, listening. Clay, seated beside Barak, merely snored, head craned back, lost to the world.

Barak answered Painter's question. "Only the local Shahra tribe know of this route down the mountains to the desert. They still collect frankincense from the trees around here in the traditional manner."

Omaha had never met anyone from the Shahra clan. They were a reclusive bunch, almost Stone Age in their technology, frozen in tradition. Their language had been studied at length. It was unlike modern Arabic, almost a reedy singsong, and contained eight additional phonetic syllables. Over time, most languages *lose* sounds, becoming more refined as they mature. With the additional syllables, the Shahri language was considered to be one of the most ancient in all of Arabia.

But more particularly, the Shahra called themselves the People of 'Ad, named after King Shaddad, the first ruler of Ubar. According to oral traditions, they descended from the original inhabitants of Ubar, those who fled its destruction in A.D. 300. In fact, Barak might be leading them down the very path to Ubar that the People of 'Ad had once used to flee its destruction.

A chilling thought, especially shadowed by the entombed graves.

Barak finished, "At the bottom of the wadi, it is only thirty kilometers to reach Shisur. It is not far."

Omaha began their descent, in the lowest gear, creeping at five miles per hour. To go any faster risked sliding out in the loose shale and rocky scree. Despite the caution, the van skidded all too often, as if traveling on ice. After half an hour, Omaha's hands were damp on the wheel.

But at least the sun was up, a dusty rose in the sky.

Omaha recognized that hue. A storm was coming. Due to strike the area in a few more hours. Already winds off the sands blew up the wadi, blustering against the less-than-aerodynamic van.

As Omaha rounded a blind bend in the riverbed, two camels and a pair of robed bedouin appeared ahead. He hit the brakes too hard, fishtailed the rear end, and struck broadside into a precariously stacked set of stone slabs alongside the road. Metal buckled. The slabs toppled.

Clay startled awake with a snort.

"There goes our collision deposit," Danny griped.

The two camels, loaded and strapped with bales and overflowing baskets, gurgled at them, tossing their heads, as they were walked past the stalled van. It looked like they were carrying an entire household on their backs.

"Refugees," Painter said, nodding to other similarly laden camels, mules, and horses moving up the dry watercourse. "They're fleeing the storm."

"Is everyone okay?" Omaha asked as he fought the gearshift knob, punching the clutch. The van lurched, rocked, and finally began to roll again.

"What did we hit back there?" Coral asked, staring at the toppled stones.

Danny pointed to other similar stone piles that peppered the graveyard. "Triliths," he answered. "Ancient prayer stones." Each was composed of three slabs leaned against one another to form a small pyramid.

Omaha continued down the road, wary of the stacked stones. This was made more difficult as "traffic" grew thicker the lower down the riverbed they traveled.

Folks were fleeing the desert in droves.

"I thought you said no one knew about this back door out of the mountains," Painter asked Barak.

The Arab shrugged. "When you're facing the mother of all sandstorms, you run toward higher ground. Any ground. I wager every riverbed is being climbed like this. The main roads are surely worse."

They had heard periodic reports over the radio as reception came and went. The sandstorm had grown in size, as large as the Eastern Seaboard, whipping up eighty-mile-per-hour winds, packed by scouring sands. It was shifting sand dunes around like they were whitecaps on a storm-swept sea.

And that was not the worst. The high pressure system off the coast had begun to move inland. The two storm systems would meet over the Omani desert, a rare combination of conditions that would whip up a storm unlike any seen in ages before.

Even as the sun dawned, the northern horizon remained cloaked in a smoky darkness. As they descended the mountain road, the storm ahead grew taller and taller, a tidal wave cresting.

They finally reached the bottom of the wadi. The cliffs fell away to either side, spilling out into the sandy salt flats.

"Welcome to the Rub' al-Khali," Omaha announced. "The Empty Quarter."

The name could not be more fitting.

Ahead stretched a vast plain of gray gravel, etched and scoured with pictographic lines of blue-white salt flats. And beyond, a red ridge marked the edge of the endless roll of dunes that swept across Arabia. From their vantage, the sands glowed in pinks, browns, purples, and crimsons. A paint pot of hues.

Omaha studied their fuel gauge. With luck, they'd have just enough gas to reach Shisur. He glanced over to the Desert Phantom, their only guide. "Thirty kilometers, right?"

Barak leaned back and shrugged. "Thereabouts."

Shaking his head, Omaha turned forward and set off across the flatlands. A few straggling folk still trudged toward the mountains. The refugees showed no interest in the van heading *toward* the storm. It was a fool's journey.

No one in the van spoke, eyes fixed forward on the storm. The only sound: the crunch of sand and gravel under their tires. With the cooperative terrain, Omaha risked pushing the van up to thirty miles per hour.

The winds unfortunately seemed to pick up with every half mile, blowing streams of sand from the dunes. They would be lucky to have any paint on the van when they reached Shisur.

Danny finally spoke. "It's hard to believe this used to be a vast savannah."

Clay yawned. "What are you talking about?"

Danny shifted forward. "This wasn't always desert. Satellite maps show the presence of ancient riverbeds, lakes, and streams under the sand, suggesting Arabia was once covered by grasslands and forests, full of hippos, water buffalo, and gazelle. A living Eden."

Clay stared at the arid landscape. "How long ago was this?"

"Some twenty thousand years. You can still find Neolithic artifacts from that time: ax blades, skin scrapers, arrowheads." Danny nodded to the wastelands. "Then began a period of hyperaridity that dried Arabia into a desert wasteland."

"Why? What triggered such a change?"

"I don't know."

A new voice intervened, answering Clay's question. "The climatic change was due to Milankovitch Forcing."

Attention turned to the speaker. Coral Novak.

She explained. "Periodically the Earth *wobbles* in its orbit around the sun. These wobbles or 'orbital forcings' trigger massive climatic changes. Like the desertification of Arabia and parts of India, Africa, and Australia."

"But what could cause the Earth to wobble?" Clay asked.

Coral shrugged. "It could be simple *precession.* The natural periodic changes in orbits. Or it could be something more dramatic. A flip-flop of the Earth's polarity, something that's occurred a thousand times in geologic history. Or it might have been a burp in the rotation of the Earth's nickel core. No one can really say."

"However it happened," Danny concluded, "this is the result."

Before them, the dunes had grown into massive hummocks of red sand, some stretching six hundred feet high. Between the dunes, gravel persisted, creating winding, chaotic roadways, nicknamed "dune streets." It was easy to get lost in the maze of streets, but the more direct route over the dunes could bog the hardiest vehicle. Something they could not chance.

Omaha pointed ahead, directing his question to Barak, meeting the Desert Phantom's eyes in the rearview mirror. "You know your way through there, right?"

The giant of an Arab shrugged again, his usual response to everything.

Omaha stared at the towering dunes . . . and beyond them, a wall of churning dark sand rising from the horizon, like the smoky edge of a vast grass fire sweeping toward them.

They had no time for wrong turns.

7:14 A.M.

Safia marched beside Kara down another tunnel. The Rahim clan spread out ahead and behind them, traveling in groups, carrying oil lanterns in the darkness. They had been walking for the past three hours, stopping regularly to drink or rest. Safia's shoulder had begun to ache, but she didn't protest.

The entire clan was on the move. Even the children.

A nursing mother strode a few steps ahead, accompanied by six children, whose ages ranged from six to eleven. The older girls held the younger ones' hands. Like all the Rahim, even the children were bundled in hooded cloaks.

Safia studied the young ones as they sneaked glances back at her. They all appeared to be sisters. Green eyes, black hair, burnished skin. Even their shy smiles carried the same dimpled charm.

And while the adult women varied in minor ways—some were wiry, others heavier built, some long-haired, others shorn short—their basic features were strikingly similar.

Lu'lu, the tribal *hodja,* kept pace with them. After announcing their journey to the Gates of Ubar, she had left to organize the clan's departure. As guardians of Ubar for centuries, none of the Rahim would be left out of this momentous occasion.

Once they were under way, Lu'lu had gone silent, leaving Kara and Safia plenty of time to discuss the revelation of their sisterhood. It still seemed unreal. For the past hour, neither had spoken, each lost to her own thoughts.

Kara was the first to interrupt the silence. "Where are all your men?" she asked. "The fathers of these children? Will they be joining us along the way?"

Lu'lu frowned at Kara. "There are no men. That is forbidden."

Safia remembered the *hodja*'s comment earlier. About how Safia's birth had been forbidden. Did permission have to be granted? Was that why they all looked so identical? Some attempt at eugenics, keeping their bloodline pure?

"It's just you women?" Kara asked.

"The Rahim once numbered in the hundreds," Lu'lu said quietly. "Now we number thirty-six. The gifts granted to us through the blood of Biliqis, the Queen of Sheba, have weakened, grown more fragile. Stillborn children trouble us. Others lose their gifts. The world has grown toxic to us. Just last week Mara, one of our elders, lost her blessings when she went to the hospital in Muscat. We don't know why."

Safia frowned. "What *gifts* are these that you keep mentioning?"

Lu'lu sighed. "I will tell you this because you are one of us. You have been tested and found to harbor some trace of Ubar's blessing."

"Tested?" Kara asked, glancing to Safia.

Lu'lu nodded. "At some point, we test all half-bred children of the clan. Almaaz was not the first to leave the Rahim, to lie with a man, to forsake her lineage for love. Other such children have been born. Few have the gift." She placed a hand on Safia's elbow. "When we heard of your miraculous survival of the terrorist bombing in Tel Aviv, we suspected that perhaps your blood bore some power."

Safia stumbled at the mention of the bombing. She remembered the newspaper reports heralding the *miraculous* nature of her survival.

"But you left the country before we could test you, never to return. So we thought you lost. Then we heard of the key's discovery. In England. At a museum you oversaw. It had to be a sign!" A bit of fervor entered the woman's voice, so full of hope.

"When you returned here, we sought you out." Lu'lu glanced down the tunnel, voice lowering. "At first we attempted to collect your betrothed. To use him to draw you to us."

Kara gasped. "You were the ones who tried to kidnap him."

"He is not without talents of his own," the old woman conceded with half a smile. "I can see why you pledged your heart to him."

Safia felt a twinge of embarrassment. "After you failed to kidnap him, what did you do?"

"Since we couldn't draw you to us, we came to you. We tested you in the old manner." She glanced to Safia. "With the snake."

Safia stopped in the tunnel, remembering the incident in the bath at Kara's estate. "You sent the carpet viper after me?"

Lu'lu halted with Kara. A few of the women continued past.

"Such simple creatures recognize those with the gift, those blessed by Ubar. They will not harm such a woman, but find peace."

Safia could still feel the viper draped over her naked chest, as if sunning on a rock, content. Then the maid had walked in and screamed, triggering it to strike at the girl. "You could've killed someone."

Lu'lu waved them onward. "Nonsense. We're not foolish. We don't stick to the old traditions in that regard. We had removed the snake's fangs. You were at no risk."

Safia slowly continued down the tunnel, too stunned to speak.

Kara was not. "What is all this about a gift? What was the snake supposed to sense about Safia?"

"Those who bear the blessing of Ubar have the ability to project their will upon other minds. Beasts of the field are especially susceptible, bowing to our wishes, obeying our command. The simpler the beast, the easier to control. Come see."

Lu'lu stepped to the wall, where a small hole opened in the sandy floor. She opened her hands. A gentle buzzing floated about Safia's head. From the hole, a small vole emerged, blind, whiskers twitching. It climbed, as docile as a kitten, into the *hodja*'s palm. Lu'lu caressed it with a finger, then let it go. It dashed back into its hole, surprised to be out.

"Such simple creatures are easy to influence." Lu'lu nodded to Kara as she continued down the tunnel. "As are those minds weakened by abuse."

Kara glanced away.

"Nevertheless, we have little control over the wakened mind of man. The best we can manage is to cloud and dull their perceptions when we are close at hand. To hide our presence for a short time . . . and then *only* of our own form. Even clothes are difficult to whisper away. It is best done naked and in shadows."

Kara and Safia glanced at each other, too amazed for words. It was some form of telepathy, mind bending.

Lu'lu adjusted her cloak. "And of course, the gift can be used on oneself, a concentration of will directed *inward*. This is our greatest blessing, securing our line back to Queen Biliqis, she who was our first and last."

Safia remembered tales of the Queen of Sheba, stories found throughout Arabia, Ethiopia, and Israel. Many involved fanciful embellishments: magic carpets, talking birds, even teleportation. And the most significant man in her life, King Solomon, was said to be able to speak to animals, like the *hodja* claimed now. Safia pictured the leopard that attacked John Kane. Could these women truly control such beasts? Was such talent the source of all the wilder tales surrounding the Queen of Sheba?

Kara spoke into the stunned silence. "What happens when you direct your gift inward?"

"The greatest blessing," Lu'lu repeated with a wistful edge to her voice. "We ripen with child. A child born of no man."

Kara and Safia shared a look of disbelief.

"A virgin birth . . ." Kara whispered.

Like the Virgin Mary. Safia pondered this revelation. *Is that why the first key, the iron heart, had been hidden at Mary's father's tomb? An acknowledgment of some sort. One virgin to another.*

Lu'lu continued, "But our births are not *any* birth. The child of our body *is* our body, born afresh to continue the line."

Safia shook her head. "What do you mean?"

Lu'lu raised her staff and passed it forward and backward, encompassing all the clan. "We are all the same women. To speak in modern terms, we are genetically identical. The greatest blessing of all is the gift to keep our line pure, to produce a new generation out of our own womb."

"Clones," Kara said.

"No," Safia said. She understood what the *hodja* was describing. It was a reproductive process found in some insects and animals, most notably bees.

"Parthenogenesis," Safia said aloud.

Kara looked confused.

"It's a form of reproduction where a female can produce an egg with an intact nucleus containing her own genetic code, which then grows and is born, an identical genetic duplicate of the mother."

Safia stared up and down the tunnel. All these women . . .

Somehow their telepathic gift allowed them to reproduce themselves, genetically intact. *Asexual reproduction.* She recalled one of her biology professors at Oxford, how he had mentioned that *sexual* reproduction was a relatively strange thing for our bodies to do. That normally a bodily cell divided to produce an exact duplicate of itself. Only the germ cells in ovaries or testicles divided in such a manner to produce cells with only half of their original genetic code—eggs in females, spermatozoa in males—allowing for the mix of genetic material. But if a woman could somehow, by sheer will, stop this cellular division in her unfertilized egg, the resulting offspring would be an exact duplicate of the mother.

Mother . . .

Safia's breath caught in her throat. She stopped and searched the faces around her. If what Lu'lu said was true, if her mother was from this clan, then all around her stood her mother. She was seeing her in all her possible incarnations: from newborn babe suckling on a teat to the mother who nursed that child, from the young girl walking hand in hand with her older sister to the elder at her side. All her mother.

Safia now understood the cryptic words of the *hodja* earlier.

All of us. We're all your mother.

It wasn't metaphor. It was fact.

Before Safia could move or speak, two women marched past. One carried the silver case holding the iron heart. The next bore the iron spear with the bust of the Queen of Sheba. Safia noted the iron countenance on the statue. The face of Sheba. The face of these women.

Sudden understanding struck Safia, almost blinding her. She had to lean against the tunnel wall. "Sheba . . ."

Lu'lu nodded. "She is the first and the last. She is all of us."

An early exchange with the *hodja* echoed in Safia's mind: *We are the Queen of Sheba.*

Safia watched the cloaked women march past. These women had been reproducing themselves asexually far back into history, tracing their genetic code to one woman, the first to produce a child in this manner, to regenerate herself.

Biliqis, the Queen of Sheba.

She stared into the face of Lu'lu, into the green eyes of the long-dead queen. The past living in the present. The first and the last.

How was this possible?

A shout rose from the front of the line.

"We're through the mountains," the *hodja* said. "Come. The Gates of Ubar await."

7:33 A.M.

Painter shielded his eyes as he stared at the stalled van, at the rising sun, at the walls of sand all around. This would not be a good place to be trapped when the coming sandstorm struck. He imagined those mountainous dunes spilling over them like crashing waves against rocks.

They had to get moving again.

A few minutes ago, the van had been careening along a stretch of flat sand, riding along the edges of dunes, a Volkswagen surfboard. The graveled "streets" they had been following had finally vanished completely, requiring them to furrow through hard-packed sand.

Only not all of the sand was *packed*.

"Camel wallow," Barak commented, on his knees, staring at the back end of the van. Its front and rear tires were mired to the axle. "Sand here is very loose. And deep. Like quicksand. Camels roll in them to clean their bodies."

"Can we dig the van out?" Omaha asked.

"There's no time," Painter said.

Barak nodded. "And the deeper you dig, the deeper the van will sink."

"Then we'll have to unload what we can. Travel on foot."

Danny groaned from his seat in the sand. "We really have to be choosier with our means of transportation. First the flatbed truck, now this junker."

Painter stepped away, too full of nervous energy, or maybe it was the electricity in the air, some cloud of static charge pushed ahead of the sandstorm. "I'm going to climb that dune. See if I can spot Shisur. It can't be more than a mile. In the meantime, clean out the van. Weapons, equipment, everything."

Painter set off up the hill. Omaha trudged after him. "I can check by myself," Painter said, waving him off.

Omaha kept climbing, every step pounded deep, as if he were punishing the sand. Painter didn't feel like arguing with him. So the pair trudged up the dune face. It was more of a trek than Painter had imagined down below.

Omaha drew a step nearer. "I'm sorry . . ."

Painter's brow crinkled in confusion.

"About the van," Omaha mumbled. "I should've spotted the wallow."

"Don't worry about it. I would've hit it, too."

Omaha continued upward. "I just wanted to say I'm sorry."

Painter sensed the man's apology covered more than the mired vehicle.

At last, they reached the knife-edged crest of the dune. It crumbled underfoot. Runnels of sand coursed down the far side.

The desert held a perfect crystal stillness. No birdsong, no chirp of insect. Even the wind had subsided momentarily. The calm before the storm.

Painter gaped at the expanse before them. Dunes stretched to all horizons. But what held his attention was the roiling wall to the north, a hurricane of sand. The dark clouds reminded Painter of stacked thunderclouds. He spotted even a few bluish flashes. Static discharges. Like lightning.

They needed to reach cover.

"There," Omaha said, and pointed his arm. "That cluster of date palms."

Painter made out a tiny patch of greenery about half a mile away, buried among the dunes, easy to miss.

"The oasis of Shisur," Omaha said.

They were not far.

As he turned away, movement caught his eye. In the sky to the east. A black gnat flew, limned in the morning sunlight. He lifted his night-vision goggles over his eyes, flipping up the ordinary lenses rather than the low-light feature. He telescoped closer.

"What is it?"

"A transport helicopter. United States Air Force. Probably from Thumrait. It's circling to land out there."

"A rescue mission, because of the storm?"

"No. It's Cassandra." Painter heard her voice in his head. *Did you really think that I'd believe you were heading to the border of Yemen?* Here was more confirmation of how high up Cassandra's group had its teeth and claws in Washington. How could Painter hope to win out here? He had only five people with him, few with military training.

"Are you sure it's her?"

Painter watched the helicopter rotor down to the sands, vanishing among the dunes. "Yes. That's the spot on the map. Six miles off course."

Painter lowered his goggles. Cassandra was too close for comfort.

"We have to get moving," he said.

Painter fixed the bearings and headed back downhill. The two men slid their way down, making faster time. Reaching the bottom, Painter eyed the stacked gear. It was a load. But they dared not leave anything they might need.

"How far?" Coral asked.

"Half a mile," Painter said.

Looks of relief spread among the others.

But Coral stepped to his side, noting his tension.

"Cassandra's already here," he said. "Off to the east."

Coral shrugged. "That's good. When the sandstorm hits, she'll be pinned down. It might buy us another day or two out here. Especially if that coastal high-pressure system crashes on top of us. The predicted megastorm."

Painter nodded, taking a deep breath. Coral was right. They could still pull this off. "Thanks," he mumbled to her.

"Anytime, Commander."

They quickly divided the gear. The largest crate held the ground-penetrating radar unit. Painter and Omaha hauled it between them. It was monstrously heavy, but if they were to search the ruins for buried treasure, they might need such a tool.

So they set off, winding around a vast dune that crested two football fields in height, then slogged up and over smaller ones. The sun continued its climb, heating the sand and the air. Soon their pace became a crawl as they were drained of adrenaline, bone-tired and exhausted.

But at last, they climbed a low dune and discovered a cluster of modern cinder-block buildings, wooden structures, and a small mosque in the valley beyond. The village of Shisur.

Down in the valley, the endless red of the Rub' al-Khali was interrupted by green. Acacia bushes grew alongside the buildings, stretches of yellow-flowering tribulus spread across the sand, along with thickets of palmetto. Larger mimosalike trees trailed flowering fronds to the ground, creating shaded arbors. And the ubiquitous date palms climbed high.

After the desert trek, where the only vegetation had been a few straggly salt bushes and wan patches of tasseled sedge, the oasis of Shisur was Eden.

In the village, nothing moved. It appeared deserted. The winds had kicked up again as the forward edge of the storm pushed toward them. Bits of refuse spun in dust devils. Cloth curtains flapped out open windows.

"No one's here," Clay noted.

Omaha stepped forward, scanning the tiny township. "Evacuated. Then again, the place is pretty much abandoned during the off-season. Shisur is mostly a waystation for the wandering Bait Musan tribe of Bedouin. They come and go all the time. With the discovery of the ruins just outside the town and the beginning of tourism here, it has grown into a somewhat more permanent village. But even that's pretty seasonal."

"So where exactly are the ruins?" Painter asked.

Omaha pointed off to the north. A small tower of crumbling rock poked above the flat sands.

Painter had thought it a natural outcropping of limestone, one of the many flat-topped mesas that dotted the desert. Only now he noted the stacked stones that composed the structure. It looked like some watchtower.

"The Citadel of Ubar," Omaha said. "Its highest point. More of the ruins are hidden below, out of sight." He set off toward the empty township.

The others began the final push to shelter, leaning against the stubborn wind, faces turned from the gusts of sand.

Painter remained a moment longer. They'd made it to Ubar at last. But what would they find? He stared at the danger looming to the north. The sandstorm filled the horizon, erasing the rest of the world. Even as he stared, Painter watched more of the desert being eaten away.

Again crackles of static electricity danced where the storm met the sands. He watched a particularly large discharge roll down a dune face, like a balloon cast before a stiff wind. It faded in moments, seeming to seep into the sand itself and vanish. Painter held his breath. He knew what he had just witnessed.

Ball lightning.

The same as had ignited the meteorite at the British Museum.

They had come full circle.

A voice spoke at his shoulder, startling him. "The blue djinn of the sands," Barak said, having noted the same natural phenomenon. "Storms always bring out the djinn."

Painter glanced to Barak, wondering if the man believed they were evil spirits or just a story to explain such phenomena.

Barak seemed to sense his question. "Whatever they are, they're never good." He set off down the hill after the others.

For a moment longer, Painter studied the monstrous storm, eyes stinging from the blowing sand. It was just beginning.

As he headed down the slope, his gaze cast off to the east. Nothing moved. The roll of dunes hid everything. A vast sea. But Cassandra and her team waited out there.

Sharks . . . circling and circling . . .

8:02 A.M.

Safia had not expected this mode of transportation, not from an ancient clan whose bloodline ran back to the Queen of Sheba. The dune buggy ramped up the sandy face, its huge knobby tires finding good traction. They shot over the crest, flew airborne for an extended breath, then landed solidly on the downward slope. Tires and shock absorbers cushioned their impact.

Still, Safia clung with her one good arm to the roll bar in front of her, like the security latch on a roller-coaster car. Kara held fast in the same manner, white-knuckled. Both women wore matching desert cloaks, hoods pulled up and secured with a sand scarf over their lower face, protecting skin from the scouring wind. They also wore polarized sun goggles, pinched over their eyes.

In the passenger seat up front, Lu'lu rode next to the Rahim driver, a young woman of sixteen named Jehd. The driver—or pilot, as the case was at times—held her lips in a firm, determined line, though a glint of girlish excitement lit her eyes.

Other dune buggies followed, each loaded with five of the clan women. They crisscrossed one another's paths to avoid the sand cast up by the vehicles in front. To either side, flanking the buggies, rode a dozen sand bikes, motorcycles with ballooned wheels, chewing through the larger vehicles' wakes, making huge leaps over the crests of dunes.

The caravan's speed was born of necessity.

To the north, the sandstorm barreled toward them.

Upon leaving the subterranean warren of tunnels, Safia found herself on the far side of the Dhofar Mountains, at the edge of the Rub' al-Khali. They had crossed *under* the entire mountain range. The passages they had traversed were old river channels, worn through the limestone bedrock.

Free of the tunnels, the buggies and bikes awaited them. Kara had commented on the choice of vehicles, expecting camels or some other less sophisticated means of transportation. Lu'lu had explained: *We may trace our lineage into the past, but we live in the present.* The Rahim did not live their entire lives in the desert, but like the Queen of Sheba herself, they wandered, educated themselves, prospered even. They had bank accounts, stock portfolios, real-estate holdings, traded in oil futures.

The group now raced toward Shisur, trying to beat the storm.

Safia had not argued against such haste. She did not know how much longer the ruse she had used to deceive Cassandra would last. If they were to gain the prize before Cassandra did, they would need every advantage.

Lu'lu and the others were counting on Safia to lead the way. In the *hodja*'s words: *The keys revealed themselves to you. So will the Gates.* Safia prayed the woman was right. She had used intuition and knowledge to lead them this far. She hoped her expertise would carry her the rest of the way.

In the front seat, Lu'lu lifted a Motorola walkie-talkie and listened, then spoke into it. All words were lost to the growl of motors and torrents of winds. Once done, she swung around in her seat-belt restraints.

"There may be trouble," Lu'lu yelled. "The scouts we sent ahead report a small band of armed strangers entering Shisur."

Safia's heart leaped to her throat. *Cassandra . . .*

"Perhaps they are just seeking shelter. The scouts found a vehicle. An old van stuck in a camel wallow."

Kara leaned forward, intense. "A van . . . was it a blue Volkswagen?"

"Why?"

"It may be our friends. Those who were helping us."

Kara glanced to Safia, eyes hopeful.

Lu'lu lifted her walkie-talkie and carried on a brief conversation. She nodded, then turned to Kara and Safia. "It was a blue Eurovan."

"That's them," Kara exclaimed. "How did they know where to find us?"

Safia shook her head. It seemed impossible. "We should still be careful. Maybe Cassandra or her men captured them."

And even if it was their friends, a new fear clutched Safia's heart. Who had survived? Painter had attempted to rescue her, risked all, stayed behind to cover her retreat. Had he made it out? The exchange of gunfire she had heard as she fled the tomb echoed in her head.

All answers lay at Shisur.

After another ten minutes of dune racing, the small township of Shisur appeared over a ridge, in a slight valley, surrounded by the rolling desert. The village's tiny mosque poked its minaret above the tumble of shacks and cinder-block buildings. The buggies all stopped below the ridgeline. A few of the women climbed out and up to the sandy crests. They dropped flat, their cloaks matching the sands, clutching sniper rifles.

Fearing a volley of accidental gunfire, Safia exited the buggy. Kara followed. She crossed up to the ridge. Caution drew her to hands and knees.

Across the village, she saw no sign of movement. Had they heard the approach of the dune buggies and gone into hiding, fearing the unknown group?

Safia surveyed the area.

To the north, ruins covered fifteen acres, surrounded by crumbling walls, excavated from the sands and reconstructed. Guard towers interrupted the walls at regular intervals, roofless stony circles, a story high. But the most dramatic feature of the ruins was its central citadel, a three-story structure of stacked stone. The castle perched atop a low hill that overlooked a deep ragged cleft in the ground. The hole encompassed most of the land within the walls. Its bottom lay in shadows.

Safia knew that the ruins of the hilltop fortress were only half of the original structure. The other half lay at the bottom of the hole. Destroyed when the sinkhole opened up under it, taking down sections of walls and half the castle. The tragedy was explained by the continual drop of the land's water table. A natural limestone cistern lay underneath the city. As the water inside it dropped from drought and overuse, it left behind a hollow subterranean cavern that eventually collapsed in on itself, taking out half the city.

Movement drew Safia's attention back to the village fifty yards away.

From a doorway below, a figure appeared, dressed in a *dishdasha* robe, his head wrapped in a traditional Omani headdress. He lifted a mug into the air.

"I just put a fresh pot on. If you want a cup of joe, you'd best get your butts down here."

Safia stood. She recognized that flash of a rakish grin.

Omaha . . .

A flush of relief washed through her. Before she knew it, she was running down the slope toward him, eyes blurry with tears. Even as she ran, the depth of her reaction surprised her.

She stumbled across the gravel roadway.

"Hold it right there," Omaha warned, backing up a step.

From windows and neighboring doorways, rifles suddenly bristled.

A trap . . .

Safia stopped, stunned, wounded. Before she could react, a figure swept out of hiding from behind a low wall, grabbed her, swung her around. A fist snatched a handful of hair and yanked back, baring her neck. Something cold touched her flesh.

A long dagger glinted, pressed.

A voice whispered with an icy ferocity. It chilled her more than the knife at her throat. "You took a friend of ours."

Omaha stepped to her shoulder. "We spied you coming. I wouldn't forget the face of someone who tried to kidnap me."

"What have you done with Dr. al-Maaz?" the voice hissed at her ear as the dagger pressed harder.

Safia realized her face was still covered by scarf and goggles. They thought her one of the women, bandits perhaps. Breathless from fright, she reached up and pulled down her scarf and goggles.

Omaha did a double take. He gaped at her face, then lunged, and pushed the man's arm away, freeing her. "Ohmygod, Saffie . . ." He hugged her tightly.

Fire flared in her shoulder. "Omaha, my arm."

He dropped back. Others appeared in doorways and windows.

Safia glanced behind her. A man stood there, the dagger in his hands. Painter. She had not even recognized his voice. She had a hard time reconciling this man with her image of him. She still felt the blade against her skin, the fist twisted in her hair.

Painter backed up a step. His face shone with relief, but his blue eyes also glowed with an emotion almost too raw to read. Shame and regret. He glanced away, to the neighboring slope.

Cycles and buggies now lined the ridge, engines revving. The Rahim had been preparing to come to her rescue. Women, all dressed and cloaked like Safia, appeared around nearby corners of buildings, rifles on shoulders.

Kara stomped down the slope, arms in the air. "Everyone back down!" she called loudly. "It was only a misunderstanding."

Omaha shook his head. "That woman doesn't need to remove her mask. I'd recognize that screech of command anywhere."

"Kara . . ." Painter said, stunned. "How?"

Omaha turned to Safia. "Are you all right?"

"I'm fine," she managed to squeak out.

Kara joined them. She removed her scarf. "Leave her be." She waved them off. "Give her some room to breathe."

Omaha pushed back. He nodded to the slope. Warily the Rahim had begun to march down. "So who are your friends?"

Kara shrugged. "That may take some explaining."

8:22 A.M.
Open Desert

Cassandra stepped up to her tent, a U.S. Army desert survival model, meant to withstand winds up to eighty miles per hour. She had reinforced it with a wind-and-sand shield on the windward side of the tent.

The team here had similar accommodations. The larger transport trucks had also been positioned as a windbreak.

At her tent, Cassandra shook sand from her fatigues. She wore a wide-brimmed hat, tied down around her ears, a scarf over her face. The winds gusted now, snapping tent lines, causing sheets of sand to course underfoot. The sandstorm rumbled like a passing freight train.

She had just returned from a final inspection of their deployment, ensuring all the copters were battened down. The men had already planted the GPS beacons to fix their position, coordinated with the fixed orbital satellites. Feed should be flowing into her computerized mapping system.

Cassandra had a couple hours before the static electricity of the sandstorm would threaten the electronics, requiring them to be shut down. Plenty of time to intercept the data from the LANDSAT satellite as it focused on her GPS beacons. The satellite's radar had the capability of delving sixty feet under the sand. It would give her an overview of what lay underfoot. Some indication of where to begin digging. As soon as the sandstorm blew itself out, her team would set to work with dozers and backhoes. By the time anyone was aware of their excavation, they'd be long gone.

That was the plan.

Cassandra pushed through the tent flap. The interior of the tent was spartan. A cot and a duffel. The remainder of her tent was an elaborate satellite communication system. She had other electronic gear stored in carryalls.

She crossed to the laptop computer and used her cot as a seat. She linked to JPL in Houston and fed the proper authorization to access LANDSAT data. The pass should have been completed five minutes ago. The data awaited her. She tapped the keys and began the download.

Finished, she sat back and watched the screen slowly fill with an image of the desert. She spotted her trucks, tents, even their trenched latrine. It was the survey pass. Perfect alignment.

A second image slowly fed into her laptop. The deeper scan.

Cassandra leaned in closer.

The terrain stripped away to display a different conformation, revealing the bedrock under the sand. It was a fossil of a different time, preserved in limestone. While most of the terrain was flat, it was etched by an old riverbed coursing along one corner of the image. It drained into an ancient lake bed buried under their site.

Cassandra studied the landscape, a snapshot from another time.

She saw nothing significant. No meteor crater, no artifact that intrigued.

She sat back. She would forward it to a pair of geologists on the payroll with the Guild. Perhaps they could read more into it.

A noise at her tent flap drew her attention around.

John Kane limped into her tent. "We've picked up Dr. al-Maaz's signal."

Cassandra swung to face him. "When? Where?"

"Eight minutes ago. It took another few minutes to get a fix. Her signal blipped into existence ten miles west of here. By the time we triangulated, she'd stopped moving. She went to ground about six miles from here."

He hobbled over to the map on her worktable and tapped. "Right here."

Cassandra leaned next to him, reading the name. "Shisur. What's there?"

"I asked one of the techs at Thumrait. He says it's where the old ruins of Ubar were found. Back in the nineties."

Cassandra stared at the map. Her lines in blue and red still looked fresh. The red circle marked her present position. She put her finger on the circle and followed the red line backward.

It crossed Shisur.

She closed her eyes. Again picturing the curator's expression when Cassandra had drawn the circle. She had continued studying the map. Her eyes had been distant, calculating in her head.

"The goddamn bitch . . ." Cassandra's finger on the map closed to form a fist. Anger burned through her. Yet deeper down, a flash of respect flared.

John Kane stood with his brows crinkled.

Cassandra stared back at the LANDSAT image. "There's nothing here. She fucked us. We're at the wrong place."

"Captain?"

She faced Kane. "Get the men up. We're heading out. I want the trucks moving in the next ten minutes."

"The sandstorm—"

"Fuck it. We've just enough time. We're moving out. We can't let ourselves get pinned down here." She herded Kane toward the doors. "Leave the equipment, tents, supplies. Weapons only."

Kane swept out of the room.

Cassandra turned to one of her carrying cases. She snapped it open and removed a handheld digital radio transmitter. She flipped it on, dialed in the proper frequency and channel to match the curator's implanted transceiver.

She held a finger over the transmit button. One touch and the C4 pellet in Dr. al-Maaz's neck would explode, severing her spine and killing her instantly. She felt an overwhelming urge to press it. Instead she switched the unit off.

It was not compassion that held her hand. Safia had proven her prowess at riddle solving. Such skill might still be needed. But more than that, she didn't know for certain if Painter was at the woman's side.

That was important.

Cassandra wanted Painter to see Safia die.

17

Picking a Lock

ⵏⵢⴱⵏⵢⵀⵉⵀⵉⵔⵔⴱⵢⵏ

December 4, 9:07 A.M.
Shisur

Safia secured her goggles in place. "Does everyone have their gear?"

"It looks like night's falling," Clay said by the open doorway. They had boarded up the windows to the cinder-block building. They had chosen this particular home because it had a solid door to close against the winds. It also opened on the south face of the structure, away from direct assault by the storm.

Through the doorway, Safia could see that the morning sky had been swept away by higher-blowing sand, darkening the world to an eerie twilight. Dust clouds shadowed the sun. Closer at hand, channels of swirling sand swept along the alleys to either side of the home, eddying in front of the door. It was the leading edge of the storm. Farther out, the heart of the sandstorm moaned and roared, like some ravenous beast, gnashing through the desert.

They didn't have much time.

Safia faced the group assembled in the plain room. Most buildings in Shisur were left open or unlocked. The seasonal residents simply stripped the place to the plaster before moving on, leaving nothing to steal, except for a few broken bits of pottery, a dirty cracked dish in the kitchen sink, and a handful of pale green scorpions. Even the curtains had been taken.

"You all have your assigned places to search," Safia said. She had a map nailed to one wall. She had divided the site into five sections, one for each of their metal detectors scrounged from the ruin's work shack. They had Motorola radios to keep in contact. Everyone, except the youngest children, had an assigned grid to help search, armed with pickaxes, shovels, and spades.

"If you detect something, mark it. Let your companions dig it out. Keep moving. Keep searching."

Nods met her orders. All the searchers were outfitted in reddish brown desert cloaks, supplied by Lu'lu. Faces were muffled. Eyes shielded by goggles. It was like they were preparing to go underwater.

"If anything of significance is found, radio it in. I'll come see. And remember . . ." She tapped the watch on the wrist of her slung arm. "After forty-five minutes, we all return here. The storm's full brunt is due to hit in just under an hour. We'll weather the worst of the storm in here, examine anything we find, and move on from there as the winds die down. Any questions?"

No one raised a hand.

"Let's go, then."

The thirty searchers set off into the storm. As the citadel was the most likely spot to search for the Gates of Ubar, Safia led a majority of the team members to the ruins of the fortress, to concentrate attention there. Painter and Clay lugged the ground-penetrating radar sled. Barak held the metal detector over his shoulder like a rifle. Behind him, Coral and Kara carried excavating tools. Trailing last, Lu'lu and the dune-buggy driver, Jehd, followed. All the other Rahim had broken up into teams to search the other grids.

Safia stepped around the corner of the cinder-block building. She was immediately blown back a step by a gust. It felt like the hand of God shoving her, rough-palmed and gritty. She bent into the wind and set off toward the entrance gates to the ruins.

She noted Painter studying the *hodja*. They had all exchanged their respective stories upon meeting, catching everyone up. Safia's story was, of course, the most shocking and seemingly fanciful: a secret tribe of women, whose bloodline ran back to the Queen of Sheba, a line granted strange mental powers by some source at the heart of Ubar. Though Painter's face was goggled and wrapped in a muffler, his very posture expressed doubt and disbelief. He kept a wary pace between Safia and the *hodja.*

They crossed out of the village proper and through the wooden gates to the ruins. Each party dispersed to its grid assignments. Omaha and Danny lifted their arms in salute as they headed toward the sinkhole below the citadel. With their field experience, the two men would oversee the search of the sinkhole. The chasm was another likely spot for a possible significant find, as a corner of the towering fortress had collapsed into the hole.

Still, Omaha had not been happy about his assignment. Since Safia's arrival, he had followed her every step, sat next to her, his eyes seldom leaving her face. She had felt a flush at his attention, half embarrassment, half irritation. But she understood his relief at discovering her alive and didn't rankle against his attention.

Painter, on the other hand, held back from her, dispassionate, clinical. He kept busy, listening to Safia's story without any reaction. Something had changed between them, become awkward. She knew what it was. She forced her hand not to rub her neck, where he had held the dagger. He had shown a side of himself, a fierce edge, sharper than the dagger. Neither knew how to react. She was too shocked, unsettled. He had closed off.

Focusing on the mystery here, Safia led her team up a steep trail to the hilltop fortress. As they climbed, the entire system of ruins opened out around them. It had been a decade since Safia had last laid eyes upon the ruins. Before, there had only been the citadel, in disrepair, just a mound of stones, and a short section of wall. Now the entire encircling ramparts had been freed from the sands, partially rebuilt by archaeologists, along with the stumplike bases of the seven towers that once guarded its walls.

Even the sinkhole, thirty feet deep, had been excavated and sifted through.

But most of the attention had been devoted to the citadel. The piled stones had been fitted back together like a jigsaw puzzle. The base of the castle was square in shape, thirty yards on each side, supporting its round watchtower.

Safia imagined guards pacing the parapets, wary of marauders, watchful of approaching caravans. Below the fortress, a busy town had prospered: merchants hawked wares of handcrafted pottery, dyed cloths, wool rugs, olive oil, palm beer, date wine; stonemasons labored to build higher walls; and throughout the town, dogs barked, camels brayed, and children ran among the stalls, bright with laughter. Beyond the walls, irrigated fields spread green with sorghum, cotton, wheat, and barley. It had been an oasis of commerce and life.

Safia's eyes drifted to the sinkhole. Then one day, it all came to an end. A city destroyed. People had fled in superstitious terror. And so Ubar vanished under the sweep of sands and years.

But that was all on the surface. Stories of Ubar went deeper, tales of magical powers, tyrant kings, vast treasures, a city of a thousand pillars.

Safia glanced at the two women, one old, one young, identical twins separated by decades. How did both stories of Ubar hang together: the mystical and the mundane? The answers lay hidden here. Safia was sure of it.

She reached the gateway into the citadel and stared up at the fortress.

Painter flicked on a flashlight and shone a bright beam into the dark interior of the citadel. "We should begin our search."

Safia stepped over the threshold. As soon as she entered the fortress, the winds died completely, and the distant rumble of the sandstorm dimmed.

Lu'lu joined her now.

Barak followed them, turning on the metal detector. He began to sweep behind her as if wiping away her footprints from the sand.

Seven steps down the hall, a windowless chamber opened, a man-made cavern. The back wall was a collapsed ruin of tumbled stone.

"Sweep the room," Safia directed Barak.

The tall Arab nodded and began his search for any hidden artifacts.

Painter and Clay set up the ground-penetrating radar as she had instructed.

Safia swung her flashlight over the walls and ceiling. They were unadorned. Someone had lit a campfire at one time. Soot stained the roof.

Safia paced the floor, eyes searching for any clue. Barak marched back and forth, intent on his metal detector, searching floor and walls. As the room was small, it didn't take long. He came up empty. Not even a single ping.

Safia stood in the center of the room. This chamber was the only inner sanctum still remaining. The tower overhead had collapsed in on itself, destroying whatever rooms lay above.

Painter activated the ground-penetrating radar, flicking on its portable monitor. Clay entered the room, slowly dragging the red sled over the sandy stone floor, pulling it like a yoked ox. Safia came over and studied the scan, more familiar with reading the results. If there were any secret basement rooms, they would show up on the radar.

The screen remained dark. Nothing. Solid rock. Limestone.

Safia straightened. If there was some secret heart to Ubar, it had to lie underground. But where?

Maybe Omaha was having better luck with his team.

Safia lifted her radio. "Omaha, can you hear me?"

A short pause. "Yeah, what's up? Did you find anything?"

"No. Anything down in the pit?"

"We're just finishing with the sweep, but so far nothing."

Safia frowned. These were the two best spots to expect to find answers. Here was the spiritual center of Ubar, its royal house. The ancient queen would have wanted immediate access to the secret heart of Ubar. She would have kept its entrance close.

Safia turned to Lu'lu. "You mentioned that after the tragedy here, the queen sealed Ubar and scattered its keys."

Lu'lu nodded. "Until the time was ripe for Ubar to open again."

"So the gate wasn't destroyed when the sinkhole opened." *That was a bit of luck. Too much luck.* She pondered this, sensing a clue.

"Maybe we should bring the keys here," Painter said.

"No." She dismissed this possibility. The keys would only become important once the gate was found. But where, if not at the citadel?

Painter sighed, arms crossed. "What if we tried recalibrating the radar, heightened the intensity, searched deeper."

Safia shook her head.

"No, no, we're looking at this all wrong. Too high tech. That's not going to solve this puzzle."

Painter had a slightly hurt look. Technology was his bailiwick.

"We're thinking too modern. Metal detectors, radar, grids, mapping things out. This has all been done before. The gate, to survive this long, undisturbed, must be entrenched in the natural landscape. Hidden in plain sight. Or else it would've been found before. We need to stop leading with our tools and start thinking with our heads."

She found Lu'lu staring back at her. The *hodja* wore the face of the queen who had sealed Ubar. But did the two share the same nature?

Safia pictured Reginald Kensington frozen forever in glass, a symbol of pain and torment. The *hodja* had remained silent all these years. She must've dug up the body, taken it to their mountain lair, and hidden it away. Only the discovery of Ubar's keys had broken the woman's silence, loosened her tongue to reveal her secrets. There was a pitiless determination in all this.

And if the ancient queen had been like the *hodja,* she would have protected Ubar with that same pitiless determination, a mercilessness that bordered on the ruthless.

Safia felt a well of ice rise around her, remembering her initial question. *How did the gate conveniently survive the sinkhole's collapse?* She knew the answer. She closed her eyes with dawning dismay. She had been looking at this all wrong. Backward. It all made a sick sense.

Painter must have sensed her sudden distress. "Safia . . . ?"

"I know how the gate was sealed."

9:32 A.M.

Painter hurried back from the cinder-block building. Safia had sent him running to fetch the Rad-X scanner. It had been a part of the equipment taken from Cassandra's SUV. Apparently Cassandra had even demonstrated it to Safia back in Salalah, showing her how the iron heart bore a telltale sign of antimatter decay, to convince Safia of the true reason for this search.

Along with the Rad-X scanner, Painter had discovered an entire case of analyzing equipment, more sophisticated than anything he was acquainted with, but there was a hungry gleam in Coral's eye as she had looked at the equipment. Her only comment: "Nice toys."

Painter hauled the entire case. Safia was onto something.

The storm fought him as he passed through the wooden gate and into the ruins. Sand peppered every exposed inch of skin, wind tore at his scarf and cloak. He leaned into the wind. The day had turned to twilight. And this was only the front edge of the storm.

To the north, the world ended in a wall of darkness, flashing in spidery crackles of blue fire. Static charges. Painter smelled the electricity in the air. NASA had done studies for a proposed Mars mission to judge how equipment and men would fare in such sandstorms. It wasn't the dust and sand that most threatened their electronic equipment, but the extreme static charge to the air, formed from a combination of dry air and kinetic energy. Enough to fry circuits in seconds, create agonizing static bursts on skin. And now this storm was swirling up a giant squall of static.

And it was about to roll over them.

Painter ducked toward the low hill, burrowing through the wind and blowing sand. As he reached the area, he headed down instead of up, following the steep trail that descended into the sinkhole. The deep pit stretched east to west along its longer axis. On the west end, the citadel sat atop its hill, maintaining a vigil over the sinkhole.

Safia and her team crouched on the other side, at the eastern end of the chasm. By now, the Rahim had gathered, too, around the rim of the pit. Most lay flat on their bellies to lessen their exposure to the wind.

Ignoring them, Painter slipped and slid down the sandy path. Reaching the bottom, he hurried forward.

Safia, Omaha, and Kara were bent over the monitor of the ground-penetrating radar unit. Safia was tapping at the screen.

"Right there. See that pocket. It's only three feet from the surface."

Omaha leaned back. "Clay, drag the radar sled back two feet. Yeah, right there." He bent over the monitor again.

Painter joined them. "What did you find?"

"A chamber," Safia said.

Omaha frowned. "It's only a remnant of the old well. Long gone dry. I'm sure it's already been documented by other researchers."

Painter moved closer as Omaha clicked a button on the monitor. A vague three-dimensional cross section of the terrain under the radar sled appeared on the monitor. It was conical in shape, narrow at the top and wider at the bottom.

"It's only ten feet at its widest," Omaha said. "Just an uncollapsed section of the original cistern."

"It does look like a blind pocket," Kara agreed.

Safia straightened up. "No, it's not." She faced Painter. "Did you bring that radiation detector?"

Painter lifted the case. "Got it."

"Run the scanner."

Painter opened the case, snapped the detection rod on the Rad-X scanner's base, and activated it. The red needle swept back and forth, calibrating. A blinking green light steadied to a solid glow. "All ready."

He slowly turned in a circle. What was Safia suspecting?

The red needle remained at the zero point.

"Nothing," he called back.

"I told you—" Omaha started.

He was cut off. "Now check the cliff face." Safia pointed to the rock wall. "Get close."

Painter did as she directed, the scanner held out before him like a divining rod. Sand swirled around inside the pit, a mini–dust bowl, stirred by the winds overhead. He hunched over the scanner as he reached the cliff face. He ran the detection rod over the rock face, mostly limestone.

The needle shimmied on the dial.

He held the scanner more steadily, shielding it from the wind with his own body. The needle settled to a stop. It was a very weak reading, barely shifting the needle, but it *was* a positive reading.

He shouted over his shoulder. "I got something here!"

Safia waved back. "We have to dig where the sled is positioned. Three feet down. Open the pocket."

Omaha checked his watch. "We only have another twenty minutes."

"We can do it. It's just packed sand and small rocks. If several people dig at the same time . . ."

Painter agreed, feeling a surge of excitement. "Do it."

In less then a minute, a ring of diggers set to work.

Safia stood back, cradling her arm in the sling.

"Are you ready to explain yourself?" Omaha said.

Safia nodded. "I had to be sure. We've been think-ing about this all wrong. We all know the sinkhole opened under Ubar's township and destroyed half the town, driving folks away in superstitious fear of God's wrath. After this disaster, the last queen of Ubar sealed its heart, to protect its secrets."

"So?" Kara asked, standing beside the *hodja*.

"Doesn't it strike you as odd that the gate was conveniently spared during the devastation here? That as the city folk fled, the queen stayed behind and performed all these secret acts: sealed the gate in such a manner that it has never been discovered, forged and hid keys at sacred sites of that time."

"I suppose," Kara said.

Omaha brightened visibly. "I see what you're getting at." He glanced to the diggers, back to Safia, grabbing her good arm. "We've been looking at this ass-backward."

"Would someone care to explain it to us layfolk?" Painter asked, irritated at Omaha's understanding.

Omaha explained. "The chronology has to be wrong. Chicken-and-egg scenario. We've believed the sinkhole was the *reason* Ubar was sealed."

"Now think about it in a new light," Safia added. "As if you were the queen. What would such a disaster matter to the royal house anyway? The true wealth of Ubar, the source of its power, lay elsewhere. The queen could've simply rebuilt. She had the wealth and the power."

Omaha chimed in, the pair working as an experienced team. "The town was *not* important. It was only a mask hiding the true Ubar. A facade. A tool."

"One turned to a new use," Safia said. "A means of hiding the gate."

Kara shook her head, clearly as confused as Painter.

Omaha sighed. "Something truly terrified the queen, enough to drive her from the wealth and power of Ubar, force her and her descendants to live a nomadic existence, existing on the fringe of civilization. Do you really think a simple sinkhole like this would've done it?"

"I guess not," Painter said. He noted the excitement growing between Safia and Omaha. They were in their element. He was excluded, on the outside looking in. A flare of jealousy prickled through him.

Safia picked up the thread. "Something terrified the royal family, enough that they wanted Ubar locked from the world. I don't know what that event was, but the queen did not act rashly. Look at how methodical her preparations were afterward. She prepared keys, hid them in places sacred to the people, wrapped them in riddles. Does this sound like an irrational response? It was calculated, planned, and executed. As was her first step in sealing Ubar."

Safia glanced to Omaha.

He filled in the final blank. "The queen deliberately caused the sinkhole to collapse."

A stunned moment of silence followed.

"She destroyed her own town?" Kara finally asked. "Why?"

Safia nodded. "The town was only a means to an end. The queen put it to its final use. To bury Ubar's gate."

Omaha glanced all around the rim. "The act also had a psychological purpose. It drove folks away, frightened them from ever approaching. I wager the queen herself spread some of the stories about God's wrath. What better way to hang a religious 'Do Not Trespass' sign on these lands?"

"How did you figure all that out?" Painter asked.

"It was only a conjecture," Safia said. "I had to test it. If the sinkhole was used to bury something, then there must be something down here. Since the metal detectors discovered nothing, either the object was too deep or it was some type of chamber."

Painter glanced at the diggers.

Safia continued, "As with the tomb sites, the queen cloaked clues in symbols and mythology. Even the first key. The iron heart. It symbolized the heart of Ubar. And in most towns, the heart of their community is the well. So she hid the Gate of Ubar in the well, buried them in sand, as the iron heart was sealed in sandstone, then dropped the sinkhole on top of them."

"Driving people away," Painter mumbled. He cleared his throat and spoke more clearly. "What about the radiation signature?"

"It would take dynamite to drop this sinkhole," Omaha answered.

Safia nodded. "Or some form of an antimatter explosion."

Painter glanced at Lu'lu. The *hodja* had remained stoically quiet the entire time. *Had her ancestors really utilized such a power?*

The old woman seemed to note his attention. She stirred. Her eyes were hidden by goggles. "No. You cast aspersions. The queen, our ancestor, would not kill so many innocent people just to hide Ubar's secret."

Safia crossed to her. "No human remains were ever found in or around the sinkhole. She must have found some way to clear the city. A ceremony or something. Then sank the hole. I doubt anyone died here."

Still, the *hodja* was unconvinced, even taking a step back from Safia.

A shout rose from the diggers. "We found something!" Danny yelled.

All their faces turned to him.

"Come see before we dig further."

Painter and the others all shifted over. Coral and Clay stepped aside for them. Danny pointed his shovel.

In the center of the trenchlike hole, the dark red sand had turned to snow.

"What is that?" Kara asked.

Safia hopped down, dropped to a knee, and ran her hand over the surface. "It's not sand." She glanced up. "It's frankincense."

"What?" Painter asked.

"Silver frankincense," Safia elaborated, and stood up. "The same as what was found plugging the iron heart. An expensive form of cement. It's stoppered the top of the hidden chamber like a cork in a bottle."

"And below it?" Painter asked.

Safia shrugged. "There's only one way to find out."

9:45 A.M.

Cassandra clutched her laptop as the M4 high-speed tractor mashed over another small dune. The transport vehicle looked like a brown Winnebago balanced on a pair of tank treads, and despite its eighteen-ton weight, it chewed across the landscape with the efficiency of a BMW down the Autobahn.

She kept the pace reasonable, respecting the terrain and weather. Visibility was poor, only yards ahead.

Windblown sand flumed all around, whipping off the tops of dunes in vast sails. The sky had darkened, cloudless, the sun no more than a wan moon above. She dared not risk bogging down the tractor. They'd never drag it free. So they proceeded with sensible caution.

Behind her the other five all-terrain trucks traveled in the tracks of the larger tractor as it blazed a trail through the desert. In the rear were the flatbeds with the cradled VTOL copters.

She glanced to the clock in the corner of the laptop's screen. While it had taken a full fifteen minutes to get the caravan moving, they were now making good time. They'd reach Shisur in another twenty minutes.

Still, she kept an eye on the screen. Two display windows were open on it. One was a real-time feed from an NOAA satellite that tracked the path of the sandstorm. She had no doubt they'd reach the shelter of the oasis before the full storm struck, but just barely. And of even greater concern, the coastal high-pressure system was on the move inland, due to collide with this desert storm in the next few hours. It would be hell out here for a while.

The other screen on the monitor displayed another map of the area, a topographic schematic of this corner of the desert. It diagrammed every building and structure in Shisur, including the ruins. A small blue spinning ring, the size of a pencil eraser, glowed at the center of the ruins.

Dr. Safia al-Maaz.

Cassandra stared at the blue glow. *What are you up to?* The woman had led her off course, away from the prize. She thought to steal it out from under Cassandra's nose, using the cover of the storm. Smart girl. But intelligence carried you only so far. Strength of arm was just as important. Sigma had taught her that, pairing brawn and brain. *The sum of all men.* Sigma's motto.

Cassandra would teach that lesson to Dr. al-Maaz.

You may be smart, but I have the strength.

She glanced to the side mirror, to the trail of military vehicles. Inside, one hundred men armed with the latest in military and Guild hardware. Directly behind, in the tractor's transport bed, John Kane sat with his men. Rifles bristled as they performed the deadly sacrament of a final weapons inspection. They were the best of the best, her Praetorian guards.

Cassandra stared ahead as the tractor ground its way inevitably forward. She attempted to pierce the gloom and windswept landscape.

Dr. al-Maaz might discover the treasure out there.

But in the end, Cassandra would take it.

She glanced back to the laptop's screen. The storm ate away the map of the region, consuming all in its

path. On the other display window, the schematic of
the town and ruins glowed in the dim cabin.

Cassandra suddenly tensed. The blue ring had vanished from the map.

Dr. al-Maaz was gone.

9:53 A.M.

Safia hung from the caving ladder. She stared up at
Painter above. His flashlight blinded her. She flashed
on the moment in the museum when she hung from
the glass roof and he was below her, encouraging her to
wait for security. Only now their roles were reversed.
He was on top; she was below. Yet once again, she was
the one hanging above a drop.

"Just a few more steps," he said, his scarf whipping
about his neck.

She glanced to Omaha below. He held the ladder
steady. "I got you."

Bits of crumbling frankincense cascaded around
her. Boulders of it lay around Omaha's feet, and the
air in the subterranean chamber was redolent with its
aroma. It had taken only a few minutes with pickaxes
to perforate into the conical-shaped cave.

Once they had broken through, Omaha had lowered
a candle into the cave, both to check for bad air and to

light the interior. He then went down the collapsible ladder, inspecting the chamber himself. Only when he was satisfied did he let Safia climb down. With her injured shoulder, she had to loosen her left arm from her sling and carry most of her weight with her right.

She struggled the rest of the way down. Omaha's hand found her waist, and she leaned into his grip gratefully. He helped her to the floor.

"I'm all right," she said when he kept a hand on her elbow.

He lowered his hand.

It was much quieter out of the wind, making her feel slightly deaf.

Already Painter had mounted the ladder, coming down, moving swiftly. Soon three flashlights shone across the walls.

"It's like being inside a pyramid," Painter said.

Safia nodded. Three rough walls tilted up to the hole at the top.

Omaha knelt on the floor, running his fingers across the ground.

"Sandstone," Safia said. "All three walls and floor."

"Is that significant?" Painter asked.

"This is not natural. The walls and floor are hewn slabs of sandstone. This is a man-made structure. Built atop bedrock of limestone, I imagine. Then sand was poured around the outside. Once it was covered, they plugged the hole at the top and covered it with more loose sand."

Omaha stared up. "And to make sure no one found it by accident, they dropped the sinkhole atop it, frightening everyone away with ghost stories."

"But why do all that?" Painter asked. "What's this supposed to be?"

"Isn't it obvious?" Omaha grinned at him, looking suddenly striking to Safia. His goggles lay draped under his chin, his scarf and hood thrown back. He had not shaved in a couple of days, leaving a bronzed stubble over cheek and chin, his hair stuck up in odd places. She had forgotten how he looked in the field. Half wild, untamed. He was in his natural element, a lion on the veldt.

All that came to her with only the flash of his grin.

He loved all this—and once, she had, too. She had been as wild and uninhibited, his companion, lover, friend, colleague. Then Tel Aviv . . .

"What's obvious?" Painter asked.

Omaha flung an arm. "This structure. You saw one of these today."

Painter frowned.

Safia knew Omaha was teasing this out, not from malice, but simply from pure enjoyment and awe.

"We banged into one of these—a much smaller one—as we descended out of the mountains."

Painter's eyes widened, his gaze swept the space. "Those prayer stones."

"A trilith," Omaha said. "We're standing *inside* a giant trilith."

Safia suspected Omaha wanted to jump up and down, and truth be told, his excitement was contagious. She could not stand still herself. "We need to bring the keys down here."

"What about the storm?" Painter cautioned.

"Screw the storm," Omaha said. "You and the others can go and hide out in town. I'm staying here." His eyes fell on Safia.

She nodded. "We've good shelter here. If someone could lower the iron artifacts, water, a few supplies, let Omaha and me figure out what to do with them. We might have the riddle solved by the time the worst of the storm blows itself out. Otherwise, we'll lose a whole day."

Painter sighed. "I should stay here, too."

Omaha waved him off. "Crowe, you're not much use to us. To use your own words from earlier, this is *my* area of expertise. Guns, military ops . . . that's *you*. Here, you're simply taking up space."

Storm clouds built behind Painter's blue eyes.

Safia placed a conciliatory hand on the man's arm. "Omaha's right. We've got radios if we need anything. Someone has to make sure everyone stays safe when the storm hits."

With clear reluctance, Painter stepped to the ladder. His eyes lingered on her, glanced to Omaha, then away. He climbed up and called, "Radio what you'll need." He then shooed everyone away, herding them back to the shelter of the cinder-block homes.

Safia suddenly became acutely aware of how alone she was with Omaha. What had seemed so natural a moment ago now seemed strange and uncomfortable, as if the air had suddenly soured in here. The chamber felt too cramped, claustrophobic. Maybe this wasn't such a brilliant idea.

"Where do we start?" Omaha asked, his back to her.

Safia lifted her arm back into her sling. "We look for clues."

She stepped away and shone her light up and down each wall. Each appeared to be the identical size and shape. The only mark was a small square hole cut halfway up one wall, perhaps a place to rest an oil lamp.

Omaha lifted a metal detector from the floor.

Safia waved him to put it down. "I doubt that's going to—"

As soon as he flipped on its power, the detector pinged. Omaha's eyebrows rose. "Talk about beginner's luck."

But as he swept the device over more of the floor, the detector continued its pinging, as if the metal lay everywhere. He lifted it to the sandstone walls. More pinging.

"Okay," Omaha conceded, dropping the detector, getting nowhere. "I'm beginning to really hate that old queen."

"She's hidden a needle in a haystack."

"All this must have been too deep for the surface detectors. Time to go low-tech." Omaha pulled free a notepad and pencil. With compass in hand, he began mapping out the trilith. "So what about those keys?"

"What about them?"

"If they're from the time of Ubar's downfall, how did they end up in a statue from 200 B.C.? Or at Job's tomb? Ubar fell in A.D. 300."

"Look around you," Safia said. "They were skilled artisans in sandstone. They must have found those holy sites, balanced whatever energy source lies within these keys. Antimatter or whatever. And burrowed the artifacts into elements already at the tombs: the statue in Salalah, the prayer wall at Job's tomb. Then they sealed them over again with sandstone with a skill that left their handiwork undetectable."

Omaha nodded, continuing his sketching.

The bark of the radio startled them both. It was Painter. "Safia, I have the artifacts. I'll be returning with water and a couple MRE rations. Anything else you need? The winds are becoming fierce."

She considered, staring at the walls around her, then realized something that might come in handy. She told him.

"Roger that. I'll bring it."

As she signed off, she found Omaha's eyes on her. He glanced too quickly to his notepad.

"Here's the best I could sketch," he mumbled, and showed her his diagram.

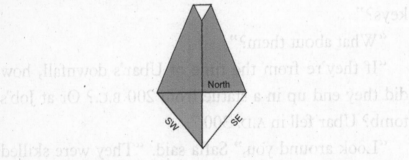

"Any thoughts?" she asked.

"Well, traditionally the three stones of the trilith represent the celestial trinity. *Sada, Hird,* and *Haba.*"

"The moon, the sun, and the morning star," Safia said, naming them as they were known today. "A trinity revered by the early religions of the region. Again the queen was showing no preferential treatment between the faiths."

"But which stone slab represents which celestial body?" Omaha asked.

She nodded. "Where to begin?"

"In the morning, I'd say. The morning star appears at dawn in the southeast sky." Omaha patted the appropriate wall. "So that seems obvious enough."

"Which leaves us two other walls," Safia said, taking over. "Now the northern wall is aligned along the east-west axis, straight as an arrow."

"The path the sun takes across the sky."

Safia brightened. "Even that little hollow square in the north wall could represent a window, to let sunlight inside."

"Then that leaves this last wall to be the moon." Omaha stepped to the southwest wall. "I don't know why this one represents the moon, but Sada was the predominant deity to the desert tribes of Arabia. So it must be significant."

Safia nodded. In most cultures, the sun was the major divinity, paramount, life-giving, warming. But in the searing deserts, it was deadly, merciless, unforgiving. So instead, the moon, Sada, was most worshiped for its cooling touch. The moon was the bringer of rain, represented by the bull with its crescent-shaped horns. Each quarter phase of the moon was named *Il* or *Ilah*, which over the years came to be known as a term for God. In Hebrew, *El* or *Elohim*. In Arabic, *Allah*.

The moon was paramount.

"Still, the wall appears blank," Omaha said.

Safia neared him. "There must be something." She joined the search. The surface was rough, pocked in places.

A crunch of sand announced Painter's arrival.

Omaha climbed halfway up the ladder and passed supplies to Safia below.

"How're things going in there?" Painter called as he lowered a plastic gallon of water.

"Slow," Safia said.

"But we're making progress," Omaha interjected.

Painter leaned into the wind. Unburdened as he was, it looked like the next strong gust might kite him away. Omaha climbed back down. Skitters of windblown sand followed him.

"You'd better get back to the shelter," Safia called up, worried for Painter's safety.

He gave her a salute and pushed away into the sandy gale.

"Now where were we?" Omaha asked.

10:18 A.M.

Out of the sinkhole, Painter fought through the storm. An eerie night had fallen. Dust covered the sun, casting the world in crimson. Visibility shut down to mere feet in front of his face. He had his night-vision goggles fixed in place, but even they gained only another yard of sightline. He barely saw the gates as he hunched through them.

Among the village buildings, sand flowed underfoot with the winds, as if he were walking along a stream-bed. His clothes spat with static electricity. He tasted it in the air. His mouth felt chalky, his lips brittle and dry.

Finally, he ducked around into the lee of their shelter. Out of the direct teeth of the storm, he felt capable of taking full breaths. Sand flumed in wild eddies, streaming over the roofline. He walked with one hand along the cinder-block wall.

Feet in front of him, a figure folded out of the swirls of darkness, a ghost taking form. A ghost with a rifle. It was one of the Rahim scouts, on guard. He hadn't seen her until he was on top of her. He nodded to her as he passed. No acknowledgment. He marched by her to the doorway.

Stopping, he glanced back. She was gone again, vanished.

Was it just the storm, or was it a part of her ability to blend into the background, to cloud perception? Painter stood in front of the door. He had heard the story from Safia, but it seemed too wild to believe. As a demonstration of their mental abilities, the *hodja* had placed a pale green scorpion on the floor and made it do figure eights in the dust, over and over again, seeming to control it. Was it some trick? Like snake charming?

As he reached to the knob, the winds took a slightly different keen. The roar had grown so constant that he barely heard it anymore. But for a moment, a deeper rumble arose, a sound carried on the wind, rather than the wind itself. He remained still, listening for it again, trying to pierce the veil of sweeping sand. The storm continued its steady growl. The grumble was not repeated.

Was it just the storm? He stared out to the east. He was certain the sound had come from that direction. He yanked open the door and twisted inside, half pushed by the winds.

The room was crowded with bodies. He heard a child crying upstairs. He had no trouble picking Coral out from among the women, an iceberg in a dark sea. She rose from a cross-legged position. She had been cleaning one of her pistols.

Recognizing his worry, she met him in quick strides. "What's wrong?"

10:22 A.M.

All the trucks gathered in the lee of a dune, lined up as if awaiting the beginning of a parade. Men hunched in the relative shelter of the vehicles, but details were murky in the gloom. They were a quarter mile outside of Shisur.

Cassandra strode with Kane down the ranks. She wore night-vision goggles, khaki fatigues, and a hooded sand poncho, belted at the waist.

Kane marched with one hand covering the earpiece of his radio, listening to a report. A company of twenty soldiers had left ten minutes ago. "Roger that. Hold for further orders." He lowered his hand and leaned toward Cassandra. "The team reached the town's outskirts."

"Have them circle the area. Both town and ruins. Pick vantages from which to snipe. I don't want anything or anyone leaving that place."

"Aye, Captain." He returned to speaking into the throat mike, relaying orders.

They continued to the rear of the line, to where six flatbed trucks carried the VTOL copter sleds. The helicopters were covered in tarps and lashed to their transport cradles. They continued to the last two trucks. Men tugged free the ropes securing the copters. A tarp went flying into the wind, billowing high.

Cassandra frowned at this.

"These are your best two pilots?" Cassandra asked Kane as he finished with the radio.

"The bastards had better be." Kane's eyes were on the storm.

Both Cassandra and Kane's lives were now staked on the success of this mission. The screwup at the tomb had cast both of them in a bad light. They needed to prove themselves to the Guild command. But more than that, Cassandra noted an idiosyncratic quality in the man, a new savageness, less humor, more deep-seated fury. He had been bested, maimed, scarred. No one did that to John Kane and lived to tell about it.

They reached the group of flatbed trucks.

Cassandra found the two pilots waiting. She strode toward them. They had helmets tucked under one arm, trailing electronic cords that would feed radar data. To fly in this weather would be to fly by instruments only. There was no visibility.

They straightened once they recognized her, difficult with everyone muffled up and bundled in ponchos.

Cassandra eyed them up and down. "Gordon. Fowler. You two think you can get these birds in the air. In this storm?"

"Yes, sir," Gordon acknowledged. Fowler nodded. "We've attached electrostatic sand filters over the engine intakes and uploaded sandstorm software into our radar array. We're ready."

Cassandra saw no fear in their faces, even as the winds howled. In fact, they both looked flushed, excited, two surfers ready to tackle big waves.

"You're to keep in constant contact with me person-ally," Cassandra said. "You have my com channel."

Nods.

"One will scout the town, the other the ruins. Kane has a software patch to load into your onboard comput-ers. It will let you pick up the signal of the primary target. The target is not—and let me repeat *not*—to be harmed."

"Understood," Gordon mumbled.

"Any other hostiles," Cassandra finished, "are to be shot on sight."

Nods again.

Cassandra swung away. "Then let's get these birds in the air."

10:25 A.M.

Omaha watched Safia crawl on her knees, sweeping sand off the floor with one hand. He found it hard to concentrate. He had forgotten how wonderful it was to work alongside her. He noted the tiny beads of per-spiration on her brow, the way her left eye crinkled when she was intrigued, the dab of dirt on her cheek. This was the Safia he had always known . . . before Tel Aviv.

Safia continued sweeping.

Was there any hope for them?

She glanced up to him, noting that he'd stopped.

He stirred and cleared his throat. "What are you doing?" he asked, and motioned to her sweeping of the floor. "The maid comes tomorrow."

She sat back and patted the wall tilted above her head. "This is the southeast side. The slab of the trilith that represents the morning star, rising each day in the southeastern skies."

"Right, I told you that. So?"

Safia had been working in silence for the past ten minutes, laying out the supplies Painter had lugged here, very methodically, her usual way of doing things. She had spent most of this time examining the keys. Whenever he tried to interject a question, she would hold up a palm.

Safia went back to her sweeping. "We've already determined which wall corresponds to which celestial body—moon, sun, or morning star—but now we have to figure out which *keys* match those celestial bodies."

Omaha nodded. "Okay, and what are you figuring?"

"We have to think in a context of ancient times. Something Cassandra failed to do, accepting modern miles for Roman ones. The answer lies in that fact." Safia glanced back to him, testing him.

He stared at the wall, determined to solve this riddle. "The morning star is actually not a star. It's a *planet*. Venus, to be specific."

"Identified and named by the Romans."

Omaha straightened, then twisted to look at the artifacts. "Venus was the Roman god of love and beauty." He knelt and touched the iron spear with the bust of the Queen of Sheba atop it. "And here's a definite beauty."

"That's what I figured. So like at Job's tomb, there must be a place to insert it. A hole in the ground." She continued her search.

He joined her—but searched elsewhere. "You have it wrong," he said. "It's the *wall* that's significant. Not the floor." He ran his palm over the surface and continued his reasoning, enjoying the match of wits in solving this riddle. "It's the slab that represents the morning star, so it is in the slab you'll find—"

His words died as his fingers discovered a deep pock in the wall. Waist-high up the slab. It looked natural, easy to miss in the shadowy darkness. His index finger sank fully into it. He crouched there like the Dutch boy at the dike.

Safia rose up beside him. "You found it."

"Get the artifact."

Safia stepped over, grabbed the iron spear. Omaha pulled his finger free and helped her insert its end in the hole. It was an ungainly process with the wall angled. But they wiggled it into place. It kept sinking farther and farther. The entire haft of the spear was swallowed away, until only the bust was left, now hanging on the wall like some human trophy.

Safia manipulated it further. "Look how the wall is indented along this side. It matches her cheekbone." She turned the bust and pushed it flush.

"A perfect fit."

She stepped back. "Like a key in a lock."

"And look where our iron queen is staring now."

Safia followed her gaze. "The moon wall."

"Now the heart," Omaha said. "Does it belong to the sun wall or the moon?"

"I would guess the sun wall. The moon was the predominant god of the region. Its soft light brought cooling winds and the morning dew. I think whatever we're looking for next, the final key or clue, will be associated with that wall."

Omaha stepped to the north wall. "So the heart belongs to this wall. The sun. The harsh mistress."

Safia glanced to the artifact. "A goddess with an iron heart."

Omaha lifted the artifact up. There was only one place to rest it. In the small window cut into the northern slab face. But before settling it in place, he ran his fingers along the sill, having to stretch on his toes to feel the floor of the niche. "There are vague indentations in here. Like on the wall."

"A cradle for the heart."

"A lock and key."

It took a bit of rolling around to find the match between the iron heart's surface and the indentations in the sandstone. He finally settled it in place. It rested upright. The end plugged with frankincense pointed at the moon wall.

"Okay, I'd say that's an important slab," Omaha said. "What now?"

Safia ran her hands along the last wall. "Nothing's here."

Omaha slowly turned in a circle. "Nothing that we can see in the dark."

Safia glanced back at him. "Light. All the celestial bodies illuminate. The sun shines. The morning star shines."

Omaha squinted. "But upon *what* do they shine?"

Safia backed up. She noted again the abnormally rough surface of the wall, its pocked moonscape. "Flashlights," she mumbled.

They each retrieved one from the floor. Safia took a post by the mounted bust. Omaha moved to the heart in the window.

"Let there be light." Holding the flashlight over his head, he positioned its beam as if it were sunlight pouring through the window, angled to match the position of the plugged end. "The sun shines through a high window."

"And the morning star shines low on the horizon," Safia said, kneeling by the bust, aiming her beam in the direction of the bust's gaze.

Omaha stared at the moon wall, lit askance by their two light sources from two different angles. The imperfections of the wall created shadows and crevices. A form took shape on the wall, painted with these shadows.

Omaha squinted. "It looks like a camel's head. Or maybe a cow's."

"It's a *bull!*" Safia stared at Omaha, her eyes bright embers. "Sada, the moon god, is depicted as a bull, because of the beast's crescent-shaped horns."

Omaha studied the shadows. "But then where are the bull's horns?"

The animal on the wall had nothing between its ears.

Safia pointed to the supplies. "Get me that while I hold the light."

Omaha placed his flashlight in the window, resting it beside the iron heart. He crossed to the gear and grabbed the device that looked like a shotgun, only with one end belled out like a satellite dish. Safia had specifically asked Painter to bring it. He was anxious to see how this worked.

He passed it to her, taking her post with the flashlight.

She strode to the center of the room and pointed the laser excavator. A circle of red light appeared on the wall. She fixed it above the shadow figure, between the ears.

She pulled the device's trigger. The red lights spun and sandstone immediately began to crumble as the laser energy vibrated the crystalline structure. Sand and dust billowed out. Also shinier bits. Flakes of metal, red.

Iron shavings, Omaha realized, understanding now why the metal detector was constantly abuzz. The architects of this puzzle had mixed iron shavings with the sand in the rock.

Back at the wall, the beam acted like a tornado, furrowing through the sandstone as if it were soft dirt. With his flashlight held steady, Omaha watched. Slowly, a brighter glitter revealed itself within the stone.

A mass of iron.

Safia continued to work, moving the laser up and down. In a matter of minutes, an arch of horns appeared, seated atop the shadowy image.

"Definitely a bull," Omaha agreed.

"Sada," Safia mumbled, lowering the gun. "The moon."

She walked over and touched the rack of embedded horns, as if making sure they were real. A shower of blue sparks erupted with the contact. "Youch!"

"Are you all right?"

"Yes," she said, shaking her fingers. "Just a static shock."

Still, she backed a step away, studying the mounted horns on the wall.

The horns certainly appeared as a sharp crescent, protruding from the rock. Sand and dust cast from the excavation swirled into the chamber as the winds above grew suddenly more stiff, seeming to blow directly down through the hole in the roof.

Omaha glanced up. Above the sinkhole, the skies were dark, but something even darker stirred the air, sweeping downward. A light suddenly speared from it.

Oh, no . . .

10:47 A.M.

Safia found herself grabbed around the waist and tackled to the side. Omaha dragged her into the shadows below the tilted slabs. "What are you—"

Before she could finish, a beam of bright light slammed through the hole overhead, casting a pillar of brilliance through the center of the trilith chamber.

"Helicopter," Omaha yelled in her ear.

Safia now heard the vague beat of rotors against the dull roar of the storm.

Omaha held her tightly. "It's Cassandra."

The light blinked off as the floodlight swept away. But the thump of the copter's rotors persisted. It was still out there, searching in the storm.

Safia knelt with Omaha. With the floodlight gone, the chamber seemed darker. "I have to alert Painter," Safia said.

She crawled to the Motorola radio. As her fingers reached to its surface, another electric spark arced from radio to fingertips, stinging like a wasp. She jerked her hand back. Only now did she notice the escalation of static electricity. She felt it on her skin, crawling like ants. Her hair crackled with sparks as she glanced at Omaha.

"Safia, come back here."

Omaha's eyes were wide. He circled toward her, keeping to shadows. His attention was not on the helicopter, but fixed to the center of the chamber.

Safia joined him. He took her hand, shocking them both, hairs tingling.

In the center of the chamber, a bluish glow billowed where the helicopter's beam had once shone. It shimmered, roiling in midair, edges ghostly. With each breath, it coalesced, swirling inward.

"Static electricity," Omaha said. "Look at the keys."

The three iron artifacts—heart, bust, and horns—shone a dull ruddy hue.

"They're drawing the electricity out of the air. Acting like some lightning rods for the static charge of the storm above, feeding power to the keys."

The blue glow grew into a scintillating cloud in the room's center. It stirred to its own winds, churning in place. The keys shone even brighter. The air crackled. Traceries of charge coruscated from every fold of cloak or scarf.

Safia gaped at the sight. Sandstone was a great nonconductive insulator. Freeing the horns from the stone must have completed some circuit among the three. And the chamber was acting like a magnetic bottle, trapping the energies.

"We have to get the hell out of here," Omaha urged.

Safia continued to stare, entranced. They were witnessing a sight set in motion millennia ago. How could they leave?

Omaha grabbed her elbow, fingers digging. "Saff, the keys! They're like the iron camel at the museum. And now a ball of lightning is forming in here."

Safia flashed back to the video feed from the British Museum. The ruddy glow of the meteorite, the cerulean roil of the lightning ball . . . Omaha was right.

"I think we just activated a bomb down here," Omaha said, pulling Safia to her feet and shoving her to the collapsible ladder. "And it's about to explode."

As she set her foot on the first rung, the world flashed blindingly bright. She flinched, tightening in place, a deer in headlights.

The helicopter had returned, hovering directly overhead.

Death waited above . . . as surely as it did below.

18
Down the Rabbit Hole

ⵀ°ⴲⵀⵉⵝⵗⵣⵝⵉⵞⵀⵑⵑⵗⵝⵉⵗ°ⵑⵣ

December 4, 11:02 A.M.
Shisur

Painter lay flat on the roof of the cinder-block building. He had bundled his cloak tightly under his legs, the ends of his scarf tucked away. He didn't want any telltale flapping of material to reveal his position.

He waited for the helicopter to make another pass over the town. He would get one shot. He had to assume the copter was outfitted with night vision. The muzzle flash would give away his position. He waited, the Galil sniping rifle at his cheek, resting on a bipod. The Israeli weapon, borrowed from one of the Rahim, had the capability to deliver a head shot at three hundred yards. But not in this storm, not with visibility so low. He needed the helicopter close.

Painter lay in wait.

The copter was up there somewhere, searching. An aerial hunter hidden in the storm. Any movement, and it would open fire with its double guns.

Painter noted the glow deeper in the storm, in the direction of the ruins. The second helicopter. He prayed that Safia and Omaha had kept their heads down. He had tried to radio them earlier, when he first suspected the danger, but something blocked the signal. Perhaps interference from the static charge of the storm. He attempted to reach them on foot, but the helicopters had swooped in, targeting anything that moved.

If there were birds in the air, then this was no small scouting party. Cassandra had somehow learned of her mistake and moved full forces in.

The radio in his ear whispered with static, the channel left open. Words formed out of the white noise. *"Commander."* It was Coral, reporting in from the field. *"As you suspected, I've hostiles coming in on all sides. They're doing a building-by-building search."*

Painter touched his transmitter, trusting that the storm kept their words private. "The children and older women?"

"Ready. Barak awaits your signal."

Painter searched the skies. *Where are you?* He needed to take out the helicopter if they were to have any hope of breaking through the noose around the town. The plan was to strike out west of the ruins, collecting Safia and Omaha along the way, risking the wild weather. Though the storm was growing worse with every minute, it could cover their retreat. If they left the ruins behind, perhaps Cassandra would be satisfied enough to make only half an effort to hunt them down. If they could get back to the mountains . . .

Painter felt a fury build in him. He hated to retreat, to hand Cassandra a victory here. Especially with the discovery of the secret chamber under the sinkhole. Cassandra would surely bring in heavy excavating equipment. Something lay down there. The Rahim were living proof of something extraordinary. His only hope was to abscond with Safia, delaying Cassandra enough for him to alert someone in Washington, someone he could trust.

And that certainly was *not* the command structure of Sigma.

Anger built in him, stoking a fire in his gut.

He had been set up. All of them had.

His mind flashed to Safia. He could still feel the beat of her heart under the blade he held at her throat. He had seen the look in her eyes afterward, as if he were a stranger. But what did she expect? This was his job.

Sometimes hard choices had to be made, and even tougher actions.

Like now.

With Coral's report of forces moving into the town's outskirts, they would be surrounded in minutes. He could no longer wait for the helicopter to show itself. It would need to be flushed out.

"Novak, is the rabbit ready to run?"

"On your go, Commander."

"Rev it up."

Painter waited, cheek against the gun, one eye peering through the telescopic lens, the other on the skies. A bright light burst down in the town, shining from an open doorway. Details were murky, but through his night-vision goggles, the light shone brilliant. A throaty engine growled and whined.

"Let her run," Painter ordered.

"Rabbit's loose."

From the building, a sand cycle burst forth. Its path was only evident as a brightness tearing down an alley between buildings. It zigzagged through the tangle of streets. Painter watched the skies to either side and above.

Then it appeared, diving like a hawk.

The helicopter's guns chattered, flashes in the storm.

Painter adjusted his rifle, aimed for the source of the gunfire, and pulled the trigger. The recoil struck his shoulder like a mule kick. He didn't wait. He squeezed off another three shots, ears ringing.

Then he saw it, a flare of flame. A heartbeat later, an explosion lit the storm. Fiery wreckage spat in all directions, but the main bulk tumbled in a steep path. It struck a building, burst brighter, then crashed into the roadway.

"Go," Painter yelled into his radio.

He shouldered the rifle and rolled off the roof's lip. The soft sand cushioned his fall. All around, engines ignited with rumbles and coughing whines. Lights flared. Bikes and buggies burst forth from alleyways, lean-tos, and out of doorways. One bike sped past Painter. A woman leaned over the bars, another sat behind her, rifle on her shoulder. The women would sweep a path ahead, guard their rear.

From the doorway, Kara appeared, carrying a girl in her arms. Others followed. Barak helped an old woman, followed by two others, supporting each other. Clay and Danny held children's hands, one on each side. Not a whimper from the lot of them. Not even Clay.

"Follow me," Painter said, and set off.

He kept his rifle shouldered but held a pistol in one hand.

As he rounded the corner of their shelter, a barrage of gunfire sounded from the ruins. Through the gloom, a floodlight flared. The second helicopter.

"Oh, God . . ." Kara said behind him, knowing what the gunfire meant.

Safia and Omaha had been found.

11:12 A.M.

"Run!" Omaha screamed as they ran across the floor of the sinkhole, but his words never reached his own ears. The rattle of guns was deafening. He pushed Safia ahead of him. They raced, blinded by the swirling sand, chased by a twin line of bullets chewing across the ground.

Directly ahead rose the western cliff of the sinkhole, shadowed from above by the citadel's ruins. The wall was lightly scalloped, coved in. If they could get under the lip of rock, out of direct line of fire, they'd have some shelter.

Safia ran an arm's length ahead of him, slightly encumbered by her sling, loping, the stiff winds tangling her cloak about her feet. Sand blinded. They hadn't even had time to pull their goggles in place.

Moments ago, they had decided that the helicopter was the lesser of two evils. The powder keg building in the trilith chamber meant certain death. So they took their chances on the run.

The chatter of guns grew louder as the helicopter swept behind them.

The only reason they had survived this long was the sandstorm. The pilot fought to keep his craft trimmed in the winds. It buffeted and fluttered, a hummingbird in a gale, throwing off the pilot's aim.

They fled for shelter, running blind.

Omaha waited for bullets to shred into him. With his last breath, he would push Safia to safety, if need be.

It wasn't necessary.

The bullets suddenly stopped, as if the craft had run out of ammunition. The sudden silence drew Omaha's attention over his shoulder, his ears still ringing. The helicopter's floodlight angled away. The copter swept back.

With his attention turned, he stumbled over a rock, went down hard.

"Omaha . . . !"

Safia came back to help. He waved her off. "Get to shelter!"

Omaha hobbled after her, his ankle flaring with pain, twisted, sprained, hopefully not broken. He cursed his stupidity.

The helicopter retreated to the other side of the sinkhole. It had them dead to rights. They shouldn't have made it. Why had it pulled back?

What the hell was going on?

11:13 A.M.

"Eagle One, don't hit the goddamn target!" Cassandra screamed into the radio. She banged a fist on the armrest of her seat in the M4 armored tractor. On her laptop, she stared at the blue glowing ring of the curator's transceiver. It had blinked into existence a moment ago.

The gunfire had flushed Safia out into the open.

Eagle One answered, the pilot's voice choppy. "I've broke off. There are two of them. I can't tell which one is the target."

Cassandra had radioed just in time. She pictured the pilot cutting down the woman. The curator was her best chance to quickly root out the secrets here and abscond with the prize. And the asinine pilot had almost mowed her down.

"Leave them both," she said. "Guard the hole they came out of."

Whatever cavern the curator had disappeared into had to be important.

Cassandra leaned close to her laptop, watching the blue glow. Safia was still in the giant sinkhole. There was nowhere she could go that Cassandra could not find her. Even if the woman vanished into another cave, Cassandra would know where to find the entrance.

She turned to the tractor's driver, John Kane. "Take us in."

With the engine still running, he shoved the gearshift. The tractor jerked, then trundled up the dune that hid them from the town of Shisur. Cassandra sat back, one hand on the laptop, holding it steady.

As they reached the dune's summit, the nose of the tractor rocked high, then fell down the far slope. The valley of Shisur lay ahead. But nothing could be seen beyond a few yards of the vehicle's xenon headlights. The storm swallowed the rest away.

All except a scatter of glows, marking the town. Vehicles on the move. A firefight between her forces and some unknown party still continued.

Distantly, echoes of sporadic gunfire reached her.

The captain of her forward forces had radioed in his assessment: *They all appear to be women.*

It made no sense. Still, Cassandra remembered the woman she had chased through the back alleys of Muscat. The one who had vanished in front of her. Was there a connection?

Cassandra shook her head. It no longer mattered. This was the endgame, and she would not tolerate anyone thwarting her.

As she watched the show of lights in the darkness, she lifted her radio and spoke to the leader of her artillery. "Forward battery, are you in position?"

"Yes, sir. Ready to light the candles on your order."

Cassandra checked her laptop. The blue ring of the transceiver persisted in the sinkhole. Nothing else mattered. Whatever they sought lay among the ruins, with the curator.

Raising her gaze, Cassandra stared at the shimmer of wavering lights where the town of Shisur lay. She lifted her radio, called the forward troops, and ordered a pull-back. She then switched back to the artillery captain.

"Level the town."

11:15 A.M.

As Painter led the others out of the village and through the gates of the ruins, he heard the first whistle. It pierced through the storm's roar.

He swung as the first shell struck the town. A fire-ball burst skyward, lighting the storm, illuminating a patch of the village briefly. The *boom* reverberated in his gut. Gasps rose around him. More whistles filled the air.

Rockets and mortars.

He never suspected Cassandra had such firepower at hand.

Painter fumbled for his radio. "Coral! Go dark!"

Whatever advantage of surprise they had gained by the sudden burst of vehicles from their hiding places had ended. It was time to evacuate.

Out in the town, the lights of the vehicles were all extinguished. Under the cover of darkness, the women were to retreat to the ruins. More rockets struck, blooming in wild spirals of fire, whipped by the winds.

"Coral!" he yelled into the radio.

No answer.

Barak grabbed his arm. "They know the rendezvous."

Painter swung around. More concussions pounded his gut.

Over at the sinkhole, the gunfire from the second helicopter had gone silent. What was happening?

11:17 A.M.

Safia huddled with Omaha under a lip of rock. The bombs rattled pebbles from the ruins of the citadel atop the cliff above them.

To the south, the dark skies glowed ruddy from fires. Another *boom* reverberated through the storm's wail. The town was being destroyed. Had the others had time to escape? Safia and Omaha had left their radios down in the trilith chamber. They had no way of knowing how the others had fared.

Painter, Kara . . .

At her side, Omaha leaned most of his weight on his right foot. She had seen him take that spill while fleeing here. He had twisted his ankle.

Omaha mumbled through his scarf. "You could still make a dash for it."

She was worn, her shoulder ached. "The helicopter . . ."

It still hovered over the sinkhole. Its floodlight had blinked off, but she still heard it. It swept a slow circuit over the sandy floor, keeping them pinned.

"The pilot broke off his attack before. He's probably half blind by the storm. If you stuck to the wall, ran fast . . . I could even take potshots from here."

Omaha still had his pistol.

"I'm not leaving without you," Safia whispered. Her statement was not all altruistic. She squeezed his hand, needing to feel his solidness.

He attempted to free his hand. "Forget it. I'd just slow you down."

She held harder. "No . . . I *can't* leave your side."

He suddenly seemed to understand the deeper meaning in her words, the raw fear. He pulled her closer. She needed his strength. He gave it to her.

The helicopter swept by overhead, the bell beat of its rotor wash suddenly louder. It angled back over the center of the sinkhole, unseen, its path described by the beat of its passage.

She leaned into Omaha. She had forgotten how broad his shoulders were, how well she fit against him.

Staring over his shoulder, Safia noted a flicker of blue across the sinkhole, a dance of lightning.

Oh, God . . .

She clutched Omaha harder.

"Saff," Omaha mumbled, lips by her ear. "After Tel Aviv—"

The explosion blew away any further words. A wall of superheated air slammed them both against the wall, to their knees. A flash of brilliance, then all vision squeezed away.

Rocks rained around them. A tremendous *crack* sounded above. A huge boulder struck the sheltering lip and thudded into the sand. More stones fell, a torrent of rocks. Half blind, Safia felt it under her knees. A shift in the earth.

The citadel was coming down.

11:21 A.M.

Painter had reached the edge of the sinkhole when the explosion ripped up from there. The only warning: a flash of blue scintillation deep in the hole. Then a column of cerulean blue fire erupted from the chamber opening, lighting every corner, shoving back the storm both with its brilliance and its hot breath.

The ground shook underfoot.

He felt the rush of heat shoot by his face, straight up, confined by the walls of the deep sinkhole, but its backwash still buffeted him backward.

Cries arose all around him.

The jetted column of cerulean fire struck the last helicopter full in the belly, knocking it skyward, cartwheeling it. Its fuel tank exploded in a wash of red flame, dramatic against the blue. The wreckage of the helicopter scattered away, not in pieces, but in liquid jets of molten fire. The entire craft had melted within the bath of cobalt flame.

Next, from the sinkhole's south rim, Painter watched the ruins of the citadel, perched precariously over the western edge, begin a slow tumble into the pit. And at the bottom, lit by the balefire flames as they petered out, two figures stumbled across the floor, rocks falling all around them.

Safia and Omaha.

11:22 A.M.

Dazed, Omaha leaned on Safia. She had an arm under his shoulders. They fought through the sands. His eyes wept from the residual burn on his retinas, but vision slowly returned. First a glow formed, dull, bluish. Then he saw dark shadows falling around him, thudding into the sand, some bouncing.

A rain of rocks. A biblical curse.

"We must get clear!" Safia yelled, sounding as if she were underwater.

Something struck the back of his good leg. They were both thrown to the sand. A deep grumble rattled behind them, above them, an angry god.

"It's coming down!"

11:23 A.M.

Painter raced headlong down the path into the sink-hole.

To his left, the back half of the citadel spilled into the chasm. It groaned and rumbled. Pouring rock and sand into one end of the pit. Painter had witnessed a mud slide during a rainstorm, an entire hillside liquefying. This was the same. Only a bit slower. Rock proving more stubborn.

In snatches through the stormy gloom, he spotted Safia and Omaha scrambling away from the avalanche as it slowly spilled toward them, chasing them across the floor. They fell down again as Omaha was struck in the shoulder and spun around.

Painter would not reach them in time.

A throaty growl whined behind him and a shout: "Out of the way!"

The shout threw him around. A light flicked on, spearing him in the face. He was blinded, but he saw enough in that split second to dive aside.

The sand bike sailed past him down the slope, spewing up gravel and sand. It leaped the path ten feet from the bottom, front wheel yanked up, rear knobby wheel spinning. It landed with a bounce, a twist, a crunch of sand—then tore off across the floor.

Painter continued down the path.

He had spotted the rider, bent over the handlebars. It was Coral Novak, cloaked and goggled, hood thrown back, white hair flagging behind her.

Painter gave chase, watching the cycle tear alongside the avalanche. Its headlamp flicked back and forth as Coral dodged around obstacles. Then she reached the pair, braking and skidding to them. He heard her shout, *"Grab tight!"*

Then she was off again, shooting straight across the floor, away from the tumbling stones, hauling Omaha and Safia, who clung to the seat's back, feet and legs dragging behind.

They raced clear of the rock slide.

Painter reached the bottom, well clear of the tumult of stone and sand. By the time he reached the floor, it was over. The collapse of the hill and fortress settled to a stop. The steep cliff was now a gentle slope.

Edging the wide delta of spilled rock and sand, Painter hurried to the idling bike. Safia had climbed to her feet. Omaha leaned one hand on the seat. Coral sat astride the bike.

They all stared at the hole in the ground ahead of them. It steamed and roiled, like some entrance to hell. It was where the trilith chamber had once opened. Only now it was ten feet across, blasted wide.

And bubbling with water.

The headlamp of the bike illuminated the steaming surface.

As Painter watched, the waters receded, draining away rapidly.

What was revealed held everyone silent.

11:23 A.M.

Cassandra stared, unblinking, through the windshield of the M4 tractor. A minute ago, they had watched a blue flash of fire shoot skyward. It had come from straight ahead.

In the direction of the ruins.

"What the hell was that?" Kane asked from the driver's seat.

They had halted the tractor a hundred yards off. To the left, the town flickered with a dozen fires. Directly ahead, the ruins had gone dark again, lost in the storm.

"That was not one of our bloody mortars," Kane said.

It sure as hell wasn't. Cassandra glanced to her laptop. The glow of the curator's transceiver continued to shine, though now it flickered, as if some interference fluttered its signal. What was going on over there?

She attempted to radio the only person who might know. "Eagle One, can you read me?"

She waited for a reply. None came.

Kane shook his head. "Both birds are down."

"Order another two copters in the air. I want aerial coverage."

Kane hesitated. Cassandra knew his concern. The storm, while already blowing fiercely, was only beginning to ratchet up. Its full might had yet to strike. And the coastal weather system was rushing up from the south, promising even wilder weather to come as the two systems collided. Outfitted as they were with only six VTOL copter sleds, to send up another pair risked half their remaining aerial force.

But Kane understood the necessity. They dared not conserve their resources. It was all or nothing. He passed Cassandra's orders over his own radio. Once done, he glanced to her, silently asking her how to proceed.

She nodded ahead. "We're going in."

"Should we wait until the birds are in the air?"

"No, we're armored." She glanced over her shoulder to the men seated in the back compartment, Kane's commando team. "And we have enough land support with us. Something's happening over there. I can smell it."

He nodded, shifted into gear, and kicked the tractor into motion. The lumbering tank ambled toward the ruins.

11:26 A.M.

Safia knelt on one knee and reached a hand over the hole's lip. She tested the heat with her palm. Winds tugged at her. Sand swirled in sweeps, but not as fiercely. The storm had abated slightly, a momentary pause, as if the explosion had sapped some strength from the gale's force.

"Careful," Omaha said behind her.

Safia stared down the hole at her feet. The waters continued to recede. It seemed impossible. As the waters had drained away, a glass ramp revealed itself, spiraling deep. The trilith chamber was gone. All that was left was *glass*, flowing downward in a corkscrew.

The entrance to Ubar.

Safia lowered her palm toward the ramp's exterior, slowly, bringing it close to the glass. It still glistened with drops of water, radiant against the black surface, reflecting the bike's headlight.

She felt no searing burn.

Daring, Safia touched a finger to the black glass. It was still warm, very warm, but it didn't burn. She placed her palm flat. "It's solid," she said. "Still cooling, but the surface is hard." She rapped on it to demonstrate.

Standing up, she reached a leg out and placed a foot on the ramp. It held her weight. "The waters must have cooled it enough to harden."

Painter stepped toward her. "We've got to get out of here."

Coral spoke, still astride her bike. She lowered the radio from her lips. "Commander, all Rahim are now gathered. We can bug out on your word."

Safia turned to the upper rim, but it was lost in darkness. She glanced down the throat of the glass spiral. "This is what we came to find."

"If we don't leave now, Cassandra will bottle us here."

Omaha joined them. "Where will we go?"

Painter pointed west. "Into the desert. Use the storm as cover."

"Are you mad? This blow is just starting. And the worst is yet to come. What about that goddamn megastorm? Out in the open desert?" Omaha shook his head. "I'd rather take my chances with that bitch."

Safia pictured Cassandra, the ice in her manner, the mercilessness in her eyes. Whatever mystery lay below would be Cassandra's to exploit. She and her employer. Safia couldn't let that happen.

"I'm going down," she said, cutting off the argument.

"I'm with you," Omaha added. "At least it's out of the storm."

New gunfire suddenly blasted up at the ridgeline.

Everyone ducked and turned.

"It looks like our decision is being made for us," Omaha mumbled.

Coral barked into her radio, Painter into his.

Along the rim, lights flared, headlamps. Engines revved. Vehicles began to descend into the sinkhole, racing down.

"What are they doing?" Omaha asked.

Painter shoved aside his radio, his expression grim. "Someone up there spotted the tunnel. One of the women."

The *hodja*, Safia imagined. With Ubar now open, the Rahim wouldn't flee. They would defend the site with their lives. Lu'lu was bringing the whole tribe down. A pair of dune buggies even bounced across the tumbled rock slide.

Vehicles closed in on their position.

The sudden eruption of gunfire died away.

Coral explained, holding her radio to her ear, "A hostile scouting party got into a sniping position atop one of the towers. They've been dispatched."

Safia heard the respect in the woman's voice. The Rahim had proven their mettle in this skirmish.

In moments, buggies and bikes, loaded with women, braked in the sand. The first buggy bore familiar faces, crammed together: Kara, Danny, and Clay. Barak followed on a bike.

Kara climbed out, leading the others. The winds were growing fiercer again, snapping scarves, flapping cloak edges. Kara held a pistol in one hand. "We spotted lights coming," she said, and pointed in the other direction, off to the east. "Lots of them. Trucks, big ones. And at least one helicopter took off. I glimpsed its searchlight for a moment."

Painter clenched a fist. "Cassandra's making her final move."

The *hodja* pushed through the throng. "Ubar is open. It will protect us."

Omaha glanced back to the hole. "All the same, I'll keep my gun."

Painter stared east. "We have no choice. Get everyone below. Stick together. Carry as much as you can manage. Guns, ammunition, flashlights."

The *hodja* nodded to Safia. "You will lead us."

Safia glanced down the dark spiral of glass, suddenly less sure of her decision. Her breathing tightened. When it was only her own life, the risk was acceptable. But now other lives were involved.

Her eyes settled to a pair of children, grasping each of Clay's hands. They looked as terrified as the young man between them. But Clay held firm.

Safia could do no less. She allowed her heart to thunder in her ears, but she calmed her breathing.

A new noise intruded, carried on the wind. A deep bass rumble of an engine, something huge. The eastern rim lightened.

Cassandra was almost here.

"Go!" Painter yelled. He met Safia's eyes. "Take them down. Quickly."

With a nod, Safia turned and began the descent.

She heard Painter speak to Coral. "I need your bike."

11:44 A.M.

Cassandra watched the blue spinning ring on the transceiver blink out. She balled a fist. The curator was on the run again.

"Get us over there," Cassandra said between clenched teeth. "Now."

"We're already here."

Out of the gloom, a stone wall appeared, crumbling, sand-scoured, more outline than substance, illuminated by their headlights.

They'd reached the ruins.

Kane glanced at her. "Orders?"

Cassandra pointed to an opening in the wall, near a broken tower. "Get your men on the ground. I want the ruins locked down. No one leaves that chasm."

Kane slowed the tractor enough for his crack team of commandos to roll out the side doors, leaping over the trundling treads. Twenty men, bristling with weapons, spread into the storm, vanishing through the gap in the wall.

Kane drove the tractor ahead, moving at a snail's pace.

The tractor crunched over the stone foundations of the ancient wall and into the inner city of old Ubar. The tractor's headlights pierced no more than a few feet as the storm wailed and cast up gouts of sand.

The sinkhole lay ahead, dark and silent.

It was time to end all this.

The tractor braked. Its headlights pierced ahead.

Men dropped flat along the rim, using the cover of boulders and tumbled bits of ruins. Cassandra waited while the team took up positions, winging out to either side, encircling the sinkhole. She listened to their radio chatter, subvocalized over throat mikes.

"In position, quadrant three . . ."

"Mongoose four, on the tower . . ."

"RPGs locked and loaded . . ."

Cassandra hit Command Q on her keyboard and twenty-one red triangles bloomed on the schematic on the map. Each of the commandos had a locator beacon tagged to his fatigues. On the screen, she watched the team maneuver into position, no hesitation, efficient, fast.

Kane directed his men from the command tractor. He stood, palms on the console, leaning forward to stare out the windshield.

"They're all in position. No movement seen below. All dark."

Cassandra knew Safia was there, hidden underground. "Light it up."

Kane relayed the order.

All around the rim, a dozen floodlights snapped on, carried by the soldiers and aimed down into the hole. The chasm now glowed in the storm.

Kane held one hand over his radio earpiece. He listened for half a breath, then spoke. "Still no hostiles in sight. Bikes and buggies below."

"Can they see any cavern entrance down there?"

Kane nodded. "Where the vehicles are parked. A black hole. Video feed should be transmitting now. Channel three."

Cassandra brought up another screen on her laptop. Real-time video feed. The image was shaky, pixilating and vibrating. Static interference. A shimmer of electric charge danced down the whip antenna strapped outside the tractor.

The storm was kicking into full blow.

Cassandra leaned closer. On the screen, she saw wavering images of the chasm floor. Sand bikes with huge knobby tires. A scatter of Sidewinder desert dune buggies. But they were all abandoned. Where were all the people? The image swung, centered on a dark hole, three yards wide. It looked like a fresh excavation, glistening, reflecting back the spotlights.

A tunnel opening.

And all the rabbits had ducked into the hole.

The video image scrambled, refocused, then was lost again. Cassandra bit back a curse. She wanted to see this for herself. She closed the jittery window on the screen and glanced at the spread of Kane's men on the glowing schematic. They had the area locked down tight.

Cassandra unbuckled. "I'm going to get a visual. Hold the fort."

She pushed to the back compartment and slid open the side door. The winds knocked her back, slamming her full in the face. She bent into the wind with a grimace, yanked a scarf over her mouth and nose, and shoved out. Using the tractor's tread as a step, she jumped to the sand.

She crossed to the front of the tractor, one hand on the tread for support. Winds battered her. She had new respect for Kane's men. When she was ensconced inside the command vehicle, their deployment seemed satisfactory: quick, efficient, no fumbling. Now it seemed extraordinary.

Cassandra crossed in front of the tractor, stepping between the two headlights. She followed the beams toward the sinkhole. It was only steps, but by the time she reached the rim, she could barely hear the growl of the tractor over the roar of the storm.

"How's things look, Captain?" Kane asked through her radio earpiece.

She knelt and peered below. The chasm stretched ahead of her. Opposite her position, the far side of the sinkhole was a tumbled slope of rock, still rolling with tiny slides. A fresh avalanche. What the hell had happened? She shifted her gaze directly below her.

The tunnel entrance stared back at her, a glistening eye, crystalline.

Glass.

Her pulse quickened at the sight of it. This had to be the entrance to whatever treasure lay below. Her gaze swept over the parked vehicles. She could not let them steal the prize.

She touched her throat mike. "Kane, I want a full team ready to enter that tunnel in five minutes."

There was no answer.

"Kane," she shouted louder, twisting around.

The tractor's headlights blinded her.

She shoved to the side. Suspicion flared.

She moved forward, only then spotting something knocked on its side, in the lee of the wall, abandoned, half covered in sand.

A sand bike.

Only one person was that clever.

11:52 A.M.

The knife stabbed at his face. Tangled, rolling across the floor, Painter turned his head, avoiding a fatal plunge to the eye. The dagger sliced his cheek, grazing the bone under his eye.

Fury and desperation fueled Painter's strength. Despite the blood flowing, he kept his legs pinned around the other man's legs, his right arm clenched around the man's neck.

The bastard was as strong as a bull, bucking, rolling.

Painter pinned him, trapping his knife arm.

As he had climbed through the side door of the tractor, left conveniently ajar by Cassandra, he'd recognized the man. Painter had been hiding, buried under loose, windblown sand piled against the crumbling wall. Five minutes ago, he had ridden the sand bike at breakneck speeds up out of the sinkhole and raced to the gap in the east wall. He knew Cassandra's forces would have to come through there with any vehicles.

He hadn't expected the behemoth of a tractor, a twenty-ton monster from the look of it. A bus fitted with tank treads. But it suited his purpose better than an ordinary truck.

He had crawled out of hiding as the tractor stopped, idling in the storm. He had ducked between the back treads. As he expected, all attention had been focused on the sinkhole.

Then Cassandra had stepped from the vehicle, giving him the opening he needed. With the door unlocked, Painter had slipped into the back compartment, pistol in hand.

Unfortunately, his wrestling partner, John Kane, must've caught Painter's reflection in the glass. He had swung around on a splinted leg and snapped out with the other, knocking the pistol from Painter's hand.

Now they struggled on the floor.

Painter maintained his choke hold. Kane tried to slam the back of his head into the bridge of Painter's nose. Painter avoided the blow. Instead, he yanked the man's head back even farther and slammed it hard against the metal floor.

A groan.

He repeated the action three more times. The man went limp. Painter continued to clamp his forearm over the man's neck. Only then did he note the blood spreading across the gray metal. Nose broken.

Time running out, Painter let the man go. He stood up and stumbled back. If that leopard hadn't tenderized the bastard first, Painter would never have won that fight.

He shoved to the driver's seat, popped the clutch, and gave the tractor some gas. The lumbering giant crunched forward, surprisingly agile. Painter checked his landmarks and aimed the tractor toward the right trajectory, straight for the sinkhole.

Bullets suddenly peppered the side of the tractor. Automatic weapons. His presence had been discovered.

The noise deafened.

Painter continued forward, unconcerned. The tractor was armored. And he had locked the side door.

The rim of the sinkhole appeared ahead. He kept the tractor moving.

Bullets continued to pound, stones against a tin can.

The front end of the tractor crawled past the lip of the sinkhole.

That was good enough for Painter. Trusting momentum, he swept out of the seat. The tractor slowed but crept farther past the edge of the sinkhole. Its forward end dipped down as the rim crumbled. The floor tilted.

Painter scrambled toward the rear door, intending to jettison before the tractor went over, taking his chances among the commandos. But a hand snatched his pant leg, yanking his feet out from under him. He fell hard, the wind knocked out of him.

Kane dragged Painter toward him, still impossibly strong.

Painter had no time for this. The floor angled steeply. He kicked out with a heel, striking Kane's broken nose. The man's head snapped back. His ankle was freed.

Painter crawled and leaped up the sloped floor, climbing a cliff of steel. Equipment and gear tumbled toward the front, knocking into him. He felt a sliding lurch. Gravity now gripped the tractor. Treads tore through stone.

It was going over.

Leaping, Painter snatched the handle to the back hatch. Unfortunately, it opened out. He didn't have good purchase to shove it open. Using his toes, his calves, he just managed to push the hatch a foot up.

The wind did the rest. The storm caught the door and flung it wide.

Painter followed, carried bodily outward.

Beneath him, the tractor fell away, diving into the sinkhole.

He managed one kick. Leapfrogging off the back end, he aimed for the cliff edge, arms outstretched.

He made it, barely. His belly struck the edge. He flung his torso on the ground, legs dangling in the pit. His fingers dug for purchase. A screeching crash sounded below him. He noted figures scrambling toward him.

They wouldn't reach him in time.

He slid backward. There was no grip. The tractor's treads had churned the edge to mush. He managed for a moment to catch a buried rock in the dust.

He hung for a breath by one hand and stared down.

Forty feet below, the tractor had slammed nose-first into the glass hole, tearing away, crumpling, a twenty-ton plug in the tunnel.

Good enough.

His rocky purchase gave way. Painter fell, tumbling into the pit.

Distantly he heard his name called.

Then his shoulder struck an outcropping of rock, he bounced, and the ground rushed up to meet him, jagged with rocks and broken metal.

PART FIVE

Fire Down Below

⬦Υ⟨Ɛⵉ⊬∘Φ⊣⎮⋂Ɛⵏ∘Φ

19

Any Port in a Storm

ᚻᚱᛈᛁᛁᚿᚩᚷᚼᛁᛉᚼᛁᚻᛁ�·ᛉᚷᚩᚷᛁ

December 4, 12:02 P.M.

Underground

Safia hurried down the spiraling ramp, leading the others. The crash above them had thrown them into a panic. Debris rolled and skittered from above: glass, rocks, even a broken rim of metal. The last had rolled like a child's hoop, skimming around the spiral, through the mass of folk in flight, and down into the depths.

Omaha followed it with his flashlight until it vanished. The noise above subsided, echoing away.

"What happened?" Safia asked.

Omaha shook his head. "Painter, I guess."

Kara marched on her other side. "Barak and Coral went back to check."

Behind them marched Danny and Clay, backs loaded with gear. They held flashlights. Clay held his with both hands, as if it were a lifeline. Safia doubted he'd ever volunteer for a field expedition again.

Beyond them marched the Rahim, similarly encumbered with supplies and packs. Only a few flashlights glowed. Lu'lu, bent in discussion with another elder, led them. They had lost six women during the fighting and bombing. Safia saw the raw grief in all their eyes. A child wept softly back there. As insulated as the Rahim were, a single death must be devastating. They were down to thirty, a quarter of them children and old women.

The footing suddenly changed underfoot, going from rough glass to stone. Safia looked down as they wound around the spiral.

"Sandstone," Omaha said. "We've reached the end of the blast range."

Kara shone her light back, then forward. "The explosion did all this?"

"Some form of shaped charge," Omaha said, seemingly unimpressed. "Most of this spiraling ramp was probably already down here. The trilith chamber was its cork. The bomb simply blew its top away."

Safia knew Omaha was simplifying things. She continued forward. If they had passed the transition from glass to stone, then the end must be near. The sandstone underfoot was still wet. What if all they found was a flooded passage? They'd have to go back . . . . face Cassandra.

A commotion drew her attention. Coral and Barak trotted up to them. Safia stopped along with the others.

Coral pointed back. "Painter did it. Dropped a truck over the entrance."

"A *big* truck," Barak elaborated.

"What about Painter?" Safia asked.

Coral licked her lips, eyes narrowed with concern. "No sign."

Safia glanced past the woman's shoulder, searching.

"That won't keep Cassandra off our tail forever. I already heard men up there digging." Coral waved forward. "Painter bought us time, let's use it."

Safia took a deep shuddering breath. Coral was right. She turned and continued down. No one spoke for another turn of the spiral.

"How deep are we?" Kara asked.

"I'd say over two hundred feet," Omaha answered.

Around another bend, a cavern opened, about the size of a double garage. Their lights reflected off a well of water in the center. It jostled gently, its surface misty. Water dripped from the ceiling.

"The source of the water flume," Omaha said. "The shaped charge of the explosion must have sucked it up, like milk through a straw."

They all entered the cavern. A lip of rock circled the well.

"Look." Kara pointed her light to a door on the far side.

They marched around the well.

Omaha placed his palm on the door's surface. "Iron again. They sure like smelting around here."

There was a handle, but a bar was locked across the door's frame.

"To keep the chamber pressure-sealed," Coral said behind them. "For the explosive vacuum." She nodded back to the well of water.

Far above them, a crash echoed down.

Omaha grabbed the locking bar and pulled it. It wouldn't budge. "Goddamnit. It's jammed." He wiped his hands on his cloak. "And all oily."

"To resist corrosion," Danny said. He tried to help him, but the two brothers fared no better. "We need a crowbar or something."

"No," the *hodja* said behind them. She nudged folk aside with her walking stick and stopped beside Safia. "The locks of Ubar can only be opened by one of the Rahim."

Omaha wiped his hands again. "Lady, you're more than welcome to try."

Lu'lu tapped her stick on the bar. "It takes someone blessed by Ubar, carrying the blood of the first queen, to affect such sacred artifacts." The *hodja* turned to Safia. "Those who bear the gifts of the Rahim."

"Me?" Safia said.

"You were tested," Lu'lu reminded her. "The keys responded to you."

Safia flashed back to the rainy tomb of Job. She remembered waiting for the spear and bust to point toward Ubar. Nothing had happened at first. She had been wearing work gloves. Kane had carried and placed the spear in the hole. It hadn't moved. Not until she wiped away the rain, like tears, from the bust's cheek with her bare fingertips. Not until she *touched* it.

Then it had moved.

And the cresent horns of the bull. Nothing had happened until she had examined them, sparking a bit of static electricity. She had ignited the bomb with the brush of a finger.

Lu'lu nodded her forward.

Safia numbly stepped up.

"Wait." Coral pulled out a device from her pocket.

"What's that?" Omaha asked.

"Testing a theory," she said. "I was studying the keys earlier with some of Cassandra's electronic equipment." Coral waved for Safia to continue.

Taking a breath, Safia reached out and gripped the bar with her good hand. She felt nothing special, no spark. She tugged on the bar. It lifted freely. Shocked, she stumbled back.

"Damn," Omaha gasped.

"Oh, *this* impresses you," Kara said.

"I must've loosened it for her."

Coral shook her head. "It's a magnetic lock."

"What?" Safia asked.

"This is a magnometer." Coral lifted her handheld device. "It monitors magnetic charge. The polarity of that length of iron changed as you touched it."

Safia stared down at the bar. "How . . . ?"

"Iron is highly conductive and responsive to magnetism. Rub a needle with a magnet and you pass on its magnetic charge. Somehow these objects respond to your presence, some energy you give off."

Safia pictured the spin of the iron heart atop the marble altar of Imran's tomb. It *had* moved like a magnetic compass, aligning itself along some axis.

Another crash sounded above.

Omaha stepped forward. "However it got unlocked, let's use it."

With the bar free, he grabbed the handle and tugged. The oiled hinges swung easily. The door opened on a dark descending staircase carved into the stone.

After closing and blocking the door, Omaha led the way with the flashlight, Safia at his side. The rest of the party followed.

The passage was a straight shot, but steep. It led down another hundred feet and emptied into a cavern four times larger than the first one. A pool filled this chamber, too, dark and glassy. The air smelled odd. Damp for sure, but also a trace of ozone, the smell that accompanies a thunderstorm.

But none of this held Safia's attention for more than a moment.

Steps away, a stone pier stretched into the water. At the end floated a beautiful wooden dhow, an Arab sailing ship, thirty feet long. Its sides glistened with oil, shining brightly in the glow of their flashlights. Gold leaf decorated rails and masts. Sails, useless here but still present, were folded and tied down.

Murmurs of awe rose among the group as they gathered.

To the left, a wide watery tunnel stretched away into darkness.

At the prow of the dhow rose the figure of a woman, bare-breasted, arms chastely crossed over her bosom, face staring down the flooded tunnel.

Even from here, Safia recognized the figure's countenance.

The Queen of Sheba.

"Iron," Omaha said at her side, noting her attention. He focused his flashlight on the boat's figurehead. The statue was sculpted entirely in iron. He moved toward the pier. "Looks like we're going sailing again."

12:32 P.M.

At the bottom of the sinkhole, Cassandra stared at the mangled body. She didn't know how to feel. Regret, anger, a trace of fear. She didn't have time to sort it out. Her mind spun instead on how to put this to her advantage.

"Haul him up top, get him into a body bag."

The two commandos lifted their former leader from the wreckage of the tractor. Others climbed in and out the back end, salvaging what could be found, setting the charges to blow apart the bulk of the smashed vehicle. Other men hauled debris out of the way, using the dune buggies.

A pair of commandos unreeled a long wire through a gap in the wreckage.

All was in order.

Cassandra swung to the sand cycle and mounted it. She tightened her muffler and goggles, then set off topside. It would be another fifteen minutes until the charges were set. She sped up the path and climbed out of the sinkhole.

As she cleared the rim, the force of the sandstorm spun her around. Fuck, it had already grown stronger. She fought for traction, found it, and raced to the command base sheltered inside one of the few cinder-block buildings still standing. The parked trucks circled it.

She skidded to a stop, propped the bike against the wall, and hopped off.

She strode through the door.

Injured men sprawled on blankets and cots. Many had been wounded from the firefight with Painter's strange team. She had heard the reports of the women's combat skills. How they appeared out of nowhere and vanished just as easily. There was no estimate even on their numbers.

But now they were all gone. Down the hole.

Cassandra crossed to one cot. A medic worked on an unconscious man, taping a last butterfly suture over the cheek laceration. There was nothing the medic could do about the big lump above his brow.

Painter might have the nine lives of a cat, but he hadn't landed on his feet this time. He had struck a glancing blow to the head. The only reason he lived was the loose sand along the inside rim of the sinkhole, cushioning his fall.

From the heavy-lidded glances from her men, they weren't so appreciative of Painter's good luck. They all knew of John Kane's bloody end.

Cassandra stopped at the foot of the cot. "How's he doing?"

"Mild concussion. Equal and responsive pupils. The bastard's only knocked cold."

"Then wake him up. Smelling salts."

The medic sighed, but obeyed. He had other men, his own men, to attend to. But Cassandra was still in charge. And she still had a use for Painter.

12:42 P.M.

"So what do we do?" Omaha asked. "Row? Get out and push?"

From the bow of the boat, he stared back. The entire company had boarded the fanciful dhow. Barak hunched over the ship's tiller. Clay knelt and scratched at a bit of the gold leaf. Danny and Coral appeared to be studying the structure of the rudder, leaning over the stern and staring down. The Rahim spread out, examining details.

The dhow was even more impressive up close. Gold leaf adorned most every surface. Mother of pearl embellished knobs. The stanchions were solid silver. Even the ropes had gold threads woven into them. It was a royal barge.

But as pretty as it was, it was not much use as a sailing vessel. Not unless a stiff wind would suddenly blow.

Behind Omaha, Kara and Safia stood at the prow, flanking the iron figurehead of the Queen of Sheba. The *hodja* leaned on her walking stick.

"So touch it," Kara urged Safia. The *hodja* had recommended the same.

Safia had her good arm crossed under her sling, her face lined with worry. "We don't know what will happen."

In her eyes, Omaha saw the flash of fire from the trilith chamber's eruption. Safia glanced to the new crew of the dhow. She feared endangering them, especially by her own hand.

Omaha stepped to her side. He placed a hand on her shoulder. "Saff, Cassandra is going to be coming down here, guns blazing. I'd personally rather take my chances with this iron lady than with that steel-hearted bitch."

Safia sighed. He felt her relax under his palm, surrendering.

"Hold on," she whispered. She reached out and touched the shoulder of the iron statue, the way Omaha was touching her. As her palm made contact, Omaha felt a slight electric tingle shiver through him. Safia seemed unaware.

Nothing happened.

"I don't think I'm the one to—"

"No," Omaha said, cutting her off. "Hold firm."

He felt a gentle tremble underfoot, as if the waters under the ship had begun to boil. Ever so slowly the boat began to move forward.

He swung around. "Free the ropes!" he called to the others.

The Rahim moved swiftly, loosening ropes and ties.

"What's happening?" Safia asked, keeping her palm in place.

"Barak, you got the tiller?"

Near the stern, the man acknowledged this with a wave of an arm.

Coral and Danny hurried forward. The tall woman lugged a large case.

The boat's speed gently increased. Barak aimed them toward the open mouth of the flooded tunnel. Omaha raised his flashlight and clicked it on. The beam was lost in the darkness.

How far did it go? Where did it go?

There was only one way to find out.

Safia trembled under his palm. He stepped closer, his body next to her. She didn't object, leaning back slightly. Omaha could read her thoughts. The boat hadn't blown up. They were still okay.

Coral and Danny were bent over the side of the boat again, their flashlights shining. "Can you smell the ozone?" she said to Omaha's brother.

"Yeah."

"Look how the water's steaming where the iron meets it."

Curiosity drew all their eyes.

"What are you guys doing?" Omaha asked.

Danny pushed back up, face flushed. "Research."

Omaha rolled his eyes. His brother was forever a science geek.

Coral straightened. "There's some catalytic reaction going on in the water. I believe it was triggered by the iron maiden. It's generating some propulsive force." She leaned over the rail again. "I want to test this water."

Danny nodded, a puppy wagging his tail. "I'll get a bucket."

Omaha left them to their science project. Right now, all he cared about was where they were going. He noted Kara eyeing him . . . no, *him and Safia.*

Caught staring, Kara glanced away, toward the dark tunnel.

Omaha noted the *hodja* doing the same. "Do you know where this is taking us?" he asked the old woman.

She shrugged. "To the true heart of Ubar."

A silence settled over the boat as they continued down the long, dark throat. Omaha stared up, half expecting a night sky. But not here.

Here they sailed hundreds of feet under the sand.

12:45 P.M.

Painter woke with a start, gasping, choking, eyes burning.

He attempted to sit up but was shoved back down. His head rang like a struck bell. Light burned icily. The room shuddered. He rolled to the side and vomited over the edge of a cot. His stomach clenched again and again.

"Awake, I see."

The voice chilled the feverish pain from his body. Despite the glare and pain of the sharp lights, he faced the woman at the foot of his bed. "Cassandra."

She was dressed in dun-colored fatigues with a knee-length poncho, belted at the waist. A hat hung by a cord behind her, a scarf around her neck. Her skin glowed in the light, her eyes shining even brighter.

He struggled to sit up. Two men held his shoulders.

Cassandra waved them off.

Painter slowly sat up. Guns pointed at him.

"We've got some business to discuss." Cassandra dropped to one knee. "That little stunt of yours cost me most of my electronics. Though we were able to salvage a few things, like my laptop." She pointed to the computer resting on a folding chair. It displayed a SeaWiFS satellite map of the region, with live feed of the sandstorm.

Painter noted the scrolling weather data. The coastal high-pressure system off the Arabian Sea had finally crossed the mountains. It was due to collide with the sandstorm in the next two hours. A megastorm of sea and sand.

But none of that mattered now.

"There's no way I'm telling you anything," he croaked out.

"I don't remember asking you anything."

He sneered at her. Even that hurt.

She shifted to the laptop and touched a few keys. The screen contained an overlay of the area: town, ruins, desert. It was monochrome, except for a small blue ring, slowly spinning, a quarter inch in diameter. Below it, coordinates along the X-, Y-, and Z-axes changed. A live feed. He knew what he was looking at. It was a signal from a microtransceiver, a system designed by his own hand.

"What have you done?"

"We implanted Dr. al-Maaz. We dared not lose track of her."

"The transmission . . . underground . . ." He had a hard time making his tongue work.

"There was enough of a gap in the wreckage to lower a weighted thread antenna. It seems once we spooled enough wire we were able to pick up her signal. There must be good acoustics down there. We've lowered booster transmitters. We can track her anywhere."

"Why are you telling me all this?"

Cassandra returned to his bed. She had a small transmitter in her hand. "To inform you of a small modification in your design. It seems with a bit more battery, you can ignite a pellet of C4. I can show you the schematics."

Painter's flesh went cold. "Cassandra, what have you done?" He pictured Safia's face, her shy smile.

"There's just enough C4 to blow out someone's spine."

"You didn't . . ."

She raised one eyebrow, a gesture that used to excite, quicken his heart. Now it terrified him.

Painter clenched fistfuls of sheets. "I'll tell you what you want to know."

"How cooperative. But again, Painter, I don't remember asking you any questions." She held up the transmitter and glanced to the screen. "It's time to punish you for your little stunt today."

She pressed the button.

"No!"

His scream was lost in a monstrous explosion. It felt as if his heart had detonated. It took him a breath to understand.

Cassandra smiled down at him, deliciously satisfied.

Laughter rose raw, with little true humor, from the men in the room.

She held up the device. "Sorry, I guess that was the wrong transmitter. This one controlled the charges placed in the tractor's debris. My demolitions experts have promised me the explosives will clear a path to the tunnel. All it requires now is a little cleanup. We'll be moving in within the next half hour."

Painter's heart still ached, thudding in his throat.

Cassandra pulled out a second transmitter. "This is the real one. Keyed to Safia's transceiver. Shall we try that again?"

Painter simply hung his head. She would do it. Ubar was open. Cassandra had no further need for Safia's expertise.

Cassandra knelt closer. "Now that I have your full attention, maybe we can have that little chat."

1:52 P.M.

Safia lounged, one hand on the iron figurehead, her hip leaning against the ship's rail. How could she be so terrified, yet so tired at the same time? It had been a half hour since they all heard the explosion, coming from the direction of the spiral ramp.

"Sounds like Cassandra's come knocking," Omaha had said.

By that time, their boat had sailed far down the tunnel. Still, tensions had escalated. Many flashlights pointed backward. Nothing came. Safia could only imagine Cassandra's frustration at finding them gone and faced with a flooded tunnel.

It would be a long swim if Cassandra and her team attempted to follow.

Though the dhow's pace was only a bit swifter than a fast walk, they had been sailing now for over an hour. They had to be at least six or seven miles away, making a slow but regal escape.

With each passing moment, everyone relaxed a bit more. And who was to say if Cassandra had even been successful in clearing the blockage atop the ramp?

Still, Safia could not let go of another fear, one closer to her heart.

Painter.

What was his fate? Dead, captured, lost in the sandstorm. There didn't seem to be any hopeful possibility.

Behind Safia, a few of the Rahim women sang softly, sadly, mourning their dead. Aramaic again. Safia's heart responded, grieving.

Lu'lu stirred, noting her attention. "Our old language, the language of the last queen, dead now, but we still speak it amongst ourselves."

Safia listened, taken to another time.

Nearby, Kara and Omaha sat on the planks, heads bowed, asleep.

Barak stood by the wheel, keeping them sailing straight as the course meandered in lazy S-curves.

Perhaps the passage had once been part of an old underground river system.

A few steps away, Coral sat cross-legged, bent over an array of equipment, powered by batteries. Her face was limned in the glow. Danny helped her, kneeling at her side, face close to hers.

Beyond them, Safia's eyes found one last member of their group.

Clay leaned against the starboard rail, staring forward. Barak and he had shared a cigarette a moment ago, one of the few left in the Arab's pack. Clay looked like he needed another.

He noticed her attention and came to join her.

"How're you holding up?" she asked.

"All I can say is that I had better get a good grade." His smile was sincere if a bit shaky.

"I don't know," she teased. "There's always room for improvement."

"Fine. That's the last time I take a dart in the back for you." He sighed, staring into the darkness. "There's a hell of a lot of water down here."

She remembered his fear of the sea, flashing back to a similar chat by the rail of the *Shabab Oman*. That now seemed like a world ago.

Danny stood and stretched. "Coral and I were discussing that. About the sheer volume of water down here. There's more than can be attributed to local rainfall or the water table."

Omaha stirred, speaking with his head down. He had not been asleep, only resting. "So what's the story then, hotshot?"

Coral answered, "It's Earth-generated."

Omaha lifted his head. "Say again?"

"Since the 1950s, it's been known that there was more water within the Earth than can be explained by the surface hydrological cycle of evaporation and rainfall. There have been many cases of vast freshwater springs found deep within the Earth. Giant aquifers."

Danny interrupted. "Coral . . . Dr. Novak was telling me about one spring found during the excavation for the Harlem Hospital in New York. It produced water at the rate of two thousand gallons a minute. It took tons of concrete to produce enough pressure to plug the spring."

"So where the hell does all this new water come from?"

Danny waved to Coral. "You know it better."

She sighed, clearly bothered at the interruption. "An engineer and geologist, Stephen Reiss, proposed that such *new water* is regularly formed within the Earth by the elemental combination of hydrogen and oxygen, generated in magma. That a cubic kilometer of granite, subjected to the right pressures and temperatures, has the capability of yielding eight billion gallons of water. And that such reservoirs of *magmatic* or *Earth-generated* waters are abundant under the crust, interconnected in a vast aquifer system, circling the globe."

"Even *under* the deserts of Arabia?" Omaha asked, half scoffing.

"Certainly. Reiss, up until he died in 1985, had over fifty years of success finding water at sites other geologists flatly predicted were impossible. Including the Eilat Wells in Israel that continue to produce enough water for a city of a hundred thousand. He did the same in Saudia Arabia and Egypt."

"So you think all this water down here might be part of that system?"

"Perhaps." Coral opened a tiny door in one of her machines. Safia noted a whiff of fog rise from it. A cooler of some sort. She fished out a tiny test tube with tweezers. She swirled it around. Whatever Coral saw deepened a frown.

"What's wrong?" Danny asked, noting her reaction.

"There's something strange about this water."

"What do you mean?"

She lifted the test tube. "I've been attempting to freeze it."

"So?"

She held up the plastic test tube. "In the nitrogen cooler, I've lowered the water's temperature to *negative* thirty Celsius. It still won't freeze."

"What?" Omaha leaned closer.

"It makes no sense. In a freezer, water gives up its heat energy to the cold and turns solid. Well, this stuff keeps giving off energy and won't solidify. It's like it has an unlimited amount of energy stored in it."

Safia stared past the dhow's rail. She could still smell the ozone. She remembered the slight steaming in the water around the iron. "Do you still have the Rad-X scanner among the equipment?"

Coral nodded, eyes widening. "Of course."

The physicist assembled the rod-and-base unit. She passed it over the test tube. Her eyes told what she found before she spoke. "Antimatter annihilation."

She shoved to her feet and held the scanner over the rail, moving from midship toward Safia's place at the bow. "It grows stronger with every step."

"What the hell does it mean?" Omaha asked.

"The magnetism in the iron is triggering some annihilation of antimatter."

"Antimatter? Where?"

Coral stared all around her. "We're sailing through it."

"That's impossible. Antimatter annihilates itself with any contact with matter. It can't be in the water. It would've annihilated with the water molecules long ago."

"You're right," Coral said. "But I can't dismiss what I'm reading. Somehow the water here is enriched with antimatter."

"And that's what's propelling the boat?" Safia asked.

"Perhaps. Somehow the magnetized iron has activated the localized annihilation of antimatter in the water, converting its energy into motive force, pushing us."

"What about the concern of it all destabilizing?" Omaha asked.

Safia tensed. She remembered Painter's explanation of how radiation from the decay of uranium isotopes might have triggered the museum explosion. She pictured the smoking bones of the museum guard.

Coral stared at her scanner. "I'm not reading any alpha or beta radiation, but I can't say for sure." The physicist returned to her workstation. "I'll need to do more studies."

The *hodja* spoke for the first time. She had ignored the excitement and simply stared forward. "The tunnel ends."

All eyes turned. Even Coral regained her feet.

Ahead, a soft flicker of light danced, waxing and waning. It was enough to tell that the tunnel ended ten yards ahead. They sailed forward. In the last yard, the roof became jagged like the maw of a shark's mouth.

No one spoke.

The ship sailed out of the tunnel and into a vast subterranean chamber.

"Mother of God!" Omaha intoned.

2:04 P.M.

Cassandra held the receiver of the satellite phone tight to her left ear and covered her right to cut out the howl of the storm. She was on the second floor of the cinderblock building that housed their command center. The storm tore through the ashes of the town. Sand battered the boarded windows.

As she listened, she paced the floor. The voice, digitally altered, made it difficult to hear. The head of the Guild insisted on anonymity.

"*Gray leader,*" the Minister continued, "*to ask for such special treatment during this storm risks exposure of our desert op. Not to mention the entire Guild.*"

"I know it sounds excessive, Minister, but we've found the target. We are steps away from victory. We can be out of Shisur before the storm even ends. That's *if* we can get those supplies from Thumrait."

"*And what assurance can you give me that you will be successful?*"

"I stake my life on it."

"*Gray leader, your life has always been at stake. Guild command has been studying your recent failures. Further disappointments now would make us seriously reconsider our need for your future employment.*"

Bastard, Cassandra cursed to herself. He hides behind his code name, sitting behind some goddamn desk, and he has the gall to question my competency. But Cassandra knew one way to spin her latest difficulty. She had to give Painter credit for that.

"Minister, I am certain of victory here, but I would also request that afterward I be able to clear my name. I was assigned my team leader. He was not of my own choosing. John Kane has mishandled and undermined my command. It was *his* lack of security that caused both this delay and his own death. I, on the other hand, was able to subdue and apprehend the saboteur. A key member of DARPA's Sigma Force."

"*You have Painter Crowe?*"

Cassandra frowned at the familiarity behind that tone. "Yes, Minister."

"Very good, gray leader. I may not have misplaced my confidence in you after all. You'll have your supplies. Four armored tractors driven by Guild operatives are already under way as we speak."

Cassandra bit her tongue. So all this browbeating was for show.

"Thank you, sir," she managed to force out, but it was a wasted effort. The Minister had already hung up. She shoved the phone down, but continued to pace the room twice more, breathing deeply.

She had been so sure of victory when she blew the tractor out of the hole. She had enjoyed tormenting Painter, breaking him so he'd talk. She now knew the others posed no real threat. A handful of experienced fighters, but also lots of civilians, children, and old women.

After the wreckage had been cleared, Cassandra had gone down the hole herself, ready for victory, only to discover the underground river. There had been a stone pier, so the others must have found some vessel in which to row away.

Alternate plans had to be made . . . again.

She had to lean on the Minister, but despite her frustration, the call couldn't have gone better. She had found a scapegoat for her past failures and would soon have everything she needed to ensure her victory under the sand.

Calmer now, Cassandra headed to the stairs. She would oversee final arrangements. She clomped down the wooden steps and entered the temporary hospital ward. She crossed to the medic in charge and nodded.

"You'll have all the supplies you need. Trucks are coming in two hours."

The medic looked relieved. The other men heard her and cheers rose.

She glanced to Painter, half sedated, groggy on the bed. She had left her laptop near his bed. The blue light of Safia's transceiver glowed on the screen.

A reminder.

Cassandra carried the transmitter in her pocket, extra insurance for his good behavior and cooperation.

She checked her watch. Soon it would all be over.

2:06 P.M.

Kara stood at the prow with Safia. She held her sister's free hand as Safia somehow propelled the dhow with her touch. They had done it, found what her father had sought for so many years.

Ubar.

The dhow sailed from the tunnel into a vast cavern, arching thirty stories overhead, stretching a mile out. A massive lake filled the cavern to an unknown depth.

As they sailed the subterranean lake, flashlights pointed in all directions, spearing out from the dhow. But additional illumination was not necessary. Across the ceiling, scintillations of cobalt electricity arced in jagged displays while gaseous clouds swirled with an inner fire, edges indistinct, ghostly, ebbing and flowing.

Trapped static charge. Possibly drawn from the storm on the surface.

But the fiery display was the least cause for their amazement. Its glow reflected and dazzled off every surface: lake, roof, walls.

"It's all glass," Safia said, gazing up and around.

The entire cavern was a giant glass bubble buried under the sands. She even spotted a scattering of glass stalactites dripping down from the roof. Blue arcs glistened up and down their lengths, like electric spiders.

"Slag glass," Omaha said. "Molten sand that hardened. Like the ramp."

"What could've formed this?" Clay asked.

No one even hazarded a guess as the dhow continued its journey.

Coral eyed the lake. "All this water."

"It must be Earth-generated," Danny mumbled. "Or once was."

Coral seemed not to hear him. "If it's all enriched with antimatter . . ."

The possibility chilled them all into silence. They simply watched the play of energies across the ceiling, mirrored in the still waters.

Finally, Safia let out a soft gasp. Her hand dropped from the shoulder of the iron figurehead and covered her mouth.

"Safia, what—"

Then Kara saw it, too. Across the lake, a shore appeared out of the darkness; it rose from the waters and spread back to the far wall. Pillars of black glass stretched from floor to ceiling, hundreds, in all sizes. Mighty columns, thin spires, and unearthly twisted spirals.

"The thousand pillars of Ubar," Safia whispered.

They were close enough for further details to reveal themselves, lit by the reflected glow of the electrical display. From out of the darkness, a *city* appeared, glinting, shining, shimmering.

"All glass," Clay murmured.

The miraculous city climbed the shore, stretching high up the back wall, scattered among the pillars. It reminded Kara of the seaside towns found along the Amalfi coast, looking like a child's toy blocks spilled down a hillside.

"Ubar," the *hodja* said at her side.

Kara glanced back as all the Rahim knelt to the deck. They had returned home after two millennia. One queen had left; thirty now returned.

The dhow had stopped after Safia lifted her hand, drifting on momentum.

Omaha stepped to Safia's side, encircling her with an arm. "Closer."

She reached again to the iron shoulder. The craft sailed again, moving smoothly toward the ancient lost city.

Barak called from the wheel, "Another pier! I'll see if I can take us in!"

The dhow angled toward the spear of stone.

Kara gazed out at the city as they drew nearer. Flashlight beams leaped the distance, adding further illumination. Details grew clearer.

The homes, while all walled of glass, bore adornments of silver, gold, ivory, and ceramic tile. One palace near the shoreline had a mosaic that appeared to be made out of emeralds and rubies. A hoopoe bird. The crested bird was an important element in many stories about the Queen of Sheba.

They were all overwhelmed.

"Slow us down!" Barak called as they approached the pier.

Safia released her hold on the iron statue. The dhow's pace immediately dropped. Barak slid the craft easily alongside the pier.

"Tie us up," he said.

The Rahim were again on their feet. They leaped to the sandstone pier and tied lines to silver stanchions, matching the ones on the royal dhow.

"We are home," Lu'lu said. Tears brimmed her eyes.

Kara helped the old woman back to the center of the ship so she could step from boat to pier. Once on solid ground, the *hodja* waved Safia to her.

"You should lead us. You have returned Ubar to us."

Safia balked, but Kara nudged her. "Do the old lady a favor."

Taking a deep breath, Safia climbed from the dhow and led the party to the glass shore of Ubar. Kara marched behind Safia and Lu'lu. This was their moment. Omaha even held back from rushing forward, though he did keep darting his head left and right, trying to see past the two women's shoulders.

They reached the shore, all flashlights ablaze.

Kara glanced up and around. Distracted, she bumped into Safia's back. She and the *hodja* had suddenly stopped.

"Oh, God . . ." Safia moaned.

Lu'lu simply fell to her knees.

Kara and Omaha stepped around them. They both saw the horror at the same time. Omaha flinched. Kara took a step back.

A few yards ahead, a skeletal, mummified body protruded from the street. Its lower half was still encased in glass. Omaha shifted his flashlight's beam farther up the street. Other such bodies sprawled, half buried in the roadway. Kara spotted a single desiccated arm poking up out of the glass, as if drowning in a black sea. It appeared to be a child's hand.

They had all drowned in glass.

Omaha moved a few steps closer, then jumped to the side. He pointed his flashlight down to where he had just stepped. His beam penetrated the glass, revealing a human shape buried below, burned to bone, curled within the glass under his feet.

Kara could not blink. It was like her father.

She finally covered her face and turned away.

Omaha spoke behind her. "I think we just discovered the true tragedy that drove the last queen of Ubar out of here, sealing the place, cursing it." He moved back to them. "This isn't a city. It's a tomb."

20
Battle Under the Sand

ⵏⵂⵅⵅⵜⴾⵛⵉⵟⵤⵀⴾⵛⴷⵉⵅⵁⵤⵜⵅⵀⵂⵂ

December 4, 3:13 P.M.
Shisur

Painter stared across the makeshift medical ward. The injection of sedatives still kept his head full of cobwebs, but enough had worn off that he could think clearer, straighter. A fact he kept to himself.

He watched Cassandra enter the room, pushing in from the storm, sand blowing in with her. It took an additional shoulder to shove the door closed.

Painter had heard enough earlier to determine that her attempt to chase down the others had hit some snafu. But he had no details. Still, from the confidence in her stride, from the way the morale here seemed high, she had not been fully thwarted. As always, she had another plan.

She noted his bleary attention, crossed to him, and plopped down on a neighboring cot. His personal guard, seated behind him, shifted straighter. The boss was here. She pulled out a pistol and rested it in her lap.

Was this the end?

From the corner of his eye, he happened to note the tiny blue ring on the laptop computer. At least Safia was still alive. She had moved well out of Shisur by now, due north. Her Z-axis coordinate grid showed her still deep underground. Over three hundred feet.

Cassandra waved off his bodyguard. "Why don't you take a smoke. I'll watch the prisoner for a bit."

"Yes, Captain. Thank you, sir." He bolted away before she changed her mind. Painter heard the trace of fear in the man's voice. He could guess how Cassandra commanded here. An iron fist and intimidation.

Cassandra stretched. "So, Crowe . . ."

Painter curled a fist under the sheets. Not that he could do anything. One of his ankles was cuffed to the cot's foot. She sat just out of reach.

"What do you want, Sanchez? Come to gloat?"

"No. But I just wanted to let you know that you seemed to have piqued the interest of my superiors. In fact, capturing you may have earned me a few steps up the chain of Guild command."

Painter glowered at her. She had come not to gloat, but to *brag*. "The Guild? So that's who signs your paychecks."

"What can I say? The salary was good." She shrugged. "Better benefits packages. Matching 401(k)s. Your own death squad. What's not to like?"

Painter heard the combination of confidence and derision in her voice. It did not bode well. She certainly had a plan in place for victory here. "Why throw your lot in with the Guild?" he asked.

She stared down at him tied to the cot. Her voice grew contemplative, but also somehow meaner. "*True* power can only be found in those willing to break all rules to achieve their ends. Laws and regulations do nothing but bind and blind. I know what it feels like to be powerless." Her eyes drifted away, into the past. Painter sensed a well of grief behind her words. Still, ice entered her voice. "I finally broke free by crossing lines few will cross. Beyond that boundary, I found power. And I will never step back . . . not even for you."

Painter recognized the futility of reasoning with her.

"I tried to warn you to back down," Cassandra continued. "Piss off the Guild too many times and they have the tendency to bite back. They've taken a particular interest in you."

Painter had heard whispers about the Guild. An organization structured after terrorist cells, a loose association with a shadowy leadership structure. They operated internationally, no specific national affiliation, though it was said they had risen out of the ashes of the former Soviet Union, a combination of Russian mobsters and former KGB agents. But since then, the Guild had dissolved across all borders, like arsenic in tea. Little else was known about them. Except that they were ruthless and bloody. Their goals were simple: money, power, influence. If they should gain access to the antimatter source, it would be a prize equal to none other. They could blackmail nations, sell samples to foreign powers or terrorists. The Guild would be unstoppable and untouchable.

He studied Cassandra. How far did the Guild's reach stretch into Washington? He remembered his test e-mail. He knew at least one man who was on their payroll. He pictured Sean McKnight. They had all been set up. He tightened his fist.

She pushed forward, leaning elbows on knees. "When this is over, I'm going to package you up, put a ribbon around you, and deliver you to Guild command. They'll pick apart your brain like a crab on a dead fish."

Painter shook his head, but he was not even sure what he was denying.

"I've seen their interrogation methods firsthand," Cassandra continued. "Impressive work. There was one fellow, an MI5 operative, who attempted to infiltrate a Guild cell in India. The chap was so broken down that all he had left to give were a few plaintive whimpers, the mewling of a beaten puppy. Then again I'd never seen a man scalped before, electrodes drilled into his skull. It's fascinating stuff. But why am I telling you all this? You'll get to experience it yourself."

Painter had never imagined the depths of depravity and cunning in the woman. How had he missed such a well of corruption? How had he almost given his heart to her? He knew the answer. Like father, like son. His father had married a woman who would eventually stab him to death. How had his father missed such a murderous soul in the woman to whom he pledged his heart, whom he slept beside each night, with whom he bore a child? Was it some genetic blindness passed from one generation to the next?

His eyes drifted to the blue glow on the screen. *Safia.* He touched the well of warm feelings there. It was not love, not yet at least, not after so short a time. But it was deeper than respect and friendship. He grasped that possibility, that potential inside him. There were good women, with hearts as genuine as his own. And he could love them.

He stared back at Cassandra. The anger bled from him.

She must have seen something in his face. She had been expecting defeat but found resolution and calmness instead. Confusion shone in her eyes, and behind it, Painter caught a glimpse of something deeper.

Anguish.

But it was only a flicker.

In a blink, fury burned away all else. Cassandra shoved up, hand on her pistol. He simply stared at her. Let her shoot him. It would be better than to be handed off to her superiors.

Cassandra made a sound between a laugh and a sneer. "I'll leave you to the Minister. But I may come to watch."

"The Minister?"

"His is the last face you'll ever see." She swung away.

Painter heard the edge of fear behind her words with this last statement. It sounded exactly like the guard who had departed moments ago. Fear of a superior, someone ruthless and ironfisted. Painter sat very still on his cot.

The last cobwebs from the sedatives burned away in a sudden flame of insight. *The Minister.* He closed his eyes against the possibility. In that moment, he knew with certainty who led the Guild, or at least guided Cassandra's hand.

It was worse than he imagined.

4:04 P.M.

"This has to be the queen's palace," Omaha said.

From across a courtyard of black glass, Safia stared up at the huge structure as Omaha splashed his flashlight's beam over the surface of the towering, vaulted structure. Its base was square, but it was surmounted by a four-story round tower, with crenellated battlements at the top. Arches of blown glass decorated the tower, opening onto balconies that overlooked the lower city. Sapphires, diamonds, and rubies decorated rails and walls. Roofs of gold and silver shone in the blue coruscations that flickered across the cavern roof.

Still, Safia gave it a critical eye. "This is a duplicate of the ruined citadel up top. Look at the dimensions. The structure of the base. They match."

"My God, Saff. You're right." Omaha stepped into the courtyard.

iron heart. Only the details of this one were not worn away. It was stunning, the intricate folds of cloth, a tiny sandstone flame perched at the tip of the lamp, the soft features of the face, clearly a young woman. Safia felt a renewed bit of enthusiasm.

She glanced to the other side of the archway. Another black glass pedestal stood there—but no statue. "The queen took it from here," Safia said. "Her own statue . . . to hide the first key."

Omaha nodded. "And planted it at Nabi Imran's tomb."

Kara and Lu'lu stood at the arched opening. Kara shone a flashlight inside. "You two should see this."

Safia and Omaha joined her. Beyond the entry, a short hallway opened. Kara flashed her light along the walls. They shone with rich, earthen hues: tans, creams, rose, umber. Splashes of indigo and turquoise.

"It's sand," Kara said. "Mixed in with the glass."

Safia had seen such artistry before, paintings done with different-colored sands, preserved behind glass . . . only in this case, the artwork lay *inside* glass. It covered walls, ceiling, floor, portraying an oasis in the desert. Overhead a sun shone with rays of golden sand, swirled with blue and white for the sky. To either side, date palms swayed, and in the distance, an inviting sapphire blue pool. Red dunes

The space was walled on both sides, with a huge arched opening in front.

Safia stared behind her. The palace—and there was no question this was the queen's palace—stood high up the cavern wall, near the back of the city, the rest of Ubar stretched in winding, crooked roads, descending below in terraces, stairs, and ramps. Pillars rose everywhere.

"Let's peek inside," Omaha said. He moved ahead, followed by Clay.

Kara helped Lu'lu. The *hodja* had recovered from her initial shock.

Still, on their journey up here, they had come across body after mummified body, buried in glass, most partially, some completely consumed. All around, at every turn, agonized poses stretched from the glass, macabre skeletal trees of desiccated, mummified limbs. The poses spoke of a misery beyond comprehension. One woman, frozen against a glass wall, sunk almost fully into it, had tried to protect her child, holding it up, like an offering to God. Her prayer had not been heard. Her child lay in the glass over her head. Such misery was everywhere.

Ubar must have once housed a population that numbered close to a thousand. The elite of the city above. Royalty, clerics, artisans, those who garnered the favor of the queen. All killed.

Though the queen sealed the place and never spoke of it, some word must have escaped. Safia recalled the two stories from *The Arabian Nights*: "The City of Brass" and "The Petrified City." Both tales spoke of a city whose populace were frozen in time, turned to brass or stone. Only the reality was much worse.

Omaha moved toward the entrance to the palace. "We could spend decades studying all this. I mean, look at the artistry in the glasswork."

Kara spoke up. "Ubar reigned for a thousand years. It had a power source at hand unlike any seen before . . . or now. Human ingenuity will find a use for such power. It would not go untapped. This entire city is an expression of human resourcefulness."

Safia had a hard time matching Kara's enthusiasm. The city was a necropolis. A city of the dead. It was not a testament of resourcefulness, but of agony and horror.

For the past two hours, their small group had climbed the city, exploring it for some answer to the tragedy. But upon reaching the summit, they had found no clue.

The others of their party remained below. Coral still worked by the lake's edge, performing arcane acts of chemistry, assisted by Danny, who had discovered a newfound passion for physics . . . or perhaps his

passion lay more for the six-foot-tall blond physicist. Coral seemed to be onto something. Before Safia and the others left, Coral had asked for something odd: a couple drops of blood from her and a few of the Rahim. Safia had complied, but Coral refused to explain why she made such an odd request and went immediately to work.

Meanwhile, Barak and the remaining Rahim had spread out to search for some means to escape the tomb.

Omaha led their group into the palace courtyard.

In the center of the open space, a giant iron sphere, four feet in diameter, rested on a cradle of black glass, sculpted into a palm. Safia eyed the sculpture as she circled it. Clearly it represented the touch of the queen upon such iron artifacts, the source of all power here.

Safia noted Lu'lu studying it, too. Not with the reverence of before. Horror still shone in her eyes.

They moved past it.

"Look at this." Omaha hurried forward.

He crossed to another sculpture, sandstone this time, perched on a glass pedestal. It flanked one side of the arched entrance to the palace. Safia stared up at the cloaked figure bearing aloft an elongated lamp on one arm. A twin to the sculpture that had once hidden the

covered one wall, done with such subtlety of shades and hues as to invite one to come strolling. Underfoot, sand and stone. *Actual* sand and stone incorporated into the glass.

The group could not help but enter. After the horrors of the lower city, the beauty here was a balm for the heart. The entry hallway was a short few steps, opening into a large chamber with arched halls leading deeper. A sweep of stairs curved to the right, heading to the upper levels.

And everywhere about the room, sand filled the glass, creating panoramic landscapes of desert, sea, and mountains.

"Was this how the original citadel was decorated?" Omaha wondered. "Did the queen try to re-create the stone abode? Turning glass into sandstone."

"It may have been a matter of privacy, too," Safia said. "A light on the inside would reveal the queen's every move."

They wandered the space, finding enough in this one room to occupy their attention. Safia found herself studying one sand painting, opposite the entry. It was the first bit of decoration one saw upon entering.

It was a sweep of desert, the sun setting, shadows stretching, sky a dark indigo. Silhouetted was a flat-topped towering structure, vaguely familiar. A cloaked figure approached, bearing aloft a lamp. From atop the structure, a spray of brilliant sand cascaded, rays of light. The quartz and silica of the sand glistened like diamonds.

"The discovery of Ubar," Lu'lu said. "It is an image passed from one generation to another. The Queen of Sheba, as a girl, lost in the desert, finds shelter and the blessings of the desert."

Omaha stepped behind Safia's shoulder. "That structure with the rays of light shining out of it. It looks like the citadel, too."

Safia now realized why the building looked familiar. It was a crude rendering, compared to the detail in other work. Perhaps it had been done much earlier than the others. To either side, the wall paintings depicted the Ubar above and the Ubar below. The palace and citadel were prominent. Safia crossed between them.

She stopped before the depiction of the subterranean Ubar, all done in indigo and black sands, a stunning depiction, the depth of detail amazing. She could even discern the two statues flanking the entryway. The only other detail in the courtyard was the figure of the cloaked girl again. The queen of Ubar. She touched the figure, trying to understand her ancestor.

There were so many mysteries here. Some would never be known.

"We should be getting back to base," Kara finally said.

Safia nodded. They reluctantly departed, heading back down. A winding thoroughfare led from lake to palace. She marched beside the *hodja*. Kara helped the old woman, especially with the stairs. Overhead, silent crackles of blue fire lit their path. Only Omaha kept his flashlight burning. None of them cared to illuminate too clearly the horrors around them.

As they hiked, the quiet of the city weighed upon them, the press of eternity, usually reserved for churches, mausoleums, and deep caverns. The air smelled dank, with a hint of electricity. Safia had once walked past a traffic accident, cordoned off, a power line down in the rain. The wire had snapped and spit. The air now smelled like that scene. It made Safia uneasy, reminding her of sirens, blood, and sudden tragedy.

What would happen next?

4:25 P.M.

Omaha watched Safia as she strode with the *hodja* around a curve in the glass road. She looked a pale shade of herself. He wanted to go to her, comfort her, but he feared his attentions would not be welcome. He had seen that look in her eyes. After Tel Aviv. A desire to curl up and shut out the world. He had been unable to comfort her then, too.

Kara moved closer to him. Her entire body expressed her exhaustion. She shook her head and spoke in a hush. "She still loves you . . ."

Omaha stumbled, then caught himself, flashlight bobbling.

Kara continued, "All you had to do was say you're sorry."

Omaha opened his mouth, then closed it again.

"Life is hard. Love doesn't have to be." She continued past him, her voice a bit harsher. "Just be a goddamn man for once in your life, Indiana."

Omaha stopped, flashlight dropped to his side. He was too stunned to move. He had to force his legs to follow, numbly. The rest of the journey through the lower city was in silence.

At last, the lake appeared ahead, down a long ramp. Omaha was glad for the company. Barak was still missing, still searching. But most of the Rahim had returned. Few could stomach the necropolis for long. Their expressions were somber at the sight of their former home.

Danny spotted Omaha and hurried over. "Dr. Novak has discovered some intriguing findings. Come see."

Omaha's group followed him back to the pier. Coral had constructed a makeshift laboratory. She had a haggard look to her eyes as she glanced up. One of her pieces of equipment was a molten ruin. It still smoked a bit and smelled like burning rubber.

"What happened?" Safia asked.

Coral shook her head. "An accident."

"What have you figured out?" Omaha asked.

Coral swiveled an LCD screen toward them. Data scrolled down one side. The main window, open on the screen, showed a few line drawings. Her first words captured their attention.

"The proof of God's existence can be found in water."

Omaha raised an eyebrow. "Care to elaborate? Or is that all you've come up with? Fortune-cookie philosophy."

"Not philosophy, but fact. Let's start at the beginning."

"Let there be light."

"Not that far back, Dr. Dunn. Basic chemistry. Water is composed of two atoms of hydrogen and one of oxygen."

"H$_2$O," Kara said.

A nod. "What's strange about water is that it is a bent molecule." Coral pointed to the first of the line drawings on the screen.

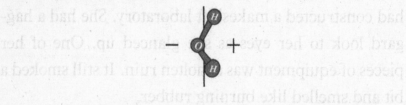

"It is this *bend* that gives water its slight polarity. A negative charge at the end with the oxygen atom. A positive one at the hydrogen side. The bend also allows water to form unusual shapes. Like ice."

"Ice is strange?" Omaha asked.

"If you keep interrupting . . . ." Coral scowled.

"Indiana, let her finish."

Coral nodded thanks to Kara. "When matter condenses from a *gas* to a *liquid* to a *solid,* it becomes more compact each time, occupying less space, denser. Not water, though. Water achieves its maximum density at four degrees Celsius. *Before* it freezes. As water actually freezes, that weird bent molecule forms an unusual crystalline shape with lots of extra space in it."

"Ice," Safia mumbled.

"Ice is less dense than water, much less. So it floats on top of water. If it were not for this fact, there would be no life on Earth. Ice forming on the surface of lakes and oceans would constantly be sinking and crushing all life beneath it, never giving early forms of life a chance to thrive. Floating ice also insulates bodies of water, protecting life rather than destroying it."

"But what does all this have to do with antimatter?" Omaha asked.

"I'm getting to that. I needed to stress the strange properties of the water molecule and its propensity to form odd configurations. Because there is another way water will align itself. It happens all the time in regular water, but it lasts only nanoseconds. It's too unstable on Earth. But in space, water will form and keep this unusual shape."

Coral pointed to the next line drawing. "Here is a two-dimensional representation of twenty water molecules forming that complex configuration. It's called a pentagonal dodecahedron.

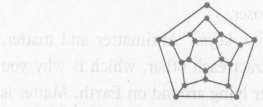

"But it's best visualized in three dimensions." Coral tapped the third drawing.

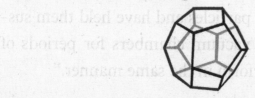

"It looks like a big hollow sphere," Omaha said.

Coral nodded. "It is. The dodecahedron goes more commonly by the name buckyball. Named after Buckminster Fuller."

"So these buckyballs are found in space," Safia said. "But last only briefly here."

"It's a stability problem."

"So why are you telling us about them, then?" Kara asked.

Danny danced back and forth on his toes behind them. He pointed to the lake. "The water here is *full* of those buckyballs, stable and unchanging."

"A good portion of the water," Coral agreed.

"How is that possible?" Safia asked. "What's holding it stable?"

"What we came looking for," Coral said, staring out at the water. *"Antimatter."*

Omaha moved closer.

Coral tapped a few keys. "Antimatter and matter, being opposites, attract each other, which is why you don't find antimatter lying around on Earth. Matter is everywhere. Antimatter would annihilate immediately. In CERN Laboratories in Switzerland, scientists have produced antimatter particles and have held them suspended in magnetic vacuum chambers for periods of time. Buckyballs perform in the same manner."

"How?" Omaha leaned over Coral's shoulder as she brought up a new drawing.

"Because buckyballs have the capability of acting like microscopic magnetic chambers. In the center of these spheres is a perfectly hollow space, a vacuum. Antimatter can survive inside there." She pointed to the *A* inside the diagram's sphere. "And antimatter, in turn, benefits the buckyball. Its attraction for the water molecules pulls the sphere tighter, just enough to stabilize the buckyball. And being perfectly surrounded by water molecules, the antimatter atom is held in perfect suspension in the center, unable to touch matter."

Coral stared around at the group.

"Stabilized antimatter," Omaha said.

Coral sighed. "Stable until it gets a good jolt of electricity or comes in close contact to a strong magnet or radiation. Either will destabilize the balance. The buckyball collapses, antimatter comes in contact with the water molecule and annihilates itself, releasing an exponential release of energy." She glanced to the smoldering ruins of one of her machines. "The answer to unlimited energy."

Silence stretched for a time.

"How did all this antimatter get here?" Kara asked.

Danny nodded. "We were talking about that just before you got here. Putting pieces together to form some idea. Remember, Omaha, in the van when we were talking about the *wobble* in the Earth that caused this region to go from a rich savannah to desert?"

"Twenty thousand years ago," he said.

Danny continued, "Dr. Novak postulated that perhaps an antimatter meteor, large enough to survive passage through the atmosphere, struck the Arabian Peninsula, exploding and burying itself into porous limestone bedrock, creating this crystalline bubble deep underground."

Coral spoke up as everyone gazed out at the cavern. "The explosion must have broken into an Earth-generated water system, cascading its effect through the deep-Earth channels. Literally shocking the world. Enough to affect the Earth's polarity or perhaps bobble the spin of its magnetic core. However it happened, it changed the local climate, turning Eden into a desert."

"And as all this cataclysm happened, the glass bubble formed," Danny continued again. "The explosion and heat of the impact triggered violent fog generation and expulsion of antimatter atoms and subparticles.

As the place cooled, self-contained and sealed, water condensed around the antimatter atoms and formed the protective, stabilized buckyballs. And this place remained undisturbed for tens of thousands of years."

"Until someone found the friggin place," Omaha said.

He pictured a tribe of nomads, stumbling upon this, perhaps searching for water. They must've quickly learned of the water's strange properties, an energy source in ancient times. They would hide it, protect it, and as Kara had mentioned earlier, human ingenuity would find a way to harness it. Omaha remembered all the wild tales of Arabia: flying carpets, magicians and sorcerers wielding incredible power, enchanted objects of every shape and size, genies bearing miraculous gifts. Had they all hinted at the mystery here?

"What about the keys and other objects?" he said. "You mentioned something about magnetism before."

Coral nodded. "I can't begin to fathom what level of technology these ancients managed. They had access to a power source that will take decades to fully understand. But they understood enough. Look at the glasswork, the stonework, the creation of the intricate magnetic triggers."

Kara stared at the city. "They had a thousand years to perfect their art."

Coral shrugged. "I wager the liquid inside the keys came from this lake. Buckyballs do have a slight charge to them. If that charge could be shifted all in one direction, then the iron container would magnetize. And as the buckyballs inside are aligned with the iron's magnetic field, they remain stable and don't annihilate in that field."

"What about the iron camel at the museum?" Safia asked. "It exploded."

"A chain reaction of raw energy," Danny answered. "The ball lightning must have been attracted to the iron and the strange polarity of its watery heart. Maybe even drawn to it. Look at the roof here, tapping static from the storm."

Omaha glanced upward as the electrical display flared with greater-than-usual brilliance.

Danny finished, "So the lightning gave its electricity to the iron, giving its energy in one jolt. Too much. The effect was dramatic and uncontrolled, leading to the blast."

Coral stirred. "I wager even that explosion only occurred because the antimatter solution had been slightly destabilized by the trace radiation given off by the uranium atoms in the iron. The radiation excited and increased the fragility of the buckyball configurations."

"What of the lake here?" Omaha mumbled, eyeing the water.

Coral frowned. "My instruments are too crude for a proper analysis. I've detected no radiation out there, but that doesn't mean it's not present. Perhaps somewhere farther out in the lake. We'll have to bring more teams down here, if given the chance."

Clay spoke up for the first time, arms crossed over his chest. "So then what happened in A.D. 300? Why all the bodies embedded in the glass? Was it one of those explosions?"

Coral shook her head. "I don't know, but there's no evidence of a blast. Maybe an accident. An experiment gone awry. There's untold power in this reservoir." She glanced to the city, then back to Safia. "But, Dr. al-Maaz, there is one last thing I must tell you about."

Safia turned her attention back to the physicist.

"It's about your blood," Coral said.

Before the physicist could elaborate, a noise drew all their eyes to the lake. A low whine. Everyone froze. The noise grew sharper, rapidly, fast.

Jet Skis.

Across the lake, a flare shot high into the air, lighting the water crimson, reflecting off the roof and walls. A second flare arced upward.

No, not a flare. It fell toward the city . . . toward them.

"Rocket!" Omaha yelled. "Get to cover!"

4:42 P.M.

Painter waited for his chance.

The cinder-block room shuddered as the brunt of the sandstorm wailed against doors, boarded windows, and roof flashings. It sounded like a ravenous animal digging to get inside, unrelenting, determined, maddened by bloodlust. It howled its frustration and roared its might.

Inside, someone had a radio playing. The Dixie Chicks. But the music was small and weak against the continual onslaught of the storm.

And the storm was creeping into their shelter.

Under the doorjamb, sand whistled in, streaming and writhing along the floor like snakes. Through cracks in the windows, it gasped and sighed in dusty puffs, now almost a continual blow.

The air in the room had grown stale, smelling of blood and iodine.

The only ones left here were the wounded, one medic, and two guards. Half an hour ago, Cassandra had cleared out the rest for her underground assault.

Painter glanced at the laptop. It showed Safia's blue spinning ring. She was six miles due north of here, deep under the sands. He hoped the glow meant she was still alive. But the transceiver would not die with her body. Its continual transmission was no assurance. Still, from the scrolling numerical axis coordinates, Safia was on the move. He had to trust she still lived.

But for how much longer?

Time pressed against him like a physical weight. He had heard the arrival of the M4 tractors from Thumrait Air Base, bringing in a shipment of new supplies and weapons. The caravan had arrived just as the sandstorm blew at its worst. Still, the group had managed to outrun the predicted megastorm.

In addition to the new supplies, another thirty men swelled the forces. Hard-eyed, fresh, heavily packed with gear. They had stomped in like they owned the place. More of the elite of the Guild. With no joking, they had stripped out of their sandy clothes and into black thermal wet suits.

Painter had watched from his bed.

A few cast stares his way. They had already heard about John Kane's demise. They looked ready to rip his head off. But they left quickly, heading back out into the storm. Through the open doorway, Painter had seen a Jet Ski being wheeled by.

Wet suits and Jet Skis. What had Cassandra found down there?

He continued to work under his sheets. He had been stripped to his boxers, one ankle cuffed to the foot of the bed frame. He had only one weapon: an inch-long, eighteen-gauge needle. A few minutes ago, when the two guards had been distracted by the room's door blowing open, Painter had managed to snag the needle from amid a pile of discarded medical gear.

He had quickly palmed it.

He sat up a bit and reached to his foot.

The guard, lounging on the next cot, lifted his pistol from the crook of his arm where he had been resting it. "Lay back down."

Painter obeyed. "Just an itch."

"Too fucking bad."

Painter sighed. He waited for the guard's attention to drift, less focused on him. He shifted his free foot to the cuffed one. He had managed to pinch the needle between his big toe and its neighbor. He now sought to pick the lock on the cuff, tricky to do blind and with his toes.

But when there's a will, there's a way.

Closing his eyes, he kept his movements minimal under the sheets.

Finally he felt a satisfying slip in pressure on his trapped ankle. He was free. He lay still and glanced to the guard.

Now what?

4:45 P.M.

Cassandra crouched in the bow of the Zodiac pontoon boat. The motor idled behind her. She had night-vision binoculars focused on the far shoreline. Three flares hung above the glass city, lighting it brilliantly through the scopes. Despite the situation, Cassandra could not help but be amazed.

Across the lake, she heard the continual shatter of glass.

Another rocket-propelled grenade arced from one of the six Jet Skis. It struck deep into the city, flashing blindingly through her scopes. She lowered the binoculars. The flares cast the city in shades of crimson and fire. Smoke billowed, hanging in the still air. Above, energy scintillated, swelling, crackling, swirling, a cerulean maelstrom.

There was such beauty in the destruction here.

A chatter of machine-gun fire drew her attention farther toward shore. A second Zodiac zipped parallel to the city, strafing the area with continuous fire.

More RPGs arced over the water, smashing into the city. Pillars of glass collapsed like toppled redwoods.

Truly beautiful.

Cassandra slipped her portable tracker from a pocket of her combat jacket. She stared at the tracker's LCD screen. The blue circle glowed, moving away from her position, seeking higher ground.

The artillery barrage was just to soften them up.

Run while you can. The fun is just beginning.

4:47 P.M.

Safia climbed with the others up a winding narrow stairway. Explosions echoed all around, amplified by the glass bubble. Smoke choked the air. They ran through the dark, all flashlights off.

Omaha kept to her side, helping Lu'lu. Safia held a child's hand, though she wasn't much reassurance to the girl. With every bomb blast, Safia ducked, fearing the end, expecting the glass bubble to come down. Small fingers squeezed hers.

The others trailed ahead and behind. Kara helped another of the elders. Danny, Clay, and Coral followed behind, leading more children. Several of the Rahim had slipped away, into side streets and terraces, dropping into sniping positions. Others simply vanished, whispering away to guard their rear.

Safia had watched one woman take a few steps down a dark street and vanish in front of her eyes. Perhaps it was a trick of glass and shadow . . . or maybe it was a demonstration of the *gift* Lu'lu had told Safia about. To cloud perception and disappear.

The group reached the top of the stairs. Safia glanced behind her. She had a panoramic view of the lower city and shoreline. Flares overhead lit the place brilliantly, bathing the city in crimson.

Down by the lake, the royal barge was a smoldering ruin of broken timber. The stone pier had been shattered, the glass shore pitted deeply.

"They've stopped the bombardment," Omaha said.

Safia realized he was right, but the explosions still echoed in her head.

On the lake, Cassandra's forces were moving in. Jet Skis and pontoon boats angled and swept toward shore, in unison, like an aerial team. Closer in, all along the shoreline itself, smaller Vs aimed through the waters.

Safia squinted, spotting men in wet suits atop motorized body boards. They struck the beach, surfed high, and rolled into crouched positions, rifles already in hand. Others darted into the streets and alleyways.

A gun battle erupted below, flashing like fireflies, popping loudly, an exchange of fire between Cassandra's forces and some of the Rahim. But it was brief, the snarl of dogs. Another grenade rocketed from one of the incoming Jet Skis, striking where the gunfire had come from. Glass shattered in a spray of brilliance.

Safia prayed that the Rahim had already fled. Shoot and run. It was their only chance. They were far too few and vastly outgunned. But to where could they run? They were trapped in a glass bubble. Even the dhow was destroyed.

Safia watched the Jet Skis and pontoons skid up to shore, off-loading more men. They would hunt and blast their way through the city.

Overhead the flares began to dim and fade, sinking into the shattered city. With the fading of the flares, Ubar darkened, lit now by the showers of blue fire above, basking the city in shades of indigo.

Safia glanced up to the arched roof. The crackles of energy and swirls of gaseous clouds had grown fierce, roiling, as if angry at the destruction.

Another spate of gunfire blasted, rattling, somewhere else in the city.

"We have to keep going," Omaha said, urging her on.

"Where?" she asked, turning to him.

He met her eyes. He had no answer.

4:52 P.M.

The sandstorm continued to pound the cinder-block building. It had worn everyone's nerves raw. Sand, dust, and grit covered everything, finding every crack and crevice to stream inside. Winds howled.

It didn't help matters that field reports radioed up from below described the battle. Clearly it was a rout. Cassandra's superior forces were sweeping through, finding little resistance, enjoying the mayhem.

And the boys here weren't allowed outside to play.

"Turn that goddamn Dixie Chicks shit off!" the guard yelled.

"Fuck you, Pearson!" the medic shouted back, fixing a seeping bandage.

Pearson swung around. "Listen, you piece of dog-shit . . ."

The second guard was back by the plastic water barrel, tilting it while trying to fill a paper cup.

Painter knew he'd never have a better chance.

He rolled from his bed with hardly a squeak, grabbed the pistol from the guard's hand, twisting the man's wrist savagely. He pumped two bullets into the guard's chest.

The impact blew the man backward onto the cot.

Painter dropped to a shooter's stance, aimed at the second guard, and fired three shots. All at the man's head. Two struck home. The guard went down, brains and blood sprayed on the back wall.

Leaping back, Painter held the gun out. He trusted that the roar of the storm had muffled the shots. He swept the room. The wounded had clothes and weapons stacked nearby, out of immediate reach. That left only the medic.

Painter kept his eyes focused on the man, his peripheral gaze on the rest of the room. On the cot, Pearson moaned, bubbled, and bled.

Painter spoke to the medic. "Go for a gun, you die. This man can be saved. Make your choice." He backed to the laptop, reached blindly for it, snapped it closed, and tucked it under his gun arm.

The medic kept his hands in the air, palms toward him.

Painter did not let his guard down. He sidled to the door, reached behind to the handle, and yanked it open. Winds almost buffeted him straight back into the room. He leaned against the onslaught and forced his way out. He didn't bother closing the door. Once out, he turned on a heel and spun away.

He aimed in the direction he'd heard the armored tractors stop, and tunneled through the sand and wind. Barefoot, he wore only his boxers. Sand scoured him like steel wool. He didn't bother keeping his eyes open. There was nothing to see. Sand choked him with each breath.

He held the pistol out in front of him. In his other hand, he clutched the laptop. It had data he needed: on the Guild, on Safia.

His outstretched gun struck metal.

The first of the tractors. As much as he would've liked to take it, he moved on. The mammoth vehicle was pinned down by the others behind it. He heard its engine running, to keep the batteries charged. He prayed they were all idling.

He continued down the line, moving fast.

He vaguely heard shouts behind him. Word was out.

Painter dug faster through the storm's headwinds, keeping a shoulder to each tractor's tread. He reached the last in the line. Its engine purred like a happy kitten, a twenty-ton kitten.

Sliding down the side, Painter found the door and struggled to open it against the wind. Not a one-handed job. He tucked the pistol into his boxer's waistband, its weight half pulling his shorts down. He set the laptop on the tread and finally got the door open enough to squeeze through. He snatched the computer with him.

At last, he slammed the door and latched it closed. Leaning his back against the door, he spit sand from his mouth and rubbed his eyes, clearing his eyebrows and lashes of grit.

Gunfire peppered the side of the carriage, stinging his back with their rattling impacts. He shoved away. *The fun never stops around here.*

He hurried to the driver's compartment and slid into the seat. He tossed the laptop onto the other seat. The sandstorm swirled beyond the windshield, a permanent midnight. He flipped on the lights. Visibility stretched for a whole two yards. Not bad.

He kicked the gear into reverse and headed out of Dodge.

He retreated straight back. If anything was back there, he'd simply have to trust that the armored behemoth could bull through it.

More gunfire chased him, like kids throwing stones.

He fled, noting when he cleared the charred remains of Shisur. He escaped into the desert, shooting backward. Eventually he'd think about forward gears. But backward worked fine for now.

As he glanced to the windshield, he noted twin glows bloom in the darkness, out in the city.

Pursuit.

5:00 P.M.

As the others took a brief rest, Omaha stared at the queen's palace. The structure had managed to escape the initial bombardment. Maybe they could make a stand here, up in its tower.

He shook his head.

Fanciful, but impractical. Their only hope was to keep moving. But they were running out of city. Not much lay above and beyond the palace. A few streets and low buildings.

He glanced over the lower city. Sporadic gunfire still flared, but it was both less frequent and closer. The Rahim's defense was wearing thin, the line being overwhelmed.

Omaha knew they were doomed. He had never considered himself a pessimist, just a pragmatist. Still, he glanced at Safia. With his last breath, he would keep her safe.

Kara stepped beside him. "Omaha . . ."

He looked at her. She never called him Omaha. Her face was exhausted, lined by fear, eyes hollow. Like him, she sensed their end.

Kara nodded to Safia. Her voice was a sigh. "What the hell are you waiting for? Bloody Christ . . ." She stepped away to the courtyard wall, slumped against it, and sank to a seat.

Omaha remembered her earlier words. *She still loves you.*

From steps away, he watched Safia. She knelt beside a child, holding both the girl's small hands between her own. Her face shone in the glow overhead. Madonna and child.

He moved closer . . . then closer again. Kara's words inside his head: *Life is hard. Love doesn't have to be.*

Safia didn't look up, but she still spoke. "These are my mother's hands," she said so quietly, so calmly, defying their situation. She stared at the child. "All these women. My mother still lives through them. An entire life. From babe to elder. A full life. Not one cut short."

Omaha dropped to one knee. He stared into her face as she studied the child. She simply took his breath away. Literally.

"Safia," he said softly.

She turned to him, eyes shining.

He met her gaze. "Marry me."

She blinked. "What . . . ?"

"I love you. I always have."

She turned. "Omaha, it's not that simple . . ."

He touched her chin gently with a finger, and turned her face back to his. He waited for her eyes to find him. "That's just it. Yes, it is."

She attempted to shift away.

He would not let her escape this time. He leaned closer. "I'm sorry."

Her eyes shone a bit brighter, not from happiness but from the threat of tears. "You left me."

"I know. I didn't know what to do. But it was a *boy* who left you." He lowered his hand, gently taking hers. "It is a *man* on his knees now."

She stared into his eyes, wavering.

Movement over her shoulder caught his eye. Figures pushed out of the dark around the corner of the palace. Men. A dozen.

Omaha leaped to his feet, scrambling to push Safia behind him.

Out of the shadows, a familiar figure strode forth.

"Barak . . ." Omaha scrambled to comprehend. The giant of an Arab had been missing since before the attack.

More men followed behind Barak, in desert cloaks. They were led by a man with a crutch under one arm.

Captain al-Haffi.

The leader of the Desert Phantoms waved to the men behind him. Sharif was among them, as hale as when Omaha had last seen him, out at Job's tomb. He had survived the firefight without a scratch. Sharif and the men dispersed down the streets, strapped with rifles, grenades, and RPG launchers.

Omaha stared after them.

He didn't know what was going on, but Cassandra was in for a surprise.

5:05 P.M.

All that was left was the cleanup.

Cassandra kept one foot on the pontoon of her boat. She listened to the open channel as various teams swept the city in quadrants, clearing away pockets of resistance. She clutched her electronic tracker, fingers digging. She knew exactly where Safia was within the city.

Cassandra allowed the curator to scurry like a mouse while her crew mopped behind her, wearing through her resistance. Cassandra still wanted the bitch alive. Especially with Painter now on the run.

She had to resist screaming her frustration.

She would have the balls of every man topside if Painter escaped.

She took a deep shuddering breath. There was nothing she could do down here. She had to secure this place, root out its secrets, which meant capturing Safia alive. And with Safia in hand, Cassandra would have a card to play against Painter. A pretty little ace in the hole.

An explosion drew her attention back to the city. She was surprised her men needed to employ another grenade. She watched an RPG sail into the air.

She blinked at its trajectory.

Fuck . . .

She leaped from her perch and sprinted down the shoreline. Her rubber soles gave her good purchase on the rough glass. She dove behind a sheltering pile of debris as the grenade struck the pontoon boat.

The explosion deafened her, making her ears ache, even stinging her eyes. Glass and water sprayed high. She rolled up and away as broken glass rained down. She covered her head with her arms. Jagged pieces fell around her, dancing off other glass, slicing skin and clothes, stinging like a rain of fire.

After the deadly shower ceased, she stared up at the city. Had someone commandeered one of her team's launchers? Another two RPGs flew by.

New automatic fire flared from a dozen places.

What the hell was going on?

5:07 P.M.

As the explosions echoed away and gunfire chattered, Safia watched Captain al-Haffi clump forward on his crutch. The shock of his arrival still held everyone speechless.

The captain's eyes settled on Lu'lu. He dropped his crutch and lowered himself to one knee. He spoke in Arabic, but in a dialect few had heard spoken aloud.

Safia had to strain her ears to recognize the words of the singsong speech.

"Your Highness, please forgive your servant for arriving so late."

He bowed his head.

The *hodja* was as mystified as anyone else by his arrival and posturing.

Omaha stepped to Safia's side. "He's speaking Shahran."

Safia's mind spun. The Shahra were the mountain clan that traced their lineage to King Shaddad, the first ruler of Ubar . . . or rather the consort of its first queen.

Barak spoke, hearing Omaha. "We are all of the Shahra clan."

Captain al-Haffi rose to his feet. Another man returned his crutch.

Safia realized what she had just witnessed: the formal acknowledgment of the king's line to its queen.

Captain al-Haffi motioned them to follow, speaking again in English. "I had thought to get you clear, but all I can offer is shelter. We must hope my men and your women can hold the marauders off. Come."

He led the way back around the palace. Everyone followed.

Omaha paced next to Barak. "You are Shahra?"

The man nodded.

"So that's why you knew about that back door out of the mountains, through that graveyard. You said only the Shahra knew of that path."

"The Vale of Remembrance," Barak intoned more formally. "The graves of our ancestors, back to the exodus from Ubar."

Captain al-Haffi hobbled alongside Lu'lu. Kara helped her from the other side, continuing their conversation. "Is that why you all volunteered for the mission? Because of its ties to Ubar."

The captain bowed his head. "I apologize for the ruse, Lady Kensington. But the Shahra do not reveal their secrets to outsiders. That is not our way. We are as much guardians of this place as the Rahim. We were given this burden by the last queen of Ubar, just before our two lines parted ways. As she divided the keys, so she divided the royal lines, each with its own secrets."

Safia stared between the two, the houses of Ubar joined again.

"What secret was left with you?" Omaha asked him.

"The old path into Ubar. The one walked by the first queen. We were forbidden to open it until Ubar was tread again."

"A back door," Omaha said.

Safia should have known. The queen who sealed Ubar after the horrible tragedy here was too meticulous. She had contingency plans stacked atop contingency plans, spreading them across both lines.

"So there's a way out of here?" Omaha asked.

"Yes, to the surface. But there is no escape there. The sandstorm rages, which makes crossing atop Ubar's dome dangerous. It was what took us so long to get here, once we learned from Barak that the gate had been breached."

"Well, better late than never," Danny said behind them.

"Yes, but now a new storm strikes the area, rising from the south. It will be death to walk those sands."

"So we're still trapped," Omaha said.

"Until the storm abates. We must simply hold out until that time."

With that sobering thought, they crisscrossed a few more streets in silence, finally reaching the back cavern wall. It looked solid, but Captain al-Haffi continued forward. Then Safia spotted it. A straight fracture in the glass wall. It angled inward, making it difficult to spot.

Captain al-Haffi led them to the crack. "The surface lies a hundred and fifty steps up. The passage can act as a shelter for the children and women."

"And a *trap* if we can't hold off Cassandra. She still outnumbers us and outguns us."

Captain al-Haffi stared across the group. "My men could use help. Anybody who can hold a gun."

Safia watched Danny and Coral accept weapons from a stash inside the crack. Even Clay stepped forward and held out his hand.

Her student caught her surprised look. "I really want that A," was all he said as he stepped away. His eyes shone with terror, but he did not back down.

Omaha went last. "I already have a pistol. But I could use a second."

Captain al-Haffi handed him an M-16.

"But this'll do."

Safia stepped up as he moved away. "Omaha . . ." She had never acknowledged what he had said back by the palace. Had his words been a deathbed confession, knowing they were doomed?

He smiled at her. "You don't have to say anything. I made my stand. I haven't earned your response yet." He moved away. "But I hope at least you'll let me try."

Safia shoved up to him and put her arm around his neck and held him tight. She spoke into his ear. "I do love you . . . I just don't know . . ." She couldn't finish the statement. It hung there between them.

He squeezed her anyway. "I do. And I'll wait until you do, too."

An argument forced them apart. Words between Kara and Captain al-Haffi.

"I will not let you fight, Lady Kensington."

"I am perfectly able to shoot a gun."

"Then take a gun with you to the stairs. You may need it."

Kara fumed, but the captain was right. The last stand might come to a fight on the stairs.

Captain al-Haffi placed a hand on her shoulder. "I owe your family a debt. Let me pay it this day."

"What are you talking about?" Kara said.

He bowed his head; his voice grew mournful and shamed. "This is not the first time I've lent my services to your family. When I was a young man, a boy really, I volunteered to help you and your father."

Kara's frown deepened.

Captain al-Haffi lifted his face to hers. "My first name is Habib."

Kara gasped and stumbled back a step. "The guide on the day of the hunt. That was you."

"I was to attend your father because of his interest in Ubar. But I failed. Fear kept me from following you and your father that day into the forbidden sands. Only when I saw that you intended to enter the *nisnases* did

I come after you, but it was too late. So I collected you from the sands and returned you to Thumrait. I did not know what else to do."

Kara appeared dumbstruck. Safia stared between them. Everything had come full circle . . . back to these same sands.

"So let me protect you now . . . as I failed to do in the past."

Kara could only nod. Captain al-Haffi moved away. Kara called after him. "You were only a boy."

"Now I'm a man." He turned to follow the others back down to the city.

Safia heard an echo of Omaha's words.

The *hodja* stared among those remaining. "It is not over yet." With those cryptic words, she entered the cleft. "We must walk the path of the old queen."

21
Storm Watch

December 4, 5:30 P.M.
Shisur

They were still on his tail.

Painter saw the glow of his pursuers back in the sandstorm. He lumbered forward, eking out as much speed as possible, which was approximately thirty miles per hour. And in the current teeth of this storm, this was a high-speed chase.

He checked both side mirrors. One truck tracked on each side. He caught the barest glimpse of his hunters: two loaded flatbed trucks. Despite their loads, they moved faster than he could, but they also had to compensate for the terrain. He, on the other hand, aimed the twenty-ton tractor in one direction, trundling over anything in his path, riding up one dune and down another.

Sand obliterated all sight lines. If this were a blizzard, it would be described as a whiteout.

Painter had set the tractor's cruise control. He checked its other features. It had a radar dish, but he didn't know how to operate it. He did find the radio. His initial plan had been to travel as close to Thumrait Air Base as necessary and contact the Omani Royal Air Force. Someone would listen. If he had any hope of rescuing the others, he had to blow his cover and alert the government here.

But the trucks had set him on a course away from the base, deeper into the storm. He had no chance to swing around. The other trucks were too fast.

As he climbed a monstrous dune, an explosion thundered on his left side. Shrapnel and a wave of sand struck that side like a bitch-slap from God Himself.

An RPG.

For a moment, an awful grating sound tore at the treads.

Painter winced, but the tractor rode through it, grinding away whatever had clogged its gears. It moved up the long slope.

Another explosion, this time directly behind him. The noise was deafening, but the armor plating proved its mettle . . . or in this case, its polycarbonate steel and Kevlar. Let them take potshots at him. The wind and storm would surely throw off their aim, and the tractor's armor would do the rest.

Then he felt a sickening lurch.

The tractor's treads still spun, but Painter's speed slowed. The M4 began to slide. He suddenly realized what his hunters' bombing had intended—not to take out the twenty-ton tractor, but to make it lose its footing.

They were bombing the slope, triggering an avalanche. The whole slope was sliding backward, taking the tractor with it. He switched off the cruise, popped the clutch, and kicked to a lower gear. He slammed the accelerator, trying to regain traction in the slippery slope.

No luck. He just churned himself into the loose sand.

Painter braked the tractor, fishtailing the back end, then hit reverse. He fled with the sand now, swimming with the riptide in the avalanche. He turned the tractor until he was parallel with the slope, the tractor tilting dangerously. He had to take care not to roll it.

He pushed the gear into neutral, braked, then back into first. The tractor moved forward again, now surfing down the slope, running along its flank, finding good traction *and speed*. He raced down to the bottom. The trucks gave chase, but they ran into the toppling sand and had to slow down.

Painter reached the end of the dune and cut around the corner.

He was done running from these fuckers.

He positioned the tractor to run straight, then reset the cruise.

Letting go of the wheel, he made sure the tractor continued its course. He then retreated quickly to the back. He found his own launcher. He loaded one of the rocket-propelled grenades, balanced the long tube on his shoulder, and crossed to the back hatch of the tractor.

He kicked the door open. Sand blew in, but not too fiercely, as he was traveling into the wind. He stared out behind him. He waited until he spotted two glows, rounding the last dune, coming at him again.

"Come to Papa," he mumbled, and aimed.

He set the crosshairs and pulled the trigger. The launcher exploded with a *whoosh*. He felt the back-wash of heated air as the grenade rocketed away.

He watched the red fire of its trail, a shooting star.

The hunters spotted it, too. Painter saw them both wheel to either side. Too late. At least for one of them. The grenade exploded. Painter enjoyed seeing one of the glows shoved high into the air and explode into a fiery ball, shining brightly in the darkness. It crashed back into the sands.

The other truck had vanished. Hopefully, in its haste, it had bogged down among the dunes. Painter would watch for it.

He returned to his seat and checked both side mirrors. All dark.

With a moment to breathe, Painter opened the stolen laptop. Slowly pixels charged and bloomed to light on the dark screen. He prayed the batteries held. The schematic of the area reappeared. Painter stared.

Oh, God, there was no blue marker.

Panic prickled. Then the familiar tiny spinning blue ring appeared. It had taken an extra minute for the wireless feed to pick up again. Safia was still transmitting. He checked the scrolling coordinates. They were still changing. She was moving. Alive. He hoped that meant all the others were safe as well.

He had to get to her . . . to them. Though the implanted transceiver could not be removed—it was tamper-proofed to blow unless deactivated—he could get Safia out of Cassandra's range, get her to a surgeon and demolition expert.

As he stared, he realized only the Z-axis coordinates were changing. That axis measured elevation or depth. The negative number was growing smaller, approaching zero.

Safia was climbing *up*. She was almost on the surface. She must have found a back door out of the caves. Good girl.

As he watched, he frowned. The Z coordinates passed zero and continued to climb into the positive numbers. Safia had not only reached the surface. She was climbing *higher*.

What the hell?

He checked her position. She was 5.2 miles from his position. As he had already been heading in the general direction, he had only to adjust his course slightly, aiming directly for her.

He crept the speed up another five miles per hour.

Breakneck speed in the current conditions.

If Safia found a back door, so would Cassandra. He had to reach Safia and the others as soon as possible. He glanced back to the blue glow. He knew one other person was surely monitoring this transmission.

Cassandra . . . and she still had the portable detonator.

5:45 P.M.

Safia marched up the long dark stairs, the others trailing behind her, climbing in twos, children and old or injured women. Kara carried their only flashlight, pointed it up the passage, casting Safia's shadow ahead of her. They sought to put as much distance as possible between them and the war below. Echoes of the fighting still reached them. A continual gunfire.

Safia fought to shut it out. She ran a hand along the wall. Sandstone. The steps underfoot had been worn by countless sandals and bare feet. How many others had walked this same path? She imagined the Queen of Sheba herself climbing or descending these stairs.

As she ascended, Safia sensed time's constriction, the past and present merging into one. More than anywhere, here in Arabia the past and present blurred. History was not dead and buried under skyscrapers and asphalt, or even trapped behind museum walls. It lived here, tied intimately to the land, merging story and stone into one.

She dropped her fingers.

Lu'lu joined her. "I heard you speaking to your beloved."

Safia didn't want to talk about it. "He's not . . . that was before . . ."

"You both love this land," the *hodja* continued, ignoring her attempt at a protest. "You've let too much sand come between you. But such dust can be swept aside."

"It's not that easy."

Safia stared down at her hand, where a ring once rested. Gone like a promise once made. How could she trust he'd be there when she needed him? *It was a boy who left you. It is a man who kneels here now.* Could she believe that? In contrast, she pictured another's face. Painter. The way he held her hand, his quiet respect and comfort, even the agony in his eyes when he frightened her.

Lu'lu spoke, as if reading her mind. "There are many men with noble hearts. Some take a little longer to grow into theirs."

Safia felt tears rising. "I need more time . . . to think things through."

"You've had time. Like us, you've spent too much time alone. Choices have to be made . . . before we are left with none."

As proof, a short way up, the storm's rush of winds moaned across the opening at the top.

Safia felt a breath of it across her cheek. She felt drawn to it. After so long below, she wanted to be free of this prison of rock. If only for a moment. To clear her head.

"I'm going to check the storm," Safia mumbled.

"I'll come with you," Kara said, a step behind her.

"As will I," the *hodja* added. "I would see with my own eyes what the first queen saw. I would see the original entrance to Ubar."

The three of them continued alone up the last flights of stairs. The winds grew stiffer, and sand swirled down atop them. The three pulled up hoods, scarves, and goggles.

Safia hiked to the top. The opening was a crack ahead. Kara clicked off her flashlight. The storm was lighter than the dark passage.

The exit stood a yard away. Safia spotted a crowbar leaning near the exit. Beyond the threshold rested a large flat boulder, partially blocking the way.

"The rock must've hidden the entrance," Kara said.

Safia nodded. Captain al-Haffi's men must have used the crowbar to pry the stone aside enough to pass through. Perhaps, if they outlasted the storm, they could all escape, push the stone back in place, and block Cassandra.

The fresh wind filled Safia with hope.

Even from here, the storm did not seem as dark as she remembered back at Shisur. Maybe the brunt of it was ending.

Safia bent through the crack but stayed sheltered behind the stone. Sand still covered the sun, but full night had become twilight again. She could see the sun again, a wan moon through the storm.

"The storm looks less severe," Kara said, confirming Safia's assessment.

Lu'lu disagreed. "Do not be fooled. These sands around Ubar are deceptive. There is a very real reason tribes avoid this area, calling it cursed, haunted, the sands of djinns and devils."

The *hodja* led them farther out of the entrance.

Safia followed, the wind tugging at her cloak and scarf. She looked around. She realized that they were atop a mesa, some thirty or forty feet above the desert floor. It was one of countless rocky prominences that poked from the dunes. "Ships of the sands," they were named by the nomadic tribes.

Safia stepped farther out, examining their perch. She recognized the shape of the mesa. It was the same as the sand painting at the palace. Here was where the first entrance to Ubar was discovered almost three millennia ago. She stared around. Both the citadel and the queen's palace had been patterned after this mesa. The most precious of all the ships of the desert.

Beyond the mesa, the storm drew Safia's eye. The swirling clouds in this area appeared strange. A mile or so out, the sandstorm darkened in bands, encircling the plateau. Safia could hear distant winds howling.

"It's like we're in the eye of a hurricane," Kara said.

"It is Ubar," Lu'lu said. "It draws the might of the storm to itself."

Safia remembered how for a short time after the keys erupted and opened the gate, the sandstorm had seemed less intense.

Kara crept dangerously near one of the rims. It made Safia nervous.

"You should get back from there," Safia warned, afraid a gust of wind might carry her over the edge.

"There's a path down this side. More of a goat track. Maybe we could make it down. I can see three trucks below, about forty yards out. Captain al-Haffi's transportation."

Safia edged closer. She could not imagine trying to traverse a cliffside path in these winds. They gusted unpredictably.

Lu'lu agreed with Safia. "It is death to attempt those sands."

Kara glanced back at the *hodja*. Her expression argued that it was just as dangerous to stay. Clearly Kara was willing to take the chance.

Lu'lu understood her thought. "Your father dismissed warnings of these sands, as you do now. Even after all you've seen."

Her words only angered Kara. "What is there to fear?"

Lu'lu swept her arms out. "These are the sands of the *nisnases*."

Both Safia and Kara knew that name. The black ghosts of the sands. It was the *nisnases* that were to blame for Reginald Kensington's death.

Lu'lu pointed to the southwest. A small whirlwind stirred, twisting, a tornado of sand. It scintillated in the darkness, aglow with static charge. For a moment, it burst more brilliantly, then vanished.

"I've seen a dust devil like that," Kara said.

Lu'lu nodded. "The *nisnases* bring the burning death."

Safia pictured Reginald Kensington's tortured body, locked in glass. It reminded her of the mummified citizens below. How were they connected?

Another devil bloomed off to the east. Another due south. They seemed to stir up from the sand and into the air. Safia had seen thousands of such whirlwinds, but never ones so brilliant with static charge.

Kara gazed out. "I still don't under—"

Directly before them, a wall of sand blew up from below the mesa's edge. They all fell back.

"A *nisnase!*" Lu'lu gasped.

The whirlwind formed just beyond the mesa, swirling in a sinuous column. Both Kara and the *hodja* retreated for the passage. Safia remained where she stood, mesmerized.

Vast waves of static charge swept up its length, chasing up from the sand and into the sky. Her cloak billowed, not from winds this time, but from the play of electricity in the air, crackling over her skin, clothes, and hair. It was a painful but somehow ecstatic feeling. It left her body cold, her skin warm.

She exhaled, not realizing she had been holding her breath.

She took a step forward, close enough to see the full breadth of the snaking whirlwind. Energy continued to jitter through the column. She saw the devil centered around one of the three vehicles. From her vantage point, she could see the sands around the truck forming a whirlpool beneath it.

She jumped a bit when something touched her elbow. It was Kara. She had strengthened her nerve to watch. Kara found and took Safia's hand. In her touch, Safia sensed Kara reliving an old nightmare.

Beneath the truck, the sands began to darken. A burning odor wafted up to them. Kara's hand clenched on Safia. She had recognized that smell.

The sands grew black. Molten sand. Glass.

The *nisnase*.

The energies in the whirlwind whipped wildly, glowing through the entire column. From their perch, they watched the truck sink into the molten pool, at first slowly, its rubber tires melting and popping— then there was a tremendous *whoosh* of static, the devil collapsed, and in the instant before it vanished, Safia watched the glass turn as black as nothingness. The truck fell away, as if through air. The black pit melted deeper into the sand, and the last winds swept fresh sand over it, wiping away all trace.

A ghost come and gone.

A moment later, a soft blast burped. The sand in the area bumped up.

"Fuel tank," Kara said.

They both raised their eyes. More of the deadly whirlwinds were popping up all over. There had to be a dozen of them now.

"What's happening?" Kara asked.

Safia shook her head. The encircling wall of storm had also grown blacker, contracting toward them, moving closer in all directions.

Lu'lu stared around them with a look of terror. "The other storm system from the coast. It has come, the two are feeding on each other, becoming something worse."

"The megastorm," Safia said. "It's forming around us."

More and more whirlwinds danced across the sands. Their glows were flames rising from the sands. It was a hellish landscape. The storm beyond grew blacker and wilder. It screamed now.

To move across those sands invited certain death.

Safia heard a sound closer at hand. A noise from her radio. She freed it from a pocket. Omaha had asked her to leave the channel open in case he needed to reach her.

She fished it out and backed toward the passageway.

A voice whispered through static at her. *"Safia . . . if . . . can hear me . . ."*

Kara leaned next to her. "Who is it?"

Safia pressed it to her ear, listening tightly.

". . . I . . . coming . . . Safia, can you hear . . ."

"Who?" Kara asked.

Safia's eyes widened. "It's Painter. He's alive."

Some vagary of the storm's static let his voice reach her clearly for a moment. *"I'm two miles from your position. Hold tight. I'm coming."*

Static erased any further reception.

Safia pressed the send button and held the radio to her lips. "Painter, if you can hear me, don't come! Do not come! Did you hear me?"

She released the button. Only static. He hadn't heard.

She stared out at the netherworld of storm, fire, and wind.

It was death to travel those sands . . . and Painter was coming here.

6:05 P.M.

Cassandra crouched with two of her men. Gunfire rattled and spat all around. After the first RPG blast had caught her off guard, Cassandra had entered the fray, moving into the wreck and tumble of the town.

Fighting continued, but her team was making steady progress.

She stared through the sights of a rifle and waited. The cluster of blocky homes lay before her, limned in shades of emerald and silver through her night-vision goggles. Having also employed an overlay of infrared, she watched a red blob move beyond a glass wall, near a corner. One of the enemy.

She studied the silhouette. Her target carried a tube on his shoulder, blazing like a small sun. Fiery hot. One of the launchers. She had instructed her men to focus their attention on such objectives. They had to eliminate the enemy's long-range capabilities.

By the wall, her target shifted, moving out into the open, positioning the grenade launcher.

Cassandra centered her crosshairs on the hottest part of the enemy's body—the head. She squeezed her trigger. Just once. That's all she needed.

Through the infrared, she saw the spray of fire blossom outward.

A clean shot.

But some twitched reflex fired the launcher.

Cassandra watched the RPG blast away, blinding on her scopes. She rolled to her back, dazzled. The grenade sailed high overhead, the aim way off course, as the enemy's body fell backward.

Angled toward the roof as the grenade was, she lost sight of it against the brilliant display of electrical discharges storming across the ceiling. She flipped away the infrared overlay and toggled off the night-vision mode. Through the regular lenses, the roof still blazed. The display had grown more violent, filling the entire cap of the dome. Small arcs of electricity speared out like bolts of lightning.

Across the lake, the misfired RPG exploded. It had struck the far wall, opposite the city. She focused the telescopic view.

Fuck . . . She could not catch a goddamn break.

The grenade struck the wall above the tunnel leading into the cavern. She watched a section of the glass wall tear away from the rock behind it, along with a portion of the tunnel room. It collapsed, sealing the tunnel.

Their exit was now blocked.

She rolled to her stomach. The surface team would just have to dig them out. The immediate concern was to secure this town, capture Safia, and extract the prize here. She flipped her infrared overlay back over her goggles' lenses.

It was time to continue the hunt.

Her two men had gone forward already to check the body and confiscate the launcher. They were ready to move on.

Cassandra paused to check her electronic tracker.

Safia lay a short distance ahead. Red triangles, the beacons from her team, closed on her position from all directions.

Satisfied, Cassandra almost pocketed the device, but the elevation reading alongside the blue glowing ring caught her eye. She froze. That didn't make sense.

Cassandra stared up again at the blazing roof. If the reading was correct, Safia was on the surface. Was there another way out?

She touched her throat mike and sent out a general alert over the open channel, reaching every man. "Close in now! Full run! Leave no one alive!"

Cassandra rose from her position and joined her men.

"Let's finish this."

6:10 P.M.

Omaha heard the cry from Captain al-Haffi, in Arabic. "Pull back to the stairs! All forces retreat to the exit."

Omaha crouched with Coral, Danny, and Clay. They had taken up a position inside the courtyard of the palace. A grenade blasted twenty yards away. They all pressed against the wall.

"We have to go," Clay said.

"I'd love to," Omaha said. "Just tell that to the two men around the corner."

They were pinned down in here. They had been for the last minute. Moments ago, Omaha and Clay had run into the courtyard from one direction, Danny and Coral from the other. Both teams chased by commandos. Now all four were pinned down.

A standoff.

Only Cassandra's soldiers had an advantage: sophisticated scopes that seemed to track their every move.

"We should pull back into the palace," Coral said, slapping a fresh magazine into her pistol. "We'd have a better chance of losing them."

Omaha nodded. They made a dash for the palace entrance.

"What about Captain al-Haffi and the others?" Clay asked as they ducked inside. "They might leave without us."

Omaha crouched on one knee, gun pointed toward the courtyard. Coral took his flank, Danny and Clay behind them.

"Leave where?" Omaha asked. "I'd rather take my chances out here than in the cramped stairwell. At least here we have some elbow—"

The shot pinged off the wall by his ear. Glass shattered, needling the side of his face. "Damn . . ."

More bullets chewed. Omaha dropped flat next to Coral. Danny and Clay retreated into the far room. The only reason Omaha was still alive was that the iron-and-glass statue of the palm holding the sphere in the courtyard's center had blocked a direct shot into the entrance.

Across the courtyard, one of the commandos ran into view, angling to the side, a grenade launcher on his shoulder, pointed at the door of the palace. Bullets continued to pepper, suppression fire for the artillery soldier. A gutsy move. Something had lit a fire under Cassandra's team in the last few minutes.

Coral twisted around and aimed her pistol at the man with the grenade launcher. She was too slow.

The gods above were not.

From the roof, a dazzling bolt of energy struck the ground near the man, crackling for half a breath, searing the retinas. It was not true lightning, just an arc of energy between the roof and floor. It did not blast a crater. It did not even knock the man down.

It did much worse.

The glass under the man instantly transmogrified from solid to liquid, changing states in one breath. The soldier fell into the pool, up to his neck. The scream that burst from his mouth was a sound only heard in the deepest pit of hell, the scream of a man burned alive.

It cut short after an instant.

The man's head fell backward, steam rising from his mouth.

Dead.

The glass was solid again.

The suppression fire died with the man. Others had witnessed it.

In the distance, the fighting continued, echoing with rifle blasts—but here no one moved. Omaha raised his gaze. The roof was on fire, filling the dome. Other bolts jumped between ceiling and floor. Somewhere across the way another scream erupted, a twin to the one heard here.

"It's happening again," Coral said.

Omaha stared at the dead man, buried in glass. He knew what she meant.

Fiery death had returned to Ubar.

6:12 P.M.

Painter bounced in his seat as the twenty-ton tractor flew over a small dune. He could see nothing now.

The visibility of a few yards had dropped to the tip of his nose. He was driving blind. He could be blithely aiming for the edge of a cliff and he'd never know.

A few minutes ago, the sandstorm had suddenly whipped up with a renewed ferocity. The buffeting winds sounded like giant fists striking the tractor. Painter's head throbbed from the concussion of the forces.

Still, he continued blindly forward. His only guidance glowed on the laptop beside him.

Safia.

He had no idea if she heard his radio call or not, but she hadn't moved since the broadcast. She was still aboveground . . . actually about *forty feet* aboveground. There must be a hill ahead. He'd have to slow once he was nearer.

A shimmer of reflection caught his eye. In the side mirror. The second pursuit vehicle. It was following the tractor's larger lights. The hunter had to be as blind as he, following in his tracks, keeping to his packed path, letting him encounter any obstacles.

The blind leading the blind.

Painter continued. He dared not leave his post. The winds suddenly whipped even more savagely. For a moment, the tractor tilted up on one tread, then slammed down. Christ . . .

For some reason, a laugh bubbled out of him. The gibbering amusement of the damned.

Then the winds ended, as if someone had unplugged the fan.

The lumbering tractor rode out into more open sands. The skies even lightened from midnight to twilight. Sand still stirred, and winds did indeed still blow, but at a tenth of the velocity of a moment ago.

He glanced to the side mirror. A solid wall of blackness blanketed the view. He must have traveled completely through its heart and out the other side.

As he watched, he saw no sign of the pursuit vehicle, its glow lost in the total darkness. Perhaps that last burst of winds had flipped the sucker.

He focused forward.

His sight line stretched for a good quarter mile. In the distance he could see a shadowy prominence of dark rock. A desert mesa. He glanced at the laptop. The blue glow lay directly ahead.

"So that's where you are."

He kicked up the speed of the tractor.

He wondered if Safia could see him. Reaching out, he took the radio in hand. He kept one eye on the road. Throughout the region, minitornadoes whipped and snaked, joining desert to sky. They glowed with a cobalt radiance. Crackles of static charge spun up from the ground. Most stood in one place, but a few meandered over the desert landscape. He was close enough to see one etch down a dune face, sand coughing up around it. In its wake, it left a trail of black sand, a squiggled sigil, a pen stroke from some storm god.

Painter frowned. He had never seen such a phenomenon.

But it was none of his concern.

He had more pressing worries. He raised the radio to his lips. "Safia, if you can read me, let me know. You should be able to see me."

He waited for a reply. He didn't know if Safia still had one of their radios. It was the frequency to which he had set the tractor's transmitter.

Noise burst from the receiver. "*—ainter! Go! Turn back!*"

It was Safia! It sounded like she was in trouble.

He hit the transmit button. "I'm not turning back. I've got—"

An arc of electricity leaped from the radio receiver to his ear. Yelping out, he dropped the radio. He smelled burning hair.

He felt a surge of static charge throughout the vehicle. Every surface shocked him. He kept his hands on the rubber-coated wheel. The laptop sizzled, then gave off a loud *pop*. The screen went dead.

The sound of a foghorn reached him, blaring, persistent.

Not a foghorn . . . a truck's horn.

He glanced at the side mirror. From the storm's black wall, the pursuit truck flew out into the open. The last winds slapped the back end. Its frame tilted, beginning to flip.

Then it was free. It struck the sands, the tires on one side, then the other. It bounced, skidded, and spun a full turn. But it was out of the storm.

Painter swore.

The truck's driver must have been as shocked to be alive as Painter was to see him. The flatbed idled. It looked like hell. One tire was flat, the bumper was curled into a steel smile, the tarp over its load in back had been blown to one side, tangled amid the ropes.

Painter pressed his accelerator, racing forward, putting as much distance between himself and the truck. He remembered the RPG bombardment. He wanted a little breathing room, then he'd take care of this truck.

In the side mirror, the truck followed, limping after him.

Painter prepared to fight, setting the cruise.

Ahead the desert was a forest of whirling sand devils, glowing in the twilight gloom. They all seemed to be on the move now. He frowned. They were all moving in unison, some unearthly ballet.

Then he felt it. A familiar lurch in the sand.

He had felt the same when the grenades had triggered an avalanche over the dune face. The shift of sands under his treads.

But he was on flat ground.

All around the whirlwinds danced, static electricity sparked, and the desert loosened under him. Against all odds, the twenty-ton tractor was becoming mired. His speed slowed. He felt its back end fishtailing. The tractor swung around, dragged by unknown forces. Then he was trapped, stopped.

His side window now faced toward the pursuit truck. It continued toward him, closing in on its wide, knobby sand tires. Then the sand under it became powder. It sank to its rims . . . then axle.

Bogged.

Both hunter and prey were trapped, flies in amber.

But this amber still flowed.

He felt it beneath him. The sand was still moving.

6:15 P.M.

Safia gave up on the radio. She could only watch in horror, alongside Kara and Lu'lu. It was a landscape out of a nightmare, a painting done by Salvador Dalí. The world melted and stretched.

She stared out at the whirlwinds, the deadly electrical discharges, pools of black sands, streaks of the same, carved out by skittering devils. The dusty clouds in the sky glowed from the amount of energy flowing into them, fed by the snaking columns of sand and static charge.

But that was not the worst.

For as far as she could see, the entire desert floor had begun to churn in one giant whirlpool, spinning around the buried bubble of Ubar. The sandstone mesa was a boulder in the current. But there were smaller rocks: Painter's tractor and another truck, mired in the churning sands.

Whirlwinds closed in on the vehicles, etching the sand with molten fire.

A crash echoed to the left. A piece of the mesa tore away, tumbling into the sand, a glacier calving into the sea.

"We can't stay here," Kara said. "It'll tear this island apart."

"Painter . . ." Safia said. Her clothing sparked and crackled with discharges as she stepped toward the mesa's edge. He had come to rescue them, driving to his doom. They had to do something.

"He's on his own," Kara said. "We can't help him."

The radio suddenly crackled in her hand. She had forgotten she was holding it. *Painter* . . .

"Safia, can you hear me?" It was Omaha.

She lifted her radio. "I'm here."

His voice sounded distant, as if from another planet. *"Something strange is going on down here. The static is arcing all over. It's zapping the glass. Melting spots. It's the cataclysm all over again! Stay away!"*

"Can you get up here? To the stairs?"

"*No. Danny, Clay, Coral, and I are holing up in the palace.*"

A commotion by the tunnel drew her eye. Sharif climbed out.

Kara moved to meet him.

He pointed to the tunnel. "We've retreated to the stairs," he said, panting. "Captain al-Haffi will attempt to hold the enemy off. You should—" His voice died as he suddenly caught a view of the desert. His eyes widened.

Another splintering crack erupted. Rocks crashed. The rim of the mesa crumbled.

"Allah, preserve us," Sharif prayed.

Kara waved him back. "He'd better. Because we're bloody damn well running out of places to hide."

6:16 P.M.

Cassandra knew true terror for the first time in ages. The last time she had felt this gut-level fear was as a child, listening to her father's footsteps outside her bedroom door at midnight. This was the same. A fear that gelled the insides and turned bone marrow to ice. Breathing was a talent forgotten.

She cowered inside a tiny glass building, more a chapel, enough for one person to kneel. Its only entrance was a short door that had to be ducked into. No windows. Past the door, the lower city spread below her.

She watched the continual arcing bolts of discharge. Some struck the lake, grew more intense, then sucked back to the roof, brighter for the effort, as if the storm above were feeding off the waters below.

The same was not true when it struck the glass. Every surface absorbed the strange energy, becoming a liquid pool, but only as briefly as a lightning flicker. Then it turned solid again.

She had watched one of her men succumb to such a bolt. He had been sheltering behind a wall, leaning on it. Then the bolt struck the wall. He fell through it, his support suddenly gone. The wall solidified again. Half his body on one side, the other half on this side. Between, he had been burned to bone. Even his clothes had caught fire, a human torch, on two sides of glass.

All across the city, the fighting had stopped. Men sought shelter.

They had seen the mummified bodies. They knew what was happening.

The cavern had gone deathly quiet, except for the occasional gunshot by the back wall, where the enemy had sequestered itself in some passageway. Anyone who approached was shot.

Cassanda clutched her electronic tracker. She watched the spread of red triangles. Her men. Or those few that were left. She counted. Of the fifty on the assault team, only a dozen were left. She watched as another blinked out. A shattering scream fluttered through the city.

Death stalked her men.

She knew even such enclosed shelters were not safe. She had seen the mummified bodies within a few of the homes.

The key seemed to be movement. Perhaps the amount of static in the room was such that any stirrings attracted a bolt to stab out at it.

So Cassandra sat still, very still. She had done the same in her childhood bed. It hadn't helped then. She doubted it would now. She was trapped.

6:17 P.M.

Omaha lay flat at the entryway to the palace. The quiet pressed upon him. Beyond the courtyard, the firestorm worsened. Bolts crackled, shattering into brilliant forks. The dome shone like the corona of a blue-white sun.

Omaha watched and knew death was near.

But at least he had told Safia he loved her. He had made his peace. He would have to be satisfied with that. He glanced upward. He prayed Safia was safe. She had relayed another short message, describing the chaos upstairs.

Death above, death below.

Take your pick.

Coral lay with him, studying the storm. "We're inside the world's largest transformer."

"What do you mean?"

They spoke in whispers, as if afraid to draw the sleeping giant's attention.

"The glass cavern with its energized antimatter solution is acting like a massive insulated superconductor. It draws energy to itself like the iron camel did at the museum. In this case, it collects the static energy of any passing sandstorm, sucking it down from above. But as energy builds in the chamber, crossing some threshold, it must need to shed its excess energy, like lightning does during a thunderstorm. Only this is aimed from sand to sky, shooting upward again in immense discharges, creating those momentary blasts of deadly whirlwinds on the desert's surface."

"Like it's draining its battery," Omaha said. "But what's going on in here?"

"A storm in a bottle. The megastorm is pouring too much energy down here. The bubble can't discharge it fast enough, so some of it's lashing back."

"Zapping itself."

"Redistributing charge," she corrected. "Glass is a great conductor. It merely takes the excess energy it can't discharge to the surface and passes it down to the floor below. The glass here captures the energy and disperses it. A cycle to keep the charge spread evenly through-out the entire glass bubble rather than just the dome. It's that equilibrium of energy that keeps the antimatter lake stable during this storm. A balance of charges."

"What about those pockets of molten glass?"

"I don't think it's *molten* glass. At least not exactly."

Omaha glanced questioningly in her direction. "What do you mean?"

"Glass is always in a *liquid* state. Have you ever seen antique glass? The flowing streaks that slightly distort the clarity? Gravity affects glass like a liquid, slowly pulling it down in streams."

"But what does that have to do with what's going on here?"

"The energy bolts aren't just melting the glass. They're changing its *state*, instantaneously breaking all bonds, liquefying the glass to the point that it borders on gaseous. When the energy disperses, it resolidifies. But just for a flash, it's in a fiery state between liquid and gas. That's why it doesn't flow. It keeps its basic shape."

Omaha hoped this discussion was leading to some solution. "Is there anything we can do about it?"

Coral shook her head. "No, Dr. Dunn, I'm afraid we're fucked."

6:19 P.M.

The fiery explosion drew Painter's attention to the mesa.

A truck parked near the sandstone prominence flipped in the air, spewing flaming fuel. One of the roving sand devils continued past it. It left a steaming trail of blackened sand.

Molten glass.

These sinuous columns of static charge were somehow discharging astronomical amounts of heat energy, burning their way across the landscape.

Painter remembered Safia's warning over the radio before it shorted out. She had tried to warn him away. He hadn't listened.

Now he was trapped inside the tractor as it slowly spun in a vast whirlpool of churning sand. For the past five minutes, it had carried him along, sweeping him in a wide arc, slowly spinning him in place. He was a planet orbiting a sun.

And all around death danced. For every whirlwind that blew itself out with a sharp discharge of static, another three took its place.

It was only a matter of time before one crossed his path, or worse yet, opened up under him. As he spun, he saw the other truck. It was faring no better. Another planet, smaller, maybe a moon.

Painter stared across the sands that separated them. He saw one chance.

It was a madman's course, but it was better than sitting here, waiting for death to come knocking. If he had to die, he'd rather die with his boots on. He stared down at his naked form. He wore only his boxers. Okay, he'd have to forgo the whole boot dream.

He stood up and crossed to the back. He'd have to travel light.

He took a single pistol . . . and a knife.

Outfitted, he stepped to the back door. He'd have to be fast. He took a moment to take several deep breaths. He opened the back door.

The clear expanse of desert suddenly erupted yards away. A devil spun up from the sand. He felt the backwash of its static. His hair flumed around his head, crackling. He hoped it didn't catch fire.

Stumbling back, he fled away from the back door. Time had run out.

He darted to the side door, shoved it open, and leaped.

Hitting the ground, he sank to his calves. The sand was damnably loose. He glanced over a shoulder. The devil loomed behind the tractor, crackling with energy. He smelled ozone. Heat pulsed from the monster.

Fleet feet, little skeet.

It was a nursery rhyme his father had often whispered in his ear when he was caught dawdling. *No, Papa . . . no dawdling here.*

Painter hauled his feet free from the sand and raced around the front end of the tractor. The whirlpool dragged at him, bordering on quicksand.

He spotted the flatbed truck. Fifty yards. Half a football field.

He sprinted for it.

Fleet feet, little skeet.

He ran, the rhyme a mantra in his head.

Across the sand, the truck's door popped open. The soldier stood on the running board and pointed a rifle at him. No trespassers.

Luckily Painter already had his pistol up. He fired and fired. There was no reason to spare the bullets. He squeezed and squeezed.

The driver fell backward, arms out.

The explosion behind Painter shoved him forward, face-first. A wave of fire seared. Spitting sand, he leaped up and away.

He glanced back to see the tractor on its side, on fire, its tank exploded by the heat of the devil as it expanded its reach. Painter pounded away. Flaming fuel rained down all around, splashing into the sand.

He simply ran, hell-bent.

Reaching the flatbed, he skipped the cab door, used the driver's body as a stepping-stone, and scrambled into the flatbed in back. The tarp was still tangled in the ropes. He used his knife to slice the lashings. They were taut and popped like overstretched guitar strings. He kicked tarps and ropes aside.

He exposed what lay underneath. What he had spotted when the flatbed mired. One of the copter sleds.

This little skeeter found his wings.

6:22 P.M.

Safia heard the staccato firing of a pistol.

Painter . . .

She had been huddling just inside the stairway passage. Kara and Lu'lu kept guard with her. She had been pondering some way to escape the doom here. She sensed an answer, just beyond reach. A clue she was missing, letting fear frazzle through her. But fear was an old companion. She took deep breaths, inhaling calm, exhaling tension.

She thought about the mystery.

She remembered her thoughts on the way up here. How the past and the present were merging in countless ways. She closed her eyes. She could almost feel the answer rising inside her like a bubble in water.

Then the gunshots.

Followed by an explosion. Like the one that had taken out one of Captain al-Haffi's trucks a minute or so ago.

Safia bolted back to the top of the mesa. A fireball billowed upward, shredding in the winds. The tractor lay on its side.

Oh, God . . . Painter . . .

She spotted a naked figure scrambling by the smaller truck.

Kara joined her. "It's Crowe."

Safia grabbed on to that hope. "Are you sure?"

"He really needs to cut his hair."

The figure climbed into something in the back of the truck. Then Safia spotted the spread of collapsible rotors. She heard a distant whine. The rotors churned. A helicopter.

Kara sighed. "That man is resourceful, I'll give him that."

Safia noted a tiny whirlwind, one of the untethered ones scribing through the dunes, swing in a wide arc, aiming for the truck and copter.

Did Painter see it?

6:23 P.M.

Painter lay flat on his belly in the sled. The controls were near his arms, one for each hand. He kicked up the rotor speed. He had flown helicopters during Special Forces training, but never one like this.

But how different could it be?

He yanked the right throttle. Nothing happened. He pulled on the left. Still nothing. Okay, maybe things were a bit different.

He pulled on both throttles and the copter lifted out of its cradle and into the air. He kept the throttles pulled and shot up in a wobbly arc, spun by the winds. The *thump-thump* of the rotors matched his heart, fast and furious.

As the copter swung, he caught a glimpse of a twister on his tail. It glowed and spat fire like a demon risen from hell.

Painter played with the controls, leaning right, left, and forward.

Forward was good.

He sped away, dipping too low, like sliding down a snowy slope. He attempted to get his nose up before he buried himself in the sand. He worked the throttle, rolled to the left, balanced it out, and finally found a way to bring the nose up.

Now he was aiming directly for a monstrously huge whirlwind.

He climbed higher and to the right—and successfully managed to spin himself in place while *still* flying toward the large devil. He felt his stomach flip. He dragged the left throttle, stopped the spin, and just managed to miss the devil.

But as a parting shot, the whirlwind spat an arc of static, zapping him. Painter felt the shock from the tip of his toes to his eyebrows.

So did the sled.

All power died. Instruments twirled. He plummeted, rotors churning uselessly. He switched all systems off, then back on again. Rebooting. A small whine answered, the motor coughed. Then died.

The mesa lay ahead. He aimed for it as best he could . . . which was at the side of its cliffs.

He rebooted again. The motor caught this time. The spinning rotors must have helped jump-start the engine. He pulled both throttles.

The copter climbed.

The cliffs rushed at him.

"C'mon . . ." he mumbled between clenched teeth.

As he reached the mesa, he caught a glimpse of its top. He willed the craft up another few inches. The landing skids brushed the edge of the lip, caught a bit, tilting the copter on its side. Rotors tore into stone.

They shattered away.

The sled compartment flipped high, and landed upside down atop the mesa. A lucky break. Painter banged his head, but he lived.

He popped the side hatch and fell out. He lay on the stone, panting, surprised to be alive. It was a good surprise.

Safia hurried over to him.

Kara followed, staring down at him, arms crossed. "Good effort, but have you ever heard of the phrase 'out of the frying pan, into the fire'?"

He sat up. "What the hell's happening?"

"We must get to a safe place," Safia said, helping him stand.

"Where?" Kara asked, taking his other arm. "The sandstorm is tearing apart the desert, and Ubar is on fire below."

Safia straightened. "I know where we can go."

22

Firestorm

◊Ƴ)ϡ੪Ӿ०)ϡ

Safia stood with Captain al-Haffi at the base of the stairs. She stared out at the azure maelstrom roiling over the arched room. It blinded. Bolts of cerulean energy lanced, forked, and speared all across the chamber. The most disturbing feature was the absolute quiet. No thunder here.

"How far to the palace?" she asked the captain.

"Forty yards."

She stared back up the staircase. The Rahim were down to fourteen adult women and the original seven children. Captain al-Haffi's dozen men were now eight. None of them looked ready to enter Ubar with its electrical wildfire.

But they stood ready to follow Safia.

She faced the path they had to walk. One misstep meant a fiery death.

"Are you sure about this?" Kara asked behind her. She was flanked by Lu'lu and Painter.

"As much as I can be," Safia answered.

Painter had borrowed a cloak from one of the Shahran men, but he was still barefoot. His lips were tight.

Far back, echoing down the passage behind them, the tumble of stones reached them. The preparation had taken longer than Safia would have liked. Already the upper sections of the stairway were falling apart.

"You're putting a lot of trust in that old queen," Painter said.

"She survived the cataclysm. The king's line survived. During the last cataclysm, the royal line was protected. They were the only ones. How?"

Safia turned and emptied the folded cloak she held in her hand. Sand poured out and covered the glass in front of her. It skittered down the path.

"*Sand* is a great insulator. The royal palace of Ubar is covered with sand paintings, on floors, walls, and ceilings. The mix of so much sand in the glass must ground the structure against the static bursts, protecting those inside." She tapped her radio. "Like it has so far with Omaha, Coral, Danny, and Clay."

Painter nodded. She read the respect and trust in his eyes. She took strength from his solid faith in her. He was a rock when she needed something to hang on to. Again.

Safia turned and stared back at the long line of folk. Everyone carried a burden of sand. They made bags out of cloaks, shirts—even the children carried socks full of sand. The plan was to pour a sand path from here to the palace, where they'd shelter against the storm.

Safia lifted her radio. "Omaha?"

"Here, Saff."

"We're setting off."

"Be careful."

She lowered the radio and stepped out onto the sand-covered glass. She would lead them. Moving forward, she used a boot to spread the sand as far as it would go and still leave good insulation underfoot. Once she reached the end, Painter handed her his bag of sand. She turned and cast the new sand down the path, extending the trail, and continued on.

Overhead, the cavern roof blazed with cobalt fire.

She still lived. It was working.

Safia crept down the sandy path. Behind her, a chain grew, passing bagful after bagful from one hand to another.

"Watch where you step," Safia warned. "Make sure sand is under you at all times. Don't touch the walls. Watch the children."

She poured more sand. The trail snaked from the back wall, winding around corners, down stairs, along ramps.

Safia stared out at the palace. They crept closer at a snail's pace.

Static charges lanced at them almost continuously now, attracted to their movements, stirring whatever electromagnetic field stabilized the place. But the glass on either side always drew away the charge, like a lightning rod. Their path remained safe.

Safia dumped a load of sand from a cloak, then heard a cry behind her.

Sharif had slipped several yards back on one of the sandy stairs. He caught his balance on a neighboring wall and used it to push up.

"Don't!" Safia yelled.

It was too late.

Like a wolf on a straggling lamb, a lance of brilliance lashed out. The solid wall gave way. Sharif fell headlong into the glass. It solidified around his shoulders. His body spasmed, but there was no scream, his face trapped in glass. He died immediately. The edges of his cloak smoldered.

Children cried out and pushed their faces into their mothers' cloaks.

Barak ran up from farther back, slipping past others, his face a mask of pain. She nodded to the women and children.

"Keep them calm," Safia said. "Keep them moving."

She took the next bag. Her hands shook. Painter stepped next to her, taking the bag. "Let me."

She nodded, falling back into second place. Kara was behind her. "It was an accident," she said. "Not your fault."

Safia understood it with her head, but not her heart.

Still, she did not let it paralyze her. She followed Painter, passing another sack to him. They crept onward.

At last, they rounded the courtyard wall. Ahead the entry to the palace glowed. Omaha stood in the archway, flashlight in hand.

"I left the porch light on for you guys." He waved them forward.

Safia had to resist the urge to run forward. But they were not safe yet. They continued at the same steady pace, rounding the iron sphere resting in its cradle. Finally, their long trail reached the entry.

Safia was allowed through first. She stepped inside and hugged her arms around Omaha, collapsing against him. He picked her up in his arms and carried her back to the main room.

She didn't object. They were safe.

7:07 P.M.

Cassandra had watched the procession, not moving, barely breathing. She knew to move meant death. Safia and Painter had passed within a few yards of her small glass alcove.

Painter had been a surprise. How could he be here?

But she did not react. She kept her breathing even. She was a statue. The many years of Special Forces training and field ops had taught her ways to remain still and quiet. She used them all.

Cassandra had known Safia was coming. She had mapped their progress, moving only her eyes, and had watched the very last red triangle on her tracker vanish a moment ago. She was all that was left. But it wasn't over.

Cassandra had watched in amazement as Safia returned to the cavern from above, returning here, passing so close.

A sand trail.

Safia had discerned the only safe haven in the cavern: the large, towering building that stood fifteen yards away. Cassandra heard the others' happy voices as they reached their sanctuary.

She remained perfectly still.

The sandy track wound only two yards from her position. Two large steps. Moving only her eyes, she watched the skies. She waited, tensing every muscle, preparing herself. But she remained a statue.

Then a bolt struck down about three yards away.

Close enough.

Cassandra sprang through the door, trusting in the old adage "lightning never strikes the same place twice." She had nothing else to go on.

One foot touched glass, only long enough to leap away. Her next foot landed on sand. She dropped to a crouch on the path.

Safe.

She took deep breaths, half sobbing in relief. She allowed herself this moment of weakness. She would need it to steel herself for the next step. She waited for her heart to stop pounding, for the shakes to subside.

Finally, her body calmed. She stretched her neck, a cat awakening.

She took a deep breath, then let it out. Now down to business.

She stood and took out the wireless detonator. She checked to make sure it hadn't been damaged or its electronics fritzed. All appeared in order. She tabbed a key, pressed the red button, then tabbed the key again.

A deadman's switch.

Rather than pressing the button to blow the chip in Safia's neck, all she had to do was lift her finger.

Prepared, she slipped her pistol from her holster.

Time to greet the neighbors.

7:09 P.M.

Seated on the floor, Painter stared around the crowded room. Coral had already reported and debriefed him on all that had happened, her theories, and her concerns. She now sat beside him, checking her weapon.

Across the room, Safia stood with her group. They smiled and soft laughter floated from them. They were a new family. Safia had a new sister in Kara, a mother in Lu'lu. But what about Omaha? He stood at her side, not touching, but close. Painter saw how Safia would lean ever so slightly in the man's direction, almost touching, but not.

Coral continued cleaning her gun. "Sometimes you just have to move on."

Before he could respond, a shadow shifted on his right, by the entryway.

He watched Cassandra step into the room. Pistol in one hand, she was calm, unconcerned, as if she had just come in from a stroll to the park.

"Now isn't this cozy," she said.

Her appearance startled everyone. Weapons were snatched.

Cassandra didn't react. She still had her pistol pointed at the ceiling. Instead, she held out a familiar device. "Is that any way to greet a neighbor?"

"Don't shoot!" Painter boomed, already on his feet. "Nobody shoot!"

He even moved to stand in front of Cassandra, shielding her.

"I see you recognize a deadman's switch," she said behind him. "If I die, poor Dr. al-Maaz loses her pretty little head."

Omaha heard her words. He had already shoved Safia behind him. "What is this bitch talking about?"

"Why don't you explain, Crowe? I mean the transceiver *is* your design."

He turned to her. "The tracker is . . . *not* the bomb."

"What bomb?" Omaha asked, his eyes both scared and angry.

Painter explained, "When Cassandra had Safia in her custody, she implanted a small tracking device.

Cassandra modified it with a small amount of C4. She holds the detonator. If she lets go of the trigger, it will blow."

"Why didn't you tell us before?" Omaha said. "We could've removed it."

"Do that and it blows, too," Cassandra said. "Unless I first deactivate it."

Painter glared at her, then back to Safia. "I'd hoped to get you somewhere safe, then have a surgical and demolition team remove the device."

His explanation did little to quell the horror in her eyes. And Painter knew some of it was directed at him. This was his job.

"So now that we're all friends," Cassandra said, "I'll ask you to throw all your weapons out into that courtyard. Everyone now. I'm certain Dr. Crowe will ensure that every weapon is accounted for. One slip and I may have to lift my finger and scold someone. We wouldn't want that to happen, would we?"

Painter had no choice. He did as Cassandra instructed. Rifles, pistols, knives, and two grenade launchers were piled into the courtyard.

As Coral threw her half-assembled gun with the others, she remained by the entry. Her eyes were on the cavern. Painter followed her gaze.

"What's the matter?" he asked.

"The storm. It's grown worse since your arrival. Much worse." She pointed to the roof. "The energy is not draining fast enough. It's destabilizing."

"What does that mean?"

"The storm is building into a powder keg in here." She turned to him. "This place is going to blow."

7:22 P.M.

From the second-story balcony of the palace, Safia stared with the others out at the maelstrom. The cavern roof could no longer be seen. The roiling clouds of static charge had begun a slow spin across the dome, a vortex of static. In the center, a small downspout could be seen, perceptibly lowering, like the funnel cloud of a tornado. It aimed for the antimatter lake.

"Novak's right," Cassandra said. She was studying the phenomenon through her night-vision goggles. "The entire dome is filling up."

"It's the megastorm," Coral said. "It must be much stronger than the ancient storm that triggered the cataclysm two thousand years ago. It's overwhelming the capacity here. And I can't help but think a fair amount of the lake water is probably destabilized like the contents of the iron camel."

"What will happen?" Safia asked.

Coral explained, "Have you ever seen an overloaded transformer blow? It can take out an entire power pole. Now picture one the size of this cavern. One with a concentrated antimatter core. It has the capability of taking out the entire Arabian Peninsula."

The sobering thought silenced them all.

Safia watched the vortex of energies churn. The funnel in the center continued to drop, slowly, inexorably. Primitive fear laced through her.

"So what can we do?" This question came from an unlikely source. Cassandra. She pulled up her night-vision goggles. "We have to stop this."

Omaha scoffed. "Like you want to help?"

"I don't want to die. I'm not insane."

"Just evil," Omaha muttered.

"I prefer the word 'opportunistic.'" She directed her attention back to Coral. "Well?"

Coral shook her head.

"We ground it," Painter said. "If this glass bubble is the insulator for this energy, then we need to find a way to shatter the bubble's underside, ground the electrical storm, send its energy into the earth."

"It's not a bad theory, Commander," Coral said. "Especially if you could break the glass under the lake itself, get the antimatter waters to drain into the original Earth-generated water system from whence it came. Not only would the energy dissipate, but it would lessen the risk of an antimatter chain reaction. The enriched waters would simply dilute away to the point of impotency."

Safia felt a glimmer of hope. It didn't last past Coral's next words.

"It's the practical application of that plan that's the big problem. We don't have a bomb massive enough to blow out the bottom of the lake."

For the next few minutes, Safia listened to the discussions of possible explosive devices while knowing what lay implanted in her own neck, knowing what had happened back in Tel Aviv, back at the British Museum. Bombs marked the turning points in her life. They might as well mark her end. The threat should have terrified her, but she was beyond fear.

She closed her eyes.

She half noted the various ideas being bandied aloud, from rocket-propelled grenades even to the bit of C4 in her neck.

"There's nothing here strong enough," Coral said.

"Yes, there is," Safia said, opening her eyes. She remembered the blast at the British Museum. She pointed down into the courtyard. "It's not a camel, but it may do."

The others stared where she pointed.

To the giant iron sphere resting in the glass palm.

"We sink it into the lake," Safia said.

"The world's largest depth charge," Danny said.

"But how do you know it will explode like the camel?" Coral asked. "It might just fizzle like the iron maiden. These iron artifacts don't all function the same way."

"I'll show you," Safia said.

She turned and led the way back down the stairs. Once in the main room, she waved to each of the sand-painted walls. "Opposite the entry is the first Ubar, a rendering of its discovery. Over on that far wall is the depiction of Ubar above. Its face to the world. And this wall, of course, is the true heart of Ubar, its pillared glass city." She touched the painting of the palace. "The detail is amazing, even down to the sandstone statues guarding the entrance. But on this picture *both* statues are shown."

"Because one was used as a vessel for the first key," Omaha said.

Safia nodded. "This depiction was done obviously before the destruction. But note what's missing. No iron sphere. No glass palm. In the center of the painting's courtyard stands the queen of Ubar. A place of prominence and importance. X marks the spot, so to speak."

"What do you mean?" Cassandra asked.

Safia had to bite back a sneer. Her effort to save her friends, to save Arabia, would also be saving Cassandra. Safia continued, not meeting the woman's eye. "Symmetry was important in the past. Balance in all things. The new object was placed on a site that matches the position of the queen in the rendering. A place of distinction. It must be important."

Omaha turned, staring out the entry to the iron sphere. "Even the way the palm is positioned. If you straightened the wrist, it would be like she's throwing the sphere toward the lake."

Safia faced them all. "It's the queen's last key. A failsafe. A bomb left to destroy the lake if needed."

"But can you be sure?" Painter asked.

"What does it hurt to try?" Omaha countered. "Either it works or it doesn't."

Coral had wandered to the entrance. "If we're going to try this, we'd better hurry."

Safia and the others crowded forward.

In the center of the cavern, a glowing funnel cloud twisted and writhed.

Below it, the antimatter lake had begun to churn, matching the vortex on the roof.

"What do we do first?" Painter asked.

"I have to place my hands on the sphere," Safia said. "Activate it like all the other keys."

"Then we get the ball rolling," Omaha said.

Omaha stood on the sandy path out in the courtyard. It had taken a minute to sweep the trail so it reached the cradled sphere. Safia stood before the four-foot-wide globe of red iron.

The skies raged above.

Safia approached the sphere. She rubbed her palms, then reached between the glass fingers of the sculpture.

Omaha saw her shoulder flinch, the bullet wound paining her. He wanted to rush to her side, pull her away, but she bit her lower lip and placed both palms on the sphere.

As her skin touched metal, a crackling blue flash arced over the iron's surface. Safia flew back with a yelp.

Omaha caught her in his arms and helped her gain her feet on the sand.

"Thanks."

"Sure, babe." He kept one arm around her and helped her back to the palace. She leaned on him. It felt good.

"The grenade is set on a two-minute timer," Painter said. "Get to cover." He had planted the explosive charge at the base of the sculpture. The plan was to blast the sphere free.

Gravity would do the rest. The avenue beyond the palace flowed all the way to the lake. *Purposeful*, Safia had said. *The ball, once freed, was meant to roll to the lake on its own.*

Omaha helped Safia back into the main room.

A blindingly bright flash flared behind them, burning their shadows on the far wall of the main room. Omaha gasped, fearing it was the grenade.

He jerked Safia to the side, but there was no explosion.

"One of the static bolts," Coral said, rubbing her eyes. "It struck the sphere."

Safia and Omaha swung around. Out in the courtyard, the iron's surface shimmered with blue energies. They watched the glass sculpture melt slowly, tilting on its own. The hand spilled the ball onto the courtyard floor. It bobbled, then rolled toward the arched entry.

It passed through and continued on.

Coral sighed. "Beautiful." Omaha had never heard so much respect uttered in one word.

He nodded. "That queen would have made a great professional bowler."

"Down!" Painter shoved them all to the side, clotheslining Omaha across the neck.

The explosion deafened. Glass shards spattered into the room from the courtyard outside. Painter's grenade had gone off on schedule.

As the blast echoed away, Omaha met his eyes. "Good job there." He patted Painter on the shoulder. "Good job."

"It's still rolling!" Danny called from above.

They all hurried up the stairs to the upper balcony, where everyone else was gathered.

Omaha pushed forward with Safia.

The course of the iron sphere was easy to follow. Its movement drew bolts from the roof, zapping it again and again. Its surface glowed with a cerulean aura. It bounced, rolled, and wended its way down the royal avenue.

Forked lightning struck and dazzled—but it kept rolling to the lake.

"It's energizing itself," Coral said. "Drawing power into it."

"Becoming the depth charge," Danny said.

"What if it blows up as soon as it touches the lake?" Clay asked, hanging back, ready to duck into the palace at the first sign of trouble.

Coral shook her head. "As long as it keeps dropping, moving *through* the water, it'll only leave a trail of annihilation. But the reaction will end as soon as the ball moves on."

"But when it stops, rests at the bottom . . .." Danny said.

Coral finished: "Then the weight of all the water above it, pressing on the stationary object, will trigger a localized chain reaction. Enough to light the proverbial fuse on our depth charge."

"Then boom," Danny said.

"Boom indeed," Coral concurred.

All eyes remained on the glowing ball.

All eyes saw it reach the halfway point, roll along a ramp, hit a tumbled pile of debris from Cassandra's bombardment . . . *and stop.*

"Shit," Danny mumbled.

"Shit indeed," Coral concurred.

7:43 P.M.

Safia stood with the others on the balcony, as dismayed as the rest. Arguments raged around her.

"What about using one of the RPGs?" Cassandra asked, staring through her night-vision goggles.

"Shoot a grenade at an energized antimatter bomb?" Omaha said. "Yeah, let's do that."

"And if you miss the debris pile," Painter said, "you'll bring down another wall and block the road even more. Right now, it's only hung up. If it could be rolled aside a couple of feet . . ."

Cassandra sighed. Safia noted the woman's finger still pressed the transmitter, protecting it from anyone's reach. Cassandra could definitely focus. With all that was going on, all the danger, she was not letting go of her trump card, keeping it in play, clearly intending to use it if everything worked out. She was a stubborn fighter.

Then again, so was Safia.

Clay held his arms crossed over his chest. "What we need is someone to go out and give it a good push."

"Feel free to try," Cassandra said with clear disdain. "The first sign of movement and you'll be bathing in molten glass."

Coral stirred, previously lost in deep thought. "Of course. It's movement that draws the bolts, like the rolling ball."

"Or my men," Cassandra added.

"The bolts must be attracted to shifts in some electromagnetic field, a giant motion-detecting field." Coral stared down. "But what if someone could move through the field *unseen*?"

"How?" Painter asked.

Coral glanced to the *hodja* and the other Rahim. "They can be unseen when they want to be."

"But that's not physical," Painter said. "It's some way they affect the viewer's mind, clouding perception."

"Yes, but how do they do that?"

No one answered.

Coral stared around, then straightened. "Oh, I never told you."

"You know?" Painter said.

Coral nodded and glanced at Safia, then away. "I studied their blood."

Safia remembered Coral had been about to mention something about that when Cassandra's forces had attacked. What was this about?

Coral pointed toward the cavern. "Like the lake, the water in the Rahim's red blood cells—all their cells and fluids, I imagine—is full of buckyballs."

"They have antimatter in them?" Omaha asked.

"No, of course not. It's just that their fluids have the capability of maintaining water in buckyball configurations. I wager the ability comes from some mutation in their mitochondrial DNA."

Dread grew in Safia's chest. "What?"

Painter touched her elbow. "A little slower."

Coral sighed. "Commander, remember the briefing on the Tunguska explosion in Russia? Mutations arose in flora and fauna of the area. The indigenous Evenk tribe developed genetic abnormalities in their blood, specifically their Rh factors. All caused by gamma radiation from antimatter annihilation." She waved an arm out toward the storm raging. "The same here. For who knows how many generations, the population residing here has been exposed to gamma radiation. Then a pure bit of chance happened. Some woman developed a mutation—not in her own DNA, but the DNA in her cellular mitochondria."

"Mitochondria?" Safia asked, trying to remember her basic biology.

"They are the small organelles inside all cells, floating in the cytoplasm, little engines that produce cellular energy. They're a cell's batteries, to use a crude analogy. But they have their own DNA, independent of a person's genetic code. It is believed that mitochondria were once some type of bacteria that absorbed into mammalian cells during evolution. The little bit of DNA is left over from the mitochondria's former independent life. And as mitochondria are found only in the cytoplasm of cells, it is the mitochondria of a mother's egg that becomes the mitochondria of the child. That's why the ability passes only through the queen's line."

Coral swept a hand over the Rahim.

"And it is these mitochondria that mutated from the gamma radiation?" Omaha asked.

"Yes. A minor mutation. The mitochondria still produce energy for the cell, but it also produces a little spark to actively maintain buckyball configuration, giving it a little juice. I wager this effect has something to do with the energy fields in this chamber. The mitochondria are attuned to it, aligning the charge of a buckyball to match the energy here."

"And these charged buckyballs give these women some mental powers?" Painter asked, incredulous.

"The brain is ninety percent water," Coral said. "Charge that system up with buckyballs and anything could happen. We've seen the women's ability to affect magnetic fields. This transmission of magnetic force, directed by human will and thought, seems to be able to affect the waters in the brains of lower creatures and somewhat upon us. Affecting our will and perception."

Coral's eyes glanced to the Rahim. "And if focused inward, the magnetic force can stop meiosis in their own eggs, producing a self-fertilized egg. Asexual reproduction."

"Parthenogenesis," Safia whispered.

"Okay," Painter said. "Even if I could accept all that, how does any of this get us out of this mess?"

"Haven't you been listening?" Coral asked, glancing over her shoulder to the vortex of storm above and now stirring the lake. They were running out of time. Minutes only. "If one of the Rahim concentrates, she can attune herself to this energy, alter her magnetic force to match the electromagnetic detecting field. They should be able to walk through safely."

"How do they do that?"

"By willing themselves invisible."

"Who would be willing to take that chance?" Omaha asked.

The *hodja* stepped forward. "I will. I sense the truth in her words."

Coral took a deep breath, licked her lips, and spoke. "I'm afraid you're too weak. And I don't mean physically . . . at least not exactly."

Lu'lu frowned.

Coral explained, "With the storm raging, the forces out there are intense. It will take more than experience. It will take someone extremely rich in buckyballs."

Turning, Coral's eyes met Safia's. "As you know, I tested several of the Rahim, including the elder here. They only have a tenth of the buckyballs found in your cells."

Safia frowned. "How is that possible? I'm only half Rahim."

"But the right half. Your mother was Rahim. It was *her* mitochondria that were passed to your cells. And there is a condition in nature called 'hybrid vigor,' where the crossing of two different lines produces stronger offspring than crossing the same line over and over again."

Danny nodded to the side. "Mutts are basically healthier than purebreds."

"You're new blood," Coral concluded. "And the mitochondria like it."

Omaha stepped to Safia's side. "You want *her* to walk to the trapped sphere. Through that electrical storm."

Coral nodded. "I believe she's the only one who could make it."

"Screw that," Omaha said.

Safia squeezed his elbow. "I'll do it."

8:07 P.M.

Omaha watched Safia standing out on the sandy path in the courtyard. She had refused to let him come. She was alone with the *hodja*. So he waited in the entryway. Painter stood vigil with him. The man looked none too pleased with Safia's choice either. In this, the two men were united.

But this choice was Safia's.

Her argument was simple and irrefutable: *Either it works or we all die anyway.*

So the men waited.

Safia listened.

"It is not hard," the *hodja* said. "To become invisible is not a concentration of will. It is the letting go of will."

Safia frowned. But the *hodja*'s words matched Coral's. The mitochondria produced charged bucky-balls aligned to the energy signature in the room. All she had to do was let them settle into their natural alignment.

The *hodja* held out a hand. "First you'll need to strip out of your clothes."

Safia glanced sharply at her.

"Clothes affect our ability to turn invisible. If that woman scientist was right with all that mumbo jumbo, clothes might interfere with the field we generate over our bodies. Better safe than sorry."

Safia shed her cloak, kicked her boots off, and shimmied out of blouse and pants. In her bra and panties, she turned to Lu'lu. "Lycra and silk. I'm keeping them on."

She shrugged. "Now relax yourself. Find a place of comfort and peace."

Safia took deep breaths. After years of panic attacks, she had learned methods for centering herself. But it seemed too small, a pittance against the pressure around her.

"You must have faith," the *hodja* said. "In yourself. In your blood."

Safia inhaled deeply. She glanced back to the palace, to Omaha and Painter. In the men's eyes, she saw their

need to help her. But this was her path. To walk alone.
She knew this in places beyond where her heart beat.

She turned forward, resolved but scared. So much
blood had been shed in the past. In Tel Aviv . . . at the
museum . . . on the long road here. She had brought all
of these folks here. She could no longer hide. She had to
walk this path.

Safia closed her eyes and let all doubt flow from her.
This was her path.

She evened her breathing, releasing control to a
more natural rhythm.

"Very good, child. Now take my hand."

Safia reached over and gripped the old woman's
palm, gratefully, surprised at the strength there. She
continued to relax. Fingers squeezed, reassuring her.
She recognized the touch from long ago. It was her
mother's hand. Warmth flowed from this connection.
It swelled through her.

"Step forward," the *hodja* whispered. "Trust me."

It was her mother's voice. Calm, reassuring, firm.

Safia obeyed. Bare feet moved from sand to glass.
One foot, then the other. She moved off the path, her
arm behind her, holding her mother's hand.

"Open your eyes."

She did, breathing evenly, keeping the warmth of
maternal love deep inside her. But eventually one had

to let go. She slipped her fingers free and took another step. The warmth stayed with her. Her mother was gone, but her love lived on, in her, in her blood, in her heart.

She walked on as the storm raged in flame and glass.

At peace.

Omaha was on his knees. He didn't even know when he fell. He watched Safia walk away, shimmering, still present, but ethereal. As she brushed through the shadow under the courtyard archway, she completely vanished for a moment.

He held his breath.

Then, beyond the palace grounds, she reappeared, a wisp, moving steadily downward, limned in storm light.

Tears brimmed in his eyes.

Her face, caught in silhouette, was so contented. If given the chance, he would spend the rest of his life making sure she never lost that look.

Painter shifted, moving back, as silent as a tomb.

Painter climbed the stairs to the second level, leaving Omaha alone. He crossed to where the entire group gathered. All eyes watched Safia's progress down through the lower city.

Coral glanced to him, her expression worried.

And with good reason.

The swirling vortex of charges neared the lake's surface. Below it, the lake continued its own whirling churn, and in the center, lit by the fires above, a water spout was rising upward, a reverse whirlpool. The energies above and the antimatter below were stretching to join.

If they touched, it was the end of everything: themselves, Arabia, possibly the world.

Painter focused down upon the ghost of a woman moving sedately along the storm-lit streets, as if she had all the time in the world. She vanished completely when in shadows. He willed her to be safe, but also to move faster. His gaze fluttered between storm and woman.

Omaha appeared from below, hurrying to join them, having lost sight of Safia from his post. His eyes glistened, full of hope, terror, and as much as Painter didn't want to see it, *love.*

Painter swung his attention back to the cavern.

Safia was almost to the sphere.

"C'mon . . ." Omaha moaned.

It was an emotion shared by all.

Safia gently walked down the stairs. She had to step with care. The passage of the iron sphere had crushed its way through. Loose glass littered the steps. Cuts pierced her heels and toes.

She ignored the pain, keeping calm, breathing through it.

Ahead the iron sphere appeared. Its surface glowed with an azure blue aura. She stepped up and studied the obstruction: a fallen section of wall. The ball had to be rolled two feet to the left, and it would continue its plummet. She glanced the rest of the way down. It was a clear shot to the lake. There were no other tumbles to block the sphere's path a second time. All she had to do was shift it over. Though heavy, it was a perfect sphere. One good shove and it would roll clear.

She moved next to it, set her legs, raised her palms, took another cleansing breath, and shoved.

The electrical shock from the charged iron shot into her, arcing over her body and out her toes. She spasmed, neck thrown back, bones on fire. Her momentum and convulsive jerk shoved the sphere away, rolling it free.

But as her body broke contact, a final crack of energy snapped her like a whip. She was flung backward, hard. Her head hit the wall behind her. The world went dark, and she fell into nothingness.

Safia . . . !

Omaha could not breathe. He had seen the brilliant arc of energy and watched her be tossed aside like a rag doll. She landed in a crumpled pile, no longer ethereal, grounded. She was not moving.

Unconscious, electrocuted, or dead?

Oh, God . . .

He spun around.

Painter grabbed his arm. "Where the hell do you think you're going?"

"I have to get to her."

Fingers tightened on his arm. "The storm will kill you within two steps."

Kara joined him. "Omaha . . . Painter's right."

Cassandra stood by the rail, watching everything through her damned scopes. "As long as she doesn't move, she shouldn't attract the bolts. I'm not sure that's a great place to be when the sphere hits the lake, though. Out in the open like that."

Omaha saw that the sphere was almost to the lake. Beyond, the titanic forces swirled. An hourglass hung in the center of the vast cavern. A tornado of charge coming down to meet a rising spout of water.

And the ball rolled toward it.

Lightning bolts chased the sphere, stabbing at it.

"I have to try!" Omaha said, and ripped away. He sprinted down the stairs.

Painter followed at his heels. "Goddamnit, Omaha! Don't throw your life away!"

Omaha landed. "It's my life."

He slid to the entryway, dropping onto his rear, skidding. He yanked off his boots. His left ankle, sprained, protested the rough treatment.

Painter frowned at his actions. "It's not just your life. Safia loves you. If you truly care about her, don't do this."

Omaha pulled off his socks. "I'm not throwing my life away." He crawled on his knees to the entryway and scooped handfuls of sand from the path and poured them into his socks.

"What are you doing?"

"Making sand shoes." Omaha leaned back and shoved his feet into the socks, squeezing them inside and massaging the sand so it covered the bottoms of his feet.

Painter stared at his actions. "Why didn't you . . . Safia wouldn't've had to . . ."

"I just thought of it. Necessity is the mother of goddamn invention."

"I'm going with you."

"No time." Omaha pointed to Painter's bare feet. "No socks."

He sprinted away, skidding and skating across the sandy path. He reached the clean glass and kept running. He wasn't as confident of his plan as he had

portrayed to Painter. Bolts dazzled around him. Panic
fueled his run. Sand hurt his toes. His ankle flamed
with every step.

But he kept running.

Cassandra had to give these folks some credit. They
did have balls of steel. She tracked Omaha's mad flight
through the streets. Had a man ever loved her with so
much heart?

She noted Painter's return but did not look his way.

Would I have let him?

Cassandra watched the sphere's last few bounces.
It now rolled toward the lake, aglow with cobalt energies. She had a job to finish here. She considered
all her options, weighed the possibilities if they survived the next minute. She kept a finger pressed to
the button.

She saw Painter staring at Safia below as Omaha
reached her.

She and Painter had both lost out.

Off by the shore, the sphere took a final hop,
bounced up, and landed in the water with a splash.

Omaha reached Safia. She lay unmoving. Bolts rained
fire all around him. His eyes were only on her.

Her chest rose and fell. Alive.

Off in the direction of the lake, a huge splash sounded like a belly flop.

The depth charge had been dropped.

No time. They needed shelter.

He scooped Safia in his arms and swung around. He had to keep her from touching any surfaces. Carrying her prone form, her head resting on his shoulder, he stepped toward the opening of an intact home and ducked inside. It might not protect him from the deadly static bolts, but he had no idea what would happen when the sphere reached the lake. A roof over his head seemed like a good idea.

The motion stirred Safia. She moaned. "Omaha . . ."

"I'm here, baby . . ." He crouched down, cradling her on his knees, balanced on his sand shoes. "I'm here."

As Omaha and Safia vanished into a building, Painter watched the flume of water geyser up after the iron sphere hit the water. It was as if the ball had been dropped from the Empire State Building. It shot toward the roof, cascading outward, water droplets igniting when they brushed the dazzle of the storm, raining back down as liquid fire.

Antimatter annihilation.

The whirl in the lake eddied and shook. The waterspout jiggled.

But overhead, the vortex of static charge continued its deadly descent.

Painter concentrated on the lake.

Already the whirlpool settled again, churning away with tidal forces.

Nothing happened.

Fire from the plume struck the lake, ignited pools, which quickly extinguished, reestablishing its equilibrium state. Nature loves balance.

"The ball must still be rolling," Coral said, "seeking the lowest point in the lake bottom. The deeper the water, the better. The heightened pressure will help trigger the localized chain reaction and direct its force downward."

Painter turned to her. "Does your mind ever stop calculating?"

She shrugged. "No, why?"

Danny stood at her side. "And if the sphere reaches the lowest point, then that's also the best place to crack the glass over any Earth-generated cistern, draining the lake water away."

Painter shook his head. Those two were peas in a pod.

Cassandra straightened next to Kara. The five of them were the last ones still on the balcony. Lu'lu had led the Rahim to the back rooms below. Captain al-Haffi and Barak led the handful of Shahra.

"Something's happening," Cassandra said.

Out on the lake, a patch of black water glowed a ruddy crimson. It was not a reflection. The glow came from deep below. A fire under the lake. In just the half second it took to look, the crimson blasted out in all directions.

A deep sonorous *whump* sounded.

The entire lake lifted a few feet and dropped.

Ripples spread outward from the lake's center. The growing waterspout collapsed.

"Get below!" Painter yelled.

Too late.

A force, neither wind nor concussion, blasted outward, flattening the lake, sweeping in all directions, pushing before it a wall of superheated air.

It struck.

Painter, half around the corner, caught a glancing shove to the shoulder. He was ripped away, tossed bodily across the room, lifted on wings of fire. Others had taken the force fully and were driven straight back. In a tangle, they hit the far wall. Painter kept his eyes squeezed shut. His lungs seared with the one breath he had taken.

Then it ended.

The heat vanished.

Painter gained his feet. "Shelter," he squeaked out, waving in vain.

The quake came next.

No warning.

Except for an earsplitting clap, deafening, as if the Earth were being cracked in half. Then the palace jumped several feet up, then down again, throwing them all flat.

The rattling worsened. The tower shook, jolted to one side, then the other. Glass shattered. An upper story of the tower went crashing down. Pillars broke and toppled, smashing into city or lake.

All the while, Painter kept flat.

A loud splintery *pop* exploded by his ear. He turned his head and saw the entire balcony beyond the archway shear and tilt away. A small limb waved.

It was Cassandra. She had not been blown through the doorway like the rest of them, but knocked against the palace's outer wall.

She fell with the balcony. In her hand, she still held the detonator.

Painter scrambled toward her.

Reaching the edge, he searched below. He spotted Cassandra sprawled in the tumble of broken glass. Her fall had not been far. She lay on her back, clutching the detonator to her chest.

"I still have it!" she hollered hoarsely to him, but he didn't know if it was in threat or reassurance.

She gained her feet.

"Hang on," he said. "I'm coming down."

"Don't—"

A bolt of charge stabbed out as she stood, striking at her toes. The glass melted underfoot. She dropped into the pool, thigh-deep before the glass solidified under her.

She didn't scream, though her entire body wrenched with pain. Her cloak caught on fire. She still held the detonator, in a fist, hugged to her neck. A gasp finally escaped her.

"Painter . . . !"

He spotted a patch of sand in the courtyard below. He leaped and landed hard, wrong, ankle turning, skidding. It was nothing. He stood and kicked sand, a meager path to reach her side.

He dropped next to her, knees in sand. He could smell her flesh burning.

"Cassandra . . . ohmygod."

She held out the transmitter, every line on her face agonized. "I can't hold. Squeeze . . ."

He grabbed her fist, covering it with his own.

She relaxed her own grip, trusting him to keep her finger pressed now. She fell against him, her pants smoldering. Blood poured where charred skin met glass, too red, arterial.

"Why?" he asked.

She kept her eyes closed, only shook her head. ". . . owe you."

"What?"

She opened her eyes, met his. Her lips moved, a whisper. "I wish you could've saved me."

He knew she didn't mean a moment ago . . . but back when they were partners. Her eyes closed. Her head fell to his shoulder.

He held her.

Then she was gone.

Safia awoke in Omaha's arms. She smelled the sweat on his neck, felt the tremble in his arms. He clutched tightly to her. He was crouched down, balanced on the balls of his feet, cradling her in his lap.

How was Omaha here? Where was here?

Memory snapped back.

The sphere . . . the lake . . .

She struggled to get free. Her movement startled Omaha. He tipped, caught himself with a hand, then yanked his arm back.

"Saff, stay still."

"What happened?"

His face was strained. "Nothing much. But let's see if you saved Arabia." He hauled her up, still carrying her, and ducked out the door.

Safia recognized the place. Where the rolling sphere had jammed. They both looked to the lake. Its surface still swirled, eddying. The skies overhead blazed and crackled.

Safia felt her heart sink. "Nothing's changed."

"Hon, you slept through a whirlwind and a major quake."

As if on cue, another aftershock rattled around them. Omaha took a step back, but it ended. He returned to studying the lake. "Look at the shoreline."

She turned her head. The water's edge had receded about twenty yards, leaving a bathtub ring around the lake. "The water level's dropping."

He hugged her tighter. "You did it! The lake must be draining into one of those subterranean cisterns Coral was yammering about."

Safia stared back up at the static storm on the roof. It, too, was slowly subsiding, grounding out. She glanced across the spread of the darkening city, both upper and lower. So much destruction. But there was hope.

"No bolts," she said. "I think the firestorm is over."

"I'm not taking any chances. C'mon." He hiked her higher in his arms and marched up the slope toward the palace.

She didn't protest, but she quickly noted Omaha wincing with every step.

"What's wrong?" she asked, arms hugged around his neck.

"Nothing. Just some sand in my shoes."

Painter saw them approach.

Safia was riding piggyback on Omaha.

Painter called to them as they reached the courtyard. "Omaha, the electrical discharging is over," he said. "You can put Safia down."

Omaha marched past him. "Only over the threshold."

He never made it. Shahra and Rahim all gathered around the pair in the courtyard, congratulating and thanking. Danny hugged his brother. He must have said something about Cassandra because Omaha glanced to the body.

Painter had covered it with a cloak. He had already deactivated the detonator and switched off the transceiver. Safia was safe.

He studied the group. Besides plenty of bruises, scrapes, and burns, they had all weathered the firestorm fine.

Coral straightened. She held one of the launchers and placed a belt buckle against its side. It stuck. She caught him staring. "Magnetized," she said, tossing it aside. "Some type of magnetic pulse. Intriguing."

Before he could respond, another aftershock rocked the palace, strong enough to shatter away another pillar, weakened by the original quake. It fell across the city with a resounding crash.

That sobered everyone up to the dangers still here.

They were not safe.

To emphasize this fact, a deep rumble rose from below, trembling the glass underfoot. A low sound accompanied it, a subway train passing underground.

No one moved. Everyone held their breath.

Then it came.

A whooshing geyser erupted from the lake, fountaining upward, three stories high, as thick around as a two-hundred-year-old redwood.

Prior to this moment, the lake had drained to a small pool, a quarter of its original size. Monstrous cracks skittered along its basin, like the inside of a broken eggshell.

Now water spewed back out again.

They all gaped.

"The aftershocks must have ruptured into the original Earth-generated springs," Danny said. "One of the global aquifers."

The lake quickly began to refill.

"This place is going to flood," Painter said. "We need to get out of here."

"From fire to water," Omaha grumbled. "This just gets better and better."

Safia helped gather the children. They hurriedly fled from the palace. The younger Shahra men helped the older Rahim women.

By the time they reached the foot of the stairs, the lake had already climbed over its original banks, drenching into the lower city. And still the geyser continued to spray.

Flashlights bobbling, the strongest men pushed ahead. Boulders and tumbled piles of rocks blocked the passage in places. They hauled and burrowed a path through them.

The rest of the group waited, following as best they could, climbing as quickly as possible, crawling over obstructions, the stronger helping the weaker.

Then a shout from above. A cry of joy. "*Hurree-ya!*"

It was a cheer Safia was relieved to hear.

Freedom!

The group fled up the stairs. Painter waited at the top. He helped pull her through and out. He pointed an arm and reached to Kara behind her.

Safia barely recognized the mesa now. It was a tumbled pile of rubble. She glanced around. The winds blew hard, but the storm was gone, its energy sucked and damped into the firestorm below. Overhead a full moon shone, casting the world in silver.

Captain al-Haffi waved a flashlight at her, motioning to a path down through the jumble, making room for the others. The exodus continued off the mount.

The group marched from the rocks and into the sands. It was uphill. The prior whirlpool in the sand had worn a declivity miles across. They passed the charred husks of the tractor and trucks. The landscape was scribed with swatches of molten sand, still steaming in the night air.

Painter darted away to the overturned tractor. He climbed inside, disappeared for a bit, then came back out. He carried a laptop in his hand. It looked broken, the case scorched.

Safia raised an eyebrow at his salvaging, but he never explained.

They continued into the desert. Behind them, water now fountained from the ruins of the mesa. The declivity behind slowly filled with water.

Safia walked with Omaha, his hand in hers. People spoke in low whispers. Safia spotted Painter, hiking alone.

"Give me a second," Safia said, squeezing Omaha's hand and letting go.

She crossed over to Painter, matching his stride. He glanced at her, eyes questioning, surprised.

"Painter, I . . . I wanted to thank you."

He smiled, a soft shift of his lips. "You owe me no thanks. It's my job."

She strode with him, knowing he was concealing a well of deeper emotion. It brimmed in his eyes, the way they seemed unable to meet hers.

She glanced at Omaha, then back at Painter. "I . . . we . . ."

He sighed. "Safia, I get it."

"But—"

He faced her, his blue eyes raw but certain. "I get it. I do." He nodded back to Omaha. "And he's a good man."

She had a thousand things she wanted to say.

"Go," he murmured with that soft, pained smile.

With no words that could truly comfort, she drifted back to Omaha.

"What was that all about?" he asked, attempting to sound casual, but failing miserably.

She took his hand again. "Saying good-bye . . ."

The group climbed to the crest of the sandy declivity. A full lake now grew behind them, the crumbled mesa almost flooded over.

"Do we need to worry about all that water having antimatter in it?" Danny asked as they paused at the top of the crest.

Coral shook her head. "The antimatter-buckyball complexes are heavier than ordinary water. As the lake drained into the massive spring here, the buckyballs should have sunk away. Over time, they'll dilute through the vast subterranean aquifer system and slowly annihilate away. No harm done."

"So it's all gone," Omaha said.

"Like our powers," Lu'lu added, standing between Safia and Kara.

"What do you mean?" Safia asked, startled.

"The blessings are gone." No grief, only simple acceptance.

"Are you sure?"

Lu'lu nodded. "It has happened before. To others. As I told you. It is a fragile gift, easily damaged. Something happened during the quake. I felt it. A rush of wind through my body."

Nods from the other Rahim.

Safia had been unconscious at the time.

"The magnetic pulse," Coral said, overhearing them. "Such an intense force would have the ability to destabilize the buckyballs, collapse them." Coral nodded to Lu'lu. "When one of the Rahim loses their gifts, does it ever come back?"

The *hodja* shook her head.

"Interesting," Coral said. "For the mitochondria to propagate buckyballs in cells, it must need a few buckyballs as patterns, seeds, like those found in the original fertilized egg. But wipe them all out, and the mitochondria alone can't generate them anew."

"So the powers are truly gone," Safia said, dismayed. She looked at her palms, remembering the warmth and peace. *Gone* . . .

The *hodja* took her hand and squeezed. Safia sensed the long stretch of time from the scared little girl lost in the desert, seeking shelter among the stones, to the woman standing here now.

No, maybe the magic wasn't completely gone.

The warmth and peace she had experienced before had nothing to do with gifts or blessings. It was this human touch. The warmth of family, the peace of self and certainty. That was blessing enough for anyone.

The *hodja* touched the ruby teardrop by her left eye. She spoke softly. "We Rahim call this Sorrow. We wear it to represent the last tear shed by the queen as she left Ubar, shed for the dead, for herself, for those who would follow and carry her burden." Lu'lu dropped her finger. "We rename it this night, under the moon, simply Farah."

Safia translated. "Joy . . ."

A nod. "The first tear shed in happiness for our new life. Our burden is finally lifted. We can leave the shadows and walk again in full sunlight. Our time of hiding is over."

A trace of dismay must have persisted in Safia's expression.

The *hodja* reached and gently turned Safia around. "Remember, child, life is not a straight line. It cycles. The desert takes, but it gives back." She freed her hand and motioned to the new lake swelling behind them. "Ubar is gone, but *Eden* has returned."

Safia gazed across the moonlit waters.

She pictured the Arabia lost to the past, before Ubar, before the meteor strike, a land of vast savannahs, verdant forests, meandering rivers, and plentiful life. She watched the flow of water across the parched sands of her home, the past and present overlapping.

Could it be possible?

The Garden of Eden . . . reborn.

From behind, Omaha settled against her, arms reaching around.

"Welcome home," he whispered in her ear.

Epilogue

⟨∏Υ1∘⊓⬛⟩

April 8, 2:45 P.M.
Darpa Headquarters
Arlington, Virginia

Painter Crowe stood outside the office doors. He watched the custodian unscrew the nameplate. It had been there since the inception of Sigma Force. Mixed feelings warred in him: pride and satisfaction certainly, but also anger and a little shame. He had not wanted to gain this position under these awful circumstances.

The nameplate fell off the door.

DIRECTOR SEAN MCKNIGHT.

The former leader of Sigma.

It was tossed in the garbage.

The custodian grabbed the new black-and-silver plate from the secretary's desk. He pressed it to the door and used an electric screwdriver to affix it in place. He stepped back.

"How's that?" the man asked, tipping back his cap.

He nodded, staring at the plate.

DIRECTOR PAINTER CROWE.

The leader of Sigma Force's next generation.

He was due to be sworn in and take his oath in half an hour. How could he sit behind that desk?

But it was his duty. Presidential directive. After all that had happened in Oman, DARPA had been shaken from top to bottom. The leader of the Guild had been a member of their own organization. Painter had brought both his suspicions and proof out of Oman. The experts here were able to recover the data from the hard drive of Cassandra's laptop. It left a trail confirming Painter's claim.

The Minister was exposed.

His plan to corrupt Sigma stopped.

He unfortunately swallowed his own pistol before he could be taken into custody. It was surely a blow to the Guild, but they were like the mythic Hydra. Cut off one head, and another would eventually arise.

Painter would be ready.

A scuff of shoe drew his attention around. Painter smiled broadly, reaching out a hand. "What are you doing down here, sir?"

Sean McKnight took his hand. "Old habits die hard. I just wanted to make sure you're settled in here."

"Fine, sir."

He nodded, clapped Painter on the shoulder. "I'm leaving Sigma in good hands."

"Thank you, sir."

Sean stepped forward, noted his old nameplate in the trash, and bent to retrieve it. He picked it up and tucked it inside his jacket.

Painter's face burned with shame.

But Sean merely smiled and patted his jacket. "For old times' sake." He strode away. "I'll see you at the swearing-in ceremony."

They would both be taking their oaths today.

As Painter was filling Sean's position, Sean would be filling the vacancy in the directorship left behind by Vice Admiral Tony "The Tiger" Rector.

The Minister.

The bastard was so vain as to use a code name derived from his own last name. Rector. Meaning a member of the clergy.

In Oman, Painter had almost pegged Sean as the traitor. But when Painter had heard Cassandra mention the Minister, he had realized his mistake. Two men sent him on this mission: Sean McKnight *and* Admiral Tony Rector. Naturally, Sean would have passed

Painter's intelligence to Rector, his boss, but it was Rector who had leaked it to Cassandra.

The laptop's data confirmed the connection.

Rector had been attempting to usurp Sigma for himself. Cassandra was his first mole. Even back at Foxwoods, she had been ordered to orchestrate and facilitate the passing of military secrets to the Chinese through Xin Zhang. The purpose was to embarrass Sigma's leadership. This failure had been intended as a crowbar to pry Sean McKnight out of office so Rector could place someone loyal to the Guild in charge.

But now it was over.

He stared at the closed door. It was a new chapter of his life.

He thought back to the long road that had led him here. The letter was still in his jacket pocket. Standing now, he took it out. He fingered its sharp edges, ran a thumb over the oatmeal envelope. His name was neatly embossed on the front. He had received it last week. If he wasn't brave enough to face this, he'd never get past the door here.

Standing still, he sliced open the seal and pulled out the contents. Translucent vellum, textured cotton card stock, hand-deckled edge. Nice.

A slip of paper fell out. He caught it and flipped it over.

Be there . . .
—Kara

With a slight shake of his head and a small smile, he opened the invitation and read through it. A June wedding. To be held on the banks of Lake Eden, the new inland freshwater lake of Oman. Drs. Omaha Dunn and Safia al-Maaz.

He sighed. It hadn't hurt as much as he'd expected.

He thought about all the others who had brought him to this door. Coral was already on another assignment in India. Danny and Clay, the best of buddies, were on a dig together . . . in India. The choice of dig sites had to be Danny's idea. The Shahra and Rahim had united their clans to much celebration in Oman. And a new *Shabab Oman* was being built. Kara was overseeing the ship's construction while financing the repairs to the British Museum. He had read in *People* magazine that she was involved with a young doctor, someone she met while in rehab.

He glanced back to Kara's note. *Be there . . .*

Maybe he could.

But first he had to get through this door.

Painter strode up, grabbed the handle, took a deep breath, and pushed.

On to the next big adventure.

Author's Note

As I've done previously, I thought I would share a few of the facts and fictions that composed this book. I hope that by doing so, I might interest a few folks in exploring some of the topics and places in more detail.

First, the whole concept of antimatter. Is it the stuff of science fiction? Not any longer. CERN Laboratories in Switzerland has in fact produced antimatter particles and has been able to hold them stable for short periods of time. NASA and the Fermi National Laboratories have also explored the development of antimatter engines, including the development of the electromagnetic Penning Traps for storing and transporting antimatter.

As to antimatter meteors, they have been postulated to exist in space, but their existence remains theoretical. The theory that the Tunguska explosion in Russia was due to a small antimatter meteor is one of many postulated explanations. However, the described effects—the unusual nature of the blast, the EM pulse, the mutations in flora and fauna—are factual.

Regarding subjects related to water: All the chemistries described in the book are based on facts, including the weird conformation of water into buckyballs. The topic of magmatic or Earth-generated water is also based on the work of geologist Stephen Reiss, among many others.

Moving to Arabia, the geology of the region is unique. Twenty thousand years ago, the deserts of Oman were indeed once verdant savannahs full of rivers, lakes, and streams. Wildlife was abundant, and Neolithic hunters roamed the lands. This desertification of the region has indeed been attributed to a natural condition called "orbital forcing" or "Milankovitch Forcing." Basically it's a "wobble" in the Earth's rotation that occurs at periodic intervals.

Most of the archaeological and historical details of Oman are real, including the tomb of Nabi Imran in Salalah, the tomb of Ayoub (Job) in the mountains, and of course, the ruins of Ubar at Shisur. Photos of all these places will be linked on my Web site (www.jamesrollins .com) for the curious or armchair traveler. Also, to read more about the discovery of Ubar, I highly recommend *The Road to Ubar* by Nicolas Clapp.

On to some minor miscellaneous details. First, the reclusive Shahra tribespeople do exist in the Dhofar Mountains and claim heritage to the kings of Ubar. They still speak a dialect considered to be the oldest in Arabia. The Omani flagship, the *Shabab Oman*, is an actual ship (sorry for blowing it up). And speaking of blowing things up, the iron camel that exploded at the beginning of the novel still resides somewhere at the British Museum. Safe and sound . . . at least for now.